In the Shadow
of the
Black Moon

Melissa Roos

D1482619

Dedicated to Kristy

If our paths had never crossed,
I would have truly missed out on
an incredible friendship.
I'm so glad we were lost together.
Thank you for always
believing in me.

Prologue

He sat and stared out into the darkness, seething with anger. The moon was barely visible in the window next to him. A glass of whiskey in his hand, and a pistol in his lap. *How did this happen? How could he have been denied?* The one thing he wanted, the one thing he coveted more than anything, taken from him with the tip of a pen pressed to paper? With the swift movement of a hand, a name was signed and his life was altered, all because of a woman.

He glanced around the room disgusted and saw his pathetic existence contained within it. There were photos, discarded clothes, and empty bottles. The only thing of value to him in the room was his beloved collection of action figures from his favorite sci-fi thriller *The Black Shadow*.

Reaching for his favorite action figure, Kage Xyon, the main character of the movie, he examined it in the dim light. Kage's hair was golden and his battle uniform was black with the moon emblem on his broad chest. He was a prince, a warrior, and the chosen one. He had everything and was everything he, himself, wanted to be, and just like Kage, he had it all taken from him by a woman.

Setting Kage back in his place, he decided right there and then he would not stand for it. Justice would be his.

He picked up a photo of her and scrutinized it. She was pretty but he saw past that to what she really was . . . cunning and manipulative. Bree Thompson . . . her name alone made him writhe with anger.

She thought she could get away with what was rightfully his but she was wrong. He felt a dark power well up inside of him. He would watch, he would wait, and when the time was right, he would take her and make her pay.

He propped the photo of her back up on the table, picked up the pistol that lay in his lap, put his finger on the trigger, looked down the barrel, and aimed it straight at her face.

Chapter 1

B ree could hear the roar of the surf the minute she got out of the car. The sound drew her forward. The smell of brine and salt swirled around her as the wind whipped past. She pulled a purple, elastic hairband off her wrist and wrangled her long, light brown hair into a ponytail. Once secured, she dug through her oversized bag in search of her sunglasses as she walked, pulled forward by the sound of the waves crashing. The sun was so brilliant overhead, the sky so blue, it made her feel a little dizzy as it reflected off every surface, the hotels, the concrete, and the sand.

She stopped and looked down. She stood at the edge of the sidewalk, where the concrete ended and the sand began. The thought raced across her mind that if she took this step, things could be . . . *would be different*, she corrected herself. *They had to be.*

She would leave one life and start another with the sand, the sun, and the water.

This was something different, something so foreign to her from where she had come. She pushed the golden wheat fields to the recesses of her mind. She couldn't keep going the way she had been. Something had to change. *She* had to change.

Bree slipped off her sandals and touched the delicate silver chain with a wave charm dangling from it that lay against her skin on her right ankle. It whispered between the tips of her fingers and gave her strength. She stood and took one step forward, letting her toes sink into the warm, coarse sand. Seagulls drifted noisily overhead, squawking as they called to each other, soaring on invisible updrafts. Swooping. Calling.

The dune blocked the full view of the ocean, yet the roar of the waves invited her forward, enticing her. Her heart hurt thinking of what she was leaving behind, but she forced herself to walk forward up over the warm sand to the top of the dune. Her breath caught as she took in the sight.

The vivid blue of the sky paled in comparison to the dazzling indigo of the Atlantic Ocean. The rays of the sun danced over the surf. It shifted, changed, and shimmered before her eyes. The waves and the endless horizon summoned her. Beckoning her forward.

Something broke in her at the sight. She struggled to stay on her feet. She trudged on, her heart heavy and hurting. She dropped her sandals one at a time, her bag, and then her pride. The surf and her emotions rushed in at her. The waves pulled away, leaving a clean smooth swatch of sand all along the edge. *If only her pain could be wiped away so easily,* she thought. She dropped to her knees as the water rushed in again. That's where she knelt, bent her head, and wept. At the edge. At the brink of sanity. And a new beginning.

• • • •

PULLING INTO THE OUTLETS, Ryker parked his truck. He reveled in the early spring warmth as he crossed and walked into Coastal Realty. He opened the door to a nautical-themed white and navy interior. Behind a large counter, made out of driftwood, sat Sheri, the receptionist.

She smiled brightly as she looked up and recognized him. She tucked her long strawberry blonde hair behind her ear and stood.

"Ryker! What a surprise. I didn't know you were stopping by today." She smoothed her grass-green silk shirt that set off her eyes and complimented her hair. "Do you have an appointment?"

He tucked his hands into the front of his jeans and grinned. "Nope, I just thought I would check in with Linda. Smells like sunscreen or maybe coconuts in here."

"That's the new diffuser I just bought," she reached out and touched a small pale aqua cylinder that sat on the counter to her left, letting out a small stream of steam, scenting the air. "Do you like it?"

"Yeah, it's nice. Reminds me of the beach."

"Exactly. Let me see if Linda has a few minutes to talk to you." Sheri picked up the phone and buzzed her, all the while keeping her green eyes locked on Ryker. "Linda. Ryker James is here to see you. Do you have a few minutes?" Placing the phone back in the cradle, she smiled. "Linda said to go right back."

"Thanks, Sheri. It was nice to see you," he tapped the counter and strolled down the short hall.

"You too," she called after him as she watched him go. She sunk back into her chair. Broad shoulders, narrow hips, and long legs that ate up the floor all too quickly as he disappeared into Linda's office. She sighed outwardly. *If only*.

Ryker gave one rap on the already open door.

"Come in."

Linda Lauer sat behind her large mahogany desk looking impeccable in a freshly pressed light pink linen suit. Her signature color. Her hair was short, dyed blonde, and neatly set, looking like she had just come from the stylist. Her face creased heavily as she smiled at him, showing her fifty-plus years spent in the sun, but her blue eyes still sparkled with spunk.

"Hey, handsome! To what do I owe the pleasure?" she asked, in her raspy voice that had been etched deep from years of smoking, a nasty habit she had picked up when she was a teenager trying to impress the boys.

Linda had quit smoking over three years ago, but her hand still reached for a pack every time a good-looking man walked in her door. Ryker was no exception. It didn't make a difference that she could be his mother. She sighed inwardly. Since she didn't have the longed-for cigarettes, she reached for her diet soda instead and took a dainty sip out of the colorful paper straw, leaving a trace of pink lipstick.

"Hi, gorgeous," he said and leaned over, giving her a peck on the cheek, pulling in the scent of lavender that always surrounded Linda.

He made her laugh, a deep throaty chuckle. "If only I was twenty years younger, I'd sure give you a run for your money, hon. Have a seat, hot stuff. Tell me what's up?"

He flopped down in her overstuffed cream-colored chair and crossed one long jean-clad leg over his knee. He sat completely relaxed and confident. "You can probably guess."

"Why don't you let me." She grinned. "Since it's after three I don't suppose you're here to take me to lunch. Instead, you're wanting to know about the offer that you put in on the Henning place?"

He nodded.

That's when her smile faded. "Wish I had better news for you. They aren't interested. They said the offer was too low."

"They won't counter?"

Linda shook her head. "Nope. Said, when you give them an offer worth considering they'll counter. But not until then. Of course, that was Mrs. Henning."

"You and I both know that was a good offer, especially with all the work that needs to be done, inside and out. What was Mr. Henning's answer?"

"Mr. Henning said they'll sell to you when hell freezes over."

"Figures. What do you recommend we do?" Ryker asked, dragging his hand through his dark brown hair. He wanted that place. He had longed to have it ever since he saw it for the first time when he was sixteen. He imagined himself ripping out the boards, replacing windows, bringing it back to its rightful glory. Not only would it be spectacular when done right but it would be the perfect place to expand the business. It had plenty of land and a to die for view.

He wrinkled his brow and looked at Linda. "Should we make another offer?"

Linda shrugged. "I say we wait. See if anyone else comes along. If they do, we make another offer. A better offer, one they can't refuse. I've made sure every realtor in the area knows we want that place. No one will show it without letting me know." She winked at him. "Just be patient, they'll come around."

"You're the expert." It irked him to let it sit. To wait. He wasn't used to that, he always went after what he wanted, full throttle. But he trusted Linda. So he would wait. Ryker started drumming his fingers on the arm of his chair, shifting gears. "How's business?"

"Really good. I'm actually looking for a new realtor to add to the company. Sheri's running an ad. Hoping to have a couple of interviews by the end of the week. I'm expecting a banner summer. All my agents are out right now showing houses. Business is good. And you?"

"We're busy too. Lots of little projects and then the big one, the Brandy beach house. We're right in the middle of it. Getting ready to hang the drywall. You should stop down and see it sometime. You'll never believe the difference already."

"And the kitchen?"

"The only snag. They couldn't agree. But I came up with a plan they both loved and got them to sign off on it this morning. Now we're back on track."

"I never doubted you for a second."

Ryker laughed, "I'm glad you didn't. I think Sam was even a little worried about this one, and he never lets it get to him." He stood. "Guess I better get back. Keep me posted if there's any news on the Henning place."

She nodded, "You're scheduled to paint my rentals Thursday and Friday, right?"

"Yes ma'am."

"Good. When you think about it, drop off some more business cards. We're down to our last one."

"Will do."

"Oh, and when you do, ask my girl at the front desk out on a date. If I can't have you, somebody might as well." She winked at him. "Now go."

Ryker laughed all the way to his truck.

Chapter 2

She sat wrapped up in a blanket, knees tucked up to her chest. The air was cold. The wind was brisk. The early hour was still dark. Her eyes were heavy, so she let them drift closed. She let herself be lulled by the ocean's melody. The night sounds of the ocean kept the nightmares at bay. When inside, she woke, drenched in sweat, heart racing, with the clash of metal ringing in her ears and the smell of gasoline and smoke burning in her nostrils.

Here, on top of the lifeguard stand, Bree relaxed and let the waves' methodical rhythm carry away the devastating images. She half dozed, trying not to completely surrender to sleep, as she knew sunrise was coming soon. Bree tried to stay awake thinking of how wonderful yesterday had turned out.

After her breakdown, she had gathered her things, took out her camera, and wandered down the beach. Noticing a sailboat in the distance she had zoomed in. Its crisp, white sails were brilliantly set off against the bright cerulean of the sky and indigo ocean. Then she readjusted the lens as the water at her feet pulled away, tumbling a cornucopia of pebbles and shells. Her camera clicked off a dozen rounds as the sea foamed and rolled the debris. A few paces further, she caught a hermit crab in her lens as he quickly buried himself into a hole.

Through her camera, Bree had watched a couple of children holding hands charge into the surf only to scamper back giggling and squealing as the freezing water swept in. She captured them with sea spray showering down around them like a thousand diamonds as the setting sun behind them caught every droplet.

The day had been relaxing, and exactly what she needed.

She had her camera with her now in hopes of capturing her first east coast sunrise. She touched it in the darkness, to make sure it was close. Satisfied, she leaned back and tuned into the sigh of the waves, making her mind focus only on that, and nothing else.

Ryker crossed the beach and quickly headed for the lifeguard chair. The morning was a little brisker than yesterday. He had pulled on a leather jacket over his sweats for the ride. Now he had to deal with the jacket. It was too heavy to run in, and he didn't want to just leave it on the bottom rung of the chair like he usually did with his sweatshirt. Not that he really thought anyone would be out this early looking to steal it, but still . . . He decided to put it on the seat, up out of view.

He climbed the chair in the dark and reached out to put his jacket down. There was a shriek and something hard connected with his jaw, knocking him backward. He lost his grip and slid down the wooden rungs, landing hard on his back in the cold sand.

"What the hell!" he shouted, rubbing his jaw. "Who's up there?" He staggered to his feet determined to get an answer.

"Stay back or I'll hit you again!" a female voice replied.

"Why'd you hit me?" Ryker looked up into the darkness and saw a dark form.

"Because you grabbed me!"

"I wasn't grabbing you. I was putting my jacket up there, so I didn't have to carry it while I was running. I didn't even know you were there."

Shaking, and feeling slightly violated, Bree leaned over the edge and peered down into the darkness. She was barely able to make out the edges of his form. Big and tall, was all she could think.

"What are you running from?" she demanded, sounding more confident than she felt. Anyone out at this hour had to be up to no good, she decided. "What have you done? I have my phone. I'll call the cops!"

Ryker let out a huff. "Not running from. Running. You know, jogging," he said in disbelief. "For exercise. I always run at this time, and in this area."

"Oh." Feeling stupid, Bree apologized, "I'm sorry."

"What the heck are you doing out here at this hour?"

"I could ask you the same thing," Bree retorted.

"I thought we already established that I'm here to go for a run. But we can go over it again if you need to."

Flustered, Bree relented. "No, that's quite all right, no need to go over it again. I came out here for the sunrise and must have fallen asleep. You startled me, that's all."

"Well, that makes two of us. I wasn't exactly looking to get punched in the face."

"Are you okay? Any blood?" she asked sheepishly, still unable to see his features clearly.

"I think I'll live. Thanks for asking," Ryker said sarcastically. "Now, am I okay to leave my jacket here while I jog? Or were you planning on turning it over to the authorities while I'm gone?"

Bree smiled to herself. "You're safe to leave it."

"You're sure? You won't steal it, will you?" Ryker asked. "I, too, have a phone and can call the cops."

She giggled softly. "Your jacket's safe with me. I'll protect it with my life. Anyone comes near and . . . well; you know what I'm capable of."

He laughed and rubbed his jaw. He liked the sound of her voice and wondered if she was as cute as she sounded. "I am indeed aware of what you're capable of. By the way, Ryker James is my name." He climbed up a couple of rungs and held out his jacket. She took it. Then, his hand.

It was stronger than she had anticipated. "Bree," she said softly. "Nice to meet you."

"Bree . . . Pretty." He held her hand a second longer. "Will you be here when I get back?" He waited a beat and added, "Because I'm concerned for my jacket."

There was a trace of laughter in her words, "Depends on how fast you run. I have other pressing matters than babysitting your . . . oh, leather." She ran her hand across it. "Nice." The sky was starting to lighten, making his face come into focus. Dark and sexy ran through her mind. "I'm a little chilly. I might just have to try this on."

He lifted a dark eyebrow. *Cute*, he decided quickly, *very cute*. "That's my favorite jacket. You can try it on, but if you leave with it, I will track you down. And believe me, I know everyone in this town. You won't get far."

She smiled wickedly at him. "How far or how long do you run for?"

"Usually about an hour." He started to climb down.

She slipped her arms in the jacket and was surrounded by the scent of man. Musky and dark. She sighed into it. "That's a pretty good head start . . . Bet I wouldn't be really easy to find."

He popped back up a rung, hoping she was teasing. He watched her lean back snuggled into his jacket. His pulse spiked. Beautiful. Sexy. But in a girl-next-door kind of way. "Guess I'll cut it back today since I'm getting a late start after being maliciously attacked by a potential jacket thief."

She laughed at that.

"Might just be back in five minutes, not sixty," he said, eyeing her.

She smiled and he felt his heart flip. He jumped down praying he could trust her, after all, it was his favorite jacket. "See you in a bit."

He didn't wait for her to answer, just jogged off as the sun slowly snuck above the horizon.

Not wasting any precious time, Bree quickly slid her camera out of the case. She adjusted the camera to a wide-angle focal length, the ISO to the lowest possible setting to capture the ambient light, and then the mode to aperture priority so she could control the depth of the field.

The horizon was changing quickly. Literally, right before her eyes. The colors: salmon, coral, crimson, and violet swirled and expanded. Shadows were created. Stretched. Elongated. The sun's fingertips reached and danced across the rolling waves. Whitecaps sparkled azure, ebony, and silver, playing tricks on the mind. The depths of the rich colors were a feast for the eyes. A balm for the soul. She prayed she could capture half the beauty she saw before her on digital film before it disappeared. She widened the aperture of the camera, allowing in more light. Her camera clicked off rounds, trying to capture every little movement and detail the exposure would allow. Letting in the light, dark, and color.

She climbed down from her wooden perch. Crossed the sand. Tried different angles. Varied her position. Stood. Squatted. Tilted the camera, all the while enthralled with the beauty before her. She was so entrenched in what she was doing, she didn't realize how much time was slipping by.

Ryker watched her as he caught his breath and walked in circles trying to cool down. He was enchanted by her grace and efficiency as she moved. He noted the blanket had been discarded and trailed behind her in the sand. She wore baggy cotton pants that whipped against long legs in the wind and his jacket. Her feet were bare and sunk into the wet sand as she moved. Her hair, long and golden in the morning sun, was pulled back into a loose braid and hung down below her shoulders.

He approached from the side so as not to startle her. His jaw still ached from where it connected with her fist from before. Despite the slender frame, she could pack a punch. He hesitated as she lowered her camera and saw one lone tear race down her cheek and drop to the sand. He felt as if he had just stepped into an intimate moment, meant only for her.

He cleared his throat loudly. "For a minute I thought you had run off with my jacket."

Slowly, she turned her head to look directly at him. An echo of sadness lingered there, but like the shutter of her camera, it was gone. Left was a whisper of a smile that didn't quite reach her summer-blue eyes.

Taking one last long look at the rising sun, she walked towards him. "I thought about it. Pretty nice leather jacket. Guess you want it back?" She slipped it off, to reveal a trim body that was hugged in a long-sleeve cotton T-shirt. "Hope you don't mind that I borrowed it," she said, handing it to him.

Their fingers brushed lightly in the exchange. He grinned. "Not at all. Anytime." He slung it over his shoulder. "I don't believe I caught your last name."

"I don't think I threw it," Bree said, slinging the camera over her shoulder, mimicking him, and walking towards the discarded blanket.

Ryker laughed. "I guess you didn't. Threw a punch instead."

She picked it up and shook the sand off, watching him over it. *A complete stranger. What had she been thinking? Putting on his jacket and flirting with him. She hadn't. He had caught her at a weak moment. That's all. She seemed to be full of them these past months.*

The sun was well over the horizon now, and Bree became acutely aware that she stood there in her thin cotton pajamas. What would her mother say if she knew? The thought made her heart hurt. She deliberately shoved it out of her mind.

She just needed to put some distance between them, and quickly. "It was nice to meet you, but I have to get going." She hugged the blanket to her chest and turned to go.

"You too. Maybe I'll run into you again sometime," Ryker called after her.

She didn't reply, just scurried across the sand towards the hotel.

"So that explains it," he thought. "The camera, the early hour. Tourist. Guess I won't see her again." Disappointed, Ryker headed back to his motorcycle, unable to shake the feeling that if he had looked in those blue eyes any longer, he might be pulled down into the depths of them, and never resurface.

Chapter 3

The week had almost gotten away from her. She had gotten caught up in the sand and sun by day, and uploading her photos by night. She had only ventured out away from the hotel to eat at a few fast-food joints. But after a few days, she craved home-cooked meals and a place of her own.

On Tuesday, Bree had inquired about a realtor, and all three behind the desk had suggested the same one. Two days later, Bree pulled up to Coastal Realty and got out of the car. She looked around at the other shops: clothing, gifts, and home accents. Another day, she promised herself she'd come back and shop. Look through each and every one. Today though, she was hoping to look for a house.

A soft bell chimed as she opened the door. She was greeted by the smell of coconut and the sound of soft music. A young woman about her age sat behind the desk and greeted her with a warm smile.

"Welcome to Coastal Realty. My name is Sheri. How can I help you?"

"Hi," Bree said awkwardly. "I was hoping to speak to someone about looking at houses."

"Have you been here before?"

Bree shook her head no.

"Okay. Are you looking to rent or to own?"

"Well, I could rent, but ultimately I want to own. I don't know if it's worth even looking at rental properties."

Sheri grabbed a clipboard with papers and placed them on the counter with a pen.

"Why don't you fill out these forms? Jot down your information: name, address, phone number, email if you have one. Also, there is a spot for location, price range, and time frame that you are looking to be in. On the right then it asks some other questions like how many bedrooms, bathrooms, and what type of home. For example, single-family, multi-housing, new construction or existing."

Bree took the clipboard.

"You can have a seat right there," Sheri said, indicating the reception area. "Are you currently working with another agent?"

"No, I'm not," Bree said, perching on the edge of the navy sofa, clipboard resting on her knees.

Sheri tapped away at the computer while Bree wrote. A soft rock station played quietly in the background.

Bree filled in her personal information and skipped over the question about preferred school districts. She had no idea about the schools here. She fantasized about the number of bedrooms and baths and felt a pang of grief when she realized she only needed one but marked three to four instead. Why not dream? Wasn't that what this was about? Plans. Dreams. Hopes for the future.

She wanted the room to grow. A place for guests and maybe a family someday. She wanted an office or space she could use as one. A place for her computer and camera equipment. Maybe even a spot for a studio. But most of all she wanted privacy with an ocean or bay view, she thought wistfully.

Her pen hovered over the box for occupancy and checked immediately.

Sheri watched her as she filled out the form. Her pen hung in midair as she stared off into space. Looking lost. Even sad. Sheri cleared her throat and asked cheerfully, "Have any questions about the form?"

"What?" Bree asked, pulled back to the present.

Sheri came around the desk. "Does one of the questions have you stumped? Seems like you're stuck on one."

"Oh no. I was just daydreaming I guess." Bree clicked the pen and slipped the papers back under the clip. "I'm finished," she said, handing it to Sheri.

"Great. Let me put this into the computer quickly." She settled down behind the desk. "It will only take a couple of minutes."

Bree stood and noticed an empty space on the wall. She thought how nice a photo of a sailboat would look in that spot. "Any chance I'd be able to go out and look today?" Bree asked, turning back to Sheri.

Typing, Sheri answered, "No, I'm sorry. All our agents are out right now. And the owner is training a new agent. The earliest would be tomorrow morning with Tina. She's great. You'll love her. Been in the business for about twenty years. I'll give her all your information. We'll pull some properties that we think best fit your needs. We like to give our sellers a couple of hours' notice before we show any properties, to make arrangements to be out of the house." Sheri continued to peck away. "What time works best for you to-morrow?"

"What's the earliest Tina could do?" Bree asked, anxious to get started.

Sheri cocked her head and really looked at Bree. "You're really in a hurry?"

"Yes, I am currently staying at a hotel through the end of next week. After that, I don't have any plans made. So, I either need to extend my stay there or find an apartment temporarily."

"I see. Maybe we should pull some temporary housing for you too." Sheri started typing again. "Tomorrow at ten. Will that work?"

"Yes, that will be fine."

"Tina will go over the ones she's pulled; you both can narrow down what's a high priority to see. Then we can arrange a time for you to visit them." She clicked a couple of times with her mouse, entering data, and then looked up at Bree who had crossed over to her desk. "Does that sound like a plan?"

"That will work. Thank you for your help."

"My pleasure." Sheri stood and extended her hand. "It was very nice to meet you, Bree. We'll take good care of you."

"Thank you," she said, shaking hands. "I guess I'll see you tomorrow at ten."

• • • •

SAM WOVE THE BOLTS & Beams truck through the parking lot in search of lunch, got lucky, and found a spot between a sub shop and a burger place. They jumped out and started across the lot, just as an older couple came out of the dry cleaners.

Sam elbowed Ryker. "Looks like it's your lucky day. Look who it is."

Ryker too had spotted them. He waved as he crossed. Neither acknowledged him, but they picked up the pace towards their own car. He heard the lock beep and smoothly maneuvered to open Mrs. Henning's car door.

"Here let me," he said, reaching for it.

Manners had her biting her tongue and murmuring, "Thank you," as she slipped in.

"My pleasure," he said, closing the door. "Mr. Henning," Ryker said, meeting the older man's cold eyes over the top of the car.

Mr. Henning hung the dry-cleaning in the backseat, slid into the driver's seat, and slammed the door, all without uttering a word to him. Within seconds the car started and pulled away.

Sam and Ryker both watched them go. Sam turned a broad grin at Ryker. "The old silent treatment. Rough."

"I didn't see him talking to you."

"Yes, but in fairness, I didn't say anything to him either."

"I don't know why they have their panties all in a wad."

"Really? You have no idea why he's that way?"

"No, I've been nothing but nice to them."

"I would say that's exactly how you get treated when you sully a girl's reputation. Especially his only daughter."

"I never sullied Tiffany's reputation."

Sam snorted out a hearty laugh. "You got caught red-handed with her in the backseat of your car, in the church parking lot no less. Need I say more?"

"Heck man, that was well over twelve years ago. We were sixteen," Ryker said with a grin, slipping his hands into his front pockets. "She's married now with a baby on the way. Aren't they ever going to let that go?"

"Apparently not. Some things get etched into a father's mind and can never be erased." Sam tsked loudly. "For instance, the sight of her half-naked and you holding her shirt in your hands," Sam shuddered. "Think of the nightmares you've given that poor man over the past twelve years!"

"Whatever," Ryker laughed. "It's not like you didn't try to go there."

"I did go there, but I was smart enough never to get caught." They started towards the strip mall. "Face it. They're never going to let you buy that place."

Not one to back down from a challenge, Ryker said, "I'll wear them down."

Sam laughed out loud. "It took over twelve years for you to get an icy glare and a huffy thank you. At this rate, it will take another ten years before they'll even look twice at your offer. Subs or burgers?" Sam asked, switching gears.

"Subs." Ryker reached for the door. He glanced at Sam. "Your turn to buy." He missed the handle and was rewarded with a quick whack to the temple. "Damn!" He cursed seeing stars.

"Oh. . . I'm so sorry! Are you okay?"

He knew that voice, had even dreamt about it. He looked down and into her face. "It's you!" he said, surprised. He grinned despite the pain. "I should have known."

She smiled back at him, reached out, and touched the red mark on his forehead. He flinched.

"I am sorry. Really. Are you okay? Should I get ice?"

"He'll live," Sam commented, cutting into the conversation. "I'm Sam Harris," he said, stretching out his hand. "And you are?"

She switched the carryout bag to her other hand. Reached out and shook his. "Bree."

"Just Bree?"

"Yeah, she doesn't give out her last name to strangers, just her right hook. This is the mighty Bree. The one I was telling you about. Took a pretty mean jab from her. She can pack a punch, so be careful."

"Ahhh," Sam nodded knowingly. "So, this is the mystery girl who punched you. Here I thought he was making it all up just to get out of work. Let me shake your hand again. Anybody who can coldcock Ryker and live to tell about it is certainly a friend of mine," Sam's green eyes gleamed as he said it.

They were like visual opposites, Bree thought. Same height and tan, but those were the only two things that they had in common. Sam was tall and slim, sandy blonde hair, grass-green eyes, and openly friendly. Ryker was tall and broad, dark, and dangerous. His eyes were as blue as the depths of the ocean. Together they gave off an air of confidence, exuded testosterone, and what else? Mischief? *An odd combination,* she thought, *but it fit.* Like salt and pepper. Dark and light. Full of spice. She decided she liked them both instantly.

"What are you up to, besides trying to take people out with doors today?" Ryker asked.

"Grabbing lunch, same as you, I guess," she said, indicating her carryout. "I don't want to hold you up." She started to go.

"Hang on," Ryker called after her. "Are you in a hurry?"

"No, why?"

"You should come inside and sit with us. You shouldn't eat alone."

Bree lifted an eyebrow. "Why shouldn't I?"

"Because . . ." Ryker hadn't thought it through. He elbowed Sam.

"Because," Sam began, "it's bad for indigestion . . . to eat alone."

"Really? That's all you got?" Ryker asked in disbelief. Sam shrugged. Bree giggled.

"Plus," Sam said, lifting a finger, clearly coming up with an idea, "Ryker shouldn't be left alone after you hit him in the head."

"Again," Ryker added. He grabbed his head and swayed a little.

"Yes, again. That's twice in less than a week you've hurt him. The least you could do is make sure he's okay for the next half hour or so. They say that's the most crucial time."

"Who says that?" Bree asked curiously.

"Doctors," Ryker said.

"Yes, doctors," Sam agreed.

"Doctors?" Bree glanced from Sam to Ryker, and back. "You've been seen by multiple doctors because I gently tapped you with my fist?"

They both nodded.

"I wouldn't say it was gentle. More like all your brute strength."

Bree laughed. "You poor baby. Well, I'd like to help and all, but it's not like Ryker here is alone. He has you." She pointed at Sam.

"Him?" Ryker asked in disbelief, aiming a thumb at Sam. "You think it's safe to leave me with him? I just got hit by a door on his watch."

"The door was more your fault than anyone's since you weren't watching where you were going. And Sam looks perfectly capable to me."

"Thanks." Sam took a slight bow. "That's me, Mr. Capable."

"There you go. You guys have a nice lunch." She turned and started to walk away.

"Try not to hurt anyone else today," Ryker called after her.

Bree turned around and walked backward a step or two, flexing her arm. "I'll try, but all this brute strength is hard to contain."

They watched her go for a minute. Sam slapped Ryker on the back. "Looks like you're two for two today, buddy. First, the shun by the ex's parents. Now her. You need to work on your game."

"Screw you." He laughed. "Let's eat."

Chapter 4

The sun was low in the west, casting dark shadows along the beach as the hotels blocked the setting sun. Ryker headed out after a long day spent painting rentals for Linda. Sam had stayed on-site at the Brandy project but texted earlier as they wrapped up for the day. They had agreed to meet for a beer and a burger at the Shark Shack, to go over the ever-increasing project load they had.

The ocean breeze swept in through the open windows of the cab as he drove, relaxing him. Maybe he needed a little extra drive time to unwind. It wasn't out of the way, he told himself, to just drive by the Henning place. Maybe it was about a five-mile round trip, but who was counting? Having made the decision, he made the appropriate turn, going away from the ocean, crossing the bridge, and heading to the mainland. The buildings gave way to homes. Then homes to trees. Before long the quiet road he wanted was just up on the right.

He pulled into the long bumpy lane despite the no trespassing sign. The foliage was low and overgrown. Scrub bushes and scraggly pine trees scraped the side of his truck as he drove down the narrow lane, curved around the circular drive, and parked the truck. The house, which tore at his wistful side, stood three stories high, dingy white and run down. Despite the lack of attention, the house still boasted a widow's walk and gables. The shingles were patched, the whitewashed shaker siding was chipped and worn, and the landscape needed work, but he didn't care. The house had character and longed to be tended. It had a past and needed a future. He wanted to be the one to give it a future.

He got out of the truck, climbed the small rise, and circled around to the back of the house. He stood on the back porch and gazed out at the bay. This is what he wanted, a house to really get his hands into, give his heart to, and make it his. This is what he needed. This view. This spot.

He stood still and took it all in. A lot of work or not, the spot itself was to die for.

After a long moment, he turned his attention back to the house, making a mental list. First, he would replace the old outdated sliders with French doors and get all new windows. Really open it up. The whole backside of the house which faced the water would be a wall of glass. Shimmering and shining in the sun. He would replace the rotted deck with all-weather materials, and the old, worn, crumbling cement patio with stamped concrete. Replace and paint all the rails on the widow's walk bright white. Replace the siding and the roof. That was only the beginning and just the outside. He hadn't been inside in years, but he doubted it was much better than the outside. Still, despite the work, forget the money, the place pulled at him. He wasn't sure if it was the water or the structure, but it was in him, unlike any other building, house, or property.

He didn't care how much he had to pay or how long the work would take. He'd make sure he got it. Somehow, he would restore the Henning's place and make it a showplace. With one last long look, he headed back to the truck.

• • • •

HOUSE HUNTING WAS EXHAUSTING. She was tired, sweaty, and hungry. She peered into the fridge of her hotel room kitchenette and was sadly disappointed at what she saw: half a container of fried rice, an orange and an apple from the fruit bowl at the front desk, and two water bottles, both half-empty. Pathetic.

She grabbed the apple and forced herself to take a bite when all she really wanted was a big thick burger and fries. She decided she would take a shower, go get something to eat, and then stop at the supermarket before she came back. After all, she still had another week, at least, at the hotel. She might as well make use of the kitchenette.

Taking another bite, she went into the bathroom and started the shower, slipped out of her clothes, and tossed the apple core into the trash. While the water ran down over her body, she mentally ran through the apartments she had seen today. Nothing seemed right. In reality, she didn't want an apartment. Bree wanted a house. A home.

Tina had been so sure that Bree had really wanted an apartment that she hadn't really pulled any houses. Was it because of her age? Maybe. She'd have to be a little more assertive in expressing what she wanted. Otherwise, she was wasting both of their time.

She washed her hair, scrubbed her body, and decided she would send Tina a quick email before she went out that she would like to look at houses. Not apartments.

Finished, she toweled off, wrapped another towel around her head, and slipped into jeans and a tee. In bare feet, she padded across the carpet, crossed to the desk, and switched on her laptop. Clicking on her email she typed a quick note to Tina. Taking the towel off her head, she ran her fingers through her hair and untangled the knots, as she scrolled down her new emails. One from her aunt caught her eye. The news from home brought tears to her eyes, so she decided to switch gears and check her website instead.

Images by Bree popped up. She checked her messages and answered a few. She had a couple of new orders to process, surprising her at how popular a couple of her photos were. One of the open wheat fields in the late setting sun was heavily requested. She hoped when she uploaded her new photos of the beach that they would be as popular. But first, she needed to edit them. She was eager to get started. That would have to wait though. Her long hair was almost dry and her stomach completely empty.

Bree decided she would walk down the street and try one of the local restaurants. A real restaurant and not a chain. If she was going to be a local, she had to start eating and acting like a local. She would need to start frequenting the local restaurants and businesses. That came with a risk though. That would mean connections. Friendships. Relationships. Could she do it? Maybe. She had to at least try. She could take her computer, do some work and soak up the local atmosphere. Start simple.

She shut her computer down, grabbed her bag, slipped her laptop in, and headed out the door, determined to try the first local place she came to.

Bree walked about a block when she came across a large building with a freshly painted sign. The Shark Shack. Sounded interesting. She could see through the windows that the place was busy. She could hear the low roll of voices and laughter through the walls. Deciding to try it she opened the door, the volume increased immensely.

Wonderful smells swirled out at her. Burgers, steaks, and seafood scented the air and made her mouth water. The entrance was dimly lit with track lighting accenting the black ceiling, deep blue walls, and fishnets that were draped on every vertical surface. They were decorated with large shells, buoys, anchors, and one large shark. It actually made Bree take a step back for a second. It was so lifelike and real. Behind the alcove was a sports bar. Big screens lined the walls, with various assorted lifelike sea creatures mounted behind the bar.

The hostess at the small stand greeted her with a big smile, big hair, and big earrings. "Hi, hon. Dinin' in ta'nite?" she asked, cracking her gum, her words laced heavily with a Baltimore accent.

"Yes."

"You alone? Or meetin' someone?" she questioned, reaching for a menu, making the large hoops in her ears dance.

"Alone. Is that shark real?" Bree asked, unable to stop looking at the black beady eyes that seemed to follow her every move.

"Sure is. The owner caught it himself. Creepy right?"

"Yeah."

"Try standing here every night. You get used to it after a while though. Deep-sea fishing is his hobby. Caught everything you see. Do you prefer to sit at the bar or maybe a booth out of the roar of the crowd?"

"I'll take the booth. One that's far away from this shark."

"Good choice." She winked at Bree. "Follow me, hon." Bree followed the tall leggy redhead as she sashayed her way through the tables. Big screens covering every wall displayed the baseball game. A roar went up as the Orioles hit a home run and cleared the bases. The atmosphere was contagious.

"Hope you like baseball. Cause it's what everyone in here is watchin' ta'nite."

"I don't watch it much, but I certainly like it."

"You're about to get your fill, hon," she smiled and handed Bree the menu after she slid in the booth. "Your waitress will be over shortly. Enjoy." With that, she turned and threaded her way back to the hostess stand.

Bree scanned the menu, but she already had her heart set on a big juicy burger. The waitress came over and she ordered.

The front door opened every couple of minutes, bringing in more customers. Bree sat back and focused on the big screen in front of her. But lost interest after only a few minutes, so she decided to get out her laptop and work, trying to ignore her growling stomach.

The waitress came and deposited her diet soda. She took a sip and glanced over as the front door opened once again. To her surprise, she actually recognized the new arrivals. Bree watched as Sam and Ryker wove their way through the tables. Both men stopped and shook hands with a few patrons as they went. There were a few catcalls from the women at the bar. They nodded and waved good-naturedly in their direction. But ultimately, they ended up at a booth with two women already seated and slipped in beside them. It took a minute for Bree to register that Ryker sat next to the receptionist from the realtor's office.

Not wanting to be seen out alone, Bree tucked herself back into the corner of her booth, suddenly very self-conscious.

She refocused on her laptop and selected a photo of the beach that had a small, black, keyhole limpet seashell dead center. She cropped the photo, capturing just the edge of the foaming wave, and enhanced the color of the keyhole shell, making it more ebony and the pale white ridges more prominent. Tiny bubbles could be seen bubbling up from the coarse sand. Bree boosted the texture of it to the point she could almost count each grain. She softened the edges of the photo and blurred the other shells and stones around it.

She was so entrenched in her work, she hardly noticed when the waitress appeared with her cheeseburger and placed it in front of her. Clearing her throat the waitress asked, "Can I get you anything else? Refill on the diet?"

Blinking, Bree looked up. "Yes, please."

"Are you new to the area?" she asked, as she reached for the glass. "Haven't seen you in here before."

"Yes," Bree answered as the wave of hunger hit her. She glanced at her burger and fries then. Her mouth watered. "This looks wonderful."

"Give it a try. I'll be back with the diet in a sec."

Bree sank her teeth in and savored the first bite. She was popping a few fries in when the waitress returned with her soda.

"How is everything?"

Bree nodded her approval with a mouth full.

"Good, glad you like it." She lingered for a moment and took in Bree and her computer. "That's beautiful."

"Thanks."

"So what? Are you a photographer or something?" she asked.

Bree dabbed at the corner of her mouth with a napkin. "Yes, I am."

"Do you do professional headshots as well as that?" she asked, pointing a finger at Bree's laptop.

Bree nodded. "I do. Are you in need of some headshots?"

"Yea, I'm putting together my resume and starting a business profile. I wanted to add a professional-looking photo, but don't want to pay a fortune to have it taken."

Bree nodded, rummaged through her computer bag, and pulled out a business card. "Here's my card. Check out my website. If you like what you see, give me a call. We can discuss a budget, and maybe a little more about what you are looking to have done. What you should wear. How to do your hair. That sort of thing."

After a quick examination, she said, "Images by Bree. Thanks." Then she tucked the card into the back pocket of her black jeans and stuck out her hand. "Nice to meet you, Bree. I'm Colette."

Accepting her hand, Bree shook it. "Nice to meet you too."

"I better let you get back to the cheeseburger before it's cold, and me to my other customers. I'll be back around to check on you in a little while."

Ryker watched the exchange from the corner of his eye as he sipped his cold beer and wondered what it was all about. He tried to pay attention to the conversation at the table but was distracted by the visible edge of the brunette sitting by herself in the corner booth.

He contemplated going over but was stopped by Colette's appearance with their food.

"All right, I have two orders of crab cakes." Colette placed one in front of Sam, the other Sheri. "Chicken sandwich for Carol. And the sirloin well done for Ryker. Can I get you anything else? A couple of refills maybe?"

"I think we're good, Colette." Ryker unwrapped his fork and knife. "Pretty busy tonight. How are things?"

"Pretty good. Graduating next week."

"That's awesome." The whole table agreed.

"It's about damn time. Took me six years, in what should have been four."

"Hey, don't beat yourself up. You did it and worked full time while doing it. Plus taking care of a sick parent. I think you rock," Sam said sincerely.

"Thanks."

"He's right, "Ryker agreed. He cut into his steak, stabbed a piece, and waved it at Colette. "Maybe we will have to get the new marketing guru to help us spruce up our advertising."

Colette blushed, "I could take a look, but I need to get a job first."

"Is that why you're collecting business cards?"

"What?"

Ryker pointed in the direction of Bree, Colette followed his gaze.

"Yes and no. She's a photographer. I need to get some professional headshots taken for my profile picture."

"Is she any good?"

"Don't know. Gonna check out her website after work and see. But if what she was working on is any indication, I would say she is. You guys enjoy. I'll be back around." With a little wave, she threaded her way back to the kitchen.

Chapter 5

Bree had a full day planned. She dressed casually and for comfort in her favorite pair of jeans, pale blue and gray striped cotton tee, and her light blue canvas shoes. She accented with small silver hoop earrings and the cross she had received from her parents for graduation around her neck. She added a smoke gray cable knit sweater because the spring air was chilly. Gone was the 70-degree weather on the day she had arrived.

She was meeting Tina to look at houses; their first appointment was at ten. They had nine listings, all shapes, and sizes. She figured that would take most of the day. Then she was going to meet Colette for the photoshoot. She was excited to get started on both.

She pulled the door open to Coastal Realty and walked into a frenzy of activity. A couple of salespeople she didn't know ran down the hall. Sheri greeted her at the door, looking frazzled.

"Oh, Bree! You're a little early. Have a seat. We have a situation." She indicated down the hall where the commotion seemed to cluster. Voices were raised in concern.

"Everything all right?"

"I hope so." Sheri pushed at her strawberry blonde hair, tucking it behind her left ear. In a hushed voice, she explained. "We have an ambulance on the way for Tina. She came in this morning with pain in her side. She tried to ignore it for a while since you have a full day of appointments. Then about twenty minutes ago she just doubled over in terrible pain, and started vomiting."

"Oh no!"

"Yeah, so I have a janitorial service on the way. Her office is a mess. She couldn't make it to the bathroom, just collapsed beside her desk."

"How awful! I hope she'll be all right. I should go. Get out of your way."

"No, don't. Linda said for Greg to take you out. It would be a shame to let all of Tina's work go to waste. And we know you are in a time crunch. Greg's new to the office so he didn't have any appointments lined up for today. If you can just be patient, we will get it sorted out."

"Of course."

"Here's the ambulance now."

Bree moved over and sank into the corner chair. Lights flashed outside and swirled around the room. EMTs came in with a gurney. Sheri escorted them down the hall. Voices were hushed as they took over. Sheri, a man, and a woman came out into the reception area and waited with Bree.

In a matter of minutes, a very pale Tina was on the gurney with Linda right beside her headed out.

Linda stopped briefly while the EMTs wheeled Tina out and loaded her onto the ambulance. "I'm going to follow the ambulance in. I'll keep you posted if there's any news. Sheri, you have everything covered?"

"Got it covered, Linda. Don't worry about anything."

"Good. Greg and Carol, you take care of all showings. Carry on!" Linda said with a flourish of her hand and scurried out the door.

Everyone stood still for a moment as silence descended over the office and the red and blue lights faded away. Sheri cleared her throat. "Greg Carpenter, this is Bree Thompson, your appointment."

Greg extended his hand, and as she reached for it. She took him in, early thirties, 5'10", thin, hair the color of hickory, and a crooked nose. His eyes were like warm syrup behind thin-rimmed wire glasses. He had a nice, friendly face.

"Like it or not, looks like you're stuck with me. Hope it's okay?"

"I'm sorry Tina isn't well, but I am completely fine with you taking me around."

"Why don't you come back to my office, and we can look over the listings quickly. I need to get myself up to date with what you're looking for. Follow me."

He led the way down the short hall whistling softly while he walked. He paused at the door. "After you. Sorry for the chaos. I've only been working here for less than a week." Greg scooped up a box and indicated she sit down. The office wasn't big but had a nice window. The walls were painted cream and contained only the basics a wood desk and a swivel chair. Matching wood filing cabinet and side chair upholstered in the same shade as the walls. He put the box on top of a couple of others and sat down across from her.

Bree noted there weren't any photos or personal items, but she figured they would come.

"All right, let's pull up what Tina had." Greg tapped away at his computer. "Looks like you want a water view. Three to four bedrooms. Oh, wait. I think Sheri mentioned Tina might have already printed out the listings. Let me check with her before I hit print."

He stepped out into the hall and disappeared. He was back in seconds with papers in hand. "We're in luck," he said, waving the stack.

"Can we look at those before we go? I think I want to add a couple of things to my list of requirements."

"Sure."

"I would like an extra space. Maybe an outbuilding or something that could be used for my studio, for business."

He glanced through the listings. I don't think there's anything like that here. Let me pull a couple of others quickly." He typed, waited for the website to upload, and found a couple of listings to fit. "We can start with a couple of these Tina already had scheduled, and I will call while we are out to see if we can get into these two new ones. Sounds good?"

"Perfect."

"Are you okay riding with me? Or would you prefer to take your own car?"

"If it's all right, I'll ride with you?"

"Works for me." He grabbed his laptop, pocketed his cell phone, and snagged his keys out of the drawer. "Let's roll."

"Have fun," Sheri called, as they went out and the cleaning crew came in.

"If you don't mind, I'm going to grab a water bottle and my sunglasses out of my car."

"No problem, take your time." Greg watched her cross to an SUV with Kansas plates. She ducked in the driver's side and reemerged carrying her items.

She crossed to him. "I'm ready."

"This is me," he said, indicating the dark green sedan. He held the door for her, and then went around. Climbed in. Punched the first address into the GPS and pulled out of the lot. "This first house isn't far. So . . . Kansas huh?"

Bree looked at him.

"You have Kansas plates. Rental?"

"No, it's mine. Yes, I'm from Kansas."

"Pretty state if you like that vast, flat, rolling plains feel. Golden wheat fields and all that blue sky."

She smiled at that. "You've been to Kansas?"

"Had some family there." Greg looked at her. *Eyes as blue as a Kansas sky,* he thought. "Do you mind me asking what brought you this way?"

She shrugged. "I needed a change. Different scenery."

When she didn't elaborate, he nodded. "I can appreciate that." He made the appropriate turns as directed by the GPS. "Now that you're here, hopefully, we can find you the perfect place to live."

Chapter 6

I t took her breath away the minute it came into view. It was worn and weathered, windswept, and haggard. It looked like she felt. Alone and abandoned against the deep battered sky, it called to her, as nothing else had. Or could.

The house stood three stories high, dingy white, and abandoned. The front porch that wrapped around the house sagged. But the lines of the house were elegant and drew her eyes up, to the dormers, peaks, and a pitched roof. And to a widow's walk.

An actual widow's walk. She couldn't believe it. Her hand went to her heart. She'd never seen anything like it in person, only in the movies. It was wistful, romantic, and a little sad. Just the sight of it created a longing in her that she'd never known.

Drawn, Bree got out of the car and the wind whipped at her hair. She stood and just took it in; the sight, the house, the water, and the sound. There were waves lapping on the shore. The smell was fresh. Pine and sea.

"Outside needs some work. The landscaping is nonexistent. But the location, secluded. Private. That's really nice." Greg walked forward, still talking. "Looks like most everything on the outside is just cosmetic: paint, patching, shore up the porch. But of course, we would have an inspector out to check it all."

He pointed to the left. "That's the carriage house over there, which is a two-car garage, connected by that breezeway. There's a space above it that could potentially be for your studio. Even has an outside entrance. On paper, the place seems to have everything you want."

He looked back and saw Bree still standing beside the car.

"Did you want to go in?"

"Yes." She shook herself. "Definitely."

"I wasn't sure for a moment. Thought seeing it in person might have actually scared you off."

They climbed four wide steps to the porch and the heavy wooden front door. He swiped his card and punched in the code to release the lock. He removed the key from the box, turned the knob and the door swung into a grand foyer. There was a sweep of dark stained stairs leading up, large identical rooms on either side of it. One a library, she guessed, the other a formal living room. Both had fireplaces made of limestone surrounded by large mantels made of driftwood stained dark. Wide tall windows from the front would bring in a wash of light on a sunny day. Now though, the walls were dingy in the measly natural light. Greg flipped switches as they entered.

"Wow," Greg exclaimed. "This is great. Lots of potential for natural light. Large rooms. High ceilings. The info sheet said ten feet high on this level. Look at the moldings." They wandered slowly across the dark hardwood floors from one room into the other. "Floors can be refinished where they're scuffed. But overall, they look good. Nice rich color."

He let out a whistle as they walked through the large archway.

The back half of the house was one big open space, which held the kitchen, eating area, and a sitting area with yet another fireplace.

The kitchen was dated, appliances missing or rusting, countertops cracking. But Bree looked past that, imagined what it could be.

The back wall had windows that ran the expanse of the room and invited the outside in, drawing her out to the water. The view. Greg stopped her before she could go out, with a light hand to her arm.

"Let's go upstairs and check out the second floor before you get sucked in by the view. Okay?"

"Yeah. Yes, you're right. I should finish the house first." Although she already knew it didn't really matter what was up there. As long as it was livable, she wanted it. She wanted this house.

Greg held out his hand indicating she should go first, so she did. Back towards the stairs and up. Her fingers trailed along the banister and railing, dark wood worn to a golden honey brown from the years of trailing hands. The large wide stairs swept up and around to a balcony overlooking the foyer. Upstairs there were four identical doors evenly spaced on either side. She imagined they led to bedrooms. But in the back, there was a set of double doors. Bree went to those first.

She swung them inward and was greeted with a large rectangular room that had a wall of windows facing the bay, just like below. This time she did cross and open the French doors. Stepping out onto the balcony she let the breeze wash over her. The sky was bruised and forlorn, the waves choppy. But the menacing sky didn't detract from it, only pulled at her aching soul. The water reflected her own self. Happy and calm one minute. Turbulent and brooding the next. This was it, a place that actually fit her and her moods. Since the accident, everything inside her was churned up, just like the sea.

"This door leads to an on-suite. Has a shower and claw foot tub. Two sinks. Pretty dated. But again cosmetic." He crossed the room, opened another door. "This one to a large walk-in closet," Greg said, from somewhere behind her.

She heard him, even acknowledged him with a nod but couldn't pull herself from the water.

Here she seemed to fit. If no one else in the world ever understood her again, the sea would. She was in heaven. Pure and honest heaven.

The rest of the upstairs consisted of three more large bedrooms and a couple of baths. The last door held worn, wooden, narrow stairs. They climbed the narrow staircase and came out into a large room. It was broken up by a few support beams and a small square set of walls directly in the middle of the room. Dormers lined both sides of the long walls.

"Attic space," Greg commented. "Probably used for storage."

The ceiling was approximately eight feet high. Open rafters. A few old pieces of furniture sat off to the side covered in sheets along with some forgotten boxes.

Bree decided it would make a fun space for kids someday, maybe even a game room. It could be enchanting with the right lighting, paint, and flooring.

"I wonder what's behind that door." Curious Bree crossed to the middle of the room. Opening it she found yet another set of stairs. This time tight compact spiral stairs made of metal. "The widow's walk," she said suddenly, breathless. "Let's look."

"Right behind you."

After climbing almost straight up they came into a small room made of clapboard and glass. There was a crude wooden bench against one side and just enough room for two or three people to stand. Bree turned a slow circle and took in the view. It was almost 270 degrees of a water view.

Green spread behind her to the west. Civilized areas sprawled across the windswept terrain. Bree racked her mind for names of towns she passed Berlin, Ironshire, Whaleyville, Bishop, and Ocean Pines. She wasn't sure which ones were which but knew these were the towns that spread out before her.

Off to the south was Assateague Island, green and lush, and east, Ocean City, between the little inlet. This was the Isle of Wight Bay that surrounded her and this little piece of land. Further up, Highway 90 cut across and divided off Assawoman Bay.

She looked back at the skyline of Ocean City, Maryland. She could see the Ferris wheel on one end. Her eyes trailed over the buildings until she reached the hotel where she was staying, and beyond that compact swipe of land? The Atlantic and the horizon lay endless and wide.

"I'll take it."

From behind her, Greg laughed. "I'm not surprised."

Greg brushed against her as he reached around her for a door, breaking her reprieve. There were two, on either side, opening out to the widow's walk that lined the top of the roof. He opened it and the wind rushed in, making her shiver.

Bree wondered what it might have been like to walk it, watch, and wait for a loved one; a father, a brother, a lover.

"Brrr, sorry. Let me close that again. It turned cold fast." His arm caressed hers as he tugged the door shut. "Probably shouldn't go out anyway. Not sure it's safe." He said, his hand still on her, his face only inches from hers.

His eyes flicked down to her mouth for a brief second. So fast, in fact, she wasn't sure if she had imagined it.

Was it the turbulent brooding weather that was making her romanticize the situation? She stepped back, unsure. *Keep it light,* she thought. She smiled. "You're probably right. I doubt anyone has been out there in years. We should go back down."

He smiled back. "After you."

They descended in silence, all the way to the first floor. She paused here and there, taking note of one thing or another. When they reached the foyer, he broke the silence.

"Let's go through the kitchen to the carriage house. Look at that space quickly. Then we can go back to the office and write up an offer."

"That sounds like a good plan."

Chapter 7

S he flipped on the lights, trying to cut the gloominess out of the room, and turned on the television. Sound on low, Bree sat at her laptop in the living room of her suite and got to work. First, she went to her website and updated her blog, "Bree's Buzz." Every Wednesday, religiously, she put something out. She always put in highlights of her week, this time though she added a few more photos of her trip east as she traveled across the country.

She posted some pictures that she had taken along the way and here at the beach. Bree gave a photography tip on how to capture a moving image. She challenged her subscribers to capture the essence of Spring and invited them to post their pictures. Lastly, she added prints to the website that were ready for purchase.

She had five different categories: landscapes, architecture, colors, textures, and portraits. Landscapes seemed to be her most popular. She got a lot of views in portraits and booked a lot of sessions. But that might slow down now that she wasn't in the Midwest. It would take a while before people knew about her here.

The photo shoot with Colette after house hunting had been fun, and she had some great shots of her to add to her site once they were edited.

At the bottom of the page, Bree had an area where clients, customers, and future photographers could make comments on her work or ask questions about photography. She scrolled through the list. Saw mostly regulars, but wasn't surprised to find a few new subscribers.

She offered praise and friendly advice to those that posted photos. Some just commented on recent posts or blogs she'd made.

Bree had a variety of subscribers, ranging from grandmothers trying to capture every precious moment, to high school students needing advice for their yearbook, or parents trying to snap pictures of their teenagers playing sports. She answered every question and read every post.

> Nannygee101: Took photos of my newborn grandson. Can't wait to share with you!

> Chocolate4ever: Set up my table like you suggested. Photos turned out great! Thanks for the idea.

> TexasTom56: Like the pictures you posted of the Appalachians. My fav was #4.

> Sunnygal: Love the pics! Safe travels.

> BigmamaMay: Great pics!

> Soccerrocks21: Miss you girl. Keep posting. Love to see your work!

> Ellisonfamily: Luv the pics of the mtns!

> Kage: This website is a piece of crap.

Shocked and hurt by the last one, Bree reread it. She couldn't understand why someone had said that. Without hesitation, Bree deleted it. It wasn't worth responding to.

She scolded herself for being so sensitive and tried to focus on the good ones, the positive ones. She closed down her website and pulled up Colette's photos from this afternoon.

She always positioned headshots in landscape format. That way she was sure never to cut off a shoulder and had plenty of area to work with surrounding her subject. Bree played with the edges, took out a blemish the camera picked up, and cropped. There really wasn't much to be done with Colette's photos. In a matter of an hour, she had the photos done. She uploaded, attached them to an email, and sent them off to Colette.

She was shutting down her laptop when her cell phone rang. "Hello?"

"Hello, Bree? This is Greg. Hope this is a good time?"

"Yes, it's fine."

"I have some news."

Bree moved to the edge of her seat. "Good or bad?"

"Definitely good. They accepted your offer."

"Already? You're kidding, right?"

"I wouldn't joke about this. You'll never believe this," he paused for effect, "They would be able to settle in a week, barring any unforeseen problems with the inspection or loan process. Will that work? I know you wanted a quick turnaround."

"Yes! That's fantastic, really. I can make anything work as long as I know I have the house. I can extend my stay here for a few days."

"We got lucky and I was able to get the inspector lined up for Monday morning at ten. Can you make that?"

"Definitely. How did you manage that so fast?"

"As I said, I got lucky. He had a cancelation, so I jumped at it. You're already pre-approved for the loan, pending the house passes inspection and the appraisal. Which I don't think should be a problem."

Greg was talking and all Bree could do was stand up and do a little jig as he listed off things to be done. She hadn't been this happy in over a year. She forced herself to concentrate on what Greg was saying.

"They don't want to leave the house empty any longer than necessary; they'd be willing to let you move in after the inspection."

"What? Wait . . . Really? That would be awesome," she exclaimed.

"If for some reason settlement won't be able to take place quickly, we'd have to draw up some papers for you to rent until settlement, they're willing to wait and see on that."

"All right."

"Also, if there's work to be done after the inspection, and most likely there will be something, you'd have to live there in the midst of that. Do you have a problem with that?"

"No, not at all."

"Okay, I've got some things to do with this yet tonight. Need to run some of this past Linda."

"Oh, how is Tina doing?" Bree asked, feeling bad she hadn't asked sooner.

"She had emergency gallbladder surgery and made it through okay. But she's going to be in the hospital for the next few days. Apparently, her gallbladder was pretty infected, ready to burst and leaking bile into her system. She's running a fever, the doctor wants to keep her at least until it breaks."

"Sounds like she was lucky," Bree commented.

"She sure was. Now . . . Let me get these details worked out and I will get back in touch with you as soon as I can."

"Thank you, Greg."

"You bet."

Chapter 8

The week was flying by. Ryker checked things off on his mental list as he drove with the windows down, letting in the soft fresh breeze, as April crept towards May. The sun inched higher in the sky, casting long golden fingers onto the water. Tempting him to come out and play. *Not today. Tomorrow,* he promised himself. He pictured his boat and his jet ski sitting in storage. The weekend promised to be sunny and 68, too chilly for swimming but just right for a day out on the water under the sun.

He savored the view for a moment longer then turned his mind back to his list. Installation was finished with the kitchen at the bungalow. The painting was completed at Coastal Realty's rentals; he'd have to send the bill over to Sheri. Everything for the Brandy beach house was ordered, with plumbing fixtures arriving on Monday, and kitchen cabinets in three weeks. Hardware was back-ordered, but should still be in on time.

Next on his list were a couple of estimates, he needed to verify the times for Monday. He consulted the calendar on his phone on his way to meet Randy Brown, the home inspector. He made a quick stop at the lumber store because it was on his way.

In a matter of minutes, he was pulling into the driveway. A white and blue Coastal Realty sign was in the middle of the lush green lawn. On top, it read "Coming Soon".

The coming soon was up to him and how long Randy's list would be today. He knew he could pass the job along to one of their employees to handle, but it was for Linda so he would most likely do it himself unless it was more than he could handle alone. She had been one of Bolts & Beams very first clients. So almost always he or Sam handled her projects themselves.

Randy was standing at the front door on the phone, waiting on Ryker. Seeing him approach he hung up.

"Hello. How's it going?"

Ryker reached out and shook Randy's hand. "Can't complain. How 'bout you?"

"Same. Ready to do this thing?"

"Yep."

"What's the situation on this one?" Randy asked.

"Repeat clients of Linda's. They want to get the house on the market ASAP and don't want a lot of hassles. We can go through, let me know what needs fixing, and we will get 'er done."

"Sounds good. From the look of the place, there might not be a lot to do."

"That's all right with me. We have enough on our plate right now. Especially since Linda is hell-bent on getting this on the market in less than two weeks."

Randy grinned his half lopsided smile. "Yeah, when Linda says jump, I always reply how high."

Ryker laughed. "That's always the best policy in my book when it comes to Linda."

Randy tucked his clipboard under his arm and slipped his pen in the breast pocket of his long-sleeve tan shirt, and ran a hand through his salt and pepper hair. "Got my ladder on the truck. Wanna give me a hand and we can go up on the roof and take a look?"

"You bet."

Ryker followed him around the truck. Both men unhooked the ladder and lifted it off the rack of the truck. They shouldered it and started towards the house. "That's why when the office called and wanted that inspection done on Cypress Lane ASAP; I said I had an opening on Monday. Had to finagle a few things around but it's fine, I made it work."

"Cypress Lane? The only thing out there is the Henning place," Ryker questioned.

They lowered the ladder, one end to the ground, and then leaned the other against the house. "Yep, that'd be the one."

"Linda called you and asked for an inspection on the Henning place?" Ryker asked in disbelief, suddenly concerned.

Sensing something in Ryker's tone, Randy turned and looked at him. He scratched his chin. "Well now, no. Sheri called, said it was for Coastal. She didn't refer to it as the Henning place, just Cypress Lane. Is that a problem?"

"I'm not exactly sure. I put an offer in on the Henning house out on Cypress Lane, but they rejected it. Said I might want to put in another if someone else is. I didn't think they would do anything without consulting me first. But . . ." he shrugged unsure.

"Maybe there's another house somewhere on that road I'm not aware of." Randy flipped through his paperwork attached to the clipboard. "10 Cypress Lane. Does that sound like the address for the Henning place?"

A knot formed in Ryker's stomach. "Yeah, that's it."

"What do you want with that big old place anyway?"

Ryker shot back, "Who wouldn't want it? That place is almost completely surrounded by water, a beach bum's paradise. It has character, great craftsmanship, and a history."

"And a ghost. Heard it's haunted," Randy said matter-of-factly.

Ryker laughed. "Hell, Randy, this is the beach, dead or alive, who wouldn't want to live here?"

Randy shook his head. "Still didn't answer my question though. What do you want with that much space?"

Ryker tucked his hands in his pockets, thought about it. Did he want it simply because the Hennings didn't want him to have it? Possibly, but that wasn't all. "It's perfect for the business, lots of space to grow, or the perfect place to have my boat. Always wanted a big house right on the water. My place is fine but doesn't have the view or the space, and I wouldn't have to pay for dock fees. But mainly, I just want to see the old place fixed up. It's a work of art, and needs to be treated as such."

Randy nodded, "Well, don't jump to any conclusions until you get in touch with Linda. Even if you don't get it, there could be some work there for you yet." Randy grabbed hold of the fifth rung of the ladder, stepped up. "Let's have a look and get this one done."

"You go on up. I'll hold it. Something you need me to see, you let me know."

It turned out that the whole roof needed to be replaced. He needed to get the go-ahead from Linda's clients to replace the roof. Punching in the office number he called to get approval.

"Coastal Realty. Sheri speaking. How can I help you?"

"Hey, Sheri. It's Ryker. How's it going?"

"Ryker! What a pleasant surprise. I was just thinking about you."

Ryker could almost hear the smile in her voice as she spoke.

"I was wondering if you were going to Sam's tonight?"

"That's correct. I'll swing by for a while."

"Carol and I are going. Should be fun." There was a pause on the other end. "What can I do for you?"

"I called to talk to Linda. Is she around?"

"She's out right now on an appointment. She's been running around trying to play catch up the past few days with Tina being in the hospital and all. She should be done around five. I'm sure you could reach her on her cell." She waited a beat when he didn't reply, she asked, "Anything I can do for you?"

"Yeah, maybe. A couple of things. First, I have a list of what needs to be fixed, repaired, and replaced at the property on Second Avenue. I just emailed it over. Can you make sure that we get approval quickly? I know Linda wants to get it on the market soon."

"Not a problem. And second?"

"Randy Brown told me today that you called him and requested a home inspection for Cypress Lane. Is that correct?"

"Yes, I believe I have him scheduled for Monday at ten. Why? Do you need him on Monday?" She tapped on her keyboard and brought up the office calendar.

"That wouldn't be for the Henning place, would it?" he asked, already knowing the answer.

He heard her make a small squeak on the other end. "Oh, Ryker. I didn't realize. I'm not sure how this happened. You need to talk to Linda."

"Believe me, I plan to."

Chapter 9

Linda didn't cook. She didn't know how to and didn't care to learn. Her skills were limited to the microwave and coffee pot. She could barely boil water, and her toast always popped up burnt. Yet somehow, she had managed to raise two healthy, grown boys on macaroni and cheese, frozen pizza, and gelatin. And not once did either of them have a complaint. Sure, she had heard her share of comments whispered between them over the years, about certain friends' moms who could cook or bake, but she didn't let it bother her. She would just give kudos to them for mastering a skill she despised. Every woman had talents, but cooking wasn't one of hers, and that was all right by her.

But in times like these, when she felt the need to deliver a decent meal to her best friend coming home from the hospital, she almost wished she could. Almost. But that's why God had seen fit to create grocery stores. So she was on a mission, a mission to provide good food without lifting a finger or a spoon.

Her need to cook was quickly squelched as she hurried into the supermarket, and the scent of coffee and fresh-baked bread hung heavily in the air. Everything you could ever want to make or hope to eat was here, all in one place, all ready done for you. That made her smile and her stomach growl.

Pushing her cart, she went straight to the deli. Linda grabbed a pound of potato salad, a container of coleslaw, baked beans, and a piping hot chicken breast from the rotisserie. She was headed towards the bakery when her phone rang.

She checked the caller id and saw that it was Ryker. "Hey, handsome. How's it going?"

"You tell me, Linda," Ryker said, his tone gruff.

"Hmmm, I'm sensing from your tone that something's wrong." Linda scooted between two shoppers and maneuvered her cart around a bin of apples.

"You could say that."

She sighed not up for his attitude. "I'm not a mind reader, Ryker. I'm old and tired. Just come straight out with it." Linda selected a package of freshly baked rolls and placed them in her cart. Suddenly famished, she went to the desserts. Probably the wrong thing to do when she was starving, but she decided to live dangerously for a change. After all, she had a huffy man on the other end of the line. And for dealing with that she required chocolate.

"First, you are not old, and be glad you are not a mind reader because I'm sure you wouldn't want to know what I'm thinking right now. My thoughts are not censored."

She stifled a laugh, only because she could tell he was fuming, and would not appreciate any comments from someone old enough to be his mother. She could almost hear him choosing his words as she examined the triple-layer chocolate cake with dark chocolate ganache dripping down the sides. She probably shouldn't get it, too many calories. She put it down, picked up an apple pie. A healthier choice. It contained fruit. Fruit was good for you. Fruit canceled out the calories of the light and airy crust. Linda placed the pie in her cart. "You don't have to mince words with me, Ryker. We've known each other for too long."

So, he didn't. "What the hell, Linda? Who are you having the home inspection for at the Henning place?"

"The Henning place?" She noted she was a little loud when a couple of shoppers glanced in her direction. She dropped her voice a notch. "We're not. I'm not. Who told you that, anyway? There hasn't been any action on that place or I would have heard."

"Don't play dumb with me. Randy Brown did. He has an inspection on Monday at ten. Said you were in a hurry to get it done. I confirmed it with Sheri. Were you hoping I wouldn't find out?"

Linda stood still in the middle of the bakery section as people walked by. She pinched the sides of her nose. Tried to think. Racking her brain. "There's some mistake. I didn't ask him either. The only thing he's inspecting on Monday for us is a house Greg sold, on Cypress Lane." Then it clicked. *Shit*, she thought. It couldn't be. Cypress Lane. The Henning place. One and the same. How had she not caught that? The address had sounded familiar, but she hadn't been able to place it. And frankly hadn't tried. The one time . . . Now it came back to bite her in the ass.

She sighed. "Ryker, I didn't realize. We never refer to it as Cypress Lane. My new guy sold it."

"How the hell did this happen?" Ryker demanded. "Didn't you go over the listings he pulled?"

Trying to juggle her thoughts and her mission. Maybe cookies for Tina. Chocolate chip were her favorite. She rubbed the spot between her eyes where a headache was forming. "It was Tina's client. I saw everything she had appointments for beforehand. I swear, the Henning place wasn't one of them."

"So how can you explain it then?"

"The only thing I can think of is . . . well, wait." Her thoughts tumbled out, "Greg took over the showings because that's the day we had to rush Tina to the hospital. I thought it would be simple. Give the new guy something to do, keep the client happy. He must have pulled it while they were out." She sighed. "He wouldn't have had any idea about your interest in the place. I simply hadn't gotten that far with him."

"Damn it! I can't believe it."

"I'm sorry, Ryker. I didn't realize. Still wouldn't, if you hadn't just brought it to my attention. I knew there was something familiar about the address, but it just didn't fully register when he ran it past me, I was distracted with all that was happening with Tina."

There was nothing but silence from the other end.

"Ryker, I'm so sorry. I know they accepted the offer and it's moving forward, and fast."

"Is there any chance it might fall through? Maybe not enough financing?"

She could hear the disappointment in his voice and felt it herself. *No wonder it was moving fast, Mr. Henning hadn't wanted Ryker to have it, so he would have accepted anything out of spite,* she imagined. *What a bastard.*

Even though he couldn't see her, she shook her head. "I'm afraid not. The financing was solid. Tina had that all confirmed."

"So that's it then?" he asked.

"We'll find you something else. Something better," Linda said, trying to sound hopeful. "I'm sorry."

"Yeah, me too." With a click, he was gone.

She stood there a moment, disgusted with herself and the situation; for not realizing, feeling the disappointment of a dear friend.

She couldn't even be angry at Greg, he hadn't known, he couldn't have.

Disheartened, Linda forced herself to look at the contents of her cart. Deemed the meal good enough. She fished out the pie, tossed it back on the shelf. To hell with fruit. After that phone call, she needed chocolate. And lots of it. She proceeded to pick up the triple chocolate layer cake, adding a container of chocolate chip cookies for Tina. She grabbed brownies too, just in case.

Chapter 10

The air was cool, but the fire took the chill out of it if she stood close as darkness descended. Groups of people gathered. Voices carried and country music played in the background, pumped out of invisible speakers.

There were a lot of people, more than Bree would have thought. She enjoyed parties, loved having them, and going to them back home. But it was completely different and a bit awkward when you were the one who was new, the one on the outside looking in. She scanned the crowd looking for familiar faces. She noticed Ryker right off. He was hard to miss in his leather and denim. Tall, dark, and mysterious was the impression Bree got from him.

She watched him move from one group to another. People, both men and women, seemed to gravitate towards him. He exchanged hugs with the women and shook hands with the guys. She watched as the girls eyed him, hoping to get his attention. He flirted, leaned in close, touched, but always moved on, leaving them drowning in his wake. *Definitely a player,* she thought.

Colette sidled up to her and handed her a wine cooler that she had unearthed from the depths of the cooler. "Anything catch your eye?" she asked, twisting the top and taking a sip of her own.

"No, I'm not in the market right now," Bree said, forcing her eyes to move away from Ryker.

"Ha! That's a good one," Colette laughed. "I'm always keeping my options open. You just never know. But I do like looking, especially if it's tall, dark, and handsome." She indicated in the direction Bree had been looking.

"He does certainly grab your attention, but I'm serious," Bree answered. "I just got out of a relationship a couple of months ago."

Colette looked at her new friend, joking aside. "Is that why you look so sad?"

"What?" Bree asked, surprised. "Do I?" here she thought she was hiding her past well.

"You do," Colette replied, looking at Bree. "I mean, not all the time, but sometimes I've noticed you are. Look, now I've made it worse." She gave her a quick sidearm hug. "I've always found the best way to get over a bad breakup is to find someone new. What was his name?"

"Chad."

"Chad, huh? Bree and Chad, nope. Doesn't fit. Was Chad that hot?" Colette tipped her bottle in Ryker's direction.

Bree laughed. "Not quite."

"I didn't think so. Come on, I'll introduce you to some hot guys. We have a plethora of them." She grabbed her hand. "But first let's get something to eat. I'm starving. And you never know who you'll bump into getting food, maybe another hot guy." She gave her a wink and pulled her along. "Here's a perfect example."

Sam came out of the house with a bowl of pretzels and a stack of napkins just as they picked up a plate.

"Good evening, ladies," he said, placing the bowl. "Glad you could make it."

"Hey, Sam," Colette said, batting her lashes. "Have you met my friend Bree? She's new to the area."

Sam grinned and stuck out his free hand. "I sure have, this woman packs a punch, or so I've heard."

Bree couldn't help but smile when she took his hand. "Not ever going to let me live that down, are you?"

"Not on your life," he laughed. Not one to forget a detail, Sam asked, "So how did the photo shoot go?"

"It was great!" Colette exclaimed, pleased he'd remembered. "Bree, here, is a pro. You need to check out my picture on her website."

"That good huh?" he asked. "I'll have to take a look."

"Well, it's not that hard when you have a great model," Bree added, putting a scoop of salsa and a handful of chips on her plate.

Colette picked up a hot dog and squirted it with mustard. Thinking out loud she added, "I took a look at your website after you mentioned it. You guys should get Bree to take some photos for your website, you know, like before and after pictures. Your website could use some updating. Maybe even a photo of both of you. I'm certain Bree here could even make you two yahoos look good."

"Who are you calling a yahoo?" Ryker asked as he strolled up.

Colette smiled. "Why, here comes the other one right now."

"That would be us," Sam answered, addressing Ryker, wagging a finger between them. "Apparently, our website is out of date and could use some work. This, from the soon-to-be marketing expert."

Colette took a little bow, leaned in, and placed a hand on Ryker's arm, flirting just a little. "Bree, here, is an excellent photographer. I know great work when I see it, degree or not."

"Is she now?" Ryker asked, giving Bree the once-over. She wore jeans that hugged every curve, a black mock turtleneck, and a gray puffy vest, with short black boots. Her long golden-brown hair hung loose and straight. It shimmered like bronze in the firelight. "How you doin', Champ?"

"Champ?" Bree questioned.

"Yes, Champ, as in Muhammad."

"Muhammad?"

"Muhammad Ali."

"The boxer?"

"That'd be the one." Ryker grinned devilishly. "You know . . . float like a butterfly, sting like a Bree."

Sam roared with laughter. "Good one!" he slapped Ryker on the back. "I wish I'd thought of that."

"You're hilarious," Bree said dryly, feeling the heat rise in her cheeks.

"In case you weren't aware, I'm the funny one." Ryker wagged his finger back and forth between himself and Sam.

Sam scoffed, "As if."

"Am I missing something here?" Colette wondered, not sure what was going on. She looked at Bree, "Are you a boxer?"

"No. Ryker, here, can't take a punch," Bree commented, reaching for a hot dog. "And apparently holds a grudge because of it."

"No grudge, but don't turn your back on this one, Colette. She won't think twice about cold-cocking you." From behind her, someone called his name. "If you'll excuse me?" He popped a chip in his mouth, winked at her, and went in the direction his name had been called.

Sam grabbed a hot dog himself, added ketchup and mustard. "How about we take a seat by the fire and you can tell me more about updating our website."

Chapter 11

The sun was bright coming out from behind large white puffs of clouds but the air was still chilly. The weatherman had promised warm and sunny weather. Bree hoped that would hold true as she followed the signs for Assateague Island, guided by her GPS.

She recognized the corner that they had taken to Sam's house last night. *The bonfire had been fun,* she thought. People were friendly, welcoming. The weather, perfect. Nights like that, though, made her ache for home, her friends, and her family.

Bree followed Route 611, and crossed Verrazano Bridge with a stretch of saltwater on either side, making her way onto the island. Despite the chill, she kept the windows down and let the smell of salt and brine flow through the small SUV. She took in the blue water, the sandy coastline, and the low brush. She spotted three ponies, on the edge of the beach, romping through the waves.

Without thinking, she said, "Look at that, Gracie!" she even pointed. "Aren't they beautiful?" But when there was no response, her heart gave a little pang. Of course, there was no response. There never would be again. Her little sister was gone.

But, if she tried hard enough, she could imagine her sister's laugh. Her giggle of delight when she saw the ponies for the first time. She'd want to ride them, or at least get close enough to feed them. Her energy was always contagious.

She could almost hear her father's lecture: "You can't feed them, they're wild animals. Beautiful, but potentially dangerous. If you do, it makes them dependent on humans. No different than feeding the bears in Canada. It's not that it can't be done. It's that it shouldn't."

Oh, dad, she thought, her eyes tearing. *What's happened to us?* The family we used to be. One wrong move by a total stranger and her whole life had changed.

Her sister would have been thirteen in May, and her parents would have celebrated thirty years in July. She wiped a tear from her cheek. She was unable to think about them without a lump in her throat, an ache in her heart, and a pit in her stomach. She couldn't believe that just out of the blue, the loss could swamp her as if it had happened yesterday.

Not today, she scolded herself. Instead, she forced herself to focus on her surroundings. Through watery eyes, she took in the sun, the sky, and the island.

She passed the State Park entrance, drove down the paved two-lane. Greeted by a park ranger, she paid the fee at the National Park entrance and drove on. She slowed to a crawl, taking in the rough landscape.

The trees were mostly pines. She recognized a few different types such as loblolly and greenbrier after she had searched the internet for what vegetation grew on the island. They were all short and scruffy, kept that way by the harsh conditions of the saltwater, wind, and sandy ground.

She noticed at least half a dozen different types of grasses. Smiling when she spotted the beginnings of a small tumbleweed, sea rocket she thought it was called, growing next to the road.

Ready to get out and explore, Bree found a little alcove, tucked inside the brush, to park. She pulled on a gray hoodie two sizes too big for her and wrangled her hair into a messy bun. She got out of the car, grabbed her camera, her backpack, and started down the little path.

Red-winged blackbirds bounced from branch to branch and swooped overhead as she threaded her way along the path. The terrain dipped down slightly, a meager impression in the ground, but enough to create a small marsh.

In the marsh, the sound of the surf softened and the grass rustled in the soft breeze. Bree stopped and turned a slow circle, taking it all in. Here the smell of damp and decay was strong, as the old vegetation rotted and new grew around it. She almost missed a Great Blue Heron standing stock-still, one leg bent among the reeds at the edge of the swampy water. Had the vegetation not swayed in the wind around him, he would have gone unnoticed. Slowly she lifted her camera, adjusted the lens, and snapped a photo of him.

She moved carefully, slowly, trying not to disturb him but kept her eye trained on him with her camera. Without warning, he lifted off. Silently. Gracefully. Quickly, Bree raised her camera, following him with the lens, and was able to capture him in mid-flight. She lowered the camera and stood watching him soar over the island.

Bree jumped at the sound of twigs breaking behind her, pivoted to find two sets of big black eyes staring at her through the reeds, not more than ten feet away.

They were both the color of nutmeg, one slightly taller than the other. The smaller pony had a long white stripe running the length of her nose. Unlike the crane, they stood staring, curious.

She moved cautiously, shifted to the side to get a better angle. Sidestepping. Their eyes followed her. Used to the intrusion of humans, they didn't move. Bree slowly lifted her camera and snapped off a couple of rounds as the breeze toyed with the wisps of their dark brown manes, the color of warm molasses. They stood as if posing. An ear twitched. A foot stomped. Bree crouched, trying to get yet another angle.

A dragonfly buzzed between them. Both bent their heads to look at it. Bree captured it. She stood then, straightened. Lowered the camera and watched them as they watched her, content to be in the moment with them.

Off in the distance drifted the sound of other horses neighing. Then, there was one long whinny. Signaled, they turned to go. The little one gave her one last look before trotting away.

So pleased with herself, Bree couldn't wait to see what else the day and the island might bring. Giddy with joy, she slung her camera over her shoulder and danced across the rest of the little marsh.

• • • •

RYKER INSPECTED THE hull of his speed boat, looking for cracks or blisters. He had already done this in the fall, but he always went over his boat again in the spring to make sure nothing new had appeared due to the change in the temperature and seasons. Finding none, he moved on to the propellers, checking diligently for pitting, cracking, and dings.

Next, Ryker inspected the battery. He refilled the battery with distilled water and checked the charge. Ryker dug through his toolbox and found a small wire brush, running it over the charge posts to make sure they were clean. He then proceeded to rub a little grease on them to keep them from eroding.

Ryker was in the middle of testing the electrical switches on the boat when a car pulled into his driveway. He looked up, recognized Linda's car, and went back to work flipping switches, and checking wires.

Linda approached in a pale pink pantsuit and small pink heels, looking impeccable.

"Good morning," she called cheerfully, crossing the yard, carrying a brown bag in one hand and drinks in the other. She smiled and shook the bag. "I come bearing sustenance."

He spared her a glance then hopped down. Determined to ignore her and her peace offering, he went deep into the shed to find his gas can. At the thought of food though, his stomach betrayed him. Returning, he hesitated and glared at her. "What's in the bag?"

"Only your favorite breakfast item from your favorite place. Plain bagel, lightly toasted, with egg, sausage, spinach, and melted Colby jack cheese. And I brought an ice-cold soda." She dangled it out in front of him. "Come on. I know you want it."

He scowled at her for a second, then snatched it out of her hand like a starving man. Ryker unfolded the bag and peered inside. "This doesn't let you off the hook, you know." He leaned back against the boat, unwrapped the bagel, and sunk his teeth into the warm, cheesy goodness.

"But it's a start, right?"

"Maybe," he said with a mouthful.

She set the cardboard tray containing the drinks down on the workbench. Slipped out her coffee and took a sip, watching him over the top. He frowned while he ate.

"Did I mention I have some rum in the car for that soda if you need it?"

He gave a little sneer. "Might need it if you have more bad news."

She sighed heavily. "Look Ryker, I really am truly sorry how this all went down. I hope you realize it was no one's fault. And if you'll let me, I can make it up to you."

He popped the last bite into his mouth and balled the paper, chucking it in the trash can behind her. "How?" he asked simply.

She twisted the soda out of the cardboard carrying case and passed it to him.

"Two things, I know it's not the same as owning it, but . . ." she hesitated. "I recommended you to the young lady that is buying the house, and she agreed to let you, Bolts & Beams, do the work on the house. I promised her that you were the best around and would give her a fair deal. You may not own it, but you would still see that the place got the TLC that it needs. There's no one better than you and Sam for that."

"That's something." Ignoring the straw, Ryker took the plastic lid off the top of the cup and took a gulp, listening. "And?"

"And . . . I pulled some other properties, ones in your price range, and with everything on your wish-list. We could go this week if you want to look?" When he said nothing, she rushed on. "I checked with Sam, and he said Thursday was the best day if you wanted to go."

He didn't answer right away, wanting to make her suffer a little bit longer.

"Well?" she questioned, "say something . . . You have to know how terrible I feel about this whole thing."

He did. He could see it written all over her face. And really, he couldn't blame her. Wanted to, but couldn't. He blamed the Henning's and the person that bought it out from under him. "Think you've thought of everything?"

"I've tried."

He didn't want to let her off the hook just yet. He really was disappointed.

Well, the Henning's had won this round but it looked like he wasn't going away empty handed. He'd still get to work on it. Improve it. Bring it back to its former glory and then some. He would push the new owner to do things the right way. His way. Make it look how he wanted it to. Then he'd have his satisfaction. His name would be stamped on it.

"Tell me who bought it?"

Linda hesitated, but then didn't see any harm in it. After all, he would find out eventually, especially if he was doing the work. "Bree Thompson."

He lifted one dark brow. *Interesting.*

"I'm sure it's no one you know. She's not from around here. Just moved to the area."

He nodded. "So, Thursday?"

She beamed. "All day Thursday if you want. I'll even take you out to lunch, my treat. Am I forgiven?"

He nodded again. "Forgiven."

"Thanks, Ryker. Your friendship and our business relationship mean everything to me. I don't want to lose you or Sam over something like this. I feel like you're my sons."

"I know, Linda. We feel the same way."

"Okay, well . . . Are you planning to get out on the water this weekend?"

"Hoping for this afternoon."

"Well then, I will let you get back to it. I have a showing soon anyway. Enjoy the beautiful day."

"You too, Linda. And thanks for breakfast." He lifted his soda in a slight toast to her.

• • • •

IT WAS DARK BY THE time Bree walked into the hotel. She carried takeout, her camera, and her backpack into the lobby. Rode the elevator to the tenth floor and got out. She fished the plastic card out of her backpack, juggling everything. Exhausted, she let herself into the room.

Flipping on lights, she dropped everything on the little round table. Went to the kitchen and dug through the drawer for a fork. Grabbing a plate and a bottle of water, she went back into the living room.

She flopped down on the sofa and opened the bag, pulling out the two white containers. She scooped out white sticky rice and smothered it in black peppered chicken. Her mouth watered at the sight. She hadn't planned to stay out at Assateague for so long today. If she had, she would have packed more than an apple and some pretzels for lunch. Bree forked in a couple of mouthfuls. She forced herself to slow down. She eased back, grabbed the remote, and turned on the television. Coming across a rerun of Friends, she proceeded to eat again, but much slower this time.

The views on the island had been spectacular. The lighting . . . perfect. The horses were everywhere, and content to let her snap their picture. She had gotten some great shots way more than she had anticipated. Cleaning off her plate, she took a drink of water.

It was silly to make herself this hungry, but it was actually good, she decided. It had been so long since she had had a real appetite, and not forced herself to eat. Maybe she was finally healing.

It wasn't that it wasn't still raw, because it was. But at least now she had some hope. Hope that life, her life, was to go on. Even without her family. And maybe this really was the place for it to happen. Things seemed to be falling into place. She had a friend here, was buying a house, and her photography business was booming.

On that thought, Bree reached for her laptop. She was excited to download her pictures from today. She couldn't wait to see them, hopeful there would be some good ones. She inserted her SD card and waited for the photos to upload. There was a lot more than she thought.

She checked orders while she waited for the upload, moved them from the inbox to the processing, setting them up for her to work on tomorrow. Reading down through some new emails that came in, she saw one from Coastal Realty confirming the home inspection on Monday, and deleted a few junk emails.

She kicked off her shoes, hummed to the theme song as a new episode started, and scrolled down a few more emails. Her heart gave a little jolt as she saw the email marked Kage. Her hand hesitated slightly, as she debated clicking on it.

She opened it and in big bold letters, it said:

YOU TOOK WHAT WAS MINE.

Bree felt a little twinge of panic surge through her body. What was that supposed to mean? She hadn't taken anything from anyone. *This is dumb,* she thought. It has to be someone playing a joke. But who?

Suddenly pissed, she fired back an email.

Who is this? I think you have the wrong email.

She hit send before she could rethink it, and then clicked marking it SPAM so she wouldn't see any from him again. Bree saw that her photos were all uploaded but instead of looking at them, she saved the file and shut down her laptop. Her good mood spoiled, she tossed her laptop onto the couch unable to work any longer.

Disgusted, her appetite gone, she carted the white containers and her plate into the little kitchenette. Glancing over her shoulder she glared at her laptop. Wracking her brain, she wondered who had sent it. And why?

Bree put the leftovers in the fridge and scrubbed the plate viciously, leaving it on the counter to dry. She looked around the suite for something else to do, anything to distract her from the laptop and the email.

Bree glanced at the time. It was only eight; she couldn't stay in this room all night wondering who had sent that message. Kage. The name bounced around her brain. This wasn't the first time he or she had contacted her, but why? *And what would I have taken?* Frustrated, she glanced at her computer again. The urge to check her email was strong, but she refused to look.

She grabbed her sweatshirt, pushed her feet into her sneakers. She searched for the plastic card that served as the room key, shoved it in her back pocket, and stormed out of the room, determined to walk off her mood on the beach.

Chapter 12

April drifted into May, mild and pleasant. Bree walked out of Coastal Realty in shock. Today, she bought a house. She had keys in her hand and butterflies in her stomach. She couldn't believe she had actually done it.

A little over four weeks ago she was sitting on her couch in Kansas completely and utterly depressed. Not knowing what to do with herself, she stared at her damn list of tasks and chores, thankful when the phone rang. It was the manager at the hotel in Ocean City, Maryland.

There had been a computer error that mixed up the room and dates. They were double booked, and he wanted to clarify when she and her family were coming.

Bree had totally forgotten that her mother had booked the trip over a year in advance in anticipation of their 30th wedding anniversary.

She had considered canceling the whole thing, unable to comprehend going without them. But for some reason she hadn't, instead, she heard herself confirming reservations, and jotting down the dates and the address. Hanging up the phone, she promised herself she'd go and added it to the list.

Thanks to the list, she stood here now, keys in hand.

She crossed the parking lot and got in her packed SUV. In a daze, she drove a few miles to her new house. Turned down the narrow lane, and came to a stop in front of the house. Her house.

She sat and just stared. It was hers. Like a mantra, she repeated it over and over in her mind, in hopes that it would sink in. She truly couldn't believe it. But it was bittersweet. It was one of the most important steps in her life and she had no one to share it with. She ached to call her mother with the news, have her go pick out paint colors and flooring with her. She wanted to show her sister the water, and the little swipe of beach. She wanted to hear her father give a long, low whistle, in awe of the place. But those things wouldn't happen. Not now, not ever.

Oh, she had others she could call that would be excited for her. Aunt Maureen, a few of her friends from home, or Chad. She wondered what Chad would think of it. He wouldn't. He would have dismissed it on sight. He'd have thought it was way too much money, and way too much work. And that's why they were no longer together. Well, one of the many reasons.

In less than a year she had lost her family, cut herself off from most of her friends due to her depression, and broke up with her boyfriend. She knew she was better off without Chad, but still it hurt. He had been a big part of her life for a long time. He'd been there those first weeks and months after the accident. He'd been supportive, sympathetic, and helpful. He had been her rock.

But she spiraled down into depression, neglecting everything and everyone, despite his quiet devotion. She was unable to think, to eat, to function. He was there forcing her to do all those things, and simply to just breathe. But nothing he did made much difference. It wasn't long before she noticed the strain it was having on him too, taking a toll on their already rocky relationship.

No, the truth. She would only acknowledge the truth, she thought. And the truth was, she hadn't noticed until her aunt had pointed it out. But she just couldn't quite make herself care.

On the first day of clear weather they had in weeks, Aunt Maureen came by. She marched in, threw the curtains back on every window in the house, and literally rolled Bree out of bed. Hands-on hips and not taking no for an answer, she told Bree to get herself up, get showered, and dressed, they were going to town. Today it was going to stop. Today she was going to get her own damn groceries, her own damn toilet paper. Enough was enough. Her family was gone, but she was still here. She needed to start acting like it.

So, she did. She did what she was told. She went through the motions, just so Maureen would stop yelling. The next thing she knew, she was in the car on the way to town. Before she knew it, they were in the grocery store parking lot when Aunt Maureen told her to go in by herself. She handed her a list, a pen, and a wad of cash, and told Bree not to come out until she had every last item on the list crossed off. She practically shoved her out of the car, unhooking her seatbelt, reaching across, and opening Bree's door. The moment Bree closed the car door, she heard the lock click. She was locked out. Aunt Maureen meant business.

She stood just inside the store, clinging to a cart, trembling. She forced herself to look at the list. She remembered thinking she couldn't do it, but then heard her mother's voice. *Yes, you can. One item at a time. Concentrate.*

The first item . . . apples. Bree remembered it clearly. It was written, neat and precise, in Aunt Maureen's beautiful script. She went to the produce section with hands shaking and looked them over. She selected five golden delicious apples without bruising and put them in a plastic bag. Twisted them closed and placed them in the cart. She took the pen and crossed them off the list. Next was lettuce. She could do this.

She concentrated. Read the list. Located the item. Placed it in the cart, and crossed it off. Slowly with each item, Bree started to feel almost normal. The pain in her chest lessened. For a moment. But just a moment.

She was standing in the bread aisle concentrating, when the conversation a row over caught her attention.

"Is Chad coming over for the party tonight?" she heard a female voice ask.

"No, it's his night to babysit Bree," said another.

Bree recoiled at the word. She recognized the voices, but couldn't quite place them.

"When is he going to dump her?" said the first.

There was a deep exasperated sigh. "He can't. Or won't. Not yet anyway. He thinks it would put her over the edge. He said she isn't stable. He wouldn't be able to live with himself if anything happened to her; she's been through so much."

"But when is enough, enough, ya know?"

"She's like this depressed old recluse. She doesn't come out of the house, sits all day in the dark, crying. Won't eat or shower."

"That's pathetic and gross."

"I know, right? Sometimes, I wonder if it's all an act, though."

"Why would you think that?"

"Well, you didn't hear this from me, but right before her family died, Chad was going to break up with her. But then the accident . . . and he felt he needed to be there for her. Felt like the whole town looked to him to get her through it. After all, they've been together since high school. But now . . . it'll be a year in May. That's a long time to keep dealing with her."

"That's a lot of pressure to put on him. I feel so sorry for him."

"Yeah, me too."

Bree had not been able to listen any longer. She threw the last few items in the cart and practically ran to the checkout. The clerk rang her up and eyed her sympathetically, as tears flowed steadily down her cheeks. She swiped at them pathetically and vowed that she would get her act together. Or at least to appear as if she did. She could fake it, for the sake of others. Especially Chad. She owed him that much.

That night, when he came over, she broke it off. For a split second, she had seen the relief wash over his face. He promised to stay in contact with her, made her swear to call him if she needed anything. When she had, he stood, hugged her, and left. He didn't look back.

She hadn't even cried after he was gone. She was numb. That's when she knew she had done the right thing. She went to the kitchen, sat at the table, and made a list of what needed to be done. She'd follow Aunt Maureen's advice, crossing one thing off every day. Give herself a purpose, a task, and eventually, time would do what it was supposed to. Heal.

And now here she was, outside of her very own house but very alone.

She got out, keys in hand, but did not go to the house. Instead, she went to the water and stood at the edge.

The water seemed to call to her. She was drawn to it. The highs and lows of the tide. The rush and pull of the waves so closely matched her emotions, her moods. It could be smooth, calm, and restful, then choppy, dark, and full of turmoil. One minute Bree had such great joy in the buying of her first home; the potential it represented. The next, she was devastated at having no one to share it with, afraid of being alone for the rest of her life.

Ryker watched her from the crumbling patio after he had stopped on his way home to drop off tools for tomorrow. He'd seen her SUV parked out front, and noticed she hadn't unpacked it yet. He figured she was in the house looking around but was surprised when he found it locked. Letting himself in with the key Linda had given him when they had gotten the contract to do the work, Ryker called out. When she didn't answer, he went in search of her. That's when he saw her out the window.

She stood by the edge of the water, in his favorite spot. A little twinge of jealousy coursed through him.

Not liking that, he went to his truck and unloaded, pushing the jealousy down.

Now, an hour later, she was still there in the same spot. *Why was she still standing there? Why hadn't she moved? Had she been there all day?* He knew the settlement had been at one. *Surely, she couldn't have been there since what? Two or three?*

Ryker went outside to talk to her, but something stopped him short. Maybe it was the way she stood, staring out at the water. Or maybe it was the perfect picture she made, that squeezed at his heart. The way the wind toyed with her long hair, the sinking sun setting it ablaze in a wash of dark gold. Her slender frame looked small and delicate against the vast dark blue water of the bay, making her seem fragile and forlorn.

He turned to go but his heart urged him not to leave, instead to go to her. So he did, cursing himself as he went. *What was he doing?* He could just leave, she hadn't seen him.

He cleared his throat, shuffled his feet on the grass, trying to make some noise. He didn't want to take the chance of getting punched again. Ryker saw her straighten, sensing him, but she didn't turn. He stopped when he came even with her. He tucked his hands in his front pockets. "Beautiful day, beautiful view," *beautiful lady,* he added silently.

"Yes, it is."

She didn't seem surprised he was there.

"Perfect spot for a couple of Adirondack chairs, so you could sit and watch the boats go by."

She turned then and gave him the most heart-piercing smile he had ever seen. It literally took his breath away.

"Those were my thoughts exactly . . . In yellow."

"Yellow?" he questioned.

She shrugged, "My mother's favorite color."

He bobbed his head. "Nice." He glanced around, not wanting to look directly at her again, because he didn't think his heart could take it. He gazed out across the bay and focused on a small boat with a couple of fishermen on it. "How long have you been out here?"

She shrugged. "Probably a half an hour or so. Why?"

"I've been here over an hour."

Bree glanced at Ryker, taking in his strong, chiseled profile. His dark hair rippled in the wind. His deep blue eyes focused on the water. "Really? What time is it?"

"After seven."

She laughed in disbelief, "Yeah, right. I can't have been standing here for . . . what? Like almost five hours. Could I?"

He shifted, shrugged his shoulders, and spared her a quick glance. "Not sure. All I know is you've been here at least an hour since I've come. And it's after seven. You do the math."

Immediately, she became aware of the sun slowly disappearing, and the warmth with it. Fatigue from hours spent standing in one spot began seeping into her bones. Suddenly, completely weary, she shivered. She turned without warning and started back to the house.

"Are you planning on staying here tonight?" Ryker asked, catching up to her in two long strides.

"I was going to, but . . . I hadn't planned on wasting the day standing by the water either. I haven't even unloaded the car yet."

Ryker could kick himself; he had a ton of paperwork to do tonight, but he asked anyway, "Do you need help?"

She must have sensed something in his tone. Bree glanced at him. "That's okay, I'm sure you have more important things to do." They rounded the house.

Surprised at himself, he was both relieved and disappointed at her answer. Before he could stop himself, he replied, "Not really. Besides, if all you're going to do is unload that SUV, it won't take long. Let me help."

"Are you sure?" she asked, pressing the button to release the back hatch of the SUV.

"Of course." He grabbed the first box. "Tell me where to go with it."

She glanced at it. "Master bedroom."

Ryker nodded and took off in the direction of the house. He came back as she went in, his cell phone stuck to his ear. He nodded and passed her. She heard him say something about a half-hour. She met him at the door again, on her way out.

"How 'bout camera equipment?"

She hesitated. "Set that in the living room there. Eventually, I'm going to make the carriage house my studio, but for now, I'll just store it all right here."

They each took a few more trips, it wasn't long and they were down to the Target bags in the front seat. They were headed in with the last load when a car pulled up behind Ryker's truck. He handed the last bag to her. "I'll go see who it is."

She nodded and disappeared into the house. Bree was unloading paper towels and cleaning supplies when Ryker walked in carrying two large pizza boxes, a plastic bag, and a bottle of wine.

"Hope you like pizza."

Surprised and touched, she asked, "You ordered pizza? When?"

"Between loads." He placed the boxes on the cracked counter of the warped little island. "I got one pepperoni and one cheese. Sorry, I didn't ask what you like, but I figured if I did, you'd tell me not to bother."

She frowned at him. "You're right, I would have. But I'm so glad you did. I'm starving."

He grinned, a dark dangerous smile that creased his chiseled face, causing two identical deep-set dimples to appear on either side. He pulled out one of the two decrepit bar stools for her to sit on, the only furniture in the entire house. He unearthed paper plates, napkins, and two plastic cups from the bag. "What's your pleasure? Cheese or pepperoni?" he asked, lifting the tops.

"I'll take one of each, I'm starving."

"Woman after my own heart," Ryker stated, getting her a slice of each. He did the same for himself. Then poured wine into the two cups. "Let's make a toast."

They both lifted their glasses. "To what?" Bree asked.

Ryker looked at her for a moment, thinking of the woman that now owned the house he had always coveted. "Why, to your new home of course. Let me think." He cleared his throat and made a show of raising his cup high. He'd do the best he could. "May God bless you and your new home and fill it with family and friends, both old and new." He tapped his plastic cup to hers.

Her eyes filled, but she was determined not to let them fall. She reached out a hand and placed it gently on his arm. "Thank you, Ryker. That was nice. Thank you for helping me carry boxes and for the pizza. But especially for being here."

Seeing she was close to tears he tried to lighten the mood. "Anytime Champ, anytime. Let's eat."

* * * *

SOMEWHERE IN THE DARKNESS, he lay awake and thought of her. He pictured her face, the light brown hair, kind, wide-set blue eyes, dark lashes, and slender nose. She was very pretty. He thought about it, pondered her a moment.

What really got him were those blue eyes. They sucked him in and made him forget what she did. What she was. How she had taken everything he had always wanted away from him.

Stole was more like it. Right out from under him. He wanted justice. He wanted revenge. He wanted what was rightfully his. Somehow, he'd get it back. Somehow, he would make her pay. After all, she was a thief, and thieves had to pay. Stealing was a sin. It was even in the Ten Commandments. Number seven.

"Thou shalt not steal," he said out loud into the quiet of the night.

He stared into the deep black. Plotting. Planning. Out of the darkness, in the deep recesses of his mind, a plan slowly started to take shape. A slow, menacing smile spread across his face. She'd be sorry. She'd beg for forgiveness before he was through with her. And he didn't plan on showing her mercy.

Chapter 13

Sam rang the bell as he and Ryker stood outside on the front porch and waited.

Ryker copped an attitude, scowling at the weathered door.

"This should be my house."

"Let it go, man."

Gulls called, swooping high above, looking pristine in the wash of morning light. When Bree answered, they were greeted with a warm smile. Her cheerfulness only made Ryker scowl harder.

"Good morning. Right on time," Bree said, opening the door wide.

"Good morning to you, too," Sam said, entering.

Ryker tipped his head. "What's up, Champ?" he asked gruffly. "How did you fare the first night in your new house?"

"Pretty good, thanks for asking. Come into the kitchen." Bree led the way.

"Ghost didn't give you any trouble, did it?"

"What?" she asked, stumbling midstride. "What ghost?"

"There's no ghost. Ryker's just being a pain in the ass," Sam said. When Bree hesitated, he added, "He's kidding, really."

"Oh, okay," Bree answered, unsure. "Very funny."

Sam jabbed Ryker in the side and glared at him, silencing him with a piercing look. Ryker smirked.

Sam pulled a pencil out from behind his ear and flipped through his clipboard. "First things first, we know you want to do the kitchen. So that's our priority today, getting the measurements and ideas down. Ryker will draw up a rough design."

Ryker pulled out a tape measure and started measuring from the entrance they just came through, jotting down feet and inches on the floor plan.

He'd give her a design all right. The best damn one. Top of the line. Nothing was too good for this house.

"Once the design is decided, you'll meet with the kitchen and bath consultant over at Seaside Kitchens where you can select the style, wood, and finish for the cabinets. They also handle the appliances, countertops, and hardware. Kind of a one-stop-shop. Ryker can go with you if you'd like."

Damn right he'd be going with her, he thought. *He wouldn't let her pick out last year's color or an outdated cabinet style.*

Bree nodded along as Sam went down his list, checking off items. "You can look at flooring over at Conway's. They handle carpet, hardwood, and tile. You name it, they have it." Sam handed her their business card. "Tell them Sam sent you. They'll help you with anything you need. They'll come out and measure, tear up the old flooring, and lay the new."

Next, Sam tugged out a window brochure from his clipboard. "I have the budget for the windows that the Hennings said they would replace." He laid the brochure on the counter and flipped it open. "Anything in this area would be covered. Anything else would be extra and we would just charge you the difference in price," he said, his finger drawing an invisible circle. "That's one of the first things I'd like to go through with you. That way we can get them ordered. We'll go through each room and take notes."

Bree held up the brochure, scrutinizing it. "I'm going to need a few minutes to look this over."

"Take a look." He checked his phone as it beeped. "I need to run out to the truck and make a phone call. I left my set of floor plans out there, too. Be back in a few."

Bree sat at the counter and flipped through the brochure, while Ryker worked his way across the kitchen. Saying nothing, Ryker took note of where the plumbing, electrical, and gas lines were.

In a matter of minutes, Sam was back. "Ready? Or do you need more time?"

"I think I can make up my mind as we go. Are we starting here?"

"Sure. Go for it."

"Well, for this back wall I pictured French doors. But now since I've seen this," Bree indicated the brochure, "I think I'd like the large slider. That way I could have the door open and still have a screen across it to let in the breeze. I like these mullions," she pointed. "Just at the top. Gives it a little design but leaves the glass and the view unbroken."

"Good choice. That style will go nicely with the overall architecture of the house. Do you want any windows on either side of the slider?"

Ryker tuned them out and was vaguely aware when they left the room. He proceeded to work his way around the rest of the large room. Taking the last measurements, he checked the ceiling height and the width of the door to the breezeway. Finished, he stepped back and envisioned the kitchen. He pulled out a pad of paper and did a rough sketch of the design he wanted.

Ryker could see there was plenty of room for a large island, twice the size of the existing one, with seating for four to six people. He'd know better once he entered the measurements into his computer and laid out his design. He pictured a large cooktop with a streamlined hood, separate wall ovens, and a double stainless-steel sink under the window.

He jotted down ideas, and mental notes that he wanted to make sure he incorporated into the design, like an angled corner lazy-Susan, glass cabinets on the far wall to display nice dishes, maybe open shelving, stained to match, next to the window. He was lost in thought when Sam walked back into the room.

"How's it going?" Sam asked, peering over Ryker's shoulder.

"I think I'm onto something here," he said, not looking up from his drawing. "Won't know for sure until I plug it into the computer program."

"Why don't you start entering it? Our next appointment canceled."

"Did she reschedule?"

"Yeah, I'll put it on our calendars."

"Works for me."

"I'm going to run over to the Brandy jobsite. The guys are installing the countertops today. Kind of want to be there when it happens."

"Need me to go?"

"No. I got it. Besides, you've got the house to yourself here. Seems as if you're in the zone. Go get your laptop from the truck and sit here and hammer it out."

"Okay, but," he glanced around. "Where's Bree?"

"She ran out to do some errands." They walked outside towards the trucks. Sam stowed his stuff while Ryker retrieved his laptop.

He liked the idea of being alone in the house. The quiet. The view. "If you really don't need me, I think I will stay. Try to work out a design or two before she gets back. If I have one and she can work with it, maybe we can get to Seaside tomorrow. Pick out cabinets. Really get rolling with this project."

"Sounds like a plan," Sam called as he climbed in. "If you get a chance, check that leaky pipe in the basement. Then we can cross that off our list of to-dos."

"On it."

"I'll touch base with you later today. And Ryker?"

"Yeah?"

"Go easy on her. She has no idea that you wanted this house."

"I know that." Not promising anything, Ryker waved over his shoulder at Sam, already lost in design ideas.

• • • •

IT WAS LATE IN THE afternoon when Bree got back to the house. She pulled up in front next to the black Bolts & Beam's truck. She'd have to remember to ask Greg if there was a garage door remote for her car, it would make it a lot easier. For now, she would have to haul all the groceries in through the front door.

Bree was gathering the bags when her cell phone started ringing. She pulled it out of the back pocket of her jeans and recognized Greg's number from Coastal Realty.

"Hi, Greg. I was just thinking of calling you."

"Really?" he chuckled. "Did I catch you at a bad time, though? Sounds like there's a lot going on."

"I'm just getting groceries out of the car." She struggled to keep the phone at her ear. "I wanted to ask you if there are any remote controls to the garage doors?"

"Actually, that's why I'm calling. I happen to have two right here. I replaced the batteries in them. Have a couple of extra sets of keys for the house too. Thought I might run them over if you're going to be around?"

Bree juggled her bags and opened the door. "I should be. I have a lot to do. But if for some reason I'm not, you can just leave them."

"I'll tell you what. How 'bout I run over now?"

"That would be great."

"See you in a few." With that, he clicked off.

Bree made her way through the house and plopped the bags down on one end of the island. A laptop, floor plans, and a tape measure sat at the other end, but the barstool was empty. She could hear noise and muffled cursing coming from underneath her feet and decided either Ryker or Sam was in the basement working. So, she went back to the SUV to haul in more supplies. When she came back in with her third and final load, Ryker emerged from the basement.

"You're home," he said gruffly.

"Nice to see you too," Bree answered, pulling out her cold items. She crossed to the refrigerator. It was old and decrepit, but it was working, and at this point, that was all that mattered to her. "What were you doing in the basement?"

Ryker set his toolbox on the floor without looking at her, and went to his laptop, and sat. "Fixing that leaky pipe. Plumbing is my least favorite thing to do. But at least it's done and we can check it off the list." And that's literally what he did. He opened the spreadsheet that contained the list of things that needed to be fixed, checked the box, and entered the date.

Bree sorted canned goods and dry foods and watched him carefully. "Is that why you're so grumpy? Because you don't like to do plumbing work?"

"What?" he asked distractedly, turning those deep, dark, blue eyes on her. "I'm not grumpy."

"You kind of seem that way. Did I do something wrong? You seemed grumpy this morning too." *Totally different guy from last night,* she thought.

He was saved from answering by the doorbell. She kept her eyes on him as she walked across the kitchen, and then disappeared down the hall to answer the door.

"Hey, Greg. That was quick."

"I was already in the car, on my way back from an appointment when I called."

"Come on in for a minute."

She held the door open; Greg came in and headed for the kitchen. Ryker still sat where she'd left him. Bree cleared her throat. "Greg, have you met Ryker?"

"No, I don't believe I have. Greg Carpenter with Coastal Realty." He extended his hand.

Ryker took it. "Ryker James. Bolts & Beams. So . . . you're the new guy," Ryker said, looking him over. "Linda mentioned she'd hired someone."

Greg grinned. "Yep, that's me. And this is my first sale." He waved his arm around to encompass the whole of the house. "Isn't she a beauty?"

"Yes, she is," Ryker answered gruffly.

"Here, Bree," Greg said, giving her the manila envelope. "Mr. Henning forgot to bring them at settlement."

"Thanks for bringing them over."

"Just part of the service," Greg said, smiling at her. "Do you have some more stuff to unload? I could give you a hand."

"You don't mind?"

"Not at all."

Ryker watched the exchange in silence. Noting how Greg leaned in a little too close. Smiled a little too broadly.

"You don't mind do you, Ryker?" Bree asked, cutting into his thoughts.

"Mind? Why would I mind if Greg helps you haul in your stuff?"

"I wasn't sure if you needed me for anything? Sam said you might have a design drawn up today."

"Oh, yeah," Ryker glanced down at his laptop. "Almost done. Give me another half hour or so, and then I'll have something to show you."

"Let's unload." Greg put his hand on the small of Bree's back and ushered her towards the door.

They went outside, Bree pressed the opener and the garage door glided up. "It works!"

"Never had any doubt. What do you have back here?" Greg asked, lifting the tailgate.

"Paint." Handing him two cans, she said, "I'm going to paint the studio myself." She looped the plastic bag filled with paintbrushes and other supplies over her arm and grabbed two more cans, heading upstairs.

Bree juggled her things and tried to open the door. "It's stuck."

"Here, let me," Greg said brushing against her. He set his cans down, turned the knob, and put his shoulder into the door. With a screech, it swung inward. "Just needed a little muscle and could probably use some WD-40."

She flipped on the light and put down the supplies. "I bought some." She dug through the bags.

"If you want, I can spray it for you," Greg said, putting down his cans next to hers.

She handed him the can.

"A little spray on each of the hinges," he said while he squirted them. "There, that should do it." He swung the door back and forth.

"Thank you."

"No problem. What else can I do?"

Bree crossed the room and opened a window. "That's it. I'm just going to clean, and try to get everything in order before I start." Bree turned to Greg, debating whether she should ask him or not. "I have a question," Bree said, looking directly at Greg.

"Shoot."

"It's something Ryker said. You're going to think I'm silly for asking, but . . ." her voice trailed off and she hesitated. "Ryker mentioned that the house was haunted. I'm not sure if he was kidding or not. Have you heard any stories about the house?"

Greg shook his head. "I haven't, but then I'm new to the area just like you. I can ask around if you'd like?"

"No, that's okay. He was probably just teasing." Bree moved to the next window. It wouldn't open.

"Here let me."

Greg came up behind her, and put an arm on either side of her, helping her lift. His body brushed up against hers and she stiffened.

"There you go."

"Thank you," Bree said softly, uncertain.

"Am I interrupting something here?" Ryker asked standing in the doorway, laptop in hand.

Greg cleared his throat and took a step back from Bree. "Not at all. The window was stuck. I'd better get going. I'll give you a call in a few days, to see how everything is going." He gave her a broad smile and made a mad dash for the door.

"Thanks, Greg," she called after him.

"Anytime."

"I think he means that too," Ryker stated. "Looks like he'd do about anything for you."

"What's that supposed to mean?" Bree asked.

"You two were pretty cozy when I walked in."

She placed her hands on her hips. "Did you want something? Or were you just spying on me?"

"Hardly spying when the door is left wide open. But yes, I did want to show you something if you're done flirting with Greg?"

"I most certainly wasn't flirting with him. He's my real estate agent, and that's all," Bree said suddenly angry.

"Whatever you want to tell yourself, Champ. Do you want to see this design or not?"

She stared at him for a hot minute. "You know I do."

He placed his laptop on the only surface available, a small table that sat squarely in the middle of the room. "Come here then."

Reluctantly, she crossed the room and stood beside him.

"Let me walk you through it."

Pointing, he started explaining the layout. She fell into the steady cadence of his voice and could visualize the design as he spoke. Bree didn't ask any questions, just followed his finger with her eyes.

He came to the last cabinet in the layout and glanced at her. "Well?" he questioned. "What do you think? You haven't said anything."

Bree laid her hand on his arm. "I love it." He glanced down at her hand and she quickly removed it.

"Really?" Ryker asked, sounding surprised. "Is there something else you wanted to see incorporated into the design?"

"The only thing I could think of, and maybe it's hard to do, but . . ."

"What?"

"Well, on the island and at these corners," Bree pointed. "Would it be possible to round them, instead of the angle? It's just that the flow and the shape of the island remind me of the ocean, like a wave or a current. And I would like to see it curved and soft, more like the water and the shoreline."

Ryker scratched his chin. "Why didn't I think of that?" He reached for his mouse. Selected a rounding tool and clicked the corners. Then took the same tool and turned the angle of the island into a soft flowing organic curve. He played with it a little, stretching, curving, and rounding it, still providing enough space for six chairs.

Ryker smiled at the visual difference. "I'll be damned, if that doesn't do the trick."

"Perfect." Bree turned to look at him, realizing suddenly that her face was only inches from his. So close, in fact, that she could see a ring of deep violet around the edges of his blue eyes. And a small scar at the hairline of his left eyebrow. She swallowed hard and stood up.

Ryker cleared his throat. "Umm . . . what time is it?"

"Five," Bree answered.

"Wonder if they're still open?" Ryker pulled out his cell phone and punched in a number.

"Who?"

"Seaside Kitchens. Hey, Julia. It's me, Ryker. Yeah, sorry I haven't called. Yes, we've been swamped. Yeah, I'm wondering if you have any appointments available tomorrow?" He waited, covered the phone, and asked, "Are you busy tomorrow?"

Bree hesitated. "I guess not. I was just going to work on the studio."

"Good. What time?" he said into the phone while looking at Bree. "Can you be ready by eight?"

She nodded.

"We'll take it. I'll email the floor plan over to you now. Thanks, Julia. You're a doll. See you tomorrow." He clicked off. "I'll pick you up just before eight." He saved the file, opened his email, and attached it to the one he had addressed to Julia, and hit send. Closing down his laptop, he stood. "And here I was, all prepared to persuade you to like the design."

"Why would you have to persuade me to like it?" Bree asked, curious.

"I'm kidding, mostly. Most clients can't visualize. And don't know a good design when they see it. A lot of times we have to convince them why something is a good idea. But not you . . . but not you," he said again softer, looking directly at her.

"For your information, I happen to know good design when I see it. I am a photographer."

"Yeah, well we'll see when we pick out cabinets tomorrow." Ryker crossed the room as if he owned it. "What's the plan for this space? There's nothing on the schedule for us to do."

"I'm going to do it myself."

Ryker raised a dark eyebrow in question but didn't speak.

"This area is in good shape. All it needs is to be cleaned and a fresh coat of paint."

"I'd agree with that. What color?" He bent over and picked up a can. "Simply White. Guess you can't get more basic than that."

"I want the space to be clean, bright, and neutral."

"Hold that thought," Ryker said as his phone buzzed. "Yeah, I'm still over here."

Bree grabbed the paper towels and the glass cleaner in a huff. "I'll show him how great this space can be," Bree mumbled to herself while she scrubbed the first window. "He doesn't think I can make it anything special without his expert advice or help. Just you watch, Mr. James."

He watched her while Sam gave him the play-by-play of his day. He liked to make her mad. And she definitely was right now, he could tell by the persistence with which she cleaned the window. He hated to admit it, but she was pretty darn cute. Under different circumstances he might pursue her. Correction . . . would pursue her if she hadn't purchased his house, *and* wasn't their client, he reminded himself.

But there had been a moment at the computer when she was right there. So close. Close enough for him to notice the small flecks of gray in her summer-blue eyes. Close enough to notice she smelled like spring, just a whisper across her skin.

He leaned against the wall and watched her, while Sam filled him in on the installation of the countertops. She was graceful and moved with purpose. There was strength there, more than what it looked like. He remembered her fist connecting with his face. Without thinking he rubbed his jaw, she definitely had some power behind it.

She finished the last window and turned with a jerk, locking eyes with him. His heart stopped for a split second. *Better get out of here,* he thought. *Before I do something I may regret, like ask her to dinner.*

Wrapping it up quickly with Sam, he stuck his phone back in his pocket. "Pick you up at eight, Champ. You better be ready." He stood in the doorway.

"I'll be ready. You'd better not be late."

His face creased into a devilish grin, *might as well finish the day as he had started it.* For a split second, he thought better of it, but then looked at her standing in his house and remembered she was the one that had it. He couldn't help himself. "Try not to let the ghost keep you awake because I won't wait." Without another word, he disappeared out the door.

Chapter 14

Bree sat on the front porch and waited. She had tossed and turned all night because of Ryker's stupid comment, hearing every creak and groan of the house as it settled down for the night. Bree could have sworn she'd heard footsteps at one point too but chalked it up to her overly active imagination.

Shivering thinking about it; she scooted a little further over into a patch of sun. It was shining but the air was cool. She wore jeans and a navy camisole with a white wool sweater that was snug and warm. She rubbed a speck of dirt off her navy Keds as she watched the trucks pull in.

Sam and Ryker got out with two other men and came across the yard like a unit. If they weren't yin and yang Bree didn't know who was. Sam was bright and cheerful while Ryker was dark and brooding.

"Good morning," Sam said cheerfully. "Beautiful day."

Ryker said nothing, only scowled at her.

"Yes, it is."

Getting right to business, Sam said, "We're going to work on the bathrooms today. The plumber will be here in a few minutes. Also, the guys are going to start repairing the front porch."

Bree stood and brushed the seat of her jeans off. "That's great. While you're at it, do you think you or the plumber could check the water heater?"

"Sure," Sam said nodding. "What's the problem? I thought the home inspector said it was in good shape."

"He did, but I had an ice-cold shower this morning that says differently. Something's happening with it." Bree thought she saw Ryker smirk from the corner of her eye, but she couldn't be sure.

"Yikes, that's a brutal way to wake up. I'll take a look."

"Thanks, Sam, I appreciate it." Bree looked at Ryker who had yet to utter a word. "Are you ready?"

"Always." Ryker motioned towards the truck.

She fell in step with him. "What's your deal? Did you have a cold shower too? Or are you always cranky in the morning?"

Ryker held the door to his truck open for her. "What do you mean? I'm a ray of sunshine."

"More like a thunder cloud."

Ryker chuckled, closed her door, and leaned in the open window, bending down slightly. His face was eye level with hers. He came within a whisper of her and said, "Maybe it's you. You seem to bring out the worst in me, Champ." He turned on his heel and went to the driver's side of the truck and climbed in.

They sat in awkward silence as they drove the few miles to Seaside Kitchens.

They parked and went into the showroom. Opening the door, a bell tinkled softly.

"I'll be out in a minute. Take a look around," came a voice from somewhere in the back.

Ryker went straight for the coffee pot like it was a lifeline. He poured a cup from the steaming pot and leaned back on the counter while Bree wandered from cabinet display to another, running her hand across the cool granite countertops, opening and closing cabinet doors, and pulling out drawers. Ryker hung back, sipping his coffee and watching her.

Within a few minutes a tall, redhead appeared. Her hair was swept up into a neat bun showing off her long, slender neck and large hoop earrings. She wore a tight pencil straight black skirt with an emerald green shirt and black heels. Her fierce green eyes swept the room from Bree to Ryker. Without hesitation, she went straight to Bree, hand outstretched. "Welcome, you must be Bree Thompson. I'm Julia. It's so nice to meet you."

"It's nice to meet you, too."

"I'm thrilled to have you here and can't wait to help you select the kitchen of your dreams." She let go of Bree and turned her attention to Ryker. "Ryker James," she said, practically purring out his name as she held out her hand. He pulled her in and kissed her lightly on the cheek.

"Julia," he replied, "Looking elegant as always."

Eyes sparkling, Julia turned her attention back to Bree. "Did you have enough time to look around?"

"Well, yes and no. I already have a good idea of what I want for color. But for door styles, I'm still open to the different profiles."

"Let's have a seat at the island here," Julia indicated, and then spread out the printed floor plan Ryker had emailed over. "This is going to be quite the kitchen. I absolutely love the design Ryker, the flow, and the incorporation of the curves in the island and at the corners. I think it's your best design yet."

Ryker smiled. "Thank you, but I can't take credit for all of it, even though I'd like to. Bree added the finishing touch."

"The combined effort is going to be spectacular. What is it that you do, Bree?"

"I'm a photographer."

"That's wonderful. Do you ever take photos of displays? We need to update our website and literature. We are currently looking for someone. We've been doing it ourselves, but feel a more professional approach is necessary."

Bree dipped her hand into the side pocket of her purse and produced a business card. "Why don't you check out my website? If you like what you see, give me a call. I would love to work with you."

Julia glanced over the card. "I definitely will look at it this afternoon. Now," she straightened the floor plan out and ran a slender hand over her blouse, mentally shifting gears. "Give me an idea of what you were dreaming of for your kitchen?"

• • • •

THE MORNING FLEW BY, and before Bree knew it, they had selected hardware, cabinets, countertops, and appliances. Her head was spinning by the time they stood to leave. But Bree wasn't too overwhelmed to notice Julia flirting with Ryker the whole time. There was the ever so slight touching of his arm, the extra little bat of eyelashes, and the sly way she smiled at him when she thought Bree wasn't looking.

They walked out into the fresh air with the promise of a price by the end of the week for Bree, a potential new client for her photography business, and a dinner date for Ryker. Bree stifled a laugh as they got into the cab of the truck.

"What are you grinning about?" he asked, starting the truck.

"Nothing."

"It's something. Now spill."

"Just wondering if every female over the age of sixteen and in a hundred-mile radius, swoons at your feet?"

"As a matter of fact, I happen to know from a reliable source that Sam's nieces think I'm cute and they're five and seven, and live in Tennessee. I reach a much larger and wider spread group than you give me credit for."

"For heaven's sake, you're a conceited one."

He laughed. "Are you gonna let me buy you lunch?"

Bree thought about it for a split second. "I'm starving so I guess I'll let you."

Ryker threw the truck in drive and swung around the parking lot, pulling into the McDonald's drive-thru. He ordered and pulled forward to pay.

"You didn't even give me a choice," Bree said, a little hurt, unable to understand what made Ryker tick.

"We always get quarter pounders from McDonald's, don't you?" he asked, pulling up to the window, not understanding the problem.

He shoved the bag and the sodas at Bree as he peeled out of the parking lot and headed back to her house. They rode in silence the entire way.

Ryker pulled into her driveway and glanced over at her. He cleared his throat, feeling like a heel. "You did a nice job selecting everything today. The kitchen will be beautiful."

"Thanks," she said but didn't look at him.

The minute he parked the truck she jumped out, left the bag of food on the seat, and set the drinks on the hood of the truck. She marched across the yard and disappeared into the garage.

Sam found her a few minutes later, soda in one hand and brown bag in the other. "I come bearing sustenance."

Bree leaned over and turned down the radio. She took the bag from him. "Thanks," she said. "I'm not sure what I'm doing to piss him off all the time."

"You're not doing anything. Sometimes Ryker just gets his panties in a wad." Sam offered the soda. "Don't pay any attention to him. He'll be fine. Ryker's going through something right now. I'll talk to him; he shouldn't be taking it out on you. It's unprofessional. He's not usually like that."

Bree perched on the table and unwrapped her burger; Sam sat beside her with his own and ate.

Taking a couple of fries, Bree looked at Sam. "I know I said I would do this space myself, and I plan to, but . . ."

Without hesitation, Sam asked, "What do you need?"

"I was thinking I should update the pedestal and toilet in the powder room, after all, clients will use it. And I was thinking I might like a waiting area for them as they enter. Maybe a wall here." Bree indicated with a fry, pointing. "Floor to ceiling. Then drop down to a half wall here. It will be a little area to put a few chairs or a sofa."

"I like that. It breaks up the large space. That's easy enough. Consider it done. We can start on it tomorrow."

"Thanks, Sam."

"You're welcome. Wanted to ask you, did you go into the basement at all yesterday?"

"No, why?"

He shrugged. "I went down to check the water heater. Got it working. The pilot light was out."

"Glad that was all. Maybe with all the doors and windows being opened up after the house was sitting empty for so long, maybe it was enough to blow it out."

"Maybe. But your case, the gas was turned off."

"Are you sure?"

"Yep, the valve was completely closed. Had to open it up to get the pilot light lit. Maybe the Henning's turned it off after the inspection, and there was just enough hot water for you to get by the first day." Sam grabbed a couple more fries. "Anyway, it's on now." He dug in his front pocket and produced a scrap of paper and handed it to Bree. "Is this of any significance to you?"

She took it from him. "It looks like part of a photograph, otherwise no. Why?"

He shrugged. "I don't know. It was lying on top of the tank. I just thought it was odd. Especially, since the basement was cleaned out well."

Bree tossed it in the trash, not giving it another thought.

Having polished off his fries, Sam wadded up his wrapper and put it back in the bag. "Well, I better get back to work. I'll send Ryker over to take a couple of quick measurements for that wall.

Then I will pick up what we need in the morning, and start it tomorrow."

"Thanks, Sam. I appreciate it."

"You bet."

He took the trash, went down the stairs and outside in search of Ryker. He found him at his truck getting out a box of nails. "Got a minute?"

Ryker looked up. "Yeah, what's up?"

"Are you going to be able to handle working on this project?"

Ryker snorted. "You know I've always wanted to get my hands on this house."

Sam ran his fingers through his sand-colored hair. "That's just it, isn't it? You've always wanted to work on this house, but you thought it would be yours. It's not."

"I'm well aware that it's not mine," Ryker said gruffly, leaning on the truck. "You don't need to remind me."

"The real question is, have you accepted that it's not yours and probably never will be?"

"Yeah, I have. That became very apparent today at the showroom. As much as I wanted to chime in and give my two cents on the kitchen, I didn't. I couldn't. They weren't my decisions to make."

"Now that you realize that, I hope you'll go a little easier on Bree. She doesn't have any idea that you had your heart set on this house, nor should she."

"You're right. I need to be nicer, more professional."

"You can start right now. She wants to add a wall to her studio. I told her you'd be up to measure."

Ryker looked at Sam ruefully. "You're making me go in there now?"

"No time like the present."

"Shit." Ryker tossed the box of nails at Sam. "What a friend." Grabbing his tape measure, he walked towards the garage, preparing to apologize.

Chapter 15

Bree sat in her new studio. The house was finally quiet after a long day of hammering and saws continuously going. The space had been transformed in a matter of days. Ryker had put up the new wall and had helped her paint the entire expanse of the room. White was her workspace color, but the small waiting area they had painted a soft sage. An ivory sofa, matching club chairs, and pillows in various patterns of ivory, sage, and black sat on top of a deep green shag rug to fill the space. She had matted and framed three black and white photographs in black and hung them on the wall. Each one was from a different category, trying to showcase her diversity and best work.

She had a few more photos that she wanted to frame and mat, but right now she was busy cropping a white sailboat she had photographed the first week she had arrived. She was going to frame it and give it to Coastal Realty as a gift. The blues of the water and sky would work perfectly in that space.

Finished, she checked her website. Clicked through the new orders, and then checked the comments from her latest blog. She had posted a few pictures from her expedition to Assateague Island and some techniques and tricks on how to capture animals.

Bree scanned down through the comments.

Sunnygal: I can't wait to see how this works on my own pets! Thanks for the tips.

Chocolate4ever: Took a pic of a doe in my yard using your tips. Turned out great!

Soccerrocks21: Love your work!

Kage: I'm watching you.

TexasTom56: The crane in flight was breathtaking.

Ellisonfamily: Loved the one of the family of horses! I gotta have that one!

Beginnerbabe: Your colors are so vivid. Mine aren't as crisp. How do you do that?

Bree's breath caught as she scrolled past it. Had she read that right? She went back up and focused on Kage.

Kage: I'm watching you.

There it was. Just three words. But Bree's heart skipped a beat. She glanced over her shoulder. The shades were drawn.

As if on cue, there was a loud bang from below. Bree pushed back her chair and ran to the top of the stairs. The door stood wide open. She raced down and slammed it shut, quickly locking it. She turned her back and leaned against it, her eyes sweeping the empty garage.

She tried to reason with herself that the door hadn't been latched properly and had simply blown it open in the increasing wind. But Ryker's voice crept into her head.

Maybe it's the ghost.

She scolded herself for letting the thought in. But the reality was a ghost hadn't typed that message.

The wind kicked up a notch outside, making the garage doors groan.

"It's nothing," she said out loud, trying to sound confident, "Just some jerk who thinks they're funny." But her words sounded hollow even to her own ears. What if this Kage wasn't kidding? What if he could see her? After all, she didn't have any of the windows covered except the studio. Half the windows had been re-placed today, the others were scheduled for next week. Suddenly she wasn't sure if the doors and windows were locked.

Bree went through the all-glass breezeway that connected the garage to the house, flipping on lights. Checking the doors and the windows, trying not to panic.

"Locking up for the night," she told herself. She walked through the kitchen, shut the door to the basement, flipped the lock, and checked all the windows in the formal dining and living rooms. The front door was the last one. It was locked. She leaned her head against it and took a long, slow breath, trying to calm her heart. She turned then and peered up the wide sweep of stairs into the dark. Her heart thudded in her chest at the thought of what might be lurking up there.

Everything is fine, she told herself. The house was locked tight. Suddenly mad at letting three little words scare her, she marched back through the well-lit house to her studio. She climbed the stairs and glanced at the clock on the wall.

It was well after eleven, suddenly tired from a long day, fatigue set in. Bree decided she might as well go to bed. She didn't think she'd be able to concentrate any longer tonight anyway, and the crew would be back early to work. She leaned over her computer and moved the mouse, the screensaver disappeared. Her hand froze as she saw another entry had been added.

Kage: Did you check the upstairs?

Frantic, Bree logged off, desperate to get away from the computer. She grabbed her cell phone and looked around for something to use to protect herself. She spotted the little hammer she had used to hang up her pictures. It wasn't much, but it was better than nothing.

Wielding it in one hand, she went to shut off the lights. She stopped, hand hovering above the light switch, shaking. If someone was watching and she shut off the light, they'd know exactly where she was. Slowly retracting her hand, she left them on. She tiptoed to the window, and lifted the corner of the shade, desperately searching the dark. She could almost feel eyes on her as she let the shade fall back into place.

Paranoid now, she tiptoed to the stairs. Peered around the corner of the doorway and scanned the dimly lit garage. Somehow the shadows seemed to shift and move. "Just my mind playing tricks," she hissed between clenched teeth.

Seeing nothing, she hugged the wall and slowly crept down the stairs, one step at a time, trying desperately to stay out of view of the windows. She got to the breezeway and knew the only way to cross without being seen was to crawl on her belly.

Bree tucked her cell phone in her back pocket and got down on all fours, hammer still in her hand. She crawled to the edge of the window and then flattened herself to the floor, elbows and legs propelling her across, scraping bare skin on the rough, chipped tile floor. It was only about eight feet but it felt like forty. A cold, slick sweat broke out across her skin. In the kitchen she kept down, staying behind the cabinets, and crawled down the hall. At the stairs, she quickly got to her feet and pressed her back to the wall. About halfway up she disappeared into the darkness.

Standing safely in the shadows, she stopped. Letting her eyes adjust to the darkness and tried to slow her breathing. She stood stock-still and listened. The wind howled. Small debris periodically hit the house, and glass rattled in their panes as the wind shook the house. But nothing seemed to be coming from inside.

The panic in her slowly subsided, and she crept up the remaining portion of the stairs. She stopped again at the top and listened. Other than the wind and the pounding of her heart she heard nothing out of the ordinary. She walked down the center of the hall, a mere shadow in the dark. Hammer in her hand, she went through the open doors to her bedroom. She stopped again and listened.

She crept to the bathroom, peered into the even darker room. Nothing. She checked the closet. Empty. Now that she was sure she was alone, she ran back across the room and closed the door. Locked it and drug the one chair she had in front of it, and wedged it under the handle.

She pulled out her phone and checked the time. Midnight. It was seven hours before someone would come to the house. Could she make it alone? She could call someone. But who? Who could she call? Colette? She'd come, but what could she do, really? Sam and Ryker? No way. Ryker would never let her live it down.

Chad? He was too far away to do any good. And he no longer cared what happened to her anyway. That truth hurt more than she wanted to admit.

Aunt Maureen? No way could she call her. She'd panic and insist she came home. Not an option. That left the police. And what would she say? Someone was stalking her by email? Maybe even that they might be outside? She had no proof. For the first time since moving into the house, she felt completely alone. And afraid.

She went to the window and peered out into the dark. Lights dotted the horizon of what was Ocean City, but there was nothing on the water. No lights close by.

No, she wouldn't call the police. She couldn't call anyone. She'd have to make it through the night. She'd wait it out. She wouldn't let herself give in to this deranged idiot who thought he could scare her with a few emails.

She went to the air mattress and crawled under the covers fully clothed. She lay there wide awake and stared into the darkness, listening intently to the sounds of the howling wind, too frightened to close her eyes.

• • • •

HE SAT IN THE DARKNESS, and watched her go from room to room flipping on lights. He chuckled to himself as he followed her with his lens. She quickly checked the doors and windows, continually glancing over her shoulder and out into the night. She was scared. He could see it written all over her face.

She went to the front of the house where he lost track of her. He waited, but no lights went on upstairs. Well, he could fix that. He typed quickly on his laptop and fired it off.

To his surprise, he watched her walk confidently back through the well-lit house. Across the glass breezeway and then disappear into the garage. He couldn't see her but imagined her climbing the stairs, going to the computer, and finding his new message.

Minutes ticked by and nothing happened. But then just when he was about to give up, he saw the corner of the shade move slightly. She peered out. He zoomed in on her face. She looked exactly the way he wanted her to. Terrified.

He smirked. The shade dropped. The house blazed like a beacon on the edge of the water, with its lights shining out into the black windy night, but there was no movement from within.

Satisfied that he had her right where he wanted her, he put the camera down. With one last glance back at the house he whispered, "You think you're scared now . . ." he laughed. "Just wait."

Chapter 16

Bree jerked, and sat bolt upright as the night came rushing back to her. She looked around, panicked as the feeble light seeped in. *It's morning. I made it.* She searched for her cell phone under the covers. Finding it, she rubbed her eyes and checked the time. It was after seven.

What was that knocking? The crew. Sam. Ryker. Bree flung off the covers, the hammer dropped to the floor with a thud as she ran to her bedroom door. The chair was still wedged under the handle. She yanked it free and flew down the stairs as the knock came again. She fumbled with the lock, yanked the door open, and came face to face with Sam and Ryker.

"Good morning!" Sam said his usual sunny self.

"Hey, Champ, you don't look so good," Ryker said, giving Bree the once over.

Relieved to see them, she couldn't respond right away.

"Did you sleep in your clothes?"

Bree pushed at her hair and straightened her shirt. "I had a rough night."

"Looks like it."

She really didn't care how bad she looked, she was just relieved they were here. "Come in," she said with an edge to her voice, then swallowed hard trying to calm her nerves. "Please, come in. Do you want coffee?"

They followed her to the kitchen.

"I would love a cup," Sam answered.

"Yeah, me too," added Ryker.

Bree went through the motions of getting out the coffee, filling the pot with water, adding the grounds. Somehow the everyday task was calming her nerves, making last night seem just like a bad dream. Relaxing as the pot started to fill, Bree turned around to find Ryker and Sam staring at her with concern.

"What? Do I really look that bad?"

"No, of course not," Sam was quick to answer.

"You look like hell."

Sam glared at Ryker.

"Well, she does. I'm just telling the truth."

"It's okay Sam; he's not hurting my feelings . . . much. I'm sure I look bad."

"You don't look bad," Sam said, trying to be a little more tactful than Ryker. "You look like you didn't sleep well, that's all."

"I didn't." Bree turned around to get down Styrofoam cups from the cabinet. Her hand trembled and she dropped the stack, scattering them.

"Do you need a hand?" Ryker asked, moving to assist.

"I got it." She scooped them up, cutting him off.

"Did the wind keep you up?" Sam asked, concerned.

"Or the ghost?" Ryker asked with a mischievous grin.

Bree turned around and pinned him in place with her eyes. "Stop that would you?"

He held up his hands in defense. "I'm only joking."

"Well, it's not funny." She poured two cups of coffee and put the pot back. She set one in front of Sam the other was for herself. To hell with Ryker. She got out creamer from the fridge and a couple of spoons from the center drawer in the island.

"Thanks," Sam said, grateful for the cup.

"Where's mine?"

Bree ignored him. "There's milk in the fridge if you would rather have that than creamer. Sugar is on the counter." Then she looked directly at Ryker while she stirred. "You can get your own. I'm going to take a shower."

"Need help with that?" he asked, lifting an eyebrow. "You've seen what I can do with a paintbrush; just imagine what I can do with a bar of soap."

Bree's face turned beet red. "In your dreams, Ryker."

"Apparently, yours too, by the look on your face."

"You're unbelievable," Bree said, walking away.

Sam stared at Ryker as Bree stomped up the stairs and slammed a door somewhere overhead. "Are you trying to piss her off so we get fired?"

Ryker laughed. "No, she's just way too fun to tease. She looks damn cute when she's mad." Plus, he didn't like seeing her upset. It was much better to have her flustered and mad than upset. He went to the coffee pot and poured himself a cup. "Something must have kept her up all night."

"How do you know?" Sam asked, taking a sip.

"Look around. Every damn light in the house is on."

• • • •

AN HOUR LATER, WITH the sound of hammering all around her, she was dressed casually in jeans and a soft butter yellow top. She pulled her long hair into a ponytail. She was feeling human again after the coffee, shower, and change of clothes, last night *almost* a distant memory.

Bree loaded the pictures that she had wrapped in brown paper into her SUV. Then jumped in, and drove the short distance to Coastal Realty. She parked in front, grabbed her packages, and went in.

Sheri was sitting at the desk when she walked in, looking pretty in her pale blue cotton dress. "Bree," Sheri beamed. "You look like pure sunshine. What brings you in?"

"Hello, Sheri. I wanted to drop this off for Linda." Bree lifted up one of the packages and laid it delicately on the counter. "Just a little something for the office, after all you have done for me."

"Oh, let me get her. I can't wait to see what it is." She punched Linda's number on her phone. "Can you come out here a minute? Bree Thompson is here." Sheri put the phone back down. "She'll be right out. How's the house? I want to come by and see the progress. Sam and Ryker have been filling us in."

"I love it and the spot. You should come over and see it now, and then come back again after the kitchen goes in."

"I think I will. Maybe I could stop by after work sometime?"

"Absolutely, send me a text. I'd love to show you."

"Wonderful." Sheri smiled. "Here she is," Sheri indicated as Linda came down the hall.

Linda stretched out her hand and greeted Bree warmly. "Hello, Bree. What can I do for you?"

"I wanted to drop off a little token of my appreciation because you accelerated closing on the house."

"It was nothing, just doing our job. You didn't have to do this, my dear." Linda glanced at the package. "But since you did. . . Sheri pass me the scissors please."

Sheri handed them to Linda, she cut the paper, unfolded it, and gasped. "This is gorgeous! Wherever did you find this?"

"Do you like it?'

"Like it? I absolutely love it!" Linda held the framed photo of the sailboat, admiring it. It was framed in the same driftwood as the reception desk. It had a double-layered mat. The first mat was navy to pull in the office colors; the second was an indigo blue that matched the water.

"I'm glad you like it. It's one of mine. I thought it would go nicely with the office decor."

"It really does," Sheri said. "It's beautiful, Bree."

"I know just where it can go," Linda said, lifting it. "Right here above the desk. It will be the first thing everyone sees when they walk in."

"That's where I imagined it too," Bree said, thrilled.

"Sam is stopping by later, I'll have him hang it when he comes." Linda handed the picture to Sheri. "Set that over there, please." Linda turned to Bree and gave her a hug. "Thank you so much."

"You're welcome," Bree said, meaning it.

The front door opened and Greg walked in. "Bree?" he said surprised. "What are you doing here?"

"I'm dropping off gifts."

"Really?"

"Look what she brought." Sheri pulled him around the counter and pointed.

He let out a little whistle. "Wow."

"I have something for you too. For all your help." She handed it to him. "You mentioned how beautiful the sunrises are here, so I thought . . . just open it."

Sheri handed him the scissors and he cut the paper off. Peeling it back he exposed the photo. It was the horizon, stretched out across in glorious color, at the peak of daybreak.

"This is spectacular, Bree."

"It's absolutely stunning. You have your own business, right?" Linda asked, admiring the photo.

"Yes, Images, Images by Bree."

"Anyone that takes one look at either of these is going to want to know where we got them. I love to promote talent and you certainly are talented."

"Really?"

"Yes, really. Do you have any business cards with you?"

"I have a few." Bree dug through her purse and produced some.

Linda took them. "That will do to start. Next time you're in the area, drop off some more." Linda turned to Greg. "Sam can put yours up in your office if you want?"

"Yeah, that'd be great. Thanks, Linda."

Bree smiled at them. "All right, I have some errands to do, so I'll let you all get back to work. Sheri, let me know when you want to stop by."

"I will."

"I'll walk you out," Greg said. He held the door for her and walked with Bree to her SUV. "Would you like to go to dinner or a movie sometime?"

Bree hesitated, unsure. She debated for a minute, then didn't see any harm in the invitation. "Sure, a movie sounds like fun. Are you an action-adventure or a comedy kind of guy?"

"I like both."

"Me too."

He beamed at her. "I'll check the shows and give you a call."

"Sounds good." She hesitated. "Greg? Have you had a chance to ask anyone about the possibility of my house being haunted?"

He cocked his head and looked at her with concern in his soft brown eyes. "Honestly, I forgot to ask. Is everything okay?"

"Just curious, Ryker brought it up again."

"Did something happen?"

"No," she brushed off his question. "Forget I mentioned it." She climbed in her SUV, backed out, and gave him a little wave.

He watched her pull away, wondering.

• • • •

RYKER FOUND BREE OUT back in *his* favorite spot. That alone almost made him turn around and go back in, but he didn't. It was hers now. There was nothing he could do about it. He might as well face it.

As he approached, he couldn't help but think how cute she looked in her big floppy hat and large dark sunglasses. She wore jeans and a yellow top that hung slightly off revealing a bare shoulder. She was sitting cross-legged on a blanket with her laptop, working.

"Can I join you?"

Bree shrugged. "Suit yourself." She scooted over, gave him half the blanket.

"What are you doing?"

Annoyed, she looked at him. "Working. Shouldn't you be?"

"Me? No, I'm taking a break. Needed some sunshine and good company." He paused for effect. "The guys were all busy, so here I am." He flashed a grin.

Bree slid her sunglasses down and glared at him. Two could play this game. "I'm flattered that I'm your second choice. You wouldn't even be on my list."

"Ouch." He clutched at his heart. "That hurt."

"Whatever." She slid her glasses back into place. "Do you mind? I *am* trying to work."

"Not at all. You go right ahead. I'm just going to sit here quietly and eat." He unzipped his small cooler and pulled out a bottle of water. Took a long pull and set it down. He inched a little closer to Bree and peered over her shoulder.

On her laptop was a picture of the beach at sunrise. It was beautiful. Taken at the split second the sun broke the horizon. Stars still hung in a black velvet sky. The moon was out and shining brightly, and the sun was a mere suggestion on the immense horizon.

"Did you take that?"

"Yes." She pulled her sunglasses off this time and rubbed between her eyes. She had a headache forming from the late night and a lack of food. Her stomach growled.

"That's one of the most intense daybreaks I've ever seen."

Bree looked at Ryker and waited for the dig. "But?"

"But what?" Ryker took a bite of his turkey club. He dug out a small bag of chips. Popped it open, and snagged one. "No buts."

"Really?" Bree asked with surprise. "You usually try to get a jab in there somewhere."

"Not this time." He pointed at the screen. "I've never seen anything that good before. I'm impressed. Didn't know you had that kind of talent."

And there it was. "I thought you said you were going to sit here quietly?"

Ryker laughed. "You should know better than that." He took half his sandwich and offered it to Bree. "Want half?"

She eyed him suspiciously. "Peace offering?"

He shrugged. "Kind of."

Bree set her computer aside and took the sandwich from him. "Thank you for the sandwich and the compliment. I'll ignore the dig."

"You're welcome for both. So, when are you going to get those Adirondack chairs? This sitting on the ground is for the birds. It's hard on the back and my ass."

This time Bree shrugged. "It's not in my budget just yet."

Ryker nodded, completely understanding, eating a few more chips. Switching gears he said, "Sam mentioned he wanted to have you update our website. Take some professional photos of us and our work. Is that something you'd be interested in doing?"

"I would."

"Can you check out our website, see what it needs, and write up a proposal?"

She nodded. "I can put something together for you."

"We can give you a list of projects that we have already done."

"That's good. I would also like to get before and after pictures of jobsites you're currently working on. Colette mentioned you

guys could use a new logo too. I could design one. Give you a couple of choices. Could probably have it for you by Friday. Would
that be soon enough?"

Ryker nodded. "Sounds like a plan. I better get back inside. We
can't all lay around in the sun all day and pretend to work."

"You can't be nice for more than five minutes, can you?"

He leaned in close. So close Ryker could feel her breath on his
lips and see the flecks of gray in her blue eyes. She sucked in a
breath.

He grinned. "What fun would that be?" He held himself there
for a few seconds. Only a hint of salt air between them. He imagined himself kissing her. Would she lean into it? Or would she
backhand him? He thought the latter, so he forced himself to back
up, and saw the flush on her face. *Maybe he should have.* Damn
if she wasn't cute when she was flustered. He was tempted, very
tempted, all the better reason to leave. He stood up quickly. "See
you later, Champ."

Chapter 17

B ree heard the knock on the door and almost skipped down the stairs. She'd slept soundly and woke to seagulls calling. The sun was shining and there was the promise of another day with temperatures in the upper sixties.

"Hey guys," Bree said cheerfully as she opened the door to Sam and Ryker. "I was just going to make coffee. Do you want some?"

"Definitely," Sam answered.

"Am I going to get a cup this time?" Ryker asked, eyeing her.

"If you're nice to me," Bree smiled sweetly at him.

"You must have gotten a good night's sleep last night."

"I did," Bree said, going to the cabinet to get the coffee grounds down. She opened the cabinet, but it was empty. Without hesitating, she went to the next cabinet, and there it was. *Huh,* she thought, *must have put it back in the wrong spot.* She filled the pot with water and put the container back where it belonged. She got out the cups as the smell of coffee permeated the air.

"What's on the agenda today?" she asked, knowing Sam would give her the rundown.

"The guys finished working on the porch yesterday, the weather is supposed to be ideal, so they're going to start painting."

Bree nodded as she went to the pantry. She had bought chocolate chip muffins yesterday at the store and decided to share. Hands on her hips she scanned the pantry. She was sure she had put them on the shelf right beside the canister of sugar, but they weren't there. "What else?" she asked, trying not to overthink it finding the muffins tucked behind a cereal box.

"Ryker and I are going to be up on the roof for a good portion of the day. We want to fix the widow's walk and patch the hole in the far corner of the roof."

Bree nodded and set the muffins down, and retrieved paper plates and napkins.

"Please help yourself to muffins." She went to the center of the island to get out silverware only to find the drawer empty. Bree stood still for a moment, and then pulled out the middle drawer. Empty. She pulled out the bottom drawer and found the silverware. A shiver ran through her.

"What's the matter?" Ryker asked.

"Nothing."

"It's something."

"It's just . . . the silverware isn't where I put it."

"What do you mean?" Sam asked, coming around the counter.

"I put all the silverware in the top drawer. I'd swear that's where it was when I went to bed last night."

"So, you changed your mind and moved it. No big deal."

"But I wouldn't. It makes no sense to put it in the bottom drawer and leave the top two empty. And I'm pretty sure I would remember doing it."

Sam bent down and scooped up the small drawer insert filled with silverware and moved it up to the top drawer. A piece of a torn photo fluttered to the floor.

"But it's not just the silverware. The coffee wasn't in the right cabinet and the muffins were moved. Everything is out of place this morning." Bree bent to pick up the scrap of paper and examined it. It looked exactly like the piece of a photograph she threw away before.

"You were probably just distracted and did it without thinking. I wouldn't worry about it."

Perplexed, Bree shrugged. "I guess but how do you explain this?" Bree waved the corner of the picture."

"I can't." Sam shrugged.

Bree tossed the paper into the trash can. Bree's cell phone rang. She looked at the caller ID and frowned. "Help yourself to muffins and coffee. I'm going to take this call."

They heard her say hello as she slipped out the slider onto the patio. Sam poured coffee into two cups, set one in front of Ryker, and took a sip of the steaming hot liquid.

Ryker eyed his cup and looked at Sam as he scrolled down his to-do list on his phone. "That's kind of odd, isn't it? The coffee and muffins are one thing, but the silverware? She doesn't remember moving it?"

Sam shrugged, clearly distracted by his agenda for the day. "I don't have an answer to that. Unless she just did it without thinking. Come on, we need to get started." He topped off his coffee and snagged a muffin.

Ryker watched Bree on the phone, and wondered what really made her move halfway across the country, and buy this house, his house. Was something going on? He took a sip of the coffee and observed her for a few minutes. She slowly walked down towards the water, still talking. Ryker hesitated a moment longer, then turned and followed Sam out the door.

• • • •

THE CREW WAS KNOCKING off for the day. The front porch was freshly painted, and sparkled in the late afternoon sun.

Sam and Ryker had spent the majority of the day on the roof. They had patched the hole and reinforced the widow's walk, making it ready to be primed.

Ryker checked his phone for the weather forecast. It was going to be sunny and seventy. If he could get the primer on the widow's walk first thing in the morning, he would still have plenty of time to take the boat out, then the guys could paint on Monday. He'd check with Bree, and make sure it was all right to come in the morning.

Sam had the truck loaded and called out to Ryker. "Wanna grab dinner and a beer later?"

"Definitely."

"I have to make a few stops on my way home. Are you heading out?"

"In a few. Need to check on something first. Send me a text when you're done, and I'll meet you at the Shack," Ryker called over his shoulder as he went around the back of the house in search of Bree.

He had seen her at the edge of the water all day which wasn't unusual. Although it was usually only for a few moments or sitting with her laptop working, today had been different. Today she had just stood there. Even now she seemed to be in the same exact spot. She was so still, stoic, and fragile looking. His heart squeezed tight, warning him not to get involved, to turn around, go back the way he had come. But his heart got the better of him and he kept walking towards her. Pulled by an invisible force that he couldn't explain.

The breeze whipped at her hair and her clothes, but that was the only movement. He came up beside her, tucked his hands in his front pockets, and waited for her to notice him.

When she didn't, he cleared his throat, "Another beautiful day."

Bree didn't say anything, just kept staring at the water.

He waited quietly another minute but couldn't take it any longer. "Are you all right?" He saw a lone tear run down her cheek and knew she wasn't. He cursed himself inwardly for coming out.

A thought occurred to him. She hadn't acknowledged his presence; maybe she truly hadn't noticed him. Maybe he could take a step back, and then another. Disappear from her line of sight. If she didn't notice his slow retreat when he was far enough back, he could safely take off, get in his truck and drive away as if he'd never even been there.

Move, you idiot. You can do it. Just turn and walk away, before it's too late. He lifted his foot, slightly convinced he could do it, but his heart took control over his mind. *Coward. She needs help, talk to her.*

He cursed himself inwardly and reached out with his hand, touching her softly on the arm. "Bree? Are you all right? You've been out here all day. Ever since that phone call. Did you get some bad news? Did something happen?"

She turned and looked at him. Her eyes shimmering blue like the bay as tears welled up in the corners. "I'm a terrible person."

At the obvious hurt in her eyes, his own self-preservation mechanism kicked in . . . sarcasm. "Tell me something I don't already know, Champ. You punch people. Won't give them coffee . . . should I go on?" When she turned away, he cursed himself for being a jackass. "I'm kidding. You're not. What's happened?"

Completely weary, she sunk down on the ground and pulled her knees into her chest. "It doesn't matter. You don't really want to know. Go away."

Believe me, I'd like to, he thought. But he couldn't without feeling like a heel. He crouched down beside her instead. "Try me. What's so devastating that has had you riveted to the same spot all day?" He waited, when she didn't answer he baited her. "Did your best friend die?"

"No . . . my parents did." Her voice broke, "And my little sister and today's my sister's birthday."

"Oh hell, Bree. I'm so sorry." He put his damn foot in his mouth again. His brain mocked him, *I told you to leave.* Ryker eased down on the ground beside her, the wind completely knocked out of him. "When? How?"

"In a car accident."

Hating himself, he hesitated, swallowed hard, and forced himself to say, "Tell me."

Not wanting to talk about it but truly needing to, she told him.

She started in a monotone, "It was Memorial Day weekend. The day was perfect. We had brunch at my favorite restaurant, and then my parents surprised me with a graduation party. I had graduated from college two weeks earlier, so I wasn't expecting anything, and I was leaving for an internship in Kansas City for the summer. I had the cars packed, mine and their minivan. We took pictures with my friends, ate cake, opened presents, and said our goodbyes. It was fun. A really good day, you know? The kind of day I'll never forget." She laughed at the irony of it.

The wind teased strands of golden-brown hair out of her clip, and Ryker tucked it behind her ear, wanting to comfort her but not knowing how. He wasn't good at this kind of thing and avoided it every chance he got. But he was stuck now and had to hear her out.

"We cleaned up and said goodbye to my friends, got in our cars, and started the drive. My dad was driving the minivan loaded down with some of my stuff, my mom, and my younger sister. I was following behind in my car. With all the excitement I had forgotten to get gas earlier. We pulled off about halfway there and filled up. We got back on the interstate and were picking up speed so my dad pulled out into the passing lane to go around a tractor-trailer. Just as he was even with the middle of the trailer the driver drifted into their lane. I laid on my horn and the semi righted itself. My dad accelerated to get around him but wasn't fast enough. The semi jerked back and swerved across both lanes and struck the minivan. Somehow dad managed to keep the van on the road." Bree hesitated, not sure if she could get the rest out.

"Go on. Then what happened?" Ryker encouraged.

"It was like a scene out of a movie, played out in slow motion, and there was nothing I could do. The tractor-trailer swerved, making contact again, pushing them off the pavement. The road curved. There was so much noise, the screech of tires skidding, of metal colliding with metal, and screams. Oh, God. The screams . . . The back hatch of the minivan came open as it rolled. My clothes, my bedding, and my books were thrown everywhere. But worse, was I could see my sister. I could see her face, she was terrified. I could hear her scream. See her reach out in my direction. And a second later she disappeared. The van rolled three times and finally came to rest upside down. If that had been it, then maybe . . . maybe they would still be here. But the semi jackknifed, came around and down into the median and struck the van again."

"The driver and I both jumped out and ran to the van, but the gas . . . the smell of gas was so strong, he grabbed me and pulled me back an instant before it burst into flames, taking my entire family with it . . . right before my eyes."

His heart ached for her.

She shook her head as tears streamed down her face. "All because I needed gas."

That shocked him. "For Pete's sake Bree, that's a bunch of shit and you and I both know it. It's not your fault. It was an accident. If anything, it's the driver of the semi's fault. Was he drunk? On drugs? Maybe texting?"

"No, he had some sort of seizure, and blacked out for a few seconds."

Ryker shook his head in disbelief. "That's rough, Bree. I don't know what to say or what you want to hear. Or need to hear, for that matter. No one should ever have to go through this, let alone witness the whole thing." He paused, wondering, did she need sympathy or tough love. He wasn't much for sympathy, so he decided to go with the latter. "But it happened. It's something that I imagine will stick with you your entire life, you have a hole that will never be filled. Shouldn't be filled. It was your family. They can't be replaced.

I imagine you think of them every day." He thought of his parents, his brothers, and couldn't imagine life without them. What a hole there would be if and when something happened to them, let alone all of them at the same time.

She nodded but didn't say anything, only looked out at the water. The sun was slowly sinking behind them. Long shadows were stretching like fingers across the vast yard.

He leaned over, closer, and nudged her with his shoulder. "But I have to ask, you started this whole conversation by saying you're a terrible person. How does any of this make you a terrible person?"

"I forgot," she laughed a soft hysterical kind of laugh. "Today is my little sister's birthday. My *only* sister. And I forgot. I didn't know what day it was. The whole month of April I've been avoiding the calendar. Not looking at it. Dreading when the calendar changed to May. But I woke up this morning and for once it wasn't the first thing on my mind. I was excited for the day, looking forward to you guys coming and working on the house, working on my photos. It never even crossed my mind that it was today." She held back a sob. "Not until my ex-boyfriend called and asked how I was doing did I remember! It hasn't even been a year and I've already forgotten them." She buried her face in her hands and sobbed. "Chad . . . of all people remembered Gracie's birthday." She sobbed harder.

His heart ripped open for her, but not his mind. His words came out a little harsher than he had anticipated. "So what? You're going to just sit here and cry all damn day and night?" He shook his head in disbelief. "I thought you were tougher than that Bree. So, you forgot what day it was. You're allowed to go on with your life. Get over yourself." He stood up, clearly disgusted.

"What?" Bree asked, shocked enough to stop crying and look at him.

Ryker almost stopped himself from saying anymore from the look of pure grief that raced across her face, but he didn't.

"Boo-hoo, you forgot the damn date. It happens. You said yourself that there isn't a day that goes by that they don't cross your mind. Hell, I've even witnessed it and I've only known you a few weeks. I didn't know what it was until now but I could see the grief, feel the sadness in you. I even know your mom's favorite color is yellow, and that your sister's name is Gracie. Now how would I know that if you hadn't mentioned it? Or them? Believe me, I don't give a damn enough to ask about such things."

Bree stood up and faced him. "What the hell do you know, Ryker James?" She shoved him. "Have you ever seen your entire family gone in mere seconds? Right before your eyes?"

He didn't say anything.

"I didn't think so. I should be able to feel sorry for myself if I want to."

"That's it then, right? Do you want sympathy? Do you want someone to feel sorry for you, Bree? If so, you came to the wrong guy for that."

"I didn't come to you! You came out here looking for me, you self-righteous ass!"

The tears were gone, replaced by white-hot rage. He smirked in spite of himself.

"Wipe that smug look off your face or I'll wipe it off for you."

"What are you gonna do, Bree? Punch me again? Or whack me with a door?"

"You ass! Go away!" she turned and stomped off in the direction of the house.

Ryker wasn't sure if he should follow or let her go. But one thing was for sure, he liked seeing her pissed off way better than sad. He decided to follow to make sure she stayed that way.

She slammed into the house with him practically at her heels.

"Get your keys, we're going out."

"Like hell I am. I'm not going anywhere with you. Get out of my house."

"I'm not leaving without you. We're going to meet Sam and get something to eat. If you stay here, you'll just sit and feel sorry for yourself all night."

"Go to hell, Ryker. I don't need you to tell me what to do."

He grabbed her arm and spun her around. "Sure you do. You got five minutes to go upstairs and get ready. Grab what you need and get back down here before I drag your sorry ass out of the house. You can go willingly or by force. It's your choice."

"Let go of me." She shook him off and they stared at each other for a hot minute.

"What's it gonna be?"

"You can't just force me to go with you."

"Try me."

"What are you going to do? Sling me over your shoulder like some big bully?"

"If I have to."

"I'd like to see you try," she said, staring him down.

"Is that a challenge?"

"Absolutely not."

He took a step towards her. "Let's go."

She let out a huff and stomped up the stairs.

"Five minutes and counting, starting now," he called up after her.

When five minutes passed and she wasn't down, he went up after her. He pounded on her door, rattling it in its frame. "Bree? You had better be ready." When there was no answer, he pounded again. "I hope you're dressed because I'm coming in." He tried the knob but it was locked. He cursed himself. He should have thought of that. He pounded again. "Bree! Get out here!"

He was about to bang on the door again when it opened. She stood in front of him, her hair brushed, left loose, and hung down just below her shoulders. Her cheeks were flushed pink and her blue eyes drilled holes through him. "Did you text Sam and tell him I was coming?" she asked harshly.

"Yes, because two against one are better odds."

"And what exactly did you say?"

"Nothing yet, but if you want it to stay that way, then you'd best be coming along willingly."

"Fine, but only because I don't want him, or anyone else for that matter, to know. I don't need anyone's pity."

"You won't get any from me," Ryker said. "Let's go."

Chapter 18

B ree woke up as the sun filled the room. She went to the French doors and looked out at the water. *Another beautiful day that I get to enjoy, I need to be thankful for that.*

Her heart hurt when she thought about her family and all the days they missed so far, and the ones she'd wasted feeling sorry for herself. As much as she hated to admit it, Ryker had been right. Feeling sorry for herself wouldn't bring them back. She was here for a reason. It was up to her to make the most of it.

First, she had to find the motivation. *Easier said than done.* Aunt Maureen had called to check on her and reminded her to keep making lists.

She went over to the air mattress and picked up her notepad. The majority of her work was outside today. She needed to clean up the existing flower beds, tear out the old bushes, pick up sticks, and rake leaves. If she got that done, maybe she could make a quick trip to the local nursery and pick up some plants, a few flowers for containers, and new shrubs around the house. The thought of that perked her up considerably.

First things first, she'd need a quick shower and a hearty breakfast if she planned on accomplishing all that today. She jumped in the shower, washed her hair, and mentally tried to decide what type of bushes she might like. She had always loved white azaleas.

She shaved her legs, thinking about tulips. It was too late for them to bloom. She'd make a list of plants and bulbs to purchase in the fall. Another of her favorites were boxwoods. The rich green would look nice against the stone foundation.

Bree toweled off and decided to blow dry her hair and pull it into a long smooth ponytail. She opened the bottom drawer in the vanity to get her hairdryer. She pulled it out and something fell to the floor. She bent and picked it up. It was another torn piece of a photograph. That was weird. She flipped it over, examining it. It had to be part of the other ones. *How would that get in with her things?* The background was plain white like the other pieces but this one contained what looked like a bare shoulder. Bree tried to shrug it off. She had no idea where it came from unless it had already been in the drawer and she hadn't seen it when she originally put her things in. She turned hastily and chucked it into the trash, trying not to give it another thought.

She dried her hair and brushed it through. She got dressed, pulling on cutoffs and a gray tank top. Grabbed an elastic hair tie and hastily put her hair in a ponytail. She spread sunscreen evenly across her face and arms before she headed downstairs.

Bree was getting the ingredients for an omelet out of the fridge when movement outside caught her eye. She crossed to the slider and saw Ryker in her favorite spot digging. "What's he doing?"

Curious, Bree grabbed her flip-flops from the breezeway and went out. Halfway there she slowed her stride, then stopped. She stood motionless as he placed a young tree into the hole he had dug, squatted and covered it with mulch, then dumped the bucket of water he had carted out at its base. Once the mulch was smoothed, he placed two Adirondack chairs on either side of it. Bree's hand went to her mouth as she realized they were yellow.

"Bless his heart," she whispered approaching him. "Good morning, Ryker."

He looked up and grinned at her. "Mornin'." He pulled off his gloves and tossed them next to his spade. Grabbed his water bottle and took a swig.

"This is beautiful, but why?" she asked, coming closer.

He shrugged. "You said you wanted to put a couple of chairs here, and you've been spending a lot of time in this spot, so I thought, why not? You'll enjoy it more with somewhere to actually sit."

"What kind of tree is this?" Bree asked, coming around to stand beside him.

"It's a weeping cherry. It blooms white in April. The blossoms are already spent for this year, but next year you can enjoy it."

"And those?" Bree asked, noticing the two little bushes on either side of the tree with reddish round leaves.

"Those are smoke bushes, specifically *Cotinus Grace*, which is a deciduous shrub. Those leaves darken over the summer and then turn in the fall to a red-orange." He could feel Bree look at him, so he kept talking. "They also get a wispy pink flower in the summer. They do well in any soil and in full sun, so I figured they'd be perfect for this spot." He tucked his hands in his front pockets and looked at her. "What?"

She looked from the quaint little spot he had created to him and back. "You thought of everything didn't you?" she said quietly. The yellow chairs for her mother, the weeping cherry for her grief, the bushes named *Cotinus Grace* for her sister, and there were three to include her dad. Bree swallowed hard. "How can I thank you?"

"It was nothing. I was really thinking of myself. Next time I want to come out here and talk to you I'll have someplace to sit beside the cold hard ground."

"Thank you, Ryker." She reached out to touch his arm, but he dismissed her.

"No big deal," and bent to pick up his tools.

"It is to me."

He smiled at that. "I'm glad you like it." He stuffed the empty plastic bags of mulch in his ten-gallon pail, slung his spade over his shoulder, and headed towards the front of the house to where his truck was parked.

Bree stood for a moment longer and took it all in. He really had thought of everything. Maybe deep down he wasn't so tough after all. She gave it one more glance and hurried after him as he disappeared around the front of the house.

"Ryker, wait!" she called after him. He was just placing everything in the back of the pickup when she came up behind him. "Have you had breakfast?"

"No. Why?"

"I was about to make myself an omelet when I saw you. Would you like one?"

"I could eat."

"Come on then."

He followed her into the house and disappeared into the powder room as Bree dug a few more ingredients out of the fridge.

"What do you like in your omelet?" she asked him when he reappeared, slicing up red pepper.

"Whatever you put in yours is fine, I like everything," Ryker said, taking a seat at the island. "Are you going to get new barstools soon? These two have seen better days." He nudged the one beside him and watched it wobble. "I have a screwdriver in the truck. I'll be right back."

Bree cracked three eggs, whipped them, and dumped them into a sizzling hot pan. In mere seconds Ryker was back. He flipped the stool over and tightened all the screws, then proceeded to do the same to the other one.

"To answer your question, after the kitchen is done, I plan on getting new barstools. Something to match the cabinets would be nice. And they need to be comfortable. Those were left in the house." As the eggs cooked, she added chopped ham, red and green peppers, onion, and shredded cheddar cheese. Then folded one side and waited for it to cook. "How long until the cabinets arrive?"

"Three or four weeks. We have the long Memorial Day weekend coming up and sometimes that affects the ship date. Another week though and Sam will have it pinned down for sure so we can schedule the install."

Bree scooped up the omelet and slid it onto a paper plate, placing it in front of Ryker. "Forks are in the island. Top drawer." She could have gotten it for him but truthfully, after yesterday she was afraid to look. She watched him out of the corner of her eye as she cooked her own omelet. The forks were right where she said they were.

"This is great," Ryker declared after savoring the first bite. "Maybe I should make it a regular habit."

"What part? Dropping by unannounced or fixing things?" She slid her omelet onto her plate, grabbed a fork, and set it beside him.

"Both."

She laughed. "Coffee or water?" she pointed to the pot on the counter. And got out a Styrofoam cup for herself, filling it.

"I already had coffee. Water's fine. Thanks."

She ran the tap and filled a cup. She couldn't wait to get some actual dishes. "What other plans do you have for the day?" She placed it in front of him then sat beside him to eat.

"I was going to prime the widow's walk since it's so nice out, that way it's ready for the guys to paint on Monday. Then hopefully take my boat out later this afternoon. What are you up to?"

"Working in the yard, raking and pulling out old shrubs."

He nodded. Finished his last bite. "Good day to do that. That hit the spot. Thanks for breakfast."

"You're welcome. Thank you for my chairs, the beautiful tree, and the plants. The spot is wonderful. I'll always cherish it." Bree got up and went to the sink. She deposited her fork in it and threw away her plate, then started to gather up all the ingredients to put back in the fridge.

Ryker came around the island, did the same as she had, then offered, "Can I help?"

"No, I got it. You go do what you came to do, so you can get out on the boat."

Despite what she said, he picked up the eggs and placed them in the refrigerator. "Do you want to come?"

"On the boat? With you?" she asked, taken by surprise.

"Yes. Would it be that bad?"

"Yes, I mean no . . . it wouldn't. I'm just surprised by the offer." She eyed him, suddenly suspicious. "What's in it for you?"

"A day with a pretty girl." He laughed at the face she made. "You know Bree, most women enjoy my company. I'm a pretty good guy. Ask anyone." He took the leftover peppers out of her hands and placed them in the fridge.

She didn't need to, she had witnessed it first-hand. They had crowded around him at Sam's party. How Sheri and Colette talked about him, even Linda. Every woman seemed to be in love with Ryker. And how couldn't they be? He was tall, with broad shoulders, dark wavy hair, deep blue eyes, and dimples you could drown in. He had naturally dark lashes that women would kill for, and a sturdy rugged face with just a slight five o'clock shadow. He was enough to make her heart stop just by looking at him.

She wasn't about to be sucked in too. She didn't need the extra heartache that would inevitably come with liking someone like him when it wasn't reciprocated.

"Well, how about it?" he asked, watching her.

She debated, despite all that she really wanted to go. A day on the water, in the sun . . . She could bring her camera and get some great photos. It *could* be a lot of fun. Bree looked at Ryker. She'd need to be careful.

Trying not to overthink it, she said, "Actually, I could use a little fun. Do you mind if I bring my camera?"

"Not at all." Ryker pulled his cell out of his back pocket and checked the time. "It's almost nine. Do you want to work until noon? Maybe grab some lunch and head out on the boat? I'll spring for the McDonalds drive-thru again. I'll even let you pick your own meal." He winked at her. "This time."

She laughed despite herself. "Sounds like a plan."

• • • •

THEY CLIMBED INTO THE truck, went through the drive-thru, as promised, then ate their cheeseburgers with the windows down. The sun was bright, the sky blue, and the breeze enticing.

It wasn't long before Ryker turned into a short lane beside a small Craftsman-style house that was sandwiched between two larger homes. It had warm brown siding with cream trim, a porch with tapered columns, and exposed rafter tails in the same cream graced the front. Ryker pulled behind the house and parked the truck.

Getting out, they walked down the short, narrow yard to a small dock where a jet black 25-foot speed boat rocked gently against it.

"Nice boat," Bree said, bending down and running her hand along the pristine black fiberglass of the hull. "The Shadow?" she questioned as she read the finely scripted lettering. "How did you choose the name?"

"It's named after my favorite ship as a kid, Shadow Jumper."

Ryker climbed in and held out his hand for Bree, she stepped in. She tried desperately to ignore the electric shock that raced up her arm and went straight to her heart at the contact.

"Have a seat."

Before Bree could ask any more questions, Ryker started the engine so she sat, stowed her bag, and slipped on her jacket. The air was filled with the smell of brine and fuel as the boat purred like a kitten while Ryker untied the ropes.

The water was smooth as they slowly maneuvered through the little waterway past the other houses. Once out on the Isle of Wight Bay, Ryker opened it up. There were at least a dozen other boats out in the immediate area, just floating. Ryker waved as they sped past.

Bree enjoyed the ride as the boat sliced neatly through the water. They raced past a pontoon that held a family. The little girls stood at the edge and waved happily at Bree as they skirted past. She waved back and smiled.

Ryker kept up the speed for a while, turning long fast arcs in the bay. Suddenly he changed course and headed for the jagged coastline. He passed large houses with small docks jutting out into the water that had boats of all sizes tethered to them. He veered away from the houses towards a heavily wooded island. Ryker followed the coastline around it, cut the motor, and drifted towards it.

"If we stay here a while and it stays fairly quiet, sometimes the wildlife can be seen. This island is actually called the Isle of Wight WMA. Which stands for Wildlife Management Area."

Listening, Bree nodded and bent to get her camera out of her bag. She uncapped the lens and set it on her lap, sitting back to enjoy the view as they drifted.

"There are about 200 acres of forests and marshlands around the Isle of Wight. Assawoman Bay is to the north," Ryker indicated with his hand. "To the south, it connects to the Sinepuxent Bay which is at the west end of Ocean City. Then narrows down to the Thoroughfare Channel. That would take us out to the Atlantic, maybe we can do that another day."

"That would be nice. I would like that." She turned back to the island and spotted a large waterfowl standing at the edge. She raised her camera, adjusted the lens, zoomed in, and captured him. "What kind of duck is that?" she asked, pointing it out to Ryker.

"That's a common loon. You can tell by the white and black checkerboard back."

"He's beautiful. Especially against the blue of the water and the green of the forest."

"This area has a lot of waterfowl. Sometimes you can see herons, swans, and black ducks. Even Canadian and snow geese depending on the time of year."

They drifted further and came across a small fishing boat nestled along the edge of the island, tucked under the overhang of a tree. Two teenage boys turned simultaneously to look at them as they drifted by. With a nod of their heads, the boys acknowledged them and turned back to fishing.

Their backs to her, Bree focused on them with her lens. She liked how the light played on the water and danced over the rocks. The boys wore faded jeans and pale T-shirts and almost blended in with their surroundings, except one had on a red baseball cap and the other had a faded patch of red on his back pocket.

Bree smiled as she thought about how she could enhance those two spots and really bring them out in her photo. Fade the edges and play with the light. She smiled as she captured the moment.

They spent the next few hours in virtual silence as they leisurely drifted around the island. Every once in a while, a boat would go speeding by and the waves would rock them closer to shore. Ryker didn't say much. He was content to let her take pictures at her leisure, answered questions about wildlife or foliage when she asked, but otherwise remained silent and watched her work.

He liked the way she moved. The way she focused on a tiny creature or moment that he didn't see, or wasn't even aware was there until she would point it out.

The sun shone down on her, casting her in a golden light as it started to dip to the west. Her cheeks flushed pink from the sun and her hair slightly mussed from the wind. There was a healthy glow about her that she hadn't had when they had started out earlier.

Ryker had never been one to sit back and let a woman run the show, especially on his own boat, but today, with her, he was completely content to let her.

As many times as he had driven his boat around this island, he had never experienced it like this before. He saw things that he hadn't, noticed details that hadn't mattered before. Even the tiniest thing held a natural beauty that had gone unnoticed until she pointed it out.

He liked the fact that she didn't pretend to be someone she wasn't in his presence. She certainly didn't fall all over him like most women did, or flirt with him relentlessly. She didn't seem to care if he took any notice of her or not, and he liked that about her. Ryker liked a lot of things about her. If only she hadn't bought his house, maybe things would be different.

He munched on a cracker as yet again she focused in on something he didn't see. The camera gave off rapid-fire as the Great Blue Heron lifted off. She followed the heron with her lens as Ryker followed her with his eyes. *Beautiful,* he thought.

She lowered the camera, turned towards Ryker, and beamed. "Did you see that? Wasn't he majestic? So graceful, didn't it just take your breath away?"

Ryker nodded, caught up in her enthusiasm. "Yes, it did." But he wasn't referring to the bird.

"I'm sorry. You must be bored out of your mind."

"Not at all. I love to sit idly in my boat all day instead of racing up and down the bay." He tried hard to put sarcasm in his voice but couldn't quite pull it off. To change the mood. His mood. There was nothing saying she was feeling as lost in the moment as he was.

Then he realized she was in the moment but her moment was in capturing the damn bird, not with him. That pissed him off a little, which helped. "Ready to go? Sun will be setting soon."

She sighed, "Whenever you are."

Without a word he stood, flipped a switch and the boat roared to life. He took off, standing at the wheel. He loved to feel the wind on his skin, the sting of it after a day spent in the sun. He noticed her snuggle down in the seat, pull her jacket on and turn out to watch the water go by. He hated to admit it, but he didn't want the day to end. He didn't want to take her home. But he couldn't think of an excuse to keep her out longer. So, resigned, he headed for her house. Her dock.

The sun was well below the horizon when he pulled up to the dock. It was hard to see. There was no light on it, only a couple of decrepit reflectors that looked like they were about to fall off. Had he not known by heart where it was, he wouldn't have found it so easily in the dark.

"Grab that rope in the back by the stern," Ryker indicated behind Bree. "Reach out and grab the post there." Bree did what she was told. Ryker maneuvered the boat effortlessly so the stern came around. "Wrap it around the post now." She did and Ryker cut the engine, then went to the bow himself and tied the other rope around the post.

He brushed against Bree as he reached around her for his flashlight. Switching it on, he sent the shaft of light up and down the length of the worn dock. "Maybe this wasn't such a good idea. This dock doesn't look safe."

"It can't be that bad, can it?" Bree asked unsure herself.

"It's not good. This thing looks like it could fall apart if you sneezed at it. Maybe I should take you back to my house and drive you home in the truck."

"Don't be ridiculous, that's what? Over a half-hour back by water, right?"

"At least."

"I'm sorry but I can't wait that long. I have to use the bathroom. And it's only like what? Twenty feet of dock that I have to cross?"

He could see the house looming large just up the hill, and the bathroom called to him too. "Okay, get your bag." He stepped out onto the dock. Testing with one foot before he put the full weight of his body on it. Got both feet out. Waited. "Step exactly where I step and hopefully neither one of us will end up taking a swim." He took a step forward then leaned back and held out his hand.

She took it and he was acutely aware of her small warm hand in his. He shoved the thought of her hand in his to the back of his mind and tried to concentrate on where he stepped. The boards groaned under his weight but held. They made steady progress across the little dock, stepping over holes and rotten boards. At last, they were across and safely on dry land.

Bree tugged his hand, "Come on, I can't wait any longer." She took off sprinting towards the house, her hand in his still pulling him along. He got his footing and ran alongside her.

He started towards the back of the house towards the slider since it was the closest door. "That's locked from inside. We will have to go around front."

"Right." They took the steps two at a time, breathing hard while she dug through her bag looking for keys. He held the flashlight over her bag. "Hurry I have to go too."

Bree laughed as she unearthed them and stuck them in the lock. "You take the powder room. I'll go upstairs." They burst through the door and she flipped on lights, taking off in separate directions.

When she came back down the stairs he was waiting. "Guess I'd better head out. They're calling for storms tonight so I want to get the boat back, fastened down, and put the tarp on before it starts."

"Are you going to be okay going back across the dock by yourself?"

"Yeah, I have the flashlight. If I'm careful I shouldn't have any problems."

Bree walked him to the door and flipped on the porch lights. "I'll put the back patio lights on too. Not sure how much they'll help." He walked out and turned back to look at her. She leaned on the door frame and smiled up at him. "Thanks for a wonderful day, Ryker. I really enjoyed myself."

"Me too," and he meant it. He wanted to say something else. Or maybe even do something else, like kiss her but he didn't. Couldn't. He might be making a fool out of himself. And he didn't do that, not when he wasn't sure how she would react. That thought alone had him taking a step down, off the porch. "I'll see you Monday, Champ. Bright and early. Don't let the ghost keep you up all night." With that, he turned and left.

"Hilarious Ryker!" she called after him in a huff and slammed the door.

True to her word though, the back patio lights came on. He made his way down to the water to the dock and picked his way carefully across it, then climbed in the boat and started it, glancing back at the house and her. He could see Bree standing, silhouetted by the kitchen lights. He untied the ropes and pushed off, speeding across the water into the dark night.

Chapter 19

The rain started after midnight, continued all through the night and into the morning. Bree stood at the kitchen slider and looked out at the choppy water, coffee in her hand, sipping. She watched as the rain streaked down the glass. The rain made puddles on her chipped and cracked patio that rippled in the blustery wind. She could barely see her little weeping cherry and the Adirondack chairs from here but the thought of them made her smile.

Turning her back on the rain, she grabbed her camera off the counter. Bree was excited to download the pictures onto her computer. She grabbed a sweatshirt because the house was a little chilly, making her way to the studio, padding softly in her socks.

Bree climbed the stairs, flipped on the lights, and adjusted the thermostat. She set her coffee down and checked her calendar. She had promised Aunt Maureen dates and a list of what she wanted from home. Settling on dates for the movers, she sent off an email to her aunt and attached the list.

Satisfied, she turned her attention to work. She slipped in her memory card from her camera and started the download of her photos.

The day passed quickly as she went through her new photos, deleted the ones she didn't like, and selected the ones she did. She loved the ones of the loon, the boys in the fishing boat, and one of Ryker he wasn't aware that she took.

First, she played with the photo of the loon. Enhanced and cropped it, adjusting the exposure and increasing the brightness. Then found two more of the same bird, and toyed with those. Finished, she placed them in a series.

Next, she worked on the image of the teenage boys fishing in the little boat. Only this time she enhanced the red baseball cap and the red patch on the back pocket, making the color really pop. She faded out the background and played up the dapple of light that hit the water. Satisfied, she clicked save and added it to her website along with the loon.

She stood and stretched, and got a bottle of water out of the mini-fridge Ryker had installed under the counter in her workstation. She had argued with him at the time about it being unnecessary, but right now while she was in the zone, she had to admit it was handy. Chalk another one up for Ryker.

Thinking of Ryker, she couldn't wait to work on the photo of him. Clicking on the tiny icon, she set her water bottle aside and scrutinized the photo. It really didn't need much because his strength and character already shone through, but she couldn't help tweak it a little.

Ryker was standing at the helm. The wheel lightly caressed between his fingers. The sun was setting off to the west, casting him in an ethereal glow. His strong features were accented by shadows.

He stood confident and sure, watching the water in front of him. She enhanced the blue of his jeans and the stripe on his shirt to match the blue of his eyes. The water was a cooler tone; she amplified the light that touched the wave behind him, making the crest a pure white. She cropped and adjusted. Playing with the photo until she felt like she could literally reach out and touch him. She sighed, falling a little for him.

A soft banging broke her concentration. She stopped working and wondered where it was coming from. She glanced at the clock and realized how late it was getting. She'd skipped lunch and now it was almost dinner time. She stretched and decided to make a quick sandwich.

She went through the house turning on the lights. In the kitchen, she noticed the rain had finally tapered off. The temperature had dropped drastically from the day before and the house was cold.

Bree was drawn to the window and looked out at the choppy water. It gave her a melancholy feeling.

The wind rushed by and banging started again. Pulling her attention away from the water she left the kitchen and walked up the stairs to the second floor. Instinctively she looked up as the sound came from overhead. Bree went to the attic door and ascended the stairs.

The air was chilly in the stairwell, the attic was colder yet, but she didn't stop. Tense, she went to the door in the center of the room and turned the knob. A cold blast of air and a loud bang made her jump.

Ryker's voice filled her head with images of ghosts and had her hesitating. Scolding herself for being scared, she forced herself to look. She left the door open behind her, and flipped the switch, illuminating the stairs in the harsh light from a single bulb that stuck out from the wall just above the door. Bree climbed the small, compact spiral stairs as the sound came again. Closer. She emerged into the tiny glass room to find the door on the left swinging in the wind.

Relieved, she grabbed the door and pulled it shut against the icy air. Sliding the latch in place she checked the other side. *Ryker must not have securely shut it yesterday,* she thought.

Letting herself relax, she stood for a few minutes and took in the view. Even in this weather, it was beautiful.

The bay was empty, void of any boats. The water was gray and choppy, looking like a jilted lover, angry and swollen with rage. She could see the lights from Ocean City as the heavy ashen clouds rolled by on a strong gust of wind. She turned a slow circle and stopped when she spotted a massive area of dark green. She wondered if that was the island that she and Ryker had been to yesterday.

A shiver ran through her as the wind rushed past. She tugged down her sweatshirt and crossed her arms, trying to hold in the warmth. Deciding she'd better go eat and finish her work, she started down the stairs. Taking a few steps, Bree noticed that the stairwell was completely dark. Her heart quickened. Had the door blown shut when she pulled the other one closed? She descended in the dark until she came even with the door. Her hand reached out and turned the knob. But it didn't turn. Bree tried again. Nothing. Her heart clenched. *Don't panic,* she scolded herself. She tried twisting it the other way. Nothing.

"It's probably just stuck. The door is old and probably warped," she said out loud, her voice sounded hollow in the stairwell. She turned the knob again and put her hip into it. It wouldn't budge. She kicked at it with her foot and banged on it with her hands. Fear crept into her body as reality set in.

She raced up the curving stairs into the glass and clapboard room. Frantically, she looked around as the feeble light dwindled. She looked out and saw the freshly primed railing of the widow's walk. It was sturdy but it led nowhere. Even if she had on shoes, which she didn't, the roof would be slick from the rain. If she fell and hurt herself there would be no one to help her. The only logical way down was the stairs.

Then she thought of her phone. She searched her pockets frantically, and remembered . . . She'd left it in the kitchen. Trying to keep her head, Bree decided to go down and at least turn on the light. *Hadn't she turned it on when she came in?*

She crept back down the stairs into the black, counting the steps as she went to keep from panicking. When she was at the bottom, she reached out and felt for the knob. She twisted it fruitlessly.

Bree ran her hands along the wall searching for the light switch. Her hand swept through a spider web and she shrieked. Disgusted, she wiped it hastily off on her jeans. Back to the wall, she felt along the rough wood again. Trying to be practical she stopped herself, thought about how high the other switches were in the house, and adjusted her search. Finding it, she had a small spike of joy. She flipped the switch, but nothing happened. She flipped it up and down several times but there was nothing but darkness. Her heart raced. Bree tried to think clearly. *Maybe the bulb came loose when the door blew shut.*

She reached up on tiptoes and found the edge of a ceramic base just above the short door. It was warm to the touch. She cupped her hand, propped herself with the other, and reached for the bulb. The socket was empty.

Bree screamed. Panic seized her. She tried the knob again and pounded on the door. Kicking it. Ramming it with her shoulder and hip, over and over, until she was bruised and battered, and her voice hoarse. There was no one to hear her. The house was empty.

She sunk down in the dark and sobbed.

Chapter 20

They all pulled into the yard, one right after the other. Parked and unloaded. The yard sparkled with a thin layer of frost from the cold front that blew through yesterday. They climbed the steps to the front porch and Sam pushed the doorbell. The chimes faintly rang out inside the house.

They stood waiting on Bree to answer, making small talk.

"Brr . . . it's cold out here!" Steve shivered.

"Got damn cold last night. Down below thirty most the night," Jerry commented. "Unusual for early May."

When Bree didn't answer, Sam pushed the button again.

"Are we early?" Jerry asked, glancing at his watch, shifting from foot to foot trying to keep warm.

"No, we're actually a few minutes late," Sam answered, checking his phone. He pushed the doorbell a third time.

"I'll text her," Ryker said. He typed in a message and then decided to call. He lifted the phone to his ear and heard it go straight to voicemail. He hung up without leaving a message. "She's not answering. Maybe she's in the shower."

"Did she leave the door unlocked?" Steve asked.

Sam tried it and shook his head no. He pushed the doorbell again. When there was no answer, he pulled out his keys. "I'll just use the key. But let's make sure we make our presence known, in case she is in the shower."

"Agreed, but let's not waste any more time and get into the heat."

They entered making as much noise as possible and stopped in the entryway. The house was cold and quiet.

"Shit, she doesn't even have the heat on in here," Steve croaked. "Gonna have to go get a sweatshirt from the truck."

145

"I don't smell coffee either, she always has some going," Ryker said, suddenly concerned. "Bree?" he called, his voice rang out in the empty house.

"Maybe she had an appointment that she forgot to mention," Sam said, trying to be reasonable.

The guys nodded putting their tools down. "We're gonna get the rest of our stuff. We'll be back."

"I'm going to check the garage and see if her SUV is here. Sam, try her cell again."

Ryker went through the kitchen towards the garage, when he heard a phone ring. Both Ryker and Sam walked into the kitchen coming from different directions and saw it lying on the island.

Sam picked it up. "Four missed calls and eight unopened text messages."

Ryker gave him a look and sprinted through the house to the garage. Within seconds he was back. "Her car is here. Something's wrong."

"I agree."

"Let's search the house and then look outside."

Sam nodded. "I'll go check the studio and you take upstairs."

"Bree," Ryker called as he took the stairs two at a time. Her bedroom door was open so he walked in calling her name. The bed was made and the bathroom door stood wide open. He poked his head in anyway and checked the closet. Empty. He yelled for her again and could hear Sam faintly calling her too.

He went into the hall and proceeded to check each of the other rooms calling her name. At the bottom of the stairs to the attic, he thought he heard something. He sprinted up the stairs calling out and followed the sound of pounding.

He went to the door that led to the widow's walk. "Bree?" he questioned.

"Ryker! Thank God! The door's stuck, I can't get out."

Ryker tried the knob. It was locked. He squatted down and took a closer look. It definitely needed a key. "Bree are you okay? How long have you been in there?"

"Since yesterday afternoon. Please get me out."

"Hang on; I need a key or some tools. I'll be right back." Ryker ran down the stairs meeting Sam at the bottom. "I've found her. She's locked in the attic. I need the keys to the house."

"What?" Sam asked as he fished them out of his pocket. "I don't know if that key works for every door. Take them though. This one's hers." He indicated the one with a red tag on it. "I'll grab my toolbox and be right behind you."

Ryker sprinted up the stairs. "Bree?" he called. "I'm back. I have the key. Let's hope this works." The key fit and turned in the lock. Ryker twisted the knob but the door still didn't open. "It wasn't just locked, it's stuck. Here comes Sam with the toolbox."

"Any luck?" he asked.

"The key worked but the door is still stuck."

"Bree, how are you?" Sam asked.

"I've been better. Last night was really cold. My fingers and toes are numb."

"I'm going to take the hinges off and see if we can use a crowbar to pry it open."

"Okay."

Ryker took a hammer and gently tapped the pins on the hinges and popped them both out, the bottom and the top. Sam used the crowbar and wedged it between the door and the frame. There was a crack and the frame splintered, but the door didn't give.

Ryker turned as Jerry and Steve came in.

"What's up?" Jerry asked.

"Bree's been locked behind this door all night," Ryker said under his breath. "Do either of you have another crowbar in your toolbox?"

"I do," Steve said, setting down his toolbox and painting equipment. He handed it to Ryker.

Both men worked their way around the frame inching the wedged door. "It's almost like it's been glued shut," Sam said to Ryker pointing at a glob of dried glue. "Does that look fresh to you?"

"Hard to tell. The lighting isn't the best up here. This damn door isn't coming out in one piece. I wish like hell I had my sledgehammer." He wiped the perspiration from his forehead.

"I don't have a sledgehammer, but I have an ax in the truck," Steve said.

"Go get it." He leaned over and put his hand on the door. "Bree? Steve went to get an ax from the truck. It'll just be a minute longer."

She half-laughed. "What's another minute. I thought this night was never going to end. I can go up and slide down the roof if that would be easier?"

He tried to keep it light, she sounded scared and tired, on the edge of hysteria. "That would be a great option if we had a long enough ladder. Didn't bring one of those with us today though. Just bear with us a few more minutes and then we will have you out. I'd have thought as hard as you punch you might have already broken the door down yourself."

"Believe it or not, I did try."

"That doesn't surprise me. What's the first thing you're going to do when we bust you out of there?"

"I'm going to kiss the first face I see, even if it's you."

"Ouch." Ryker clutched at his heart.

"I call breaking the door down," Jerry chimed in.

"Looks like we have a volunteer to wield the ax now that you're going to pass out kisses," Sam chuckled.

"After you kiss all of us, then what are you going to do?"

"Make a run for the bathroom. And I never said I was going to kiss *all* of you. If Jerry's the one holding the ax, he'll be rewarded."

"Now wait just a minute, Sam and I have been working hard. Jerry's just standing here looking pretty like usual; it's only fair that if he gets kissed, then we do too."

Bree laughed. "I'll think about it."

"Here's Steve with the ax."

Ryker held out his hand for it. "You need to stand back. Move to the top of the stairs. Yell down when you're out of the way."

"Okay, give me a minute my legs are so stiff and cold I can barely move."

"Take your time."

They heard her call from the top of the stairs. Ryker didn't hesitate; he brought the ax down in one wood splintering crack. The door was old but solid. Ryker chopped away, trying desperately to make a hole big enough to get through without tearing up skin. Out of breath, he stopped. Gloves on, Sam pulled a large chunk of wood out and let Ryker step through.

"Bree? We're in. I'm coming up for you." Ryker took the stairs quickly. She sat at the top shivering in the morning light. He was acutely aware of how cold it was. "You're bleeding. Why are you bleeding?" he asked, concerned, reaching for her battered hands.

She looked down. "I wasn't aware that I was." She shrugged, "I told you I tried to knock the door down."

"Looks like you put up one hell of a fight but the door obviously won. Let's get you out of here." He pulled her slowly up.

"How long did you say you've been up here?" he asked, guiding her down the stairs.

"Around four yesterday afternoon. I heard something so I came up to check it out. Turns out one of the doors blew open. You must not have shut it tightly on Saturday."

He was about to argue with her because he was positive he had but decided it wasn't the time.

"Be careful," Sam said as they reached the bottom. "We tried to clean up most of the splinters, but there could still be some, and you're in socks."

"Thanks, guys," Bree said, stepping through the rough opening. "I owe you one."

"You can put it right here," Jerry said tapping his cheek.

Bree laughed and leaned over and gave the older man a quick peck on the cheek. "I'm sorry I can't stay right now and kiss you properly, but I really need to get down to the bathroom."

Jerry's ruddy face turned beet red. "You go on, Miss Bree. Take a hot shower while you're at it. Thaw out those bones. We'll get this cleaned up. Don't you worry."

"Thanks, you're lifesavers. Literally," she smiled at them.

"I'll help you down the stairs," Ryker said, taking her arm. "Why don't you have the heat on?" he asked, as they descended the stairs.

"I do. Maybe it's not working."

"I'll check it. You okay from here?" he asked as they stepped into her bedroom.

"Yes, I'm fine. I owe you one. Lunch is on me, okay?"

"You don't have to do that."

"I know. But I want to. I'm not going to stand here and argue with you because at this point the bathroom is an emergency."

"Yes, go."

"I'm doing lunch and that's final." Bree gave him a definite look and hobbled off, closing the door behind her.

• • • •

BREE STOOD IN THE SHOWER longer than necessary, letting the hot water run down her aching body. She had tried not to overthink her situation when she sat in the cold and dark, completely alone. The isolation had started to overwhelm her and the mere thought that no one would find her terrified her. The only glimmer of hope she had was that the guys were coming bright and early. That's what had kept her sane, the idea that Ryker would find her in the morning.

Her mind played tricks on her in the dark. She was positive she had turned on the light in the stairwell, but the socket was empty, she shuddered at the fact that she couldn't have. Was she losing her mind? Hadn't she put a lightbulb in there earlier in the week when she knew the guys would be working up on the roof? She'd have to check the package of lightbulbs she'd bought. She had bought light bulbs, hadn't she? Suddenly she wasn't sure.

Sitting in the dark, she was in tune with every creak and groan of the house. The house had been locked up tight all day. And yet she could have sworn she had heard footsteps. She would stake her life on it.

Bree shut the water off and stepped out. She could hear music playing and was comforted by the voices overhead. Drying off she rubbed lotion over her entire body, taking extra care of her bruised and scuffed hands.

She got dressed and reached into the bottom drawer for her hairbrush. She froze when she saw her blow dryer and the same piece of photo as yesterday. Her hand shook as she reached for it. She was sure she had thrown it away. *Or had she?* No, she was certain she had. *But then how did it get back in the drawer?* Thoughts swirled around her mind.

She trembled slightly as she plugged in the hairdryer. She was losing it. Again. She felt like she was in a fog like right after her family had died. Days blurred together; nights crept by in loneliness. Things disappeared, reappearing days later where she didn't remember putting them. She had slept for hours on end drifting from one day to the next. Finally, Aunt Maureen took control.

Why was it happening now? She was happy here. Was it too much stress from the move, buying the house, and now the remodeling? Or was there really a ghost, like Ryker joked about? Was something or someone in the house?

She pulled her hair back into a long ponytail examining her pale face in the mirror. Picking up the scrap of photo, she took it out to the bedroom, deliberately making it a point to place it on the windowsill, in plain sight.

She took a deep breath, sucking in courage. There were people in the house; she'd have to at least act like she was okay.

Descending the stairs, Bree went straight to the laundry room, opened the cabinet, and pulled out the brand-new package of light bulbs. Relieved that they were there. She noticed one was missing, the one she had used for the stairwell.

But how. . . She couldn't even complete the thought. She heard someone come in from outside. Putting the package back, she closed the door. She'd think about it later.

Ryker put his tools down when he noticed Bree coming into the kitchen. "How ya feelin', Champ?"

She looked tired and her knuckles were covered in bruises. He crossed the kitchen and reached for her hands. "Let me see these." He held them in his and examined her bruised knuckles. "Just how long did you bang on that door?"

She pulled her hands free from his. "I don't know. I lost track of time."

He watched her, taking her completely in. The quiet beauty, the silky golden-brown hair, and the shimmering blue eyes. He hadn't wanted to, but somewhere, somehow, she had gotten under his skin, slid her way into his heart. "After a couple of hits, you had to have known you couldn't budge it. But by the look of those hands, it seems you kept trying. Why?"

"Because I thought I heard . . ." she clamped her teeth together to stop herself. She hadn't planned on saying anything. "It doesn't matter."

He raised a dark eyebrow. "Heard what?"

Bree turned and went to the fridge. "Nothing." She dug out turkey, ham, and provolone from the fridge, mayo, lettuce, and tomatoes too. "It doesn't matter, it was just my imagination." She turned her back on him, grabbed the rolls, a serrated knife, and set to work.

Ryker came up behind her. Reached for her arm and turned her around to face him. "What did you hear?" he asked her patiently. "Tell me."

"Why? So you can make fun of me?"

"Bree, I wouldn't . . ." his voice trailed off as he registered the look of disbelief on her face. He chuckled, "Okay, so I might tease you a little, but I really do want to help. Tell me. What did you hear?"

She let out a breath. "Footsteps. I thought I heard footsteps, okay? I thought someone was in the house."

She looked scared, and he didn't like it. "Like a person?" He tried to lighten the mood. "Or a ghost?"

She glared at him.

"Okay, sorry," he held up his hands in surrender. "That wasn't funny. I apologize."

Sam entered through the slider and spotted them. "What's going on?" he asked, looking from one to the other.

"Bree thought she heard someone in the house last night while she was locked in the attic."

"I said I heard what sounded like footsteps," she corrected.

Sam tilted his head, thinking. "The house was locked this morning when we got here. I had to use the key to get in. Is it possible you just thought you heard footsteps?"

Bree shrugged, put the knife down, and stepped away from Ryker. "Yes. It was really rainy and cold yesterday. The house was creaking, shifting in the wind, so it might have been my imagination." *Or it might not have been.* The alternative made her shiver inwardly. Bree reached over and grabbed the plate of rolls, then set them on the island with the other fixings to make her subs. She tried to keep her voice neutral, as she selected a roll and started to spread mayo.

"How many keys do you guys have?"

"I have one, and Ryker has one," Sam answered. He dug his out of his front pocket. He held it up. "That's how we got in this morning."

"Mine's in the truck, in the glove box. I haven't used it since the first day you moved in. I always let Sam carry the keys to the projects. No one else working for us would have keys."

Bree nodded. "It was probably just my imagination. Add that to my circumstances, the dark, and the wind . . ." her voice trailed off as she layered turkey and provolone.

"That's completely understandable," Sam said. "Just so you know, I put in an order for a new door for the staircase to the widow's walk. We can pick it up in the morning, and install it tomorrow. The whole door and frame are trashed. Jerry and Steve are going to finish ripping it out, and will bring down the pieces."

Bree continued to fix the sandwiches as Sam updated her on the progress of the house. She was acutely aware of Ryker's watching her every move. *Did he think she was imagining it? Did he think she was crazy?* The thought nagged at her. She was putting the finishing touches on the last sub when the doorbell rang, saving her from her own thoughts, and Ryker's scrutinization.

Bree hurried to the door and opened it, surprised to find Greg. "Good morning, Bree," he said cheerfully.

"Hello, Greg. What a pleasant surprise." Bree opened the door wide. "Come in." He stepped in, carrying a basket full of goodies. "Go on back to the kitchen. Ryker and Sam are in there. I was just making lunch."

Greg set the basket down on the island and shook Sam's hand then Ryker's. "Hello, nice to see you both. Are you taking a break?"

"Yeah, just knocking off for lunch and getting Bree up to date on our progress."

"Well, I don't want to interrupt, but . . ." Greg swung his attention around to Bree. "I wanted to bring over this house warming gift from Coastal Realty."

"Oh, that's so sweet. Thank you, Greg."

"No problem. It was supposed to be here when you moved in but it all happened so fast." He shrugged. "You can look through it when you have time. By the way, the front porch looks great. And I see you've gotten the flower beds cleaned out around the house. Things are really starting to shape up."

"Yes, they've replaced all the windows and my studio is done."

Greg nodded his head, laid his hand on Bree's arm. "Saw the guys on the roof. What's happening up there?"

"They're painting the rails to the widow's walk. Ryker and I are working on the patio," Sam answered.

Greg let out a little whistle. "That patio is a big job. Better you than me. I need to run, have an appointment to get to. Bree, walk me out?" He didn't wait for her to answer, just guided her to the door, whistling softly.

He led her out of the house, down the steps, and to his car. He glanced around the yard and saw that they were alone. Clearing his throat he said, "I've debated whether I should tell you this or not, but I have come to think of you as a friend, so I feel I should."

"Okay," Bree said carefully. "What is it?"

Greg ran his hand through his brown hair. "You know how you asked me about the possibility of a ghost in your house?"

She nodded.

"There's no real easy way. . . I'm just going to say it . . . Ryker James made that up. There's no such story or any facts to prove it."

Bree narrowed her eyes and asked, "Are you sure?"

Greg nodded. "Apparently Ryker has been spreading that little rumor around for years."

"But why? Why would he do that?" Bree asked, clearly shocked.

"Because he wanted this house," Greg pointed. "He's wanted to buy it for years."

"Then why hasn't he?"

"Because the Hennings wouldn't sell to him. He's tried. So, to keep prospective buyers away he started the rumor." To drive home his point he asked, "Isn't he the one that mentioned the ghost to you?"

"Yes, he is. But that doesn't make sense. Why would he have to do that? Why wouldn't they sell to him? A sale is a sale, isn't it? Didn't he have enough money?"

"Oh, he has the money, even offered a really good price. They turned him down flat."

"Why? And how do you know all this?"

"I asked Sheri. She knows all the gossip." He shifted from one foot to the other, uncomfortable with what he was about to say. "When Ryker was in high school, he dated Henning's only daughter. I don't know all the details, but it didn't end well, they have never forgotten it, and refuse to sell their house to Ryker. Evidently, all the real estate agents in the area know Ryker and that he wants this house. Ryker's well-liked and his company has done business with virtually everyone. The other realtors all had an agreement with Linda that if they had clients with any interest in the Henning place they would contact Coastal Realty first, so Ryker could make a counteroffer, hopefully, to give him a fighting chance."

Bree contemplated this for a moment. "Then how did I end up with it so easily?"

"Sheer dumb luck." He brushed at a speck of dust on his black pants. "Basically, because I'm new and I didn't know. If you remember correctly, I wasn't even supposed to take you out. Tina was. She had all the listings that I showed you, already approved by Linda. But I pulled this one right before we went out, not knowing. It's no wonder the Hennings jumped at the offer. Seems they would have taken anything to make sure Ryker James didn't get it."

If that was true, it explained why Ryker was so gruff a lot of the time. It also explained why he kept mentioning the ghost. The thought that he was deliberately trying to scare her crept into her mind. *Why?* She answered her own question. In hopes that she would sell. *Of course.* He couldn't buy it from the Hennings but he could easily buy it from her. "Thanks for telling me."

"Can we keep this conversation between us? I don't want to get Sheri in any trouble or myself. I like this job. And I don't think Sheri would like Ryker to find out she told me. Apparently, they have a little thing."

Bree nodded. "Of course."

Greg got in the car and rolled down the window after he started it. "I'll give you a call, we'll get to that movie soon."

She waved as he pulled out and went back into the house.

Bree wasn't quite sure how to act around Ryker, now knowing what she did. Was he in the house yesterday? Did he purposefully leave the widow's walk door open on Saturday? She didn't want to believe it was him, just because he started the rumor didn't make him the kind of person that would go around sneaking into people's homes. She had no real proof that anyone had even been in the house. It was old. Doors warped and stuck all the time when the weather changed. But it hadn't just been stuck, it had been locked too. And Ryker had a key.

Bree went into the kitchen and finished making the sandwiches while Sam and Ryker talked. It was only a matter of minutes before Steve and Jerry came down carrying pieces of the door. They took a load out to the dumpster and came back as Bree finished the sandwiches.

"Sorry guys, I only have the two barstools," Bree said looking at the four men. She dug out sodas from the fridge, and chips from the pantry. "If you'd rather have water, I can get out cups."

"No, this is great, Miss Bree," said Jerry. "I need a little pick me up. I'm gonna have a soda."

"You didn't have to go to so much trouble," Steve said, taking a sub.

"No trouble at all. It's the least I could do for my rescuers," she said smiling as she set out a bowl of fruit.

"You might want to put a light bulb in those stairs, it gets pretty dark when you're coming down and you've been outside. Hard on my old eyes to adjust from the sun."

"Yeah," Ryker chimed in. "I thought you had one in there on Saturday when I worked up there."

"I thought so too," Bree commented. She looked at him, suspiciously.

"We have the widow's walk's first coat on and the door frame ripped out. The supply company called my phone by mistake," Jerry said, directing his comment to Sam. "They have that door you wanted, found one back in the warehouse. We could run in, get it, and put it on this afternoon."

Sam nodded between mouthfuls. "That would be great. These sandwiches are great, Bree. Thanks for doing this."

"You're welcome."

It didn't take long for the guys to finish eating while she tidied up the kitchen and put away the sandwich fixings.

The guys walked out while Bree wiped down the counters. Ryker hung back.

"Hey, I checked your heat. There's nothing wrong with it. It was just switched off."

Bree stopped wiping the counter in mid-swipe and looked at him, suddenly furious. "I wonder if your ghost did that. You're unbelievable." Bree threw her dishrag in the sink. "By the way, I want your key on my counter by the end of the day. Bolts & Beams only needs one, and I'd feel better knowing Sam was the one with it." Bree didn't wait for him to reply, she just walked out.

Chapter 21

The guys were gone. The house was quiet. Bree got up and stretched. She peered out the window and noticed the late afternoon sun was dropping lower. She wanted to go outside, but she had yet to check her website or write her blog for the week.

She glanced at her computer then back at the window and knew she wasn't about to get any more work done if she didn't go out for a little while. Grabbing her camera and a light hoodie, she went down the stairs and out the back door of the garage.

The light was at the perfect angle for taking pictures. It slanted across the yard playing with the different levels of the landscape. She noticed as she walked down to the bay that the spiky textures of the grass seemed even more heightened, the rocky sand near the wooden dock more pronounced, and the water sparkled just a little brighter in the long rays of the sun.

Bree snapped a couple of pictures of the rickety dock in the enchanting light, the shadows made an interesting contrast against the wood. But after a couple of shots, Bree lost interest.

Feeling a little melancholy, she walked back to her favorite spot. The one Ryker had made extra special. She touched the delicate green leaves of the weeping cherry with her fingertips, then ran her hand over the warm wood of one of the Adirondack chairs, sinking into it. She tried to shake the feeling that the spot was a little tainted, now that she knew he had made up the ghost.

Angry with him, she tried not to let that affect the beauty of the spot or the sincere gesture he had made. Reasoning that he had made the story long before her. *And* he had made this spot after he had found out about her family. That had to count for something.

Her phone chimed. Bree looked down and saw a text from Sam.

Sam: FYI Locked up when we left. Our keys are on the island. We will be back 7:30

Bree: Thanks. See you then.

Sam: Have a good night.

Bree felt guilty for having them leave their keys, but she needed to eliminate any possibility that it was either one of them. Part of her was nervous now though, realizing no one she knew had a key. Had they not had one this morning, who knows how long she would have been stuck in the stairwell.

That reminded her, she made a mental list of a couple of things she wanted to get from the hardware store. An escape ladder was one of them. She'd make sure if she got caught up on the widow's walk again, she'd have an alternate way down.

Trying to relax by soaking in the soothing sounds of the water, she snuggled down into the chair, wishing she'd grabbed a blanket. Lights blinked on across the bay. She could see neon signs, streetlights, and headlights became more prominent as the sky darkened behind her. On the bay, small fishing boats and pontoons trawled the waters, slowly headed in for the night.

Time slowly ebbed by like the steady rhythm of the waves methodically lapping the rocky shore. As she relaxed, the toll of a sleepless night took over. Bree closed her eyes, giving in to the enticing pull of sleep.

She dozed off and slept heavily.

When she awoke the sun was gone, completely snuffed out behind the horizon.

Bree stood, groggy and disoriented for a moment. She adjusted her hoodie, trying to ward off the chill of the night air. Remembering she hadn't written her blog, Bree decided to head in. Turning to go, she hesitated, hearing a soft whistle drift on the wind. A shiver raced over her. She glanced around feeling like she was being watched but saw no one in the spongy darkness, even the boats were off the water now. The bay was empty, void of any lights.

Her heart quickened.

She stood stock-still and listened intently, straining her ears but there was nothing except the lap of the waves. She grabbed her camera and sprinted to the house.

Bree couldn't help it, she ran up the slight incline to the patio. She reached for the slider, but it was locked.

Then she remembered Sam's text. She'd have to go in the way she came out. *Don't panic, there's no one here. The house is locked like it's supposed to be.*

Taking a deep breath, she tried to slow down her racing heart. She rounded the house, stumbling over the flagstone pavers that were stacked on the patio. She breathed a sigh of relief as she reached the back door of the garage. She turned the knob and found it locked.

She let out a little squeak. *How?* The guys had left before she came out this door, and she had left it unlocked. Hadn't she? Bree frantically tried the knob again, she even put her hip into it, trying to force the door open. But she couldn't. It didn't budge.

Images of last night bounced around her mind and panic snaked its way in.

Bree raced around to the front and tried the other doors, the breezeway, and the front door, only to find them locked just like Sam had said. Despair overtook her. What was she to do? Who could she call? No one had keys... But Ryker and Sam had tools.

She couldn't call Ryker. He would think she was crazy. She'd seen the way he had looked at her this morning with the locked door, the lightbulb, and the furnace. No, she wouldn't call him. She'd call Sam. Yes, Sam. He'd come, she was sure of it. She could make a joke out of it. Ask him to come over and pick the lock. Then she'd give him a key back. And they'd have a good laugh. Yes, that's what she'd do.

Thank God she had her cell phone this time. The wind shifted, stirring a stash of old dry leaves across the front porch. Bree turned and slunk down in the corner. Her back to the wall, with her eyes on the vast dark yard, she made the call.

• • • •

RELIEF WASHED OVER her as Sam's headlights cut through the night. She cringed at the thought that he had been at Ryker's, but after sitting in the eerie darkness all alone, she didn't care anymore.

Bree stood at the top of the steps as the truck came to a halt in front of the porch. She took a deep breath to soothe her nerves and tried to appear calm. Both doors swung open.

Crap, Ryker came too. She should have known he would. Bree brushed at her clothes trying to look presentable, not like a woman who'd been cowering in the corner for the last thirty minutes.

"First, you're locked in, and now you're locked out. Way to go, Champ," Ryker said.

He gave her a smile that could melt a weaker woman's heart. She wouldn't fall for his charm. Instead, she turned her attention to Sam.

Sam spared Ryker a glance as he grabbed his toolbox out of the backseat. "Any idea how this happened?" He set his tools down and fished out a flashlight, handing it to Ryker. "Hold that, will ya?"

She shrugged. "Well, after everyone left, I decided to go outside and take some pictures. I went out the back door because I was in the studio."

"Naturally," Sam said. "I'm going to try the old credit card trick first. If that doesn't work . . . well, we'll just see where we're at."

Bree nodded.

"Then what happened?" Ryker prompted as Sam took out his wallet.

"I took some photos, went and sat in my Adirondack chair, and fell asleep. When I woke up the sun was down. I went around to the garage, the door I came out of, and found it was locked. Only, I don't remember turning the lock. I went around the house, but as you can guess, all the doors were locked. So, I called you, and here we are."

"Got it," Sam said victoriously as the spring lock unhooked. He turned the handle but the deadbolt held. "Huh?"

"What?" Bree asked.

"Did you flip the deadbolt? Because I know I didn't."

"No, I told you I didn't go through the house. I went out the garage door."

Sam set back on his haunches. "I don't have any tools to unlock a deadbolt. Which doors don't have them?"

"The garage door and the slider."

Sam nodded. "Let's head around back then."

A few minutes later Sam used his credit card on the garage door and they were in. He flipped on the lights and looked around.

Ryker grabbed the door and examined the handle. The lock was a push-button that should have popped when turned if it had been locked when Bree went out, not a turn button that will let you out and remain locked. So, either she pushed it without thinking or someone else did.

"I think we should have a look around, just to be safe," he said, making eye contact with Sam.

"My thoughts exactly."

Ryker pushed past her. "I'll lead."

They checked the studio, then went through the garage, to the breezeway, and into the kitchen. The keys were on the counter in the kitchen where they had left them. Nothing seemed out of place.

Sam poked his head into the laundry room while Ryker walked down the hall. Bree scooped up the keys, determined to give them back.

Ryker was flipping on lights as he went, and let out a long, low whistle as he entered the living room. "I think you guys had better come look at this."

"What's the matter?" Bree asked, coming up behind him, and gasped as she saw it for herself. Her new sheers were shredded and hung in tatters. Chunks of material were strewn about. Her first thought was blood as she saw the red smeared on the walls and the floor, but quickly realized it was paint as fumes hung heavily in the air. Her body trembled as her eyes landed in the middle of the room. A steak knife was stuck in the hardwood. The blade gleamed in the pale light next to crude, jagged words carved into the floor.

You ToOk WhaT wAs MiNe

Fear coursed through her. She had seen that before. Kage.

Bree stepped forward, and then Ryker grabbed her arm. "Don't go any further. We need to call the cops."

"I'm on it," Sam said, punching in 9-1-1 and stepping into the hall.

"I don't understand," Bree whispered, barely audible. She could hear Sam in the next room talking to the dispatcher, giving her name and address. "What could I have possibly taken?"

"I'm not sure," Ryker said looking at the mess, reaching out for her.

The sound of his voice and the touch of his hand both comforted her and disturbed her. Something clicked in her brain. *The house.* She took a small step away from him not able to trust him. She tried to think through it quickly. *He had been with Sam. Both had left their keys. Had they left at the same time?*

Sam came up beside Bree. "The police will be here in a few minutes. Come out of there."

Ryker guided her by the arm. "Let's go to the kitchen."

"Yes," Bree agreed, gently shaking off his hand. "I should put on some coffee."

But once in the kitchen she just sat. Both Ryker and Sam stood watching her, not sure what to do.

Without looking at them she asked, "What time did you guys leave today?"

"Right around five," Sam replied.

Bree nodded and turned to face them. "Did you all leave together?"

"No, Jerry and Steve left before us. We worked about a half-hour longer and then knocked off. We drug some of our tools in," Sam pointed at the pile by the slider.

Red and blue lights cut through the room from outside. "Looks like the cops are here. I'll let them in," Ryker said. walking down the hall. He opened the front door to reveal an officer. "Hey, Kilpatrick," Ryker said, recognizing him.

"Ryker James." The police officer stuck out his hand to Ryker. "I wasn't expecting to see you here tonight."

"Wasn't expecting to be here."

"Are you the owner of this house?"

"No, I am," Bree said, coming up behind Ryker with Sam following, she wasn't about to let Ryker take charge. "I'm Bree Thompson. Please come in."

"What seems to be the problem?"

"Please have a look for yourself." Bree stepped back and indicated for him to look in the living room.

Kilpatrick stepped into the room and looked around. "Were you in the house when this happened?"

"No, I was outside. I was locked out."

"Has the house been searched?" Kilpatrick directed his question to Ryker.

"Not completely."

"I'm going to ask you to step outside. If you could please wait in the truck with the doors locked until we tell you to come out, I would appreciate it."

• • • •

AN HOUR LATER A MAN in khakis and a white button-down shirt led them back into the house. He was short, stocky, and had skin the color of warm caramel. Intelligent, dark brown eyes shone out from a friendly face that was lined slightly around the eyes and mouth. He extended his hand to Bree.

"Ma'am. I'm Detective Savard. Officer Kilpatrick called me. I understand you've had some trouble tonight. Can you tell me about it?"

"Of course. Let's go into the kitchen." Bree averted her eyes as she walked past the living room. She needed something to do with her hands to keep herself steady. "Would you like some coffee, Detective?"

"Yes, please."

Bree got out the coffee, put a paper liner in the basket, and scooped out two heaping measuring cups full of fresh grounds. She filled the pot with water and poured it into the cavity. Only when the dark liquid started to drip out, did she turn back to the detective and start her explanation.

Bree ran through it quickly for him.

"How long do you think you were outside until you came back up to the house?" Savard asked, taking notes.

"I went out before six and woke up in the dark after nine."

"Tomorrow I'd like you to show me how far you were from the house; I'm not going to drag you down there tonight." He glanced down at his notepad. "You tried all the doors and found them all locked?"

"Yes, that's when I called Sam." Bree pointed in his direction.

Savard turned his attention to Sam. "You have a key?"

"We," Sam motioned between him and Ryker, "Had keys up until this afternoon."

"Why were you given a key?"

"We own Bolts & Beams. We're doing the renovations on the house. We've had the keys since Bree moved in, until today."

"I've seen your black trucks around. Hear good things about your work." He glanced down at his notepad and made another note. "What changed today?"

"Because of what happened last night," Bree answered.

He lifted a dark bushy eyebrow. "Walk me through it," Savard said.

Again, in a calm steady voice, Bree started with working in her office, hearing the banging, following it through the house. Then getting locked in the stairwell, sitting all night in the cold and dark, up to the guys rescuing her this morning. She finished with, "While I was sitting there in the dark, I swear I could hear footsteps in the house. I asked the guys to leave their keys today."

"You've lived here for about a month? Is that correct?"

Bree turned to the full coffee pot and poured four cups of coffee, placing them on the island. "I've been in the area almost six weeks. I arrived in Ocean City on the first of April. Settled on the house a few weeks later." Bree got out the cream and sugar. "Please help yourself," she said, indicating the cups of hot coffee.

"Thank you," Savard said, picking up a cup. "Where did you move from?"

"Kansas."

"Mind my asking why you moved?"

Bree looked at Savard, into his kind brown eyes. She sighed, "My family was killed in a car accident almost a year ago. I wasn't handling it well." She shrugged, looked down and into her cup, staring blankly at the dark liquid, then back at him and attempted a weak smile.

Detective Savard looked at her with compassion, not pity like a lot of people did.

"I'm sorry to hear that." He shifted gears quickly, steering the conversation back to matters at hand. "Is there anyone you can think of that might want to cause you harm? An old boyfriend? Anyone you dated or are dating there, here, or now?"

Bree shook her head, all too aware that Ryker shifted in the corner and his dark blue eyes watched her.

"My ex-boyfriend's name is Chad Warner. There's nothing to worry about there. It was a mutual break up."

"What about something that has come into your possession lately? Any jewelry? Real estate? Or money? Anything like that, that someone could possibly think you took from them?"

The only thing Bree could think of was the house, *this house*, and she wasn't about to say that in front of Ryker. She'd have to tell the detective in private. "I can't right now."

"I'm going to want a list of anyone you've had contact with since you moved here. Also, a list of old boyfriends, friends, coworkers, or relatives you've had a falling out with."

Bree nodded.

"We've gone over the crime scene. We have what we need, so you can clean up when you're ready." He lifted the bagged steak knife. "This looks familiar?"

"Yes," Bree said. "It looks like mine. I only have two. I didn't bring a lot of silverware with me. Most of my kitchen equipment is still back in Kansas."

"Let's take a look."

Sure enough, there was only one, and the bagged item matched perfectly.

Savard switched gears, and looked at Ryker and Sam. "I want phone numbers from both of you, names and numbers of your employees, and any other subcontractors you may be using."

"We'll get that together for you." Sam pulled out his wallet. "I can give you our business card now. Both our numbers are on it." He handed him a card.

"Thank you." Directing his attention to Bree, he said, "I'll be out tomorrow around ten." He slipped a card of his own into her hand. "Please don't hesitate to give me a call if you think of anything before."

"Thank you, Detective."

"I'll see myself out."

They heard the door close and stood in silence for a few minutes. Bree was emotionally and physically drained. She glanced at her phone. It was after one. "I'm sure you guys are exhausted and ready to go. I want to thank you for rescuing me, yet again."

Sam smiled at her, came across the room, and gave her a hug. "Anytime. You know we're always here for you." She hugged him back. He leaned out and put her at arm's length. "I'm so sorry this is happening to you."

"Thanks. Me too."

"Do you want us to go in and help you clean that up?"

"No, I'm tired, and I just can't face it anymore tonight. I'm sure you guys are too. It can wait until the morning. You guys go."

"Are you sure you'll be okay by yourself?"

"It's only a few hours, then you'll be back." She laughed. "How much trouble could I possibly get into in six hours? On second thought, don't answer that." She slipped her hand into her pocket and produced a key. "I'd feel better if you had this back." She handed it to him. "Just in case."

"You're sure?"

She nodded and Sam slipped it in his pocket.

Ryker watched the exchange and felt a twinge of jealousy. How easy it was for Sam to enfold her in a hug. *Why couldn't he do that?* He wanted to. Felt the need to all the way down to his toes. And that's why he didn't.

Sam gave Bree one more hug and turned to go. "Ready?"

He unfolded himself from the wall where he'd propped himself for the last hour. "I'll be staying here."

Bree stopped short. "What?"

"You heard me. I'm staying. I'm not leaving you alone in this house with some lunatic out there."

"That's completely unnecessary. Besides, I don't have anywhere for you to sleep. There's no beds or a couch if you haven't noticed."

"Then go pack a bag and come to my house. You can have my bed; I'll sleep on the couch."

Sam quickly jumped on board. "That's a great idea. I don't like the idea of you being here alone."

"You've got to be kidding?" Bree said suddenly furious. "This is my house. I won't let some sicko drive me out. That's just what he or she wants. They want me to be afraid."

"Simmer down, Champ. We know you're perfectly capable and not afraid to be alone. But humor us, please? Just tonight, until we are able to either change the locks or get some other safety measure in place. Hell, you don't even have a dog out here to alert you to someone driving in."

"He's right. You are isolated here. And somebody, other than us, might possibly have a key, and without any other way to secure the house, you need to be careful."

"If you don't want to stay at my place, call Colette. I'm sure she'd put you up."

"Are you crazy? I'm not about to call Colette this late."

"Then march upstairs and throw some things in a bag and let's get a move on. I'm tired. And stubborn, I won't take no for an answer."

Bree looked at Ryker in disbelief.

"You might as well, he won't budge, and then none of us will get any sleep," Sam said.

She looked from one man to the other. Ryker stood between her and the door with his arms crossed and a devilish, cockeyed grin. The five o'clock shadow on his face was more prominent than normal, making him seem dark, dangerous. . . and sexy. Sam stood to the side looking apologetic yet firm.

"Are you going to grab some stuff, or am I going to haul your ass out of here over my shoulder?"

She narrowed her eyes at him, "You wouldn't dare."

"Try me."

They stared each other down as her blue eyes shot daggers in him, but he didn't relent. Suddenly, he took a step towards her, she let out a little shriek.

"I'm going! Keep your hands off me," Bree said haughtily as she pushed past him.

"You got five minutes to get packed and back down here, or I'm coming up for you," Ryker called after her, watching her stomp off. He turned back and saw Sam shaking his head. Ryker grinned at his friend. "She's comin' ain't she?"

• • • •

BREE STOOD STARING at the red taillights disappearing in the darkness, wishing she was still in the truck.

"You comin'?" Ryker asked, grabbing her bag and heading into the house. "Or are you gonna stand there all night?"

Bree let out a deep sigh. "Do I have a choice?"

"Not if you want some sleep." Ryker held the door open for her as she walked past. "Not sure what your problem is, you're getting a comfy bed for a change. That air mattress of yours can't be too comfortable. Follow me." He led the way through the house and up the stairs.

"It's actually not that bad. But I did order a mattress online the other day. Should be arriving by the end of the week."

"If you need help breaking it in, let me know," he said, glancing over his shoulder at her. He had the instant satisfaction of seeing her turn red.

Ryker walked into the first room. "This is mine. You can have the bed. I'll sleep on the couch." He placed her bag on the dresser. "Lucky for you I changed the sheets this morning. The bed is freshly made."

The room was spacious and sparsely decorated like the downstairs and smelled faintly of him. His furniture was gorgeous. It was a deep, rich walnut with organic lines and a distressed textured stain. The large king-sized bed with headboard and dresser stood proud and masculine against the plain white walls, just like the man.

The room was clean and tidy except for the two baskets full of folded laundry, and a stack of dog-eared books scattered on the nightstand.

"Do you actually read?" Bree asked, picking up the top book. "Or are these just here to impress women?"

"Any woman that makes it to my bed isn't up here to be impressed by what I read. They're here for . . ."

Bree raised her hand and cut him off. "That's quite all right. I get the picture."

Grinning, Ryker cleared his throat. "Right then, the bathroom's through there. There are towels and washcloths beneath the sink. Use whatever you need." He went into the bathroom and flicked on the light. "Let me grab my toothbrush and paste, and I'll be out of your way."

She sat down on the edge of the bed completely exhausted and waited for him to gather what he needed. As he turned to go, she said, "Thanks Ryker for coming over and helping me tonight, you certainly didn't have to. And . . . thanks for letting me stay here."

Ryker could see she was tired, even a little forlorn. But there was something else there too, a vulnerability he hadn't seen before. He didn't like to see her like that; it made his heart ache for her.

He grinned a mischievous smile that creased his whole face. "If you're really appreciative you'll let me sleep in my own bed . . . with you," he added, "And not on the couch."

She straightened then, a little spark racing through her. "Not on your life."

He crossed the room in three long strides, bent down to her level. Placed an arm on either side of her. Her breath caught as he reached around her, brushing against her body. "Then you can't have my favorite pillow."

His face hovered inches from hers. Her pulse spiked.

"Goodnight Bree. Try not to dream about me." His breath whispered on her lips, and he had the satisfaction of seeing her cheeks flush. *Much better,* he thought, *keep her rattled then she won't look so sad.* As quickly as he had reached her, he pulled back, and he retraced his steps. "If you need me," he cocked his eyebrow suggestively. "For anything . . . I'm right downstairs."

"Believe me, I won't."

He clutched at his heart. "Wounded, I am." Then he shut the door laughing.

Bree flopped back on the bed and tried to calm her racing heart.

• • • •

HE LAY IN THE DARK, staring at the ceiling, and thought of her. He thought of how she had awakened in the waning light, slightly off balance. Disoriented from having slept too long in a chair. Hustling up to the house. Finding the first door locked, then the next. Wondering if she had punched the lock herself. He snickered picturing it.

But the night before had been better. Standing within inches of her, only the door separating them. Hearing her jiggle the knob. Then flip the switch off and on to the one lone lightbulb. Wondering why it wouldn't turn on. Then realizing it was gone. Her breath had hitched. Then the pounding began, and the screaming. Screaming until she was hoarse. She had beat on the old wooden door until her knuckles were bruised. He had stood there well over an hour until she finally gave up, hearing her sink down into a puddle behind the locked door, and begin to sob. He pictured her in a heap, wrapping her arms around her legs trying to stay warm as the air around her cooled and turned frigid. And the night, completely black. He smiled wickedly at the memory.

Then he remembered the living room. His little housewarming gift that she found tonight. What had she thought? Did it frighten her? Did it make her angry? He hoped it pissed her off that someone had done that to her beloved house. Her home. Taken something she considered shiny and new, then defiled it. The way she had with his life.

What had she thought of the knife stuck in the hardwood floor? Had it made her shiver, thinking of the possibility of it sliding across her throat? Or maybe plunging into her heart? Did the red paint make her think of blood? Her blood that could be easily spilled?

Or had she shrunk back and wondered what she had done? What she had taken? Did she even have a clue as to how she had ruined his life?

She played sweet and innocent. The kind of person everyone wanted to do everything for and give everything to. But not him. He saw through her. He knew exactly what she was. A conniving, greedy bitch. She was a manipulator, plain and simple.

He knew what she was capable of. Had seen first-hand what she was, knew what she had taken. And that was everything. She had. Taken. Everything. Everything that was his. Everything that had mattered. But no longer. He couldn't . . . no change that, wouldn't allow it to go on any longer. He would take back what was rightfully his. Strip her of everything. Her house. Her money. Her dignity. Her pride. Once she had paid, paid in full, he would take what was left of her. Only when he had it all and she was dead would he be satisfied.

Chapter 22

Bree stood at the patio door sipping her second cup of coffee, feeling the caffeine flow into her system. Entranced, she watched Ryker and Sam work on the pavers. It was like watching a well-oiled machine. Ryker lifted and shifted, while Sam placed and leveled. Both guys had muscles well-toned from years of manual labor.

Her heart did a little flip as she watched Ryker. Despite everything, all the questions and concerns she had about him, she was more afraid that she actually might be falling for him, than the idea he might be dangerous. She just couldn't bear to give her heart to someone else that would hurt her, leave her, or destroy her. Losing her family nearly had.

The doorbell rang, pulling her away from the window and Ryker.

"Detective Savard, right on time," Bree said, opening the door wide. "Please come in."

"Good morning, Miss Thompson."

"Please, call me Bree."

He smiled at her, making the corners of his dark brown eyes crinkle. He wore jeans today, with his white button-down shirt and brown jacket. Sunglasses were perched on his shiny bald head, and a pen was in his front shirt pocket. His phone was clipped on his brown belt that matched his shoes, and he carried a small notepad in his hand.

Getting down to business he said, "Okay Bree . . . How 'bout we take a walk? You can show me where you were at last night."

"Do you mind if we go through the house? My shoes are in the breezeway."

"That's fine. We can go out the same door and retrace your steps." He indicated for her to go first. He glanced into the living room as they walked by. "I see you took down what was left of the sheers."

"Yes, but that's as far as I've gotten. Sam brought me some turpentine to clean up the paint. I'll probably do that this afternoon. I just didn't have the energy to start that this morning." Bree slipped on her shoes. "Ready." They walked into the garage. "As I told you last night, my studio is upstairs. I came down, and went out this door."

"Anyone could have come in this way without a key because you left it unlocked, correct?"

"Yes, but it was locked when I came back up, so they must have slipped back out this way and turned the knob, then pulled it shut."

Savard looked around. "The door isn't visible from the front of the house, but easy enough to find. Okay, you came out this way. Then what?"

"I walked down to the dock. The lighting was perfect so I took some pictures but I wasn't really in the mood after being up all night, instead I decided to relax." Bree pointed to her spot.

They walked the rest of the way in silence.

"Take the seat you had last night," Savard said, indicating the chairs. She did as she was told. "Was it this quiet out here last night?" he asked, taking note that the wind had died down and sounds were carrying. They could hear voices and music drift towards them, as well as the occasional clink of tools.

"The wind was stronger, the waves more turbulent."

Savard did a slow 180, taking in the whole of the yard. "You can easily see the whole back of the house from here, even though we're at a lower grade. But if your back is to it, you're far enough away not to notice anything going on up there. Certainly not someone trying to go unseen. It would be easy to slip in and out unnoticed."

Savard sat down beside her. He pulled his ink pen out of his pocket and flipped open the pad glancing out at the shifting blue water. "I can see why it was so easy for you to fall asleep here; you could, even if you weren't tired. It's peaceful."

"Yes, it is. This spot is one of the many reasons I bought the house."

"Have you given any thought to what I asked last night? About the possibility of who or what?"

Bree fished a folded piece of paper out of her back pocket and handed it to him. "Here are all the names you requested: ex-boyfriend, family, friends, and people I've met since coming here, along with the phone numbers I have."

"Thank you. Any ideas?" he asked, scanning it quickly.

"Maybe," Bree shifted in her chair, suddenly uncomfortable. "I can only think of one person, but honestly I hate to mention it because it just doesn't feel right."

"You let me worry about figuring it out. Give me as much information as you can."

She wasn't sure how to say it, so she decided to explain it, trying hard not to have to say his name just yet. "I have a website for my business. It's called 'Images by Bree'. I post pictures, write a blog, have photos for purchase, and a place for my followers to leave remarks. They can comment on my work or ask questions they may have regarding photography."

He jotted it down. "Go on."

"Well, I received an unkind comment on my blog a few weeks ago. I didn't think too much about it. And then a couple of days later another nasty comment through my email, it said exactly what was carved into the floor. *You took what was mine.* Then two more comments on my blog." She gave him almost word for word what the other comments had been.

"The one was exactly the same as what was carved into your floor?"

She nodded.

"Do you still have the emails?"

"I deleted them, but I don't think I've emptied my trash in a while, so they should still be there."

"Good. I'll need to see them. Is there a reason you didn't report this?"

"I just thought . . . I don't know what I thought. I guess that it was someone a million miles from here. Or if I ignored it, they would stop."

"And now? Now that it's actually carved into your floor? What do you think now?"

"Now it's real. Up close and . . ." she couldn't finish.

"Was there a username?"

"Yes, Kage."

"Cage?" he questioned. "How did they spell it?"

"K.A.G.E."

"That's kind of a unique name. It reminds me of the main character in the movie the Black Shadow?"

"Maybe." She shrugged. "Now that you mention it, I think you're right. I've seen those movies."

"Any other ideas? Someone's last name, or nickname from back home perhaps? Or someone you know that's really into the Black Shadow?"

"Well, my one cousin was when we were younger. He had every action figure, and a spaceship too, I think it was called the Shadow Jumper." She smiled at the memory but shook her head. "I think every boy my age loved those movies, but . . ." she hesitated.

"Tell me."

"It may not really matter . . ."

"Right now, we don't know what matters, or what's important. Anything, no matter how small, you need to tell me. Understand?"

It didn't feel right to think about it, let alone say it out loud, so she blurted it before she could change her mind. "It's Ryker James.

I don't have any proof that he's Kage, or why he would pick that name, but . . ."

Savard leaned forward, closer to Bree, and dropped his voice low so it wouldn't carry. "What makes you think it might be him?"

"I found out he wanted this house." Now that she'd started, the words tumbled out quickly. "Apparently, he's been trying to get it for some time, but for some reason, the Hennings wouldn't sell to him. I was told he even invented a story about a ghost to keep prospective buyers away from the property." Bree ran her hands through her long hair, suddenly self-conscious as Savard watched her.

"Go on."

She sighed, she felt like she was betraying her best friend. How had she come to care for someone so quickly, and yet still have so many doubts about him? *Focus,* she scolded herself. *Just state the facts, let Savard figure it out.*

"He was pretty miffed the first couple of times they came to the house to work. I didn't know why. And he kept making these little snide comments about a ghost."

"How do you know he started this rumor?"

"My real estate agent told me."

He looked at his notes. "Coastal Realty, right?"

Bree nodded.

He asked, "Was it Linda?"

"No, Greg Carpenter. He's new. He's on the list. There." She pointed. "I guess Sheri, she's the receptionist, told him. It was some sort of fiasco at the office. Ryker had been in a big uproar over losing the house." Bree wrung her hands together. "By the way, Ryker doesn't know that I know. Greg asked me to keep it confidential. He doesn't want to risk losing his new job."

"I see."

"The thing is Detective, it doesn't seem to fit. Ryker's also been very kind to me. He put in this spot for me." She indicated the chairs and the landscaping. "Rescued me out of the attic, and let me stay at his house last night after what happened."

"Things and people aren't always what they seem. I think I have enough for now." He held out a hand to Bree. She took it, and he placed his other hand on top of hers. "I'll get to the bottom of this, I promise you. For now, stay alert. Might be best to not be alone with Mr. James though, until I've had him checked out."

Bree nodded, "Thank you, Detective."

"Just doing my job. I'm going to send Kilpatrick back out to take a look at those emails. Is this afternoon good for you?"

"Yes, that would be fine." She started to stand.

"Don't get up, stay here and enjoy the sunshine. I'll find my way back to the car."

He left her sitting there, a lot of things running through his mind, as he walked back towards the house and approached the two men on the patio.

"Good morning," he called loudly to be heard over the music. Both heads turned. Ryker reached over and cut the radio.

"Detective," Ryker brushed his hands on his pants, stuck out his hand. "How are things this morning?"

Savard shook his hand, then Sam's. "Could ask you both the same thing. Did you guys get any sleep?"

"Not much. You?"

"Probably about the same as you did. Heard Bree spent the night at your place." Savard directed the statement at Ryker. "That was kind of you."

"I wasn't about to leave her here alone, after what had happened."

Savard nodded. "Understandable." He looked from one man to the other. "You two were together then from the time you left the jobsite until you got Miss Thompson's call?"

"No," Sam answered. "I went home. I showered, changed, and then picked up pizza on the way over to Ryker's."

"What time did you get to Ryker's place?"

"I'd say around seven."

"And you?" Savard asked Ryker. "What did you do after you left here at five?"

"I stopped at the hardware store and picked up a couple of things, then went home."

"What time did you get there?"

"Right at six. I took a shower, and then did some paperwork until Sam got there with the pizza at seven."

"Either of you have your receipts from last night?"

"Mine's in the truck. I can get it for you," Sam said.

"Can you get it now?"

"Yes, I'll be right back."

Ryker pulled out his wallet from his back pocket and thumbed through it. A second later he handed it to Savard.

Savard glanced at the time stamp and returned it to Ryker, jotting it down in his notebook. "Bree said that you were over here Saturday morning working on the roof. Is that correct?"

"Yes, the weather was nice, and I wanted to get the rails primed, that way Monday morning the guys could paint."

"Is it possible you didn't secure the door properly before you left, causing it to swing open in the strong winds we had Sunday?"

Sam came back and handed the receipt to Savard.

Ryker hesitated a moment, contemplating the question. "It's possible, but not likely. Sam and I are pretty diligent when cleaning up or closing down a jobsite for the day. We were burned once when we first started. Had a situation where we didn't secure a couple of rooms properly. The owner had dogs and was gone overnight; the dogs got loose and tore up the entire house. They caused thousands of dollars of damage. Had we been more careful, more diligent when closing up for the night it wouldn't have happened. We almost went bankrupt replacing everything. That's why we always make sure we're the last to leave, the last to lock up. If we aren't on-site, one of us typically drives by after and checks."

"Would you agree with that?" Savard asked Sam, giving back his receipt.

"I would, I never worry when it's one of us locking up," Sam said with a jerk of his thumb between the two of them. "Wish I could say the same with the others."

Savard decided to test the waters a little. "What have you two heard about a ghost?"

Ryker chuckled despite himself, and Sam just shook his head.

"What? You don't believe in that sort of thing?" Savard asked, watching their reactions carefully.

"Tell him," Sam said, looking directly at Ryker.

He laughed. "Fine." He raised his hands in defense. "There's no ghost. It was me. I started the rumor."

Savard wasn't expecting Ryker to come right out and admit it. "Really? Why?"

Ryker sighed deeply. "I started the rumor about the ghost years ago. At first to get girls. Senior year of high school, or summer right before to be more accurate. We'd come out here, the house was already empty. The place was quiet and secluded . . ." Ryker shrugged, smiled devilishly. "It started as a little white lie to get a cute girl to snuggle closer. I think you get the picture."

"I do," he agreed knowingly. He'd been seventeen once too. "But that doesn't explain why you're still telling that same tired story, some ten years or more later." Savard couldn't help baiting Ryker. "Still having a hard time getting girls?"

Sam roared with laughter, Ryker shot him a dirty look. "Not quite. Changed my reasons. I wanted the house."

Savard raised an eyebrow. "Why?"

"Because I like the look of it. The house, its architecture, it's a rare find. A place like this with its character and age, withstanding time and weather. I love the location, the property itself. I've always wanted to own a place like this. And what better way to keep people away from it, and keep old man Henning from raising the price?" Ryker reached for a water bottle, took a drink. "Most people know it's just a story. No crime in telling stories, is there?"

"No, can't say that there is. But I say it's childish and I'd even go as far as saying unethical. A man who owns his own business needs to build a good reputation. One that his clients and colleagues respect. I assume you get a lot of your business by referrals, I wouldn't want potential customers to find out that you start vindictive rumors, could be bad for business."

Ryker's blood pressure rose. "It wasn't like that."

Detective Savard stepped up close to Ryker, so they were only a foot apart. "That's how it seems. Someone who does that . . . who knows what they're actually capable of? Maybe they're vindictive enough to get back at an innocent woman who just happens to have bought the house he's coveted for years? Try to scare her out. . . maybe into selling." Savard registered a flicker of guilt race across Ryker's face. *Just how guilty was he?*

They stood there for a hot minute, toe to toe, not saying anything. Savard's intelligent brown eyes searching Ryker's.

"Gentlemen," Detective Savard said, stepping back. He slipped on his sunglasses. "I'll let you get back to work." He didn't look back as he disappeared around the side of the house.

Chapter 23

Savard sat at his desk and worked. He couldn't find anything on Ryker James or Sam Harris, not even a parking ticket. He Googled Bolts & Beams. Their ratings were all five stars, there was nothing but good reports on the Better Business Bureau and social media. Bolts & Beams lived and breathed on good referrals.

Tapping away at his computer, Savard checked out Chad Warner, the ex-boyfriend. There was nothing of any interest there either. Just an average guy from the Midwest, working a nine to five.

Kilpatrick walked into Savard's office unannounced. "Got the printout of the emails and blog comments off Bree's computer," he said waving a sheet of paper.

Savard looked up at him. "Any luck on where they came from?"

"No, running a trace on it now, trying to find where they originated." Kilpatrick put the single piece of paper on his desk. "You need me, let me know." He was gone as quickly as he had come.

Savard searched Bree Thompson. He got a couple of hits. Her website was first. Images by Bree. He followed the link. He was surprised when a cover photo of a lush gold wheat field graced the initial contact. The picture was so crystal clear he could see individual grain heads and he swore it looked like it shifted in the wind. The wheat field did a slow fade into a gorgeous sunset. The warm vibrant colors of the sun bled into the deep dark blues of the ocean. The image shifted again and he was captivated by a whitetail deer standing in a flower-filled meadow. Then the meadow zoomed in, enlarging the flowers until they were a faded image in the background. There was a small photo of Bree in the upper left-hand corner and her name in the top banner. The navigation bar had tabs for portraits, landscapes, events, a bio, and a blog.

Savard clicked through the website, impressed by her talent, captivated by the unique photos for purchase. He read through a few of her blogs which were on different techniques on lighting, or moving objects, how to create more depth, and get crisper photos.

When he had exhausted the website, he went to the next post about her. The tragic accident that took her family. He jotted down any names that were mentioned in the article including the driver of the semi, Garth Snader.

He was so engrossed in the world of Bree Thompson; he wasn't aware of how much time had passed until his wife called.

"You're meeting me at the hospital, right?" she asked.

He pulled his eyes away from the computer. "Hospital?" he questioned.

"Lamaze class. Remember?"

Savard glanced at his watch. "Class. Right. Seven o'clock. I'll be there in fifteen minutes. Are we going out to eat after?" he asked, suddenly famished.

"Yes."

"Right. See you soon." He hung up, logged off his laptop, and grabbed his keys.

• • • •

BREE WAS LOOKING FORWARD to tonight. Colette had invited her to go out with the girls for dinner at the Shark Shack. They were celebrating, Colette had landed herself a job at an advertising agency. Little did Colette know what was really going on, Bree smiled to herself, thinking of the surprise Sheri had included her in.

Bree glanced at the time, needing to get ready. She shut off the lights and left the studio. Taking special care to check the locks on the doors as she went through the house.

She went upstairs to her room, walked outside, and stood on the deck for a few minutes, checking the temperature and taking in the view. Content, she went back in and slipped into her favorite pair of faded jeans and a white knit top that clung to her and set off the start of her summer tan. She applied a trace of makeup and straightened her hair. She put in small silver hoops that glittered in the light. She latched a silver chain around her neck when she heard a car.

She slid on her white sandals, adjusted her silver anklet, and went down the stairs as the doorbell rang.

Bree opened it to find Colette standing there with a bundle of mail in her arms.

"Hey, girl! Are you ready?"

"I am, just let me grab my purse. Come in a second." Bree held the door wide.

"Oh, wow," Colette said, sucking in a big breath. "This place is gorgeous."

"Thank you. What do you have there?" Bree asked, indicating the armful of newspapers and envelopes Colette held.

She looked down. "It's your mail. I hope you don't mind, but the box was full. The door was hanging open, so I thought I'd grab it for you." She handed Bree the bundle.

"Thanks, I guess I haven't gotten the mail in a while. Hadn't actually thought about it with everything going on." She tossed it on the counter. Grabbed her empty purse, slipped in her camera, her wallet, cell phone, and lip-gloss. Then slung it over her shoulder. "With the mailbox out by the road, I don't even think about it unless I'm driving past it. Do you want a tour?"

"I definitely do." Colette glanced at her phone. "But we don't have time right now, I told the girls we'd be there in fifteen minutes, so we'd better go. How about when we come back?"

"Sounds good. I'm ready then." They walked past the living room and Colette hesitated. "Is this where it happened?" she asked, noticing the bare windows, the scarred floor, and the freshly painted walls.

Bree nodded.

Colette shivered. "That gives me the willies. I can't even imagine how you begin to sleep at night."

"I'm going to stay up really late, and go to bed completely exhausted," Bree said grimly. "Let's not think about it tonight."

Bree ushered Colette out the door, flipping on the outside lights, and making sure to lock up. They both climbed in Colette's car and started down the bumpy lane.

"How was the first week of work?" Bree asked.

"It was great! Everyone is so nice and friendly. I have my own cubicle and my very first assignment."

"How exciting! What is it?"

"Have you ever seen those books they have in hotel rooms?" Colette glanced over at Bree. "You know, the ones that have advertisements in them for places to eat, things to do, sights to see?"

"Yes, there was one in my room at the hotel. I looked through it several times. I found a few good places to eat, as well as some stores. Is that what you're going to be working on?"

"Yep. I think mostly it's a no-brainer. You know, give the new girl something she can't possibly screw up, but whatever." She shrugged. "All I have to do is contact the existing business and try to get them to buy back into it. Update the events page; change the layout to make it more user-friendly and inviting. There are a few pages for new businesses, also just some pages for a few scenic photos of the area."

Colette glanced over at Bree as she flipped on her blinker to make the right turn. "They have a photographer they've used forever. He gives them the same tired photos year after year. They said if I knew of someone else, I could use them at my discretion."

"Really?"

"Yeah, so I thought, I know a new and upcoming hotshot photographer that I might be able to collaborate with . . . maybe trade a few photos for an ad advertising her business." She pulled into the lot behind the Shark Shack and parked the car. "What do you think, hotshot? Want to collaborate?"

Bree laughed. "I'm no hotshot, but yes, I'd love to."

"Awesome! We can talk about it more later. Let's go eat, I'm starving!" With that, they both got out of the car and headed into the restaurant.

The place was packed and noise wafted out as the door opened. The hostess greeted them and ushered both women back to the party room.

"There must be a mistake; we're just meeting a couple of friends."

"No mistake, follow me hon," she winked at Bree as she opened the door to the party room.

"SURPRISE!"

The room was bursting at the seams with all Colette's friends and family.

"Oh, you guys!" Colette shrieked and was pulled into the throng of people.

Bree stood just inside the door, unsure where to go or what to do. She hadn't been expecting this many people. She didn't see anyone she recognized.

"Hey, Bree," Sam said, coming up beside her.

"Oh, hey Sam! I'm so glad to see you. For a second I thought I wasn't going to know anyone."

"Might as well get yourself something to drink," he raised a cup. "And eat, it will be a while before you see her again. Come on, I'll go with you."

They threaded their way through the crowd and got in line at the buffet. "Where's Ryker?" she asked, picking up a plate. "You two are usually inseparable."

Sam scoffed, "No we're not." He met Bree's eyes across the buffet and laughed. "It just seems that way. He's coming in a little while. He had a few errands to run."

Bree selected a sandwich and placed it on her plate, moving slowly down the table. "By the way, the patio looks beautiful. I can't believe you guys are almost finished."

"Yeah, it's turning out nice. 'Bout another half day's work and we will be done. Then we can start the hardwood floors and tear out the kitchen cabinets."

They came to the end of the buffet and looked for a spot to sit. Sam balanced his loaded plate, spotted Sheri, and motioned towards the table in the back. Bree nodded and followed.

· · · ·

RYKER ENTERED THE ROOM and was engulfed in noise. Music, laughter, and conversation made it impossible to hear himself think. Someone had turned on a disco light that was suspended from the center of the room, casting the crowd in dancing light. He was surprised to see a few couples actually dancing.

He threaded his way through the crowd greeting familiar faces and stopping to chat for a few minutes, but in search of a specific one. From across the room, he saw her.

Her golden-brown hair hung straight as an arrow, shimmering in the pale light. Her blue eyes sparkled like sapphires as she laughed at something someone said. She was surrounded by people he knew. Sam, Sheri, Carol, and Greg Carpenter.

He grabbed a drink from the bar and worked his way to the table. To her. The table was full, but he snagged a chair from the one next to it. "Got room for one more?" Ryker asked.

Sheri looked up. "Ryker, of course. Make room everyone."

Chairs scraped the floor, bodies shifted, and somehow space between Bree and Sheri opened up. Ryker sat and his leg bumped hers. He looped an arm over the back of her chair and reached across Bree to shake Greg's hand.

"Carpenter, nice to see you," he said, shaking his hand. "Didn't know you knew Colette."

"Only in passing," Greg answered. "Carol and Sheri invited me. And who can pass up a party?" He was interrupted by the appearance of Linda.

"Well, look at that, the gang's all here." She smiled sweetly and bent to hug Ryker and Sam. "Bree, I wanted to tell you, we have been getting so many compliments on the picture you gave us. Everyone who comes in just raves over it."

Bree beamed, "Thank you, Linda, that's great to hear."

"It made me think that we should update the pictures in the conference room. They're old and faded. I was wondering if you had anything you thought would go in there?"

"I'm sure I could find something."

"Great! Stop by sometime next week and take a look. Let me know your thoughts." Linda looked up as she heard her name called. She waved. "I gotta make my rounds. You kids have fun, but not too much." She gave Ryker a wink and disappeared into the crowd.

Sheri leaned over to Ryker and whispered something in his ear. His lips quirked effortlessly into a smile, making Bree wonder what Sheri had said. She tried not to let it bother her but a little prick of jealousy formed in the pit of her stomach. *Was he interested?* Sheri placed her hand on his thigh and left it. Bree forced herself to look away. Only to make eye contact with Greg. He smiled coyly, making her cheeks flush.

Ryker said something to Sheri that only she could hear and it made her giggle, then she ran a hand up his arm. Bree couldn't stand it. She slid her chair back, cleared her throat. "I'm going to walk around and take some photos of the party. Does anyone need anything while I'm up?"

"No, we're good."

Bree nodded, pulling out her camera, and disappeared into the crowd.

She moved slowly among them, looking for clusters of friends. Bree snapped a few candid pictures, and others she asked people to pose. She photographed them in groups of threes and fours. Lifting cups in salute or wrapping arms around each other. She found Colette and made her the focal point.

From his vantage point, he watched her moving effortlessly among the crowd. He sipped his beer and politely listened to Sheri chatter on. Making the appropriate comments or gestures when needed, but his real focus was Bree. To say she worked the crowd was an understatement. She created magic, she was magic, friendly, graceful, and oozed pure charisma as she worked the crowd.

She was able to get people to pose without interrupting the flow of the conversation or the party, to laugh and smile genuinely at the camera, at her. She took one group after another, whether dancing, sitting, or eating. No person went unnoticed. No group too small or too large for her to aim her camera at.

When she had the camera pointed in someone's direction, they had her undivided attention. He wanted that. He wanted her to look at him, and no one else. To have her focus solely on him. To be framed in a moment of time, just with her.

"Earth to Ryker," Sheri said, deliberately leaning in close and touching his arm. "You're a million miles away. Can I come too?" she asked softly.

His face etched into deep masculine lines of concern, then he gave his attention to Sheri and flashed a dynamite smile. "Nowhere special. I'm going to grab a sandwich. Be back in a few." He got up and left the table quickly. He knew Sheri was into him, and up until recently, he thought he might be into her too. But then Bree had walked into his life and everything had changed. That thought alone made him want a beer. He didn't like being focused on one woman. He liked to roam, to wander, to enjoy each and every woman and what they had to offer. He loved all women, no matter their shapes or size. He appreciated each one and their individuality. He had never craved one in particular. Until Bree.

• • • •

THE CAKE HAD BEEN CUT and served, the music slowed, and the crowd thinned. Cans and bottles were collected, the buffet was cleaned up, trash was whisked away, and tables were starting to break down. Colette stood by the doorway, a little tipsy, giving hugs to each and every person as they wished her well and left for the night.

Bree aimed her camera one last time as Sam hugged Colette. Bree captured the intimate moment and thought, *there just might be something there.* Ryker came up beside her making her jump as he leaned down, so close she could feel his breath on her neck. "Do you mind?" she asked, as he leaned over her shoulder, trying hard to keep her heart from fluttering.

"Not at all. Why? Do you?"

She shrugged him off. "Yes, you're a little too close. I need some space to work."

Bree glanced over to see both Sheri and Greg standing together, watching them.

"Besides, I don't think Sheri would appreciate it." Bree took a noticeable step away from him.

"Sheri's not the boss of me."

"What are you, three? Not the boss of you? Are you kidding?" she looked at him and arched a delicate brow.

He flashed a deeply etched smile, making him dangerously appealing.

Bree swallowed hard. "Besides, by the look on Sheri's face, I would say she disagrees with that statement."

Ryker didn't even look in Sheri's direction, just kept his eyes locked on Bree. Her breath caught, she felt like he could see right through her. That he knew exactly how attracted to him she was.

She cleared her throat and inched back a little further. "If you'll excuse me, I need to see if Colette is ready to go." On cue, Colette walked over with Sam.

"Hey," she said bumping her hip into Bree's. "You 'bout ready to go?"

"When you are. But I think I should drive."

Colette smiled. "Yeah, I think you're right. I've had a few too many."

"I can take you," Sam chimed in. "It's on my way."

It took a few minutes to get it all sorted out, but in the end, Bree drove Colette home with Sam following behind. Then Sam took Bree home.

The moon was hidden behind some clouds as Sam pulled into her driveway. Bree was glad she had left the outside lights on as they came up to the house, but still, it was dark, and it made her think of what could be waiting inside.

"I was thinking, maybe we could put some lights along the driveway. Light it up a little bit. What are your thoughts?"

"I think that's a great idea. We could even put a couple of lights on the front to accent the roof at the peaks. Make the house have a romantic, yet dramatic feel. You could use some on the back too. It would look spectacular from land and sea. Really show the place off. I'll get you a price with some options."

"That sounds great." Bree opened her door. "Thanks for the ride."

"You're welcome. Do you need me to come in?"

"I'll be fine. Thanks though."

"I'll wait until you're in."

She unlocked the door and gave a wave, he pulled around and disappeared down the lane. Bree locked the door behind her and went to the kitchen, flipping on lights. She glanced in each room, a little paranoid, hoping she wouldn't find anything. With a sigh of relief, she was satisfied that everything looked in order. The mail was where she left it, piled on the island, and nothing else seemed to be out of place.

Bree got a glass of water and leaned back against the counter, and savored the quiet and the dark. Her ears were still ringing from the loud music. Not quite ready for bed, Bree decided to check the photos she had taken tonight. She reached in her purse to get her camera and felt a piece of paper. She pulled out the folded sheet and knew that it hadn't been in there when she left the house. She unfolded it, only to reveal a photo of herself. She was standing in her bedroom in her bra and jeans, the white shirt that she wore now, in her hands. She started to shake as she read the big, bold typed message across the bottom.

I'm watching you.

She dropped the paper on the counter like it was on fire. She tried to think. To reason. He had to have been at the party. There were so many people at the party. So many she didn't know and only a handful she did. He could have been any one of them. He could have been anywhere, watching her, waiting to slip the photo into her purse.

And he'd been here earlier, outside when she was getting dressed. He'd seen her half-naked. He'd been at the house and at the party. Fear slicked through her, causing her to shake uncontrollably. She grabbed her cell phone and dialed the detective, suddenly afraid of the quiet and the dark.

Chapter 24

The rest of the week passed quietly. She had called a locksmith; he changed all the locks on the outside doors and installed a security bar on the slider. Next had been the electrician. He had installed solar accent lights that ran the length of the driveway and spotlights on the front of the house that pointed and accented every peak. In the back, he had attached floodlights on each corner of the house with motion sensors. When on, they flooded the backyard in soft light, reaching as far out as her favorite spot.

Other projects were coming along nicely, too. The guys had finished the patio and all the hardwood floors. Bree had ordered patio furniture and a fire pit that had been delivered yesterday afternoon; she couldn't wait to try it out.

They were scheduled to start the kitchen next week. The cabinets were going to ship early and Sam promised they'd be ready.

The remodeling that started when she moved in had ceased temporarily. It would start again on Monday but for today there was no hammering, no music, and no voices. Today there was only quiet.

Bree went through the house pulling back sheers, opening windows, and inviting the sunshine and the bay breeze in. On a day like today, how could someone not be happy, she wondered.

She grabbed her laptop, sunglasses, sunscreen, and placed her floppy hat on top of her head. She walked out of the house, across her new stone patio, and down through the grass. She noticed that the grass was getting long, and needed to be cut. *A mower,* she thought. *I need to buy a mower.* The mower made her think of her father.

Oh, daddy, I wish you were here to see my place, to enjoy it with me. She swallowed and wiped at a single tear that threatened to fall.

Not today, she thought. Fear and sorrow had no place on this beautiful day.

She eased down into her chair, placing her stuff in the one beside her, and sat for a moment gazing across the water. It was smooth today. The water was the color of cyan and shimmered like a mirror, bouncing back the intense rays of the sun.

There were already a few boats out, racing up and down the bay. She figured by noon the bay would be full. She wondered what it would be like in a year from now to sit here and watch them. Would she still find it peaceful, relaxing, captivating? Or would she tire of the wind, the sand, and the sun? She didn't think she would. Not when she sat here now in awe.

She snagged her laptop from the chair and leaned back, thankful she had a career she loved and a business she could really delve into. To think it all started when she had joined the school yearbook, and volunteered to take pictures because no one else would.

From the moment she picked up her first camera, she was in love. She loved everything about it. The cool black metal finish of the camera, the weight of it in her hands as she aimed it, and the feel of it on her shoulder as she carried it from event to event. It became a part of her as nothing had before.

She loved capturing the special moments. The way it made her feel connected to what was happening right before her, even if she didn't know the people or understand the sport. It was like she was stepping into an intimate moment with those she held in her lens, one that no one else could feel. But if she did her job well, others would be able to see, feel, and relive it too. Whether it was on the soccer field, at the football stadium, or the auditorium stage, she relished it all. And then the compliments started coming.

She started the website for herself, her family, and her friends. It had just been a way to organize and keep track of the photos. She simply posted the pictures and soon she had some followers, and the whole thing snowballed from there. And here she was almost eight years later, still loving it. There was that old phrase that said a picture tells a story, and that's what she strived for with every click of her camera. A story people could relate to, and feel as they looked at her images.

With that in mind, Bree set to work. She wanted to work on a couple more sailboat photos. She pulled them up and kept them side by side, wanting to turn them into a set.

They were similar to the one she had already given Linda at Coastal Realty, but a little bit more serene, more subdued, making them perfect for the conference room.

The room was decorated in the same blues and repeated the theme of the reception area, but it was darker, richer. Bree edited the sailboats that way. She enhanced the shadows, produced more depth, and blurred out the edges. But kept her sails so crisp and white she could almost hear them snap in the ocean breeze.

Satisfied, she saved her changes, added her watermark, and then attached them to an email and sent them to Linda.

Inspired, Bree went ahead and wrote her blog. She focused solely on how to properly crop photos. Giving tips and showing some examples.

Next, she checked her website and processed a few orders. She was pleased; orders had been steady since she had moved. She needed to increase her advertising though, really get her name out there. The coffee table book that Colette was talking about working together on would be a great start, but that would be a while before it was finished.

For now, she thought she would make a quick post on social media. She scrolled through her photos and found one of the broken-down dingy next to her dilapidated dock. She edited it. Cropping out some of the surrounding water. Changed the filter to black and white, and used vignette to soften the edges. She enhanced the dapple of sunlight on the bow, and adjusted the sharpness, to the point it looked like a tiny spark set on the point. Finished, she enlarged the final product, examining it for flaws.

And flaws it did have. Beautiful, real flaws. The boat itself was beaten and weathered. The dock was worn and aged. The rope that tied them together frayed and unraveled. The photo showed every pockmark, every chip and crack, it was fragile and breathtaking. *Like life,* she thought. Pleased, Bree added her watermark, posted it on her feed, and captioned it "Tethered."

• • • •

RYKER DROVE WEST, AWAY from the coast, away from the water, when he really wanted to be headed towards it and be out on it. But this job wouldn't take long, or so Linda said. It was a friend of hers from the bridge club, Mrs. Peters. She was old and frail, in fact, she was the oldest member of the bridge club. Linda had gone on and on until he'd said yes. It was only three things that needed to be done. A very short list, Linda promised.

He mentally ran through the list. One, fix the railing on the porch, so Mrs. Peters had the support she needed to go down the short set of stairs. Two, repair the screen door. It needed new mesh and the rusty hinges replaced. And three, tighten a cabinet door in the kitchen. *Simple enough,* he hoped.

Ryker took note of the place as he pulled in. The grass was too long, the house needed painting, and the white picket fence needed mending. He sighed. This wasn't going to be a quick job. There's no way he could leave the house looking like this.

He knocked on the door, heard a dog bark inside, and the shuffle of feet. A long moment later, the door opened, and out peered two sets of eyes. One set big, brown, and almond-shaped, the other faded blue. The blue eyes belonged to Mrs. Peters and the brown to her cocker spaniel.

"You must be Ryker. Linda told me you were coming at eight sharp and look at that. Right on the dot." She shuffled backward and opened the door wider. She was hunched at the shoulders and fragile-looking, but there was a sparkle in her eyes that couldn't be squelched by age. Ryker could still see the beauty she once had been under the heavily etched lines of her face.

"Yes, ma'am. That's me." He stuck out his hand and took her petite one. "Ryker James. And who's this beauty?" he asked, shaking the cocker spaniel's paw.

"This here's Millie, my best girl."

"Hey there, Millie," he said, patting her on the head. Millie reached up and licked his hand.

"Why Ryker James, if you ain't the most handsome thing I ever seen, I don't know who is. Even Millie here is taken by you, and she's a hard sell. My Harvey, he was good-looking too, a real James Dean, but you? You make this old heart flutter."

Ryker smiled. "You flatter me, Mrs. Peters. Linda mentioned you had a few things that needed to be fixed?"

"Oh, yes. I almost forgot why you were here. Don't mind me if I don't look at you when we speak. You're making my mind all fuzzy."

Ryker laughed. He liked her instantly.

She put the dog down and shuffled through the house to the kitchen. "This cabinet door needs fixin'." She pointed at it and kept moving. "This back screen door needs work and those stairs. That's all. You think you can handle that?"

"You bet, Mrs. Peters. I got everything I need in the truck for those jobs, but first let me ask, who's been cutting your lawn?"

"Why? You in the mowin' business too?"

He smiled broadly. "No ma'am, but your lawn is looking a little long. If you wanted, I could cut it quick before it gets hot, and then still get to these other jobs. It's up to you."

She eyed him knowingly. "That'd be very kind of you. The neighbor boy has been doin' it, but he fell off his skateboard last week and sprained his ankle real bad. Be at least another week before he can mow."

"I'd be happy to do it for you if you have a mower?"

"Sure do, it's outback. Be nice to get it cut, otherwise, the bugs start getting bad in the high grass. I worry about ticks and mosquitoes."

They walked back to the shed with Millie trailing; next to it was a small dog house with a little fence around it.

"Wanna see my pups?"

"You have puppies?"

"Yep, Millie here had four puppies."

Ryker peered over the little fence and saw four little cocker spaniels. "They're certainly cute."

Mrs. Peters bent down and patted Millie. "My Millie makes good babies. Cute as a button, they are," she said, scooping the littlest one up. "All spoken for too, 'cept this one." She handed her to Ryker. "Cute, ain't she?"

"That she is," Ryker said, holding the runt of the litter at arm's length. He examined her long floppy ears that were the color of copper. She had pure white patches on her face and her sides. Cute was an understatement. Her little stub of a copper tail wiggled fiercely as she snuggled against his chest. "Very cute." He handed the puppy back before he could get sucked in. "Right then, the mower?"

She laughed heartily, reading him. "You're a softy. Mower's in the shed."

The little swatch of a yard only took him an hour to mow and weed whack. He fixed the stairs, the cabinet, and the screen door. She made him a sandwich and chatted the whole time he ate; asking questions about his business, his family, his friends, his health, and his love life. There wasn't a subject she was afraid to broach.

When he was done eating, he replaced lightbulbs in two of the bedrooms and in the hanging light fixture in the entryway. He asked her for batteries, which she dug out of a junk drawer, and he replaced them in all the smoke detectors. He even fixed the picket fence out front and scheduled a time to come back to paint the house.

Mrs. Peters was pleased. "Why Ryker James, you have done a wonderful job and I'll be sure to tell Linda and all my friends. Now," she went to the closet and pulled out her purse. "How much do I owe you for today?"

"Not a thing, ma'am." He patted her on the hand. "Just doing a favor for a friend."

"You're so sweet. And lucky."

"Lucky?" he questioned.

"Yes, lucky. Cause if you had said an old friend, I would have had to hit you over the head with my pocketbook."

Ryker laughed. "There isn't anything old about you, Mrs. Peters." Ryker stood and packed up his toolbox. "I need to get going. It's been a real pleasure."

"Now, Ryker James, what kind of woman do you take me for, if you think I'm gonna let you walk out of here empty-handed?" She tsked loudly. "No sir, I gotta give you somethin' for your troubles."

He thought for a second. "There is one thing."

She pointed directly at him with a crooked finger. "Name it and it's yours."

Chapter 25

He gave her a puppy, and not just any puppy. The cutest little cocker spaniel she'd ever seen. Bree fell in love instantly, and a little more with the man. She cuddled her close. "Ryker, she's so sweet. But I can't take her from you."

"Nonsense, I got her *for* you."

"But why?" Bree held her up, cradled in the palm of her hand, looked into her big brown eyes, and saw nothing but pure love, as only a puppy can give. "Why would you do that?"

"Because, you're out here all alone, and with everything happening," he shrugged. "I thought you could use a watchdog."

Bree laughed and snuggled her close again. "Yeah, because she's *so* fierce. She's barely more than a handful."

"Okay, well not now, but dogs, even small ones, can sense other people. She may not be much of a watchdog now, but that yapping could be an alarm."

"What will I call her?"

"My first thought was Zylah. But you name her whatever you want, she's yours."

"Zylah?" Bree looked at her again. "Zylah, that fits her. Small or not, I love her already." So moved by the gesture, without thinking Bree reached up and kissed Ryker on the cheek. "Thank you."

He didn't even hesitate, his arm slipped around her waist. He pulled her in fast. One hand on her face the other moved to her hip.

Her breath caught as his lips caressed hers, sealing hers in a hot, passionate kiss. Sparks shot through her from her head to the tips of her toes. It was like nothing she had ever experienced before. Gentle, yet demanding. He tasted like soda and desire. Smelled like fresh-cut grass and aftershave. She forgot about everything, and just let herself fall into the kiss. Into what was Ryker. Strong, stubborn, compassionate, sexy Ryker.

He didn't let up until the little cocker spaniel whimpered and started to squirm between them.

She pulled back, realizing they were crushing the puppy. Bree stood breathless and speechless, her face flush and her pulse racing. She eased back a step trying to catch her breath, and put some space between them, afraid he could hear the hammering of her heart.

Ryker couldn't believe how beautiful she looked at that moment. The sun setting behind her, her honey-brown hair set off like gold. The adorable puppy in her arms, the color in her cheeks, and the blue of her eyes seemed to pull every ounce of desire out of him. He wanted her as he'd never wanted anyone before. He took a step towards her, determined to kiss her again, but she stepped back and held out her hand.

"Ryker, wait," she whispered breathlessly.

"Why? I've wanted to do that since the first time I saw you, at the beach, in the morning light."

Surprised, she asked, "You have? I don't believe you."

"Then let me show you." He stepped toward her and she quickly stepped back.

"This isn't a good idea. You're working on the house. This should stay professional."

"I can separate business from pleasure, can't you?" he teased.

"No, I can't." She could see he didn't buy it. She thought quickly and switched tactics as he took another step towards her. "What about Sam?"

That stopped him.

"What about Sam?" Ryker tucked his hands in his pockets. "Do you like Sam?"

"Of course, I like him. What's not to like?"

"Let me get this straight. You'd rather be kissing Sam?"

"What? No, I just meant that he's your business partner, he won't like you kissing the clients."

He smirked. "You let me worry about Sam. I don't think he'll have a problem with it."

"Then what about Sheri?"

"Sheri?" he questioned. "What about her?"

"Aren't you dating her?"

"No, I'm not."

"Well, that comes as a surprise to me, and probably Sheri as well."

"What in the hell is that supposed to mean?"

"Every time I see you two, I get the impression that you're together."

He cocked an eyebrow. "Damn it, Bree, now you're just making things up. We're not together, never have been."

"Well, you could have fooled me. And like I said, Sheri's into you. I saw the way she looked at you at Sam's party, at the Shark Shack, and even the other night at Colette's surprise party, she couldn't keep her eyes or her hands off you. You can't tell me you didn't know."

He stayed silent.

Bree read him like a book. "That's what I thought." She stared at him, waiting for him to deny it. But he didn't.

Ryker crossed the yard and went to the truck. "I stopped and bought her a bowl, a bed, and some dog food. This is the right kind for puppies, the woman at the store said." He lifted them out of the truck bed and placed them on the porch. "I figured you didn't have any of these things since I've seen your scantily furnished house. This should at least get you through the night." He turned on his heel then and went back to the truck. "You're probably going to want a collar and a crate, but you'll have to get that yourself." He climbed in and started the engine. "Oh, and one other thing, she's had all her shots."

Bree looked down at the puppy and softened. "Ryker, thank you. And I'm sorry."

"Me too. It was just a damn kiss, Bree. Don't read too much into it. It's not like I slung you over my shoulder and drug you off to bed."

"But Sheri . . . I don't do that to friends."

"Like I said, it was just a kiss. I'm a guy and I took advantage of the situation. Don't flatter yourself that much." He threw the truck in drive and pulled off, leaving her standing there with the puppy.

• • • •

HE WATCHED HER THROUGH his camera going about her day, working outdoors, and playing with her new puppy. Smirking, he thought how easy it would be to take her or kill her if he wanted to.

Little did she know that he knew her property like the back of his hand. He spent the days and nights before she moved in scouring the place, looking for hiding places, easy passages in and out. He knew the quickest way by land and by water. He knew where he could sit and watch the back of the house and where to see the front.

He'd seen the locksmith arrive the other day and change the locks. He'd seen where she hid the key outside. That too had made him laugh. There wasn't anything she could do that he wasn't prepared for. He was always one step ahead of her.

When the electrician installed the spotlights on the front and the floodlights on the back of the house, he'd been watching.

Day and night he watched her and knew she was starting to relax again. She felt safe and reassured that the home improvements she had made could keep him at bay. Little did she know there wasn't any way to keep him out if he wanted in. . . and he wanted in.

Chapter 26

Asoft whimper drifted in and out of her dreams. Unable to fully wake up, Bree tried to ignore it until it started again, and something warm, wet, and a little rough touched her hand. Bree screamed and sat straight up. She heard the scamper of little feet. She glanced around and saw the little cocker spaniel cowering in the corner of her cloth bed.

"Oh, Zylah!" She swung her legs off the mattress and went over to her. "I'm sorry sweetheart," she said, scooping her up. "You scared me. I'm not used to having a puppy." The morning sun shone through the curtains, casting the room in a soft glow. "I'm guessing you need to go out."

Bree carried her down the stairs and went straight for the back door. She had heard that if you went to a certain spot every time when training a puppy, they would always go there when they needed to do their business. "Let's give it a try, girl."

Bree picked a spot away from the patio, set her down, and waited. It didn't take long and Zylah was scampering back towards her. Bree bent down and lavished the puppy with praise. "I'll need to get you some treats to reward you when you've done such a good job, like just now."

She scratched her behind the ears, and Zylah rolled over and wanted her belly rubbed. "You're too cute. Let's go in and get some breakfast. Then we can make a trip to the store and get you everything you need."

Bree put puppy chow in one bowl and fresh water in another, Zylah pounced on it, hungry. Bree started her coffee and sat down to write her list.

Since Zylah was busy, she went to the pantry and got a large box. She needed something for the puppy to stay in while she was busy taking a shower and getting dressed.

Somehow Bree managed to shower, throw on some clothes, and pull her damp hair into a ponytail, all the while corralling the puppy in the box. Zylah had managed to crawl out twice tipping the box over. The puppy got into her clothes, pulled the towels down off the bar, and chewed up a pair of socks.

Already exhausted, Bree grabbed the escaping puppy, the box, the socks, her purse, and headed out the door.

Pulling into the parking lot of the strip mall, she parked in front of the pet store. Bree wasn't sure if she should be cursing Ryker or thanking him. Zylah certainly was a handful.

She buzzed through the store with Zylah in her arms, and with the aid of a clerk selecting the things on her list. She glanced down as her phone chimed and was surprised to see it was a text from her aunt.

> Aunt Maureen: Your things are packed and coming on the moving truck. Should arrive tonight.
>
> Bree: So soon?
>
> Aunt Maureen: Yes. Did some spring cleaning this week and got it done. Meant to text sooner.
>
> Bree: Wow! Thanks! What time?
>
> Aunt Maureen: Around 7:00pm. U R Welcome. Sending our love!

Bree stood there for a moment and contemplated the message. That meant her furniture was to arriving tonight. She didn't have anyone lined up to help her unload, she hadn't been expecting it for a couple of weeks. Panicked, Bree threw a couple more things in the cart, thanked the clerk, and headed for the checkout. She paid the cashier, a million things running through her mind, and headed out to the SUV with Zylah and her purchases.

She was loading everything in the back when Zylah started to squirm. "Oh Zylah, sorry, you probably have to go. Hold on." She dug through the bag and found her new collar and leash. Slipping them on Zylah, she walked her over to the grass. Bree looked over as she heard her name called and saw Colette coming towards her.

"Hey, girl! I was going to call you later. And here you are, with a puppy no less." Colette gave Bree a hug and squatted down to pet the little cocker spaniel. "Isn't she the cutest?"

"She is, isn't she?"

"When did you get her?"

"Yesterday. Ryker gave her to me."

Colette wiggled her eyebrows. "I guess someone has a crush."

"I wouldn't say that."

"Oh really? You don't see him giving me a puppy, do you?"

"Well, no . . . but you don't have a stalker either."

"Yeah, about that," Colette placed a hand on Bree's arm. "I'm so sorry that's happening to you. If you need something, or someplace to stay until this is over, please don't be afraid to ask."

"I'm fine, I appreciate the offer though. He's not going to chase me out of my home."

Colette nodded in understanding. "Just don't be naive about the situation either." Switching gears, Colette turned the subject back to the puppy. "What's her name?"

"Zylah."

"Was that Ryker's suggestion?"

"Yes, how did you know?" Bree scooped up the puppy.

"Those guys are always naming stuff after their favorite movie."

Bree looked at Colette, not sure what she meant.

"You know," Colette said, "Princess Zylah, from the Black Shadow."

That comment triggered something in Bree. "Who, Ryker and Sam?"

"Yep. They both love it. It's their all-time favorite. They've seen all the movies dozens of times. That's not the first thing they've named after the Black Shadow either. And I'm sure not the last. After all, Ryker's boat is Shadow." Colette shook her head when Bree didn't respond. "Shadow Jumper. Surely, you've heard of Theo Knight, the character that piloted Shadow Jumper?"

"Yes, I have." Apprehension coursed through Bree, making her want to ask more, but she didn't have the time or the courage. Asking more would only incriminate Ryker; maybe even link him to Kage. She didn't want it to be true. The thought made her nauseous. Zylah started to squirm. "I don't mean to be rude Colette, but I really gotta run."

"Okay, but I was going to see if you wanted to do something tonight."

"I would love to, but I can't. I just found out my furniture is arriving around seven, and I don't have anyone lined up to unload it."

"Don't they have movers coming with the truck?"

"You would think so, but we didn't do that. We only hired a guy to deliver. My relatives loaded it all on the truck on their end, and I said I would line up movers here. Cheaper that way. That's my aunt, pinch every penny." Bree shrugged. "Anyway, my aunt sent the truck early, a lot earlier than I expected, and I don't have anyone lined up to unload. I have no idea who's going to be available at such short notice or where to even start looking."

"How much stuff is it?"

"A dining table, a couple of bedroom sets, the rest of my clothes, books, dishes, additional camera equipment, and lord only knows what else my aunt put on."

"Doesn't sound that bad. If you buy some beer and wine, order pizza, I'll supply the workers."

"Seriously?"

"Yep. We will move some furniture, drink, eat, and be merry! It'll be fun."

Bree gave her another hug. "You're a lifesaver! Thank you!"

"That's what friends are for. I'll see you tonight."

. . . .

BREE OPENED THE DOOR to find Colette, Sam, and Ryker. She should have known Ryker would be asked to help. After all, he and Sam were best friends, and Colette was definitely interested in Sam. But still, she was surprised that Ryker had come, considering how they left things last night.

Sheri and Greg arrived right behind them.

"Hey!" Sheri said, hopping out of her car. She gave Bree a quick hug. "Carol wanted to come and help because she's dying to see the place, but she couldn't. She had a family thing."

Bree turned to Greg. "Thanks for coming, Greg."

"Glad to help," he said, smiling broadly. "Anything for a friend. When does the truck arrive?"

"Should be here any minute. Wanna get yourselves a drink while we wait?"

They followed her into the kitchen.

"Would anyone like a beer or a glass of wine? I also have soda and water."

"I think the drinks are going to have to wait. Looks like the truck is here," Sam said, with a jerk of his thumb towards the door.

From that moment on, it was a flurry of activity. The driver helped unload, but the guys did the heavy lifting. Bree gave direction, and the girls toted smaller boxes, clothing, garden tools, dishes, and camera equipment.

It only took a couple of hours to unload. Bree paid the driver and he was on his way. They were assembling the king-size four-poster bed in Bree's room when she slipped out and ordered pizza.

Colette found her in the kitchen, setting out plates and napkins. She picked up a box of dishes. "Do you want me to put some of these in the cabinets?"

"No, thanks. They're going to tear out the cabinets on Monday. There's no point in putting dishes away. If you want, you can set them over there in the corner."

The doorbell rang.

"Must be the pizza. I'll be right back." She yelled up the stairs. "Pizza's here." She paid the delivery guy, carried the hot pizzas into the kitchen, and set them on the island.

They all came down from upstairs.

"If you want to fix a plate, you can go sit outside on the patio. It's beautiful out tonight."

"Is there a place to sit out there?" Sam asked. "Last time I checked there wasn't."

"Won't you be surprised? I actually bought patio furniture and it was delivered yesterday after you left."

"Good for you," Sam said.

"Actual furniture inside and out. You're finally moving up in the world, Champ," Ryker said in a sarcastic tone, picking up a plate.

This was the first time he had said anything to her since he had arrived. Even though he had worked hard and took direction, he let Sam or Greg ask questions. He had simply picked up the other end of a piece of furniture and assisted. He'd been standoffish when he arrived, but the comradery of working with everyone had taken the edge off his attitude.

"You bet I am." She smiled at him, grateful for his help, and glad he was here. "Surprised?"

"You could say that. Thought maybe you were going to continue to live like a nomad indefinitely."

"I'm here to stay. Despite the fact that someone wants me gone."

They were silent for a moment while everyone loaded their plates, got drinks, and went outside. When they were alone, Ryker moved towards her. Caught her in the corner.

"For what it's worth Bree, I'm glad you're here to stay."

"Really?" she asked, a little suspicious. "You of all people seem most likely to want me to leave. I heard through the grapevine you wanted to buy this house. Is that true?"

Ryker shifted his plate from one hand to the other, looking uncomfortable. "That's true, I did. I'm not going to lie. I wanted this house pretty bad. And I was mad when I heard it had been bought out from under me."

He smiled at her then, a deep, heart-wrenching smile that creased his whole face, turning his deep-set dimples into caverns. "But I've gotten over it, or mostly. I think this house suits you. Plus, what I really wanted was to help restore it. Work on it with my own hands. Turn it from something that's falling apart to something that stands out, and that people will envy as they pass by on their boats, craning their necks to see. I think your ideas, all the things we've done here so far, and what you plan to do will achieve that. This place is going to be spectacular. Something we can both be proud of."

Bree's heart softened at that.

Someone cleared their throat.

"I don't mean to interrupt."

Bree broke the connection with Ryker and turned to find Greg standing there. "You're not. What can I do for you?"

Greg looked from Bree to Ryker, and back. "I was going to grab a beer if that's okay?"

Ryker slipped out as Bree went to the fridge.

"Certainly." She grabbed an ice-cold can and handed it to Greg.

"You comin'? I saved you a seat."

"Yes, I'll be right there," Bree said, pulling out a soda for herself. She watched Greg go out the slider. She leaned back on the counter a minute to think. If Ryker was into the Black Shadow, it could certainly be him sending the messages. He admitted to wanting the house, but he also sounded genuine when he said he was glad she had gotten it. She didn't like the idea that Ryker was behind all this, not one bit. But . . . and it was a big but, if he was, maybe now it would stop.

Bree went outside; the only two spots left were next to Ryker and Greg. Bree opted for the one next to Greg as she didn't trust herself when it came to Ryker. She was already being sucked into the entity of what was Mr. James, even though Detective Savard had warned her to be careful.

She took a bite of pizza, letting the tangy sauce sit on the tip of her tongue. She watched Ryker and wondered, could she trust him? She wanted to. The blue eyes, the dark hair, the way his whole face creased into his smile. She sighed inwardly. She felt like she was standing at the top of a cliff looking down into a deep, wide magnificent valley, into an abyss.

She could see the greens and golds, inviting lovely spaces, as well as dark, enchanting, mysterious places. Wanting to glide and soar above it, and slowly drift down into the sweet chasms and explore the depths. Knowing full well at the bottom it would be a little dangerous only enticed her. All she had to do was take one step and she would tumble head over heels into the abyss of Ryker James.

• • • •

RYKER WATCHED BREE. He couldn't help it. He liked how the last rays of the sun made her honey-brown hair shimmer like gold. The slenderness of her face, how the shadows played with the angles, and the slight pout to her lips. The intense blue of her eyes had him mesmerized.

He felt a surge of jealousy course through him as Greg leaned over and whispered something in her ear, and she laughed. He wanted to throttle that guy. There was just something about him he didn't like. He tried to rationalize it to himself. The only reason, he told himself, that he didn't like Greg, was because he had sold Bree the house and because he was cozying up to her now. Flirting. He tried to look away, but he couldn't. He was caught like a deer in the headlights staring, watching, waiting for the inevitable.

Did she like Greg? Ryker couldn't help but wonder. Then he remembered the kiss. The way she had felt. Soft and warm. Inviting. The way she had tasted. Like sweet ripe cherries on a hot summer day. He was trying hard to follow the thread of conversation around him, but couldn't. He was so lost in Bree he was having a hard time remembering his own name. Until he heard it.

"Hello, Ryker? Are you in there?" Sheri asked, leaning in close and waving her hand in front of his face.

Ryker pulled his eyes off Bree and turned to face Sheri.

"You were a million miles away just now. Everything okay?"

Ryker glanced over at Bree, then back to Sheri. "I'm fine. Just thinking about . . . work," he finished lamely.

"How about I grab you another beer?"

"Naw, I'm good." He glanced back at Bree and didn't like how Greg had his arm draped behind her. He stood. "Bree, you want me to light that new firepit of yours? It's getting a little chilly."

"That's a great idea, let me help you." Bree stood, and carried her plate into the kitchen, Ryker followed. "I have a newspaper and matches somewhere."

"Point me in the direction of the newspaper, while you dig for the matches."

"Over in the corner." She pointed. "In that pile of mail."

Ryker sifted through the mail and pulled out the newspaper. "Geez, don't you ever go through your mail?"

She shrugged, located the matches then turned to him. "Not really. It's usually all junk mail. I pay all my bills online."

Ryker picked up a thick envelope and waved it at her. "This looks important. Has Heffner Attorney at Law in the upper left corner."

"Really?" She crossed to him. "Let me see."

He hid it behind his back. "How bad do you wanna see it?"

Bree put her hand on her hip and cocked her head. "What are you, three? Give me that."

"I feel like you ask me that a lot."

"Then don't act so immature."

"What's he being immature about now?" Sam asked, carrying in plates.

Caught, Ryker handed the envelope to Bree. "You know me. Give me the matches."

Bree examined the official looking envelope. "The wood is stacked behind . . ."

"I know where the wood is," Ryker said, cutting her off as he disappeared out the door.

"Everything all right?" Sam asked.

"Yeah, I guess." Bree shrugged and put the envelope on the window sill. "Let's get that fire started."

Chapter 27

It was late when she locked the door behind Ryker, then turned and scooped up Zylah. "Need to go out before we go to bed, sweetheart?" The puppy nuzzled into her neck. "Okay, let me get your leash. I don't want to lose you in the dark. There could be some tempting sounds and smells out there."

All the windows in the house were open and a cool breeze blew in off the bay that carried a hint of smoke. Bree shivered and shrugged a little deeper into her hoodie. For a split second, she thought she heard a soft, eerie whistle flit by on the breeze. She scolded herself and tried to convince herself it was the wind blowing through the reeds as Zylah wiggled, needing to go out. She grabbed the leash and walked out the back. A scream ripped from her throat as she saw flames tear across the yard.

Thinking quickly, she sprinted back to the house and closed Zylah inside. She pulled her phone out of her back pocket and dialed 9-1-1 as she scrambled for the garden hose. Zylah let out a stream of little yips as the flames reached higher and raced in crazy patterns across the yard. She yelled her information into the phone at the dispatcher and hung up. Turning on the hose she drug it across the lawn. She didn't think she could reach the fire but she sure as hell was going to try to keep it from getting close to the house.

She was spraying water as far as she could when Ryker and Officer Kilpatrick came running up beside her.

"What the hell happened?" Ryker demanded taking the hose from her. "Never mind, there's no time. Where are the hoses the movers brought?"

"In the garage."

"Get them."

Kilpatrick grabbed her arm. "Are you okay?"

"I'm fine. Come help me get extra hoses. Where did you both come from?" Bree asked as he ran beside her.

"I was patrolling in the area and decided to drive in and check on you. Did you call it in?"

Bree nodded. "Firetrucks are on the way." She flipped on the lights in the garage. She had two more hoses thanks to her aunt; she prayed they'd be enough. "There," she pointed. Kilpatrick slung a hose over one shoulder and ran.

Bree followed suit, but she couldn't keep up. The hose was heavy and slippery.

Out of breath, she dropped it at Ryker's feet and doubled over with a massive side stitch. The men were already connecting the second hose. They worked quickly connecting the final hose, stretching them out as far as they could. They started the spray, running it back and forth across the grass trying to outsmart the fire.

Sirens rang out through the night, announcing the arrival of the firetrucks.

A low layer of smoke rolled across the yard and crept out over the water as the last embers smoldered and sputtered out. Bree cleaned up the small puddle Zylah had made, no longer able to contain her tiny bladder, since she hadn't given the puppy a chance to go after she had seen the fire.

She discarded the paper towels and washed her hands, unable to keep them from trembling. *It could have been so much worse,* she told herself. The fire had only scorched half the yard but the little dock had all but disintegrated.

If it had reached the reeds and brush. . . or if it had raced up the hill towards the house, she shuddered to think what could have happened. If Officer Kilpatrick hadn't turned into the driveway and stopped to talk to Ryker, she would have been stuck further back with the one hose instead of a hundred feet closer they had gotten by attaching the additional hoses.

She vowed she would go out and mow what was left of the lawn today. If the grass had been shorter, it might not have spread so quickly. Her dad would give her a lecture if he were here right now. Thank goodness Aunt Maureen had had enough foresight to send her father's zero-turn lawn mower on the truck.

Officer Kilpatrick came into the kitchen through the slider followed closely by Ryker. "How are you holding up?" he asked.

"I'm fine."

Ryker leaned against the counter nonchalantly and looking disinterested, but Bree could feel him assessing her.

"Chief said the fire's out. They are pulling up hoses now. Should be packed and out of here shortly," Kilpatrick said.

"Do they have any idea how it started?"

Kilpatrick shook his head no. "But the Chief said he would be around first thing, as soon as it's light enough to investigate."

"I should go out and thank them."

"I'm going out, I'll let them know. Get some sleep. Morning will be here before you know it." He started down the hall. "You need something, let me know."

"Thank you," Ryker said.

"Yes, thank you," Bree called after him. She turned to Ryker, afraid to be alone. She tentatively asked, "Are you leaving, too?"

"No, I'm staying. I'm too tired to drive home on my motorcycle, and I have a feeling you don't really want to be alone."

"I really don't, but . . ."

"But what?" He moved a little closer to her. "Thought maybe we could have a sleepover. What do you think?"

She lifted an eyebrow and considered him a moment. He had a smoldering intensity about him that made her body warm just by looking at him. "Just where do you think you're going to sleep?"

He flashed a mischievous grin at her. "I seem to remember un-loading and carrying a very heavy king-size bed-frame up those stairs," he said, pointing. "It looked awfully comfortable."

"I don't think so. And that's exactly where I thought you might be going with this whole sleepover thing." She slouched against the counter completely exhausted. "If you insist on staying there's a per-fectly good mattress just down the hall."

"What? Don't you trust yourself to share that big, old bed with me?" He inched towards her. "You wouldn't even know I was there."

She held up her hand, stopping him. "I trust myself, it's you I don't trust."

Pretending to be wounded, he clutched his chest. She pushed off the counter, turned on her heel, and gently scooped up the sleepy puppy.

"If you're staying, come on then, I'm exhausted."

Silently, he followed her up the stairs and watched her delicate-ly lay Zylah in her little cloth bed. She backed up slowly, trying not to wake the puppy, and bumped into him. She shifted back, all too aware of him. "I'm sure my aunt put some sheets in the box marked guest bed. Let me put them on."

She started to pass by him, but he caught her arm and gently pulled her into him. He slowly lifted his hand and brushed her hair back over her shoulder. She held her breath, and her pulse quick-ened. He dipped his head and his lips hovered just inches from hers, but instead of kissing her on the mouth as she expected, he lifted his head and laid a protective kiss on her forehead.

He pulled her in tight holding her. A flash of longing rushed through her. She melted into his warm body, and simply let him. She eased into his arms, his embrace. She could feel the toned mus-cles of his chest and stomach through his thin shirt, relishing in his strength and gentleness. For the first time in months, she felt safe and protected.

He kissed her forehead again even more softly and drew back. "I'm going to run out to my bike and get a fresh set of clothes. I always keep a set in the storage compartment. If you don't mind, I could really use a shower, I reek of smoke."

She reluctantly pulled back too and nodded, unable to make direct eye contact with him, in fear that he would be able to see right through her. She suppressed an urge to reach out to him and managed to say, "I'll get the towels and sheets."

· · · ·

RYKER COULDN'T SLEEP a wink. He just lay there in the dark staring up at the ceiling. He rolled over and punched his pillow a couple of times, and flopped back down. How was he supposed to sleep with Bree just down the hall? He thought about slipping in next to her, sliding up next to her warm, slender body. He couldn't help noticing those long legs in her skimpy shorts and a cotton tee. Alone, there was nothing provocative about her clothing, but on her . . . he had to stop. He'd never get any rest if he kept picturing her lying in that big bed all alone.

He rubbed at his temples, mentally shifting gears, and thought about the fire. He was grateful that he'd stopped to talk to Kilpatrick before he got on his motorcycle and left. They had been talking about baseball when they'd heard her scream. It had been like a shot to his heart. He had taken off around the house like a bullet, desperate to get to her.

He smiled in the darkness now though, thinking of her trying to battle the fire with her garden hose. If he had had time, he would have loved to see her in action.

There was time now. He marveled at her bravery and determination to save what was hers. Despite it all, all that she'd been through with losing her family and with this mad man on the loose, she had an inner spark that couldn't be squelched, by anything or anyone.

Ryker tried to imagine how the fire had even started. A spark from the firepit? Maybe drifting ash? He didn't think it was likely. He'd made sure the fire was out before he'd gone inside. A cigarette or a match thrown overboard by a passing boat? Possible. But it would have been almost an impossible throw to get it to land and light that wood on fire. But the thing that got him most was the way the flames had zigzagged across the grass as if it was following an invisible line or had a mind of its own. And a couple of times as the wind shifted and changed direction, Ryker could have sworn he smelled gasoline. But if it wasn't one of those things, how had it started? Was it this crazy man that was stalking her? Was he capable of this? That thought alone scared the shit out of him.

He lay on his side and watched as the room slowly lightened around him, a million questions running through his mind. The bay breeze drifted in through the open window, and birds started to chirp. The morning was here whether he wanted it to be or not. He rolled over and groaned, swung his legs out of bed, and stretched. *Coffee,* he thought, he needed coffee.

He crept down the hall so he wouldn't disturb Bree, but when he saw the door cracked, he couldn't help himself, he peered in. The sun cut a long triangle across the room casting her in an enchanting glow, making her look like an angel. He opened the door just a little wider, tempted to wake her with a long, slow kiss. Would she welcome it or punch him?

He heard the crunch of tires on gravel, signaling someone's arrival. He backed up, turned, and tiptoed downstairs, disappointed he wouldn't get to find out.

• • • •

BREE PUT ZYLAH ON HER leash and led her outside. They vis-ited the spot, and the puppy did her business, then walked down to where the three men stood. The sun shone bright and inviting, re-flecting off the water. The green grass quickly gave way to scorched grass that had been burned the previous night. Bree stopped at the edge beside them and noticed other officers. Some were in the brush, one was scouring the water's edge, and another taking pho-tos.

"Good morning, Bree," Detective Savard said, reaching out to shake her hand. "Looks like you had another rough night."

"You could say that. I'm surprised to see you here, for a fire."

"Well, the Chief called me. He said I'd better come take a look."

Bree turned to the older man and shook his hand too. "I want-ed to thank you and your crew from last night. I don't know what I would have done if you hadn't gotten here so quickly."

"All in a day's job, Miss Thompson. Glad we could help."

"Do you have any idea how it might have started?" Bree asked the chief.

"We were just going over that," he said slowly. "Looks like it started right at the edge of the dock there." He pointed.

"What are those spikes sticking out of the ground? And why isn't that grass as burnt as the other areas?" She took a step closer. "Are those pieces of paper stuck in the ground?" Bree questioned.

Ryker caught her arm. "Don't. They haven't finished pho-tographing the area."

There was a whistle and a wave from an officer down by the dock. "Excuse us a moment," Savard said to Bree, exchanging a look with the Chief. They walked into the charred grass toward the offi-cer.

"Ryker, what's going on?"

"Those stakes," he pointed. "They're holding down photos." He turned and looked at her, and dropped his voice low, "Of you."

"Me? I don't understand."

"They think it's some sort of warning. From what I gather, the fire was set and connected by some sort of chemical. Deliberately going wide in those areas leaving the photos almost untouched."

"What?" Without warning, Bree marched across the burnt ground and stopped at the first stake.

"Bree, you can look, but don't touch anything," Detective Savard called over to her.

Bree nodded, handed Zylah to Ryker, and squatted down. She gasped as she saw the first photo. It was an 8X10, slightly melted from the intense heat of the fire, but intact. It was her in the studio sitting at her computer. There was another a few feet away of her pulling weeds, her back to the camera. Bree went to another photo, an eerie feeling creeping slowly through her. This photo was of her and Zylah. That had to have been yesterday, she concluded. She moved carefully to the next one.

"Bree, you don't need to look at these right now," Ryker said, standing beside her with a wiggling puppy.

"I'm fine." She looked down. This one was of her asleep in her Adirondack chair. It had words scrawled on it, "I'm watching." A shiver ran down her spine. She stepped back. She steeled herself and forced herself to go look at the last one. Her stomach turned. It was a photo of her in her bra and underwear walking across the kitchen, carrying a basket of laundry. Scrawled at the bottom was "Always."

She stepped back, sick to her stomach.

"Are you okay?" Ryker asked.

"I'm fine. I just need a minute." She grabbed for the puppy and hurried back to the house.

Inside she let Zylah down. Her hands trembled as she poured puppy food into Zylah's bowl. She put it down, and then leaned over the sink, shaking; afraid she was going to be sick. What was she going to do? Who was doing this and what did they want? She needed to think. She was smart, or so she thought. She could figure this out. Needed to. Had to.

Ryker let himself in the slider. "Bree?" he asked tentatively. "Are you all right?"

She nodded, turned, and got out the coffee. "Would you like a cup?" she asked, trying to keep her hands from shaking and her voice even. She didn't want him to see her frightened.

"Yeah, I could use one."

He crossed over to her. He laid his hands on her shoulders. She stiffened.

"Let me help."

She sidestepped him. "No, I need to do it. I need to do something."

"Okay," he said and backed off.

The coffee was coming out in a steady stream when Detective Savard came to the back door, plastic bags in one hand. "Knock, knock," he called. "Bree, can I come in?"

"Of course."

Zylah scampered across the floor and yipped at him. He bent and rubbed her ears. "Cute puppy. Just get her?"

"Yes," Bree said, with a hint of a smile, "A gift from Ryker. Coffee, Detective?"

"Yes, please." He petted the pup and waited until Bree had poured him a cup, then brought it over to him. "I see you got some furniture."

"My aunt sent some of my things. They arrived yesterday."

"Can we sit at the table?" He indicated the dining room.

"Certainly." She led the way and took a seat.

"Do you mind if I join you?" Ryker asked.

"It's okay with me, as long as Bree doesn't mind."

Somewhere along the lines, Ryker had wiggled his way into her house, into the investigation, and into her heart. And right now, she didn't care. She hated to admit it, but she really did want him here. "It's fine with me."

Savard laid the photos in the bags on the table. "I know this is upsetting, but I need you to look at these. And tell me what you see."

Bree braced herself to look at them again. There was nothing menacing about them except for the cryptic handwriting on the bottom of two of the photos. Otherwise, it was just her carrying on with everyday life, completely unaware someone was watching her. Stalking her. She took a deep breath. "Well, they're all obviously of me. Taken at different times of the day and from far away. This one's my studio, taken through the window." She lifted it, shifted it over. "This one is me outside, back by the garage. These other two, I'm outside also," she said, lifting one of her and Zylah, the other in the Adirondack chairs.

The one that made her pause was the one of her in her bra and underwear. This was the second time he had caught her half-naked. Suddenly, she was pissed. She should damn well be able to walk around her own house half-naked without wondering if some pervert was watching her. "And this one," she tossed it back down disgusted, it slid across the table and stopped in front of Ryker. "Is me in the kitchen."

Savard watched her and Ryker, trying to judge their different reactions to the photographs. Bree had gone from scared to pissed in an instant, and Ryker sat back silently watching, a noncommittal look on his face.

He straightened, reached out, and piled the pictures together. Handing them to Bree, he asked, "Do you think you could put these in chronological order?"

Bree shrugged, "I guess. This one of me and Zylah is the newest. That was yesterday."

"Let's put it at the end." Savard slid it over. "Zylah? That's an interesting name. How did you come up with that?"

"It was Ryker's idea."

"Really?" He scrutinized Ryker as he asked, "So what made you think of Zylah?"

Ryker shrugged. "She looks like a little princess. And I'm not into Disney, so the only other one I know is Princess Zylah from the Black Shadow."

"The Black Shadow?" Savard questioned, then looked at Bree.

"I know how it sounds. But in his defense, he doesn't know and it fits her." They all glanced over at the little puppy sprawled out on the rug, chew toy clenched in her teeth, fast asleep.

"What don't I know?" Ryker asked.

"We'll get to that in a minute," Savard said. "Back to the pictures. Which one do you think is first?"

"I would say . . . this one." Bree picked up the one of her half-naked. "Because it doesn't look like I have any curtains or blinds up yet. Then I would say . . . the studio." She looked at the others and tried to remember when she had pulled weeds. "I'd say this one when I was asleep, then this one. And again, the one with Zylah last."

"Okay, that was my guess as to the order too."

"Why does it matter?"

Savard held up a finger. "Flip them over, keep them in order."

She did as he asked. That's when she noticed the words scrawled on the back. Each picture had one or two words scribbled on it. And since she had them in chronological order, they made a short phrase. *In the shadow of the black moon.*

"What's that supposed to mean?" Bree asked with a sharp hitch to her voice.

"I was hoping you could tell me," Savard said.

"I don't have any idea."

"And what about you, Ryker? Any thoughts?" Savard asked.

"No, should I?"

Savard didn't answer directly. "The Black Shadow, huh? Are you a big fan?"

"Yeah, Sam and I have seen them all."

"Who's your favorite character?"

Ryker laughed. "Not sure what this has to do with anything." He sat back in his chair and crossed his arms. "But what the heck, I'll bite. Theo Knight is my favorite."

"Not Kage Xyon?"

"Nope. That was Sam. Can you see me as a warrior prince? I'm definitely more of a pilot, a smuggler. More of a love 'em and leave 'em kinda guy like Theo." He winked at Bree.

Savard nodded and waited for him to go on. "Anything else?"

Ryker cocked his head. "I already told you my favorite Princess is Zylah. Can't get the princess if I'm her brother, now, can I?" Ryker glanced down as his cell phone chimed. "I need to take this if you'll excuse me a minute?"

Bree waited until they heard Ryker go out the door. "Where are you going with all this? Do you think Ryker is Kage?"

"I don't know Bree, but I have to check all my facts, look in every direction, and treat everyone as a suspect." He waited for her to say something, but she didn't. "Aren't you the one who told me he had a motive? That he wanted this house. The one *you* own?"

"Yes, but . . ."

"But what? Go with your instincts, Bree." He waited. "Tell me what you're thinking."

"Well, it's like he said. He doesn't fit the Kage profile. He *is* more of a Theo Knight. The way he's built, the way he acts, the way he looks. His boat is even named after the Shadow Jumper, Theo Knight's spaceship."

"Let's suppose he just picked Kage as a decoy, a way to throw us off. It still doesn't change the fact that he loves the Black Shadow, or that he's always around when these . . . we will call them crimes . . . for lack of a better term, happen to you. He was here last night."

"Yes, but he never left. Ryker couldn't have done it. He was the last one to leave and was outside talking to Officer Kilpatrick when the fire started. Ryker never had a chance because I was with him all night."

Savard knew she was right. Kilpatrick had corroborated that same story earlier. But it didn't change the fact that he wanted the house and he was a big Black Shadow fan. But then according to Ryker, Sam Harris was too. He had all the same access to the house that Ryker James had. Maybe Sam was secretly mad because his friend didn't get the house, and was taking it out on Bree. Or maybe Harris wanted it for himself.

Savard felt like he was going in circles.

The detective's beeper went off, just as Ryker stepped back into the house. "Bree, I have to run. And Ryker, I'm going to need your shoes. There was a boot print found down by the center of the fire. My man will be in shortly to get it. Since you spent the night, I'm assuming those are the same shoes you had on last night?"

"Yes, they are. Am I a suspect?"

"Everyone's a suspect until they're not." Savard turned to Bree. "Call me if you need anything." Savard let himself out the door.

Chapter 28

Bree placed her hands on either side of the motorcycle and laced her fingers through the little metal bars on the side of the seat. Ryker took his time and drove slowly along Ocean Gateway, crossing the Harry W. Kelley Memorial Bridge into Ocean City. The streets were full of cars and people as tourists descended in anticipation of the upcoming Memorial Day weekend.

He turned right at Entry Park and drove south down Philadelphia Avenue, curved around First Street, and pulled into Inlet Park. They saw a few old men fishing off the Inlet Jetty, families unloading strollers, and teenagers talking they leaned against cars as Ryker parked the bike. He cut the engine as a group of guys hanging out near a truck yelled his name. He gave a nod and kicked the stand into place.

The ocean air caressed Bree's skin as she swung her leg off the motorcycle. She needed to get out, away from the house. Even though she had hesitated when Ryker suggested it, she was already glad he had talked her into coming. She needed to be around people.

They walked through the parking lot towards the Boardwalk, as others called out, and waved to Ryker. Bree took note of how many women turned their heads to watch Ryker walk by.

Luscious scents like french fries and fudge drifted toward her as they walked the Boardwalk. They passed the rides, carnival games, and a sideshow.

People sat on benches eating ice cream, popcorn, or large slices of pizza. Bree's mouth watered.

"What's your favorite thing to eat at the Boardwalk?" Bree asked Ryker as they strolled down the concrete walk.

"Probably pizza if I want actual food. Otherwise, I like to get taffy."

"Taffy?"

He nodded. "Yeah, saltwater taffy." He reached for her hand and pulled her past a few T-shirt and souvenir shops. "Here," he pointed.

There was a small brightly colored glass storefront with huge glass cases filled with taffy that looked like large pieces of confetti piled behind the glass. Decorative paper bags and buckets were filled with specific kinds of taffy or an assorted mix, ready for purchase. Long, silver, metal beaters churned behind the counter and stretched pink and blue taffy in large drums.

"Want some?" he asked.

She nodded.

He pulled out his wallet and purchased a mixed bag. He thanked the cashier who smiled up at him sweetly and turned to Bree. "Try one."

She pulled out a yellow one, unwrapped it, and popped it in her mouth. "Oh, yum. It's banana."

"Good, right?" he put a pink one in his mouth and chewed.

Bree nodded reaching for a white with a red stripe. "I could eat the whole bag."

He laughed. "How about we get some real food?"

"I could eat."

"We could grab a slice of pizza or a hot dog. What do you think?"

"Pizza's good."

Ryker handed her the paper bag of taffy. "Hold that and I'll get the pizza. Do you want a soda?"

"I'll split one with you."

Ryker ordered two slices and a soda. He handed the soda to Bree as a couple of women called his name. He waved. They then proceeded to carry the pizza over to the concrete wall that bordered the edge of the boardwalk, looking for a place to sit. They wandered down until the concrete turned to boards, and found an opening big enough for both of them and sat, their legs hanging over the side, facing the Atlantic.

Bree inserted two straws into the tiny hole on top of the soda and placed it between them and asked, "Do you know everyone?"

Ryker handed her a slice and took a gooey bite of his, savoring it. "Not everyone."

"It seems like you do, especially the women. I think you've turned every woman's head and melted every young girl's heart that we passed."

He laughed his deep sexy laugh. "Not quite."

Sitting here amongst a crowd, Bree relaxed and was able to really enjoy sitting next to a sexy man that others couldn't keep their eyes off of. Was he aware of his pure magnetism? How others were drawn to him, turned to look at him, just so he could briefly acknowledge them? She doubted he knew the real power he held, which in Bree's eyes made him all the more attractive.

"So," he said, drawing out the word. "Do you want to talk about what's been happening? Maybe fill me in on what I've missed?"

Bree didn't answer. She just took another bite and stared out at the ocean.

Ryker cleared his throat and tried again. "I got the feeling Savard considers me a suspect." He waited for a beat. "Do you?"

Bree turned to face him and said bluntly, "I have."

"Why?" Ryker asked the surprise evident in his voice. "What have I done to make you think I would be the one behind this?"

It was now or never. Bree decided to confront him point-blank. But first, she wanted to get away from the crowd. She glanced around. "I think we should walk. Go down by the water, where it's more private."

He agreed and finished the last of his pizza, took a drink, and handed the soda back to Bree. He jumped down off the wall landing in the sand, then turned and helped her down. The soda finished, they tossed the cup and the rest of their trash into a receptacle.

They walked in silence to the water's edge. Slipping off their shoes, they walked on the wet sand for a while not saying anything as the waves rushed in and out pulling the sand from beneath their feet.

"Okay, I can't take it any longer." Ryker reached for her arm and gently turned her toward him. "Let's have it. Why do you suspect me?"

She took a deep breath, looked up into those blue eyes, and asked, "Is it true you started the rumor that my house is haunted?"

"Yes," he answered truthfully.

She looked at him seriously. "You admitted you wanted my house. That could be considered a motive, add in the ghost."

"Wanting a house is a far cry from stalking you and trying to burn the place to the ground."

She shrugged, mentally changed directions. "I was told the Hennings wouldn't sell to you. Why?"

"I dated their daughter."

"That's it?" When he didn't elaborate, she added, "There has to be more to it than that."

This time he shrugged. "Apparently, I was just some misunderstood, dark, and dangerous teenage boy that their precious, only daughter got caught up with."

Bree raised both her eyebrows, questioning him.

"It's really more innocent than it's been made out to be. We got caught making out in my car in the church parking lot by the pastor. Her parents were humiliated. They forbid us to see each other again." He smiled at the memory. "But as I'm sure you're aware when teenagers are forbidden to do something, it only makes them want it more. We started sneaking around. She started climbing out her bedroom window to meet me. One thing led to another . . . The next time we got caught, we were . . . Let's just say, the minister saw a lot more than he bargained for." He grinned.

Bree tried not to smile; she could picture Ryker as the bad boy, the rebellious teenager all too well. She mentally shifted back to the present and assessed the situation.

"You couldn't buy the house from the Hennings, but no one could stop you from buying from the next owner. And lucky for you the next owner was a single woman that you could either manipulate or scare into selling." She watched him struggle to keep his face neutral. She straightened and placed a hand on her hip. "Don't pretend the thought didn't cross your mind."

Ryker cocked his head and gazed down at her. "I'd be lying if I said it didn't. But I hope you know me well enough by now to know I wouldn't stoop to breaking into your house and destroying your property. Or watching you and taking photos of you half-naked. Believe me when I say, if I want to see you naked, I'll do it without the aid of a camera. And you'll be fully aware of my intentions."

He looked at her so intently, Bree couldn't help but blush.

"But what he's doing . . . these stalking or peeping tom tendencies, whatever you want to call it. Seeing those photos of you today really disturbed me. You were completely unaware of being photographed. That's a total pervert in my book. Whoever did that is plain sick."

A shiver ran up Bree's spine. "I agree with that statement."

"Then there's the fire last night. That's some serious shit, Bree." He looked at her intently. "You can't possibly think I did that?"

She looked away from those deep blue eyes and out to the ocean, watching the waves roll, contemplating. "No, I don't. Actually," she looked back at him. "That's what turned the tide for me, so to speak. There's no possible way you would have had time to do that because I was with you the entire time . . . but," her voice trailed off.

"But what?"

"If you're not doing it, it seems like someone is trying to make it look like you are."

He scrubbed his hands over his face. "This is disturbing on so many levels. I need to sit down."

"Where?"

He pointed. "The lifeguard chair. It's big enough for both of us and has a great view."

They walked in silence, left their shoes at the bottom, then climbed up the wooden rungs and sat. No matter how Bree shifted, she couldn't create any space between them. The heat radiated out from him and made it hard for her to focus. All too aware of Ryker, Bree fidgeted, nervous. She opened the taffy bag and dug through it to give herself something to do other than think about how close she was to him.

"Tell me, what else points to me? What besides wanting to buy the house has given you a reason to think I might be behind it?"

She unwrapped a green piece and popped it in her mouth, giving herself a minute. She swallowed hard. Did she trust him? The answer was yes, despite the evidence.

"First, you have access to the house. It would make it easy for you to come in anytime you wanted, move stuff around. For example, my silverware or the coffee."

"Do you think I would do that petty stuff?"

"I'm not saying you would, but you have access, is what I'm saying." She shifted sideways, tucked her leg up under her, and looked directly at him.

"I'm not the only one with access. Sam had a key. And what about the real estate office? They might have still had keys."

"That's a good point. We will have to revisit that thought, but right now you're the only one with a motive." She placed a hand on his arm seeing him tense. "Just listen."

He shifted too, held her gaze. "I'll try, but it's not easy to sit here and feel like you think I'm some psycho or pervert."

"I know. I'm sorry . . ." She hesitated, not sure how to soothe him. "Try to be objective and listen to how incriminating it all sounds. Try to look at it from my point of view."

He grunted, clearly put off.

She held out her fingers and ticked off points. "First, my water heater is shut off. You were the last one down there the day before. Second, I get locked in the attic stairwell because I go up and check on a noise which turned out to be the banging door. Again, you were the last one up there. Next, I get locked outside of my own house. You were the last one to leave that day," Bree paused, watching him process it.

"You're right. I didn't realize all that. It really does make me look bad."

Bree nodded, a little softer she said, "Add in the ghost story . . . and the Black Shadow thing."

"Wait," he cocked a dark eyebrow. "What about the Black Shadow?"

"I've been getting threatening emails from someone named Kage, and you're into the Black Shadow."

"You're kidding, right?"

"I wish I were. Now that I think about it, that's actually how it started."

"What did the emails say?"

"At first they were about my work. They came in on my website. He said that I wasn't a good photographer. Then it switched to creepy, he was watching me, and then that I took something from him. He specifically said "*You took what was mine*" in an email and that's also what he carved into my floor. I just assumed once I found out that you wanted the house, that's what Kage was referring to."

Ryker leaned forward and tucked a wisp of her long brown hair behind her ear.

"Let's take the house out of it for a moment. Assume it has nothing to do with it. What else could it possibly be that you might have taken from someone? Man or woman."

"That's just it. I don't have anything else."

"Does Savard have any ideas?"

Bree shrugged. "He asked about my family's will, but that's a dead-end, literally. Everything my parents had was left to me and my sister. And my sister . . ." Bree's voice hitched.

Ryker put his hand on top of hers. "It's all right, don't say it. There's no one else that stands to inherit?"

"No."

"There has to be something else. Something we're missing. Something you either don't know you have or that's not of much significance to you, but is to him."

"What do you think this last message means? You're a Black Shadow fan. Does a black moon mean anything to you?"

"Not really. The only thing I can think of related to the Black Shadow is that there were Black Moon Warriors." Ryker reached for his phone. He Googled *Black Moon* and the *Black Shadow.*

Bree leaned in close to see.

"Here . . . looks like Kage Xyon was Grand Master of the regiment. I don't remember that in the movies. Looks like it was just referred to in comic books. But there was a black moon emblem on all their uniforms."

"We're back to square one."

They fell silent for a moment, thinking, and the world around them slowly came back into focus. The sun had sunk behind them as they talked, casting long shadows across the cooling sand. Off in the distance, lights winked on the Boardwalk. The Ferris wheel spun in a slow, enchanting circle of neon lights. People screamed as a slingshot catapulted them into the night sky. The long cables stretched tight and shot them plummeting back towards the ground with another round of screams.

The air was growing chilly, and Bree shivered.

"Come here," Ryker said, pulling her close and slipping his arm around her. His body heat engulfed her as she relaxed into him. His voice was deep but softer. "I'm sorry this is happening to you, Bree. I truly am. You don't deserve this. I hope you know by now I would never do anything like this to hurt you." He kissed the top of her head, and she fell a little further for him.

The moon was up and it was bright, and hanging low over the Atlantic. The pale moonlight shimmered across the darkening water. Bree melted into Ryker laying her head on his shoulder, drawing in the scent of his aftershave. It was a deep musky scent, dark and seductive, much like the man. She felt as if she could stay next to him forever.

But she shouldn't, she scolded herself. She needed to keep her distance, just in case. In case he was somehow tied to what was happening, and he really was the playboy she suspected.

She still didn't have an answer to the whole Sheri question either. Were they or weren't they a couple? What if it was truly only one-sided? Sitting here with him now, she felt like it was. Prayed it was. She was already headed down the road to heartbreak if it wasn't.

Straightening, she said, "We should probably go home. Zylah will need to go out soon."

"You're probably right. It will take a little while to get back to the bike. I didn't realize we walked this far." He climbed down and helped her. His hands were on her waist. He smiled at her. "Not going to punch me, are you?"

"No, why would I?"

"Because the last time we were near a lifeguard stand, you did."

"Last time you gave me a reason to. Are you going to this time?"

He cocked his head to one side and gave her that heartbreaking smile. "No Champ, I learned my lesson." His hands were still on her waist and his eyes flicked down to her lips and lingered. When they returned to lock with hers, they were dark with desire.

A vision of them dropping down on the sand ran through her mind. With great effort, she stepped back. His hands dropped to his sides.

"We should go."

He didn't say anything, just stuffed his hands in his pockets.

She bent and picked up her shoes, and they started back.

• • • •

HE SAT ON THE EDGE of his chair and dug through the cardboard box. Of course, the one he wanted was at the bottom. Wasn't that always the way? He took them out one by one and lined them up on the window sill placing each action figure. He had them all: warriors and side characters. He placed Theo Knight in the middle, and right beside him, directly in the center, the one he'd been looking for: Kage.

He held him up and examined him from every angle. Kage Xyon. The chosen one. The good guy. The hero. But he had an evil side to him too that tugged at him. Just like his father, who'd once been good and decent until he'd met a beautiful woman. A woman that had corrupted him and turned him against his family.

He pulled out a photograph he had taken of Bree and examined it. Bree Thompson was that kind of a woman. She had big kind eyes, long golden hair, and a tender heart. He had to physically shake himself to keep from falling for her himself. She was just a woman after all. *The* woman who had changed everything.

And that was what had happened to his father too. He'd been a decent guy, even though his mother never talked about him much, or let him see him. He had sent gifts religiously for his birthday and for Christmas. He would call on Easter and Thanksgiving, and send chocolate on Valentine's Day.

On his eighth birthday, his father called and asked if he could come to take him out for lunch and maybe catch the new Black Shadow movie that was out. Surprisingly, his mother had said yes. From then on, they bonded over the Black Shadow. It was their thing, something his mother didn't understand as she had never seen a movie or read the comics. It became so important to them that his father even came up with a CB handle of Shadow Man. Which fit perfectly because his dad drove a black semi and drove the night shift, joking he only drove by the light of the moon which was the Black Shadow's symbol. And he was his Kage Xyon the prince of the Black Shadow.

But then almost a year ago, that fateful day on the highway changed everything.

He lifted the picture of Bree and scrutinized it. He thought about how naive she was. How she walked around the house half-naked like she didn't have a care in the world. Didn't she sense him watching? She did now; he smiled at that thought but then frowned.

Why couldn't Bree Thompson have been in the minivan with the rest of her family? Why couldn't she have died like the rest of them? If she had, his father would have never met her. He would have never held Bree back from the fire and felt sorry for her or wept for her family.

She would have simply perished in flames with the rest of them. And then, maybe, his father would still be alive.

He tossed her picture to the side and twirled Kage Xyon in the palm of his hand. Like Kage, he could feel the dark power inside him. Only unlike Kage, he would let it consume him, he couldn't resist. He held the prince up into the light of the moon.

The moon was shining its pale luminous light through the window. He looked at it and smiled. Would she get his clue? Would she figure it out in time? Did she realize she only had days left to live?

Five days. That wasn't much time. He had a lot to do, a lot to plan. He didn't have all the details ironed out yet, but it was forming in the back of his mind. It wouldn't really be like the Black Shadow, even though he so wanted it to be. But he would do his best.

Kage had been changed by the loss of his father, and so had he.

He pulled out a small handgun from the box under his bed. The gun his father had left him. The circle of life would be complete when it snuffed out the enemy. He stared down the short barrel of the gun and aimed it at a photo of Bree Thompson. Once the enemy was vanquished then all would be right with the world.

Chapter 29

It started small. Just a tiny spark in a great vast void of ebony darkness. Then it grew, casting a glow. At first, it seemed inviting, enticing even. It looked like a sparkler on the Fourth of July. But it grew quickly, getting larger. It started to snake out in every direction as if it had a life of its own. It snapped, popped, and hissed. The small sizzle grew and grew until it was a roar. The sound engulfed her. Then the screams started. She could hear them. Her mother. Her sister. Could hear her father calling out.

She could see shadows reaching, clawing. Arms outstretched. Hands. She saw metal twist and warp. Flashing in the bright light of the fire. Then the smells came. Smoke. Gas. Ash. And hot metal burning.

The pure white-hot heat poured over her. She writhed and wriggled. The fire touched her skin and scorched her hair. She cried out in terror as the flames engulfed her.

Bree sat upright in bed, drenched in sweat and panting. She fumbled in the darkness trying to get out of the tangle of sheets. Zylah padded over and yipped at the edge of the bed, paws outstretched, and tail wagging.

"Oh, Zylah!" Bree said scooping up the puppy and snuggling her in close. "I'm so glad I have you." The puppy lavished Bree with kisses all over her hands and arms as Bree sat in the darkness and wept.

Minutes passed and the crying jag ended. Bree sniffed and wiped at her eyes with the back of her hand. The sun was just peeking out over the horizon, and spongy light filtered through the drawn curtains.

Bree went over to the window and drew them back, unlatching the French doors she stepped out into the early morning air. She stood for a moment and enjoyed the fresh air, but then the thought flooded through her. What if he was watching? What if he was somewhere out there right now, searching for her with his lens? Bree shuddered and quickly turned on her heel. Calling Zylah to follow, she disappeared back inside, locking the door behind her.

Downstairs, she took the dog out, and then made coffee. She fed Zylah and was about to sit and drink her coffee when the large envelope on the windowsill caught her eye. She had completely forgotten about it. She picked it up and read the return address again. *Heffner Attorney at Law, Kansas City, Kansas.* This wasn't her lawyer. She pulled out a butter knife and slit the end of the manila envelope. Bree pulled out the paperwork and gasped as she realized what she held. With a shaky hand, she picked up the phone and dialed Savard's number. He answered on the first ring.

"I think I just found out what I took," she said in a wary voice.

Savard didn't hesitate, "I'll be right over."

After only twenty minutes Savard arrived. Followed closely by Ryker, because Bree had called him shortly after Savard.

"So, this is about money. A will?" Ryker questioned.

"Looks that way," Savard answered.

"Can you catch me up here? Remind me, who is Garth Snader?"

"He's the man that was driving the tractor-trailer that killed my family," Bree answered softly.

"Was he convicted?"

"Yes, he was convicted of vehicular manslaughter. Which, Bree, I know you are aware he paid the maximum fine, lost his driver's license, but didn't serve any jail time."

"Why didn't he serve time?" Ryker demanded. He didn't know the Thompsons, but he knew Bree, and that was enough for him to be on the defensive. "He killed three people."

"It was an accident," Bree whispered. "He had a seizure, causing him to blackout for a few seconds, which caused him . . ."

"To lose control," Savard finished for her. "They ruled it an accident due to a medical condition." Savard looked from Ryker to Bree. "I'm not sure if you heard? But I guess now, with this you might have figured it out. Mr. Snader passed away about three months ago."

"He actually was a very nice man," Bree said quietly. "I wanted so much to dislike him, hate him even, but I couldn't. He was genuinely as devastated as I was. He begged for my forgiveness and offered to help me in any way he could. I told him there wasn't anything he could do." Bree lifted the papers. "This . . . I never expected. I can't believe he did this."

"The lawyer needs to be contacted. Do you think you could make the call now, Bree? See if we can get some answers?" Savard asked.

Bree swallowed hard. "Yes, I guess I can."

Ryker handed Bree her cell. "Make the call."

Chapter 30

It didn't take long for the day to turn warm and sunny. After Savard and Ryker left, Bree took Zylah out for a long walk along the edge of the water. The puppy ran and explored to her heart's delight.

It took all of Bree's willpower to go in around lunchtime and head upstairs to the studio to work. She had a lot to get done. There were orders to fill, emails to check, and a blog to write.

With two of the three things on her list done, she allowed herself a half hour to upload the photos she took of her own house; the before and after shots. She pulled up the original photo she took the day she had bought the house, split the screen, and placed the current updated one beside it. She marveled at the difference. Gone was the weather-beaten broken house that had withstood the elements. It was replaced by a freshly painted, pristine, and elegant home, yet the wistful and romantic side of it still shown through in all its glory.

She smiled at the next one that Greg had taken of her next to the sold sign. She enlarged it and focused on her face. What had she been feeling at that moment? Nervous. Proud. Excited. And even sad. She could remember those feelings perfectly as they tumbled around and twisted her stomach in knots. Thrilled to have the house. Nervous about sinking so much money into it. And sad because her family wasn't there with her. That they wouldn't see it . . . ever, and share in her joy.

She had been scarred and in need of repair just like the house. And somehow in the slow day-by-day process of remodeling the house, and building the studio, not only was the structure transformed but so was she.

She wasn't a fool. She wasn't completely healed. Bree feared she never would be, but she was healing, and this house, this place, these friends she was making were a good start.

Bree scrolled through the rest of the pictures. She had the before and after of the widow's walk, her studio, and the patio. She wanted to make sure she got pictures of the kitchen as tomorrow was demo day.

She opened a new file and saved the photos and labeled it. She would show them to Ryker and Sam, let them choose so Colette could update their website.

Before she closed out, Bree clicked on the photo she had taken of both men just for fun.

Her heart skipped a beat as she enlarged it. They stood on her patio, shirts off and posed, sledgehammers slung over their outside shoulders. The sun glistened off their tanned bodies, as they stood bare-chested, slightly sweaty, muscles flexed, side by side, grinning. Even if you didn't know them you would be able to tell they were best friends, loving what they did. If Bolts & Beams used this as a cover photo on their website, they'd have every female between the ages of sixteen and sixty hiring them.

She tried not to think about Ryker's arms around her, holding her on the beach. She sighed, letting her chin rest in the palm of her hand, and just admired him. Bree jumped as if caught ogling when her cellphone rang.

"Hey, Champ. What are you doin'?"

Bree blushed at the sound of his voice. "Working. And you?"

"Same. You doin' all right after what you found out this morning?"

Bree thought of the will and the sweet man that had bequeathed her his life savings, trying desperately to replace something, anything, of what she'd lost. "I guess. I just can't help but wonder . . ." she couldn't finish the sentence.

"Wonder what?" He waited, when she didn't say anything, he prompted her. "Tell me, Bree."

"No, not now. I'm not ready to talk about it. I'm still digesting something that Savard told me earlier today."

"Do you have plans for tonight?"

"I'm emptying my kitchen cabinets in anticipation of tomorrow. Why?"

"That won't take long, I've seen the inside of your cabinets. They're practically bare. Let's have dinner together. I'll pick you up around six."

"Ryker . . . You can't just expect me to drop everything when you say. I have work to do. I have to finish my blog, clear out the cabinets, walk and feed Zylah. . ."

He cut her off. "You have an hour and a half to finish your blog and take Zylah out for a walk. If you don't get the cabinets cleared out before I get there, I'll come thirty minutes early and help you in the morning. It's going to be a beautiful night. I want to take you out on the water. I'll drop anchor and we can eat on the boat. There's nothing that the wind and the waves can't cure. At least for a little while, anyway. Plus, what better company could you ask for?" He waited a beat. "Come on, what do you say? You know you want to. You can't say no to me."

"I most certainly could say no to you. You're not irresistible, you know?" She wondered if he knew it was a lie. She couldn't say no, even if she wanted to. But she didn't want to. She wanted to go. More than anything. She tried to come across as aloof, but appreciative. "Actually Ryker, that sounds wonderful. I could use a break." *From work. From her thoughts.*

She could hear the smile in his voice. Could tell he was pleased. "I'll order Chinese. See you at six."

The next hour and a half flew by. She wrote her blog, walked Zylah, and changed her outfit at least half a dozen times, settling for her favorite pair of white capris, and a blue blouse that had a softly scooped neckline. Since she was going to be on the water, she swept her hair up into a messy bun, determined to pin it down and keep it out of her face. She put small silver hoops in her ears and silver around her neck.

Bree heard the motorcycle coming and knew the minute it turned down her lane. She checked her appearance in the mirror. Casual, simple. *Not overly done,* she thought. She didn't want to come off like she was trying too hard since she wasn't sure if this was a real date or not. Nonetheless, she all but skipped down the stairs in anticipation.

When she opened the door, he was instantly at a loss for words. Damn if she didn't look good enough to eat. He cleared his throat and ran a hand across his mouth, afraid he was drooling. *Keep it light, you idiot.* "You clean up pretty good, Champ."

She smiled, melting his heart.

"Thanks."

"You ready?"

"Yes, but come in for a minute. I want to let Zylah out one last time. I hate for her to have an accident when she's been doing so well."

She held the door open for him and he caught the soft, alluring scent of her that whispered over her skin as he passed. It was all he could do to keep walking, and not turn around and pin her to the wall. He needed to keep his distance until the blood returned to his head.

"I'll take the dog out to do her business," he said gruffly, cursing himself inwardly. "You grab your shoes and a jacket. It gets cold out on the boat after sunset." He scooped up Zylah, carried her out, and deposited her in the spot.

It only took a couple of minutes and Zylah came bounding back. She scampered at his feet, trying desperately to lavish his boots with puppy kisses. His demeanor softened. "You're all right, for such a little thing," he said, reaching down to pet the puppy.

She dashed in front of him and darted back into the house. Bree was waiting with fresh water, a puppy treat, and a chew toy. When she had Zylah situated in her crate, she stood, ready to go.

"Takeout should be arriving just as we get back," Ryker said, waiting for Bree as she flipped on the outside lights and locked the house.

"You good?" he asked as he watched her tuck the keys in her purse and slip it over her shoulder. She nodded. He swung his leg over his bike and hit the throttle. Revving the engine, he gave her a nod, and she climbed on.

The second she wrapped her arms around his waist, he hit the gas and they tore off down the driveway spewing gravel. He slowed and took the corner easily. He drove through the back roads and onto a few city streets, working his way across to his house. They cruised into his neighborhood and pulled up at the same time as the carryout did.

Ryker stopped, pulled out his wallet, and handed Bree a twenty. "Can you pay while I put my bike away? I'll meet you out back."

Bree accepted the twenty and went to get the takeout. Ryker emerged from the detached garage at the same time Bree came around the house. They grabbed a few more things then loaded up the boat.

He stowed the food in a cooler, untied the boat, and started the engine. "Take a seat anywhere you like. There's not much of a breeze, and the sky's clear so I thought we could go out to the Atlantic and eat if you're all right with that?"

"Sounds good to me." Bree took the seat next to him and settled in for the ride.

Ryker glided away from the dock and out to where the inlet opened into the bay. Bree waved at a couple of little boys who were perched on the end of the dock fishing, they eagerly waved back.

They passed a family on a pontoon coming back in. Once safely past them, Ryker opened it up. The front of the boat lifted as he increased the speed, then leveled out as the 25-footer cut neatly through the water. They made their way across the bay, passing several other boats that were anchored. The waves from Ryker's boat sent them all gently swaying as they sped by.

Riding in silence they enjoyed the warm air, the waves, and the scenery. White fluffy clouds drifted overhead looking pure white against the soft blue. Ryker slowed as he came to the Ocean Gateway Bridge. They waited with other boats as it lifted, the line of cars increased, and then they passed under. He puttered along the Inlet until he could see nothing but blue and the horizon. Through the no-wake zone, he once again opened it up and swung a wide arc, heading south down along Assateague Island.

Bree watched Ryker as he stood at the helm looking carefree and comfortable, tall and confident. He had an edge of cockiness about him as he half grinned and swung wide again. She could tell that this was what he lived for. Moments like these spent in pure pleasure. After about ten minutes of pure speed, Ryker cut the engine and let the boat glide and come to a slow drift.

He turned to Bree, beaming. "Hungry?"

"Starving."

"Then let's eat." He dropped anchor as they floated about a hundred yards off the coast, then proceeded to grab the cooler that was filled with the takeout. "There are drinks under the bench," he indicated with a point of his finger.

Bree stood and lifted the seat, snagged a couple of sodas, and replaced the cushion.

"Let's eat in the bow."

Bree walked up and sat next to Ryker. He flipped the lid on the cooler and unearthed the food.

"I hope you're not too picky. I got a couple of different kinds."

"I'm not."

"There are plates, utensils, and napkins in the bag."

They sat, knees touching, as the boat slowly rocked and they dished up.

"Not a chopstick kind of guy?" Bree asked, in between bites.

"No, I don't have the patience to try to figure them out. You either?"

"Nope, my fingers aren't that coordinated. But my mom could," Bree stated, and then had a tiny pang in her heart. "She tried to teach us all, but without any success. Too impatient, I guess. We would always break out the silverware after only a couple of minutes." Bree wagged her fork at Ryker. "You never told me. Do you have a big family?"

"I'm the youngest of three boys. My oldest brother Rick is married and has a baby on the way. Ron's engaged. Both my parents still work. Mom's a nurse, and dad has his own accounting firm. Everyone lives in the area. Always have, and always will." He scooped a second helping of sticky rice on his plate.

"It's beautiful here. I can see why." They ate in silence for a couple of minutes, enjoying the food as the boat slowly rocked.

"So how about you?" he asked, stabbing a piece of General Tso's chicken. "Born and raised in Kansas?"

She nodded and took a sip of her soda. "Yes, all my family is there. My grandparents, aunts, uncles, and cousins. The Thompsons and Ellisons have lived there for generations. I'm the first to move this far away." She sat back, full.

"Did you get enough?"

"Yes, thank you."

He folded one white container shut. She leaned forward to help him. His fingers brushed hers accidentally while tucking the containers back into the cooler. He had to try hard to concentrate on what he was doing and not how soft her hands were. He pulled out a trash bag from a side pocket and they stuck their plates in it. "Were you planning on leaving, moving away before the accident?" he asked, deciding this was a delicate subject. But he wanted to know. Correction, he needed to know if this was a short-term, knee-jerk reaction for her, or if she planned on making this move permanent.

She hesitated, then sat back, slipping off her sandals and curling up protectively on the long bench. She smoothed the tiny pieces of her hair that had escaped.

"I always wanted to travel, to explore. See new places and have new experiences. But as far as actually moving away from Kansas? I don't know."

"But now that you're here? Seems like you're making it a permanent thing. Or is this just a project for you? The house. Something to do to keep your mind off the loss you've experienced?"

She hesitated. "I'd say I came here out of desperation. Out of a need to get away. Change the scenery, change my outlook. I needed someplace to go, to be, that every time I turned around, I didn't have something or someone reminding me of what I had lost."

He shifted over and sat closer to her. The boat rocked in the movement. "And now?"

She shrugged, gave him a whisper of a smile. "It was only supposed to be a two-week vacation. Something my mother had planned for their anniversary. It was something we had dreamed about for months. My sister and I had always wanted to see the ocean. To lie on the beach in bikinis. To ride the waves on boogie boards or go parasailing over the water."

He reached for her long legs, she let him uncurl them, placing them over his lap. He toyed with the delicate chain around her right ankle. "Is that why you wear this?" He fingered the charm.

She smiled. "Yes, my mother gave my sister and me both matching wave charms for Christmas when they told us of the trip. Neither of us ever took them off once we got them. Gracie was buried with hers."

He saw the shimmer of tears. "Hey, I'm sorry. I didn't mean to upset you."

She reached over and touched his arm. "It's okay. Even though it makes me sad, it still feels good to talk about them. Every day it gets a little better."

He placed his hand there on her bare skin and left it. "Let's go back and talk about you on the beach in a bikini. I'm imagining a little white skimpy thing. Showing off every curve, every inch of tanned skin." His blue eyes shot hot, intense, dangerous darts through her heart. "You don't happen to have it underneath there, do you?" he said, reaching for her.

She swatted him and laughed. "Keep it clean Mr. James. I can see where your thoughts are going."

Movement across the water caught his eye. "Look," he pointed, "On the beach."

Bree turned her gaze in the direction he indicated. There were half a dozen ponies in varying shades of nutmeg and brown, walking along the edge of the beach. All of them had their heads down, grazing on the short grass, except one. He was a little taller than the others and his head was facing out towards the water, towards them.

"Oh, I wish I had my camera," Bree whispered. "I can't believe I didn't bring it."

Ryker chuckled. "Do you take that camera everywhere?"

"Pretty much. That way I don't forget or miss moments like this. A photo like that would sell."

"There are other ways to capture a moment, and know that you will remember it forever."

"Like what?" Bree asked, tearing her eyes away from the simple beauty of the horses.

Ryker leaned over and slipped his hand under her chin, lifting it slightly. The other slowly slipped behind her back and pulled her into him. Her breath caught a second before his lips took hers. She tasted like cherry soda and felt soft, warm, and enticing. His hand moved from her chin to the back of her neck, holding her gently in place so she wouldn't pull back. He wasn't ready for the kiss to end. He wanted more. Needed more. His pulse spiked and felt hers do the same.

"Ryker," she whispered, breaking the connection. Her hand slid between them and lay on his chest, easing him back. She cleared her throat. "I'm not sure I could sell that. But if I could, it would definitely go for a high price."

He grinned, causing his deeply chiseled features to crease. "I noticed you always caption your photos on your website." He ran a thumb over her lips. "How exactly would you caption that?"

She smiled up at him, batted her lashes. "Hmmm . . . 'The Kiss' by Ryker James. Sufficiently adequate."

"Ouch." His hand clutched his heart. "Sufficiently adequate? Really? I guess I'll have to do better." He tugged her forward and drew her onto his lap, capturing her mouth with his.

She was instantly taken hostage by his lips, and his hands. Bree's senses were overwhelmed as her mind filled with only Ryker. His strength, hard but gentle. His passion and tenderness. He was seductive and dangerously sexy. Inch, by precious inch, she could feel her body surrendering to him, willing and wanting him to take more.

Just when she didn't think she could take much more but couldn't imagine it stopping, it did. He pulled back but hovered just a whisper away from her lips. "Would you like to amend your caption now?"

She nodded slightly, breathless, unable to speak.

"Well?" he waited with dark desire in his eyes. "What do you say now?"

She swallowed, desperately trying to catch her breath. "Breathtaking and heart-stopping."

He smirked. "Much better."

She shivered despite the heat of his body next to hers.

"Are you cold?"

"A little," she fibbed, unwilling to let him know just how much he had affected her.

He reached around her into a compartment and pulled out a fluffy blanket. "Here," he said, draping it over her legs.

"Thank you." Bree shifted, snuggling into him as the world was slowly darkening around them. "Look at that sunset."

He followed her gaze and saw that the horizon was set on fire. The pinks and purples bled into deep crimson and violet as the sun sank below the coastline.

They watched in silence as the minutes crept by and the sky shifted and changed before them. Leaving them in soft spongy darkness as stars winked on all around.

The moon was a sliver overhead, pale but dominant in the vast ribbon of navy blue. In only a matter of days, it would be gone, and a new moon would begin. Even though it wasn't much more than a thumbnail, it still seemed larger somehow out over the ocean.

Gazing at the slice of moon, Bree suddenly had a thought. "I hate to bring this up, but . . ."

"But what?"

"Well, you're into the Black Shadow, have you had a chance to give any thought to the whole 'In the shadow of the black moon' statement?"

He shook his head. "No, sorry. I couldn't find any other reference in the Black Shadow other than what I already told you."

"Oh, okay. It's just a weird expression. Now, had he said something about a blue moon, I would have known what he was talking about."

"What's a blue moon?" Ryker asked.

"You haven't heard that expression?"

"I've heard it, but never really understood it."

"It's used to explain or to reference two full moons in a month. It doesn't happen very often. So that's why they say - once in a blue moon. My dad used that expression all the time."

"What would the opposite of that be?"

Bree straightened. "I don't know . . . the opposite of a full moon would be a new moon, I guess."

Ryker pulled out his phone. "Hey, Siri," he said. "Is it possible to have two new moons in a month?"

"*Okay, I found this on the web for 'Is it possible to have two new moons in a month,'*" came the automated reply. "*Check it out.*"

Bree peered at Ryker's phone with him. She gasped as the answer was displayed. She read, "Two new moons in a month - the second new moon is known as a black moon. Ryker, is there going to be a second new moon this month?"

They both stared up at the slice of moon in question that shone overhead. "I think you're right. That's it. That's the answer. It has nothing really to do with the Black Shadow; he's using that to throw us off. It's more about the actual moon." Ryker raised his phone, "Hey, Siri - how many days until the new moon?"

"*Okay, I found this on the web for 'How many days until the new moon?' Check it out.*"

"Five days." He glanced at Bree. "That's this Saturday."

A chill raced through her. Five days. "Now we don't know this for sure. We're just guessing. It could still be something to do with the Black Shadow."

"I don't disagree with you. Either way, I don't like it." Changing the subject he said, "How about we head back? The wind's starting to pick up, and I don't want it to get too rough."

Bree glanced at his phone, checking the time. "I should get home anyway. Zylah will probably need to go out again soon. If I take her out around midnight, she can make it until seven."

He leaned over and kissed her gently on the mouth, lingering just a little. Tasting, tempting. He stood up and held out his hand, pulling her up. "Let's go."

Ryker started the boat, letting it idle, he hauled in the anchor. When she was snuggled into the seat next to him, he swung the boat around and headed towards the city lights.

Chapter 31

It was just after midnight as they threaded their way through the quiet streets, the only sound was his motorcycle. Bree relaxed and laid her head on Ryker's back, enjoying the ride. Loving the smell of his cologne and the feel of his warm body, she wrapped her arms around him.

Bree smiled to herself as she remembered his lips on hers, and wondered if he would kiss her again at the front door.

They turned down her lane and bumped along the rutted driveway. He pulled up in front of the house and killed the engine. Quiet descended around them.

Her body hummed as she climbed off the motorcycle. The house was dark. She hesitated, looking at it. *Didn't she flip the lights on when they left?* She could swear she had. An eerie feeling crept up her spine.

As if reading her mind Ryker said, "I thought you left the outside lights on."

"I'm almost positive I did."

She took a step toward the house. Ryker grabbed her arm. "Bree don't. Let me call Savard first."

She started to agree but then thought of Zylah. A sick feeling snaked through her. She wrenched loose and ran towards the house.

"Stop!" Ryker yelled, running after her. "Bree, wait!" He caught her at the bottom of the stairs. "What the hell? I told you to wait."

"Zylah's in there," she hissed. "Something's happened; I can feel it in my gut. I have to go in."

"Damn it," he swore. "Okay, but I'm going first." He looked around for something, anything to use to protect them. But there was nothing. "Get behind me."

They could see the door was cracked before he even reached for the knob, Ryker nudged with his foot. It swung silently open.

He reached inside, feeling along the wall for the light switch. The minute the lights were on Bree pushed past him, headed for the kitchen, and Zylah.

"Ryker!" Bree screamed.

He got to her in three long strides. She had dropped to her knees, kneeling and cradling the limp puppy to her chest, traces of fresh meat lay in chunks on the floor. He hit 9-1-1.

"Bree let's get in your car and take her to the vet."

"This is 9-1-1. What's your emergency?" he heard in his ear as he followed Bree to the garage.

"There's been a break-in at 10 Cypress Lane. Please alert Detective Savard."

"Is anyone hurt?"

"A small puppy. Looks like she's been poisoned. We are on our way to the vet now. Send someone over." Ryker clicked off, not waiting for a response. He googled emergency vets and dialed the first number. "Get in Bree. I'll drive."

• • • •

SAVARD SQUATTED AND scooped up all the little chunks of raw meat that were scattered on the inside of the puppy's crate and placed them in a plastic container. He marked them as evidence and tucked them into his bag. He waited patiently while the photographer took photos, documenting the kitchen, and then dusted the front door and the crate for prints.

He received a text from Ryker saying they'd be back shortly from the vet. Savard made himself as comfortable as possible, took off his jacket and slung it over the back of the barstool, and unbuttoned his top button. It was three in the morning, he didn't think

Bree would mind if he had shown up in his pajamas, let alone loosened his collar.

Alone in the house, he took his time and walked through every inch, taking it all in with a detective's eye.

Snader Jr. or Kage, whatever you wanted to call him, had to have a key or he was damn good at picking locks. The question was, if he had a key, where did he get it? Bree had changed the locks at least a week ago so the only ones that had keys now were Sam Harris, Ryker James, and Bree herself.

They hadn't found any evidence of forced entry, so either he had walked right in the front door like he let them believe, or he had found another way in. If he really waltzed in the front door, then he was bold and stupid. But being bold and stupid might actually help in catching him. When criminals got arrogant, they made mistakes.

Savard heard the SUV pull in and walked to the front door. He saw Ryker pull around to the garage and went through the house to meet them.

"Detective," Ryker greeted him solemnly and stuck out his hand.

Savard shook it, then turned to Bree. "How's Zylah?" he asked, reaching out for Bree's arm and guiding her through the breezeway.

"They had to pump her stomach," Bree said with a hitch in her voice. "She's pretty bad. But the vet said she's strong and healthy despite her size, and we got her there quickly, so she has hope that she'll make a complete recovery. They're going to keep her there for at least the next 48 hours."

"Let's sit down and you can run through what happened tonight."

Ryker and Bree took turns filling in the details of the events of the night, while Savard took notes.

"Who knew you were going out tonight?"

"No one. I didn't speak to anyone after Ryker called me," Bree stated.

"And you, Ryker? Who did you mention it to?"

He shrugged, "Just Sam. I called him on my way home. We always touch base at the end of the day."

Savard opened a manila folder and produced a photo. "Take a look at this photo." He pushed it across the table. "Recognize him?"

Bree picked up the 8X10 and studied it. Shaggy blonde hair the color of sand. Blue eyes. Crooked nose. Full face. "He looks familiar, but I can't place him. Why? Who is it?" She handed the photo to Ryker.

"That's Garth Snader Jr. taken about a year ago or, most likely Kage, whatever you prefer to call him."

"You're sure now Kage and Snader Jr. are one and the same?"

Savard nodded.

"Maybe that's why he looks familiar. Now that you say that, I can see the resemblance to his father. He has the same color of hair, same blue eyes but I'd say that's where resemblance ends." Bree looked at Ryker. "What is it?"

"He looks familiar to me too, but obviously I've never met Snader Sr."

"What about him catches your eye?" Savard asked.

"I'm not sure."

"Give yourself some time. It may come to you. In the meantime, I'm going to run this photo through our computer and have it change hairstyles, hair and eye color. They can add a little weight to his face and even thin it out. See if we can come up with a composite picture that one of you might recognize. It may take a little time, but I'll make sure we get it done." Savard looked from one to the other. "What else?"

Bree started, "We had an idea about the warning."

"You mean - In the shadow of the black moon?" Savard asked. "Let's hear it because I didn't get anywhere with it."

"What if it's about an actual black moon, nothing to do with the Black Shadow?"

"I'm listening."

"When there are two new moons in one month, the second one is called a black moon," she paused. "And there just happens to be two new moons this month."

Thinking of the sliver of moon he had noticed on the drive over, he asked, "This coming weekend?"

"Saturday to be exact."

"Interesting." Savard sat back and ran his hands over his bald head. Even in the dim light of the dining room, it shone like a polished bowling ball. He watched Bree for a hot minute. "What are you thinking, Bree?"

"I just . . . it's been bothering me ever since you mentioned that Mr. Snader took his own life. Maybe if I had been kinder, more understanding, more forgiving . . . maybe he would still be here. Maybe none of this would be happening."

"You can't blame yourself for him taking his own life. He had a brain tumor that caused him to blackout right before the accident. It was inoperable. He knew that. He knew he was going to die anyway. He chose to die sooner than later. The kind of tumor he had would have inevitably caused seizures, more blackouts, memory loss, and ultimately loss of control of his own body." Savard sighed. "I guess Mr. Snader felt this was a much better way for him to go. And personally, I would have to agree with him. No one wants to live like that. Don't blame yourself for what he did."

"You're right, she shouldn't blame herself but someone sure does," Ryker stated.

"I think you're right and I believe it's Garth Jr."

Chapter 32

"I'm headed out to an appointment," Tina said, poking her head into Linda's office. "Do you want to grab a late lunch when I get back?"

The sun shone in through her window, illuminating the tiny dust particles that stirred when the central air circulated. She looked away from her paperwork for a moment and made eye contact with her friend, and noticed she was a little peaked yet. She was happy to have Tina back, and glad that she had made a full recovery. They were in the middle of a very busy stint but Linda couldn't help but worry. "You're not doing too much are you?"

"I'm fine, Linda. Stop worrying."

"If you have too much on your plate, give something to Greg."

Tina made a face. "No thanks. I think I'll keep it. I like my clients too much to hand them over to him."

Linda lowered her reading glasses and cocked an eyebrow at Tina. "You don't like him?"

"Let's just say there's something about him that makes my skin crawl. I can't put my finger on it, but . . ." her voice trailed off. "I need to go. Wait for me for lunch?"

"Will do."

Linda slipped her glasses back on and tried to focus on her paperwork. She jotted down notes and divided up duties that she would cover tomorrow in the morning meeting. They would have a quick meeting following the photoshoot.

She looked through the list of clients versus agents and noticed everyone was out either showing a house or meeting with potential clients to list their homes. Everyone except Greg. He didn't have anything until two. And now that Tina had brought Greg to her attention, she couldn't let it go.

Linda stretched, stood, and smoothed down her light gray linen skirt, tucked in the tail of her pink blouse that had worked its way free and glanced at her watch. She walked down the hall with her heels clicking on the tile floor, towards the reception area. She walked past Greg's closed door, hesitated when she saw it was dark, and realized she hadn't seen him yet this morning. "Sheri?" she called.

Sheri looked up from her computer as Linda entered the room. "Have you seen or heard from Greg this morning?"

"No, Linda, I haven't. Did you need him for something?"

"Is he out on an appointment?" she asked.

Sheri checked the schedule. "No, I don't believe so."

Linda tapped her pink nails on the top of the receptionist desk. "He came in late yesterday too," she said, thinking out loud. She turned to the younger woman and knew behind that pretty face was a sharp mind. Sheri paid attention. Linda knew there wasn't anything that went on in this office that Sheri wasn't aware of. "How many times was he late last week?"

Sheri looked directly at Linda. "Every day but Wednesday."

"He's only been here six or seven weeks now and he's already slacking off. I don't like that. Not one bit." Linda started to pace back and forth in front of the desk. Then turned to look out at the parking lot.

"Do you want me to try his cell phone?"

"Don't bother. Here he comes now."

Linda stepped back and anchored herself at the front desk. She gave him the once over when he came through the door. "Good morning Greg. Nice of you to finally join us this morning," Linda said with a briskness to her words. Noticing his dirty hands and rumpled clothes she asked, "Car trouble?"

He grinned, a lopsided toothy smile. "You could say that. Flat tire. Took me a while to get it off and the spare on. A mechanic I'm not."

Linda eyed him. "After you get cleaned up, come into my office."

"You bet."

Linda watched him disappear into the bathroom. She walked down the hall to her office, leaned over and plucked a sheet of paper off the desk. When he came in, she handed it to him.

"I have several listings that I need you to stop by. These top five, I need lockboxes put on and signs placed in the yards. These seven need the signs removed. You can use the signs from those houses to put on these. And then this one, it's way out." She pointed to the last listing. "They decided to take it off the market for now. Just pull the sign from the road. There's no lockbox or anything. It's just a little outbuilding way back in the woods, off the beaten path."

"Yep, I can do that. Do you have extra lockboxes?"

"Yes, here." She reached for an ocean blue tote with Coastal Realty stamped on it in white, and handed it to him. "They're all in there with the appropriate keys inside and Sheri has them all labeled."

"Got it."

"What you don't get done before your appointment you can do after. You'd better get going."

"Right."

She watched him walk away. He had an excuse for today, but what about yesterday? Or last week? She'd need to keep better tabs on him, she decided.

• • • •

THE RADIO PUMPED OUT hard rock, and despite the cool breeze blowing in from the open windows, sweat dripped down

Ryker's back. All the appliances had been taken out except the re-frigerator. It still ran so Bree had decided to keep it and put it out in the garage for a backup. They would move that as soon as Bree came down for lunch and emptied it out.

All the base cabinets were out and most of the wall. The island had been removed and the counters were gone. *The room is almost bare,* Ryker thought, taking another cabinet to the dumpster fol-lowed out by Sam.

"That's the last one," Sam said, hefting it over the side of the metal container. "I'm surprised we got that all done before lunch, as large as that kitchen is."

"Yeah, me too. I guess it's because we had an early start." Ryker ran his dusty hands through his hair. "Looks like we can patch the walls and get started painting this afternoon."

They walked in through the slider as Bree came in carrying lunch.

"Perfect timing," Sam said. "We just finished ripping out the cabinets."

"Why don't you come into the dining room and eat?"

"You'd probably rather have us sit outside, we're covered in dust," Ryker said, indicating their clothes. He noticed the dark smudges under her eyes but didn't say anything. It gave him a small fist to the gut to think of little Zylah, and what might have hap-pened to Bree if she had been home when it happened.

She nodded and followed them out. They sat and she doled out food. "I can't believe how far you guys have gotten already."

"We have patching and painting to do this afternoon. Cabinets arrive bright and early tomorrow morning," Sam said, taking a bite of his sub. "Have you gotten any news on Zylah?"

"I spoke to the vet a little while ago. She made it through the night without any further complications. The vet said she should make a full recovery. They're going to keep her at least through to-morrow, just to be safe," Bree said, with relief evident in her voice.

They ate in silence for a few minutes, enjoying the sunshine and the breeze. Boats dotted the bay, anchored, or slowly trolling by, fishing.

"Did you two ever decide if you were going to have Colette update your website?"

Ryker nodded, taking a swig of his soda. "We are. We need to get some photos together."

Bree beamed. "I'm one step ahead of you. I already have quite a few before and after photos from my own house that you could use. If you let me know some other jobsites, I can stop and take photos there too. Also, we should take professional shots of the two of you."

Sam wadded up his trash. "I can give you a list of some of our projects. Then maybe you could meet one of us at a site."

"Just let me know when and where."

Bree folded her unused napkin and crumpled up her wrappers. "Did you guys get enough to eat?"

"Yeah, I'm good," Sam said. "Thanks for getting that for us." He looked at Ryker. "I'm going to wash up, then grab the cans and paintbrushes out of my truck."

Having finished too, Ryker stood and walked over to Bree. "How are you holding up, Champ? You look tired."

She smiled up at him, but it didn't quite reach her eyes. "I am, but you must be too. Thanks for everything last night. I never got to tell you how much I enjoyed the evening. Thank you for that. And thanks for being there with Zylah, and for staying after Savard left. I know you have to be as exhausted as I am."

"I had a thought."

"Only one?"

"More than one, especially when it comes to you. But for the moment I want to concentrate on just this one thought."

"Let's have it."

Ryker rubbed at his neck. "I'm not sure how you're going to take this idea, but please believe me when I say I have your best interest at heart and there are no ulterior motives."

"Hmmm . . . that sounds like a setup if I've ever heard one for something you know I'm going to hate. I'm listening, but tread carefully." She put her hands on her hips and waited.

He grinned sheepishly. "With you? Always." He cleared his throat and prepared to tell her his idea. "On your cell phone there are these apps." He swiped through his and held it up for her to see.

"Yes," she said hesitantly.

"Well, I was thinking we could link our phones. There's this app in particular . . ." he touched the screen of his phone and pulled it up to show her. "You can turn it on and share your location with certain people. I thought it might be wise if we linked ours so I could find you if . . ." he hesitated, not sure how to actually say it.

Bree didn't hesitate though. "In case something happens to me?"

Ryker nodded.

"That's a good idea." Without a second thought, she handed him her phone.

He made the appropriate adjustments and gave it back. "That actually makes me feel better."

"Me too."

She moved to go, but he reached out, and turned her towards him. Looking down at her, he grinned, causing the deep-set dimples to appear. "Now about those other thoughts . . . maybe we should sneak off and take a nap. We both could use it."

"Why do I get the impression there wouldn't be much sleeping in your version of a nap?"

He tugged her in fast so her hips were instantly pressed to his. His smile grew wider, the creases in his cheeks, deeper. "Why Bree, if I didn't know better, I'd think you were after my body. I had every intention of sleeping . . . eventually." He dropped his mouth and hovered just a whisper above hers. He could feel the warmth of her breath on his lips.

She tried to step back but he held her firmly. "Ryker, don't. Sam's right inside."

"What? You don't think Sam has ever seen me kiss someone before?"

She half laughed. "No, I'm sure he has. It's just, you're working. We shouldn't."

"So? I like to mix business and pleasure whenever I can. Don't you?" He didn't wait for a response. He dropped his mouth to hers and seized it.

He went down fast. Like a man drowning in a sea of pleasure. Ryker lost all sense of time and feeling. The outside world slipped away, and all that was left was Bree. The feel of her lips on his, the warmth, the tenderness. The taste of soda lingered on her tongue, and the hint of fresh flowers whispered over her skin. His hands were on her face, caressing it and tilting her back gently, his mouth eager for more.

He pulled back with a smile as he heard Sam clear his throat.

"Are we going to do any more work today? Or should I just pack up and call it quits?"

Bree flushed red and pushed back. "No, we're done. You can get started. I have work to do also." She took another step back. And then another, until she was out of arm's reach, then turned and bolted inside.

Ryker stood grinning after her. It was all he could do not to follow her and sweep her up. "Damn it, Sam. You've scared her off."

"My apologies, I was under the impression we were here to work. How is it you always get the girl?" Sam asked in disbelief, going back inside.

"Ha! Don't you know by now?"

"Why don't you enlighten me."

"It's my rugged good looks and my undeniable charm."

Sam snorted and choked back a laugh. "Undeniable charm, my ass."

"Would you rather I said sex appeal?" Ryker asked, popping the top on a tub of spackle and grabbing a putty knife. He stirred the thick material, scooped a small amount, and went to the first divot in the wall. "And I wouldn't say I've gotten this one."

"You could have fooled me. She looked pretty comfortable in your arms." Sam took a screwdriver and started removing outlet and light switch covers, preparing to paint. "You need to be careful. I get the impression Bree isn't a one-night stand."

"I know that. She's different. Give me a little credit, won't you? I haven't been playing around lately." Not since he had seen Bree. The day she had punched him in the jaw on the lifeguard stand, something had shifted in him. And not just his jaw.

There had been something about her voice, her attitude, which had him cutting his run short. When he had returned and saw her taking pictures on the beach . . . a longing had ripped open in him as wide as the ocean. Anyone and everything paled in comparison to the desire he experienced when he simply looked at her. He'd been trying desperately to shake the feeling ever since.

"If I didn't know any better, I'd say you might actually have feelings for Bree."

He didn't want to. Up to this point he'd been happy and content with how his life was going. Since she'd come along, things had been turned upside down for him. He didn't like it. Not one bit.

"And what makes you think that?" Ryker asked, methodically spreading spackle, trying to sound noncommittal.

"She's different. For starters, she doesn't drool all over you or chase after you like other women."

That was for damn sure. She definitely played hard to get.

"I'm just guessing here, so feel free to correct me if I'm wrong, but you haven't successfully talked her into bed yet, either."

Disgusted that Sam could read the situation so well, Ryker scraped off a chunk of spackle and flung it back into the bucket with the knife. "Think you've got it all figured out?" He defiantly turned to Sam. "Spent the night here, didn't I?"

Sam smirked. "Yes, but if you'd gotten lucky you wouldn't be so pissy now."

"Fuck off, Harris. I'm going out to the truck and make some phone calls."

Sam laughed as Ryker strode off, pissed.

"Man, it's good to be right!" he called out as Ryker slammed the front door.

Chapter 33

Bree worked steadily the rest of the afternoon, trying desperately to keep busy and not let her mind stray to Ryker. She wasn't quite sure what to make of him. One minute he was all business, gruff, and to the point, the next he was protective, sweet, and seductive.

She'd run the gamut of emotions with him. One moment finding him irresistible and kind, the next she'd like to beat him over the head with her shoe. If the man didn't make her crazy, she didn't know who did.

She tried to picture her life with him and could easily see it. Spending weekends out on the water on his boat or working together on projects around the house. Taking long walks on the beach or going for a ride on his motorcycle. It was so clear in her mind it almost hurt to think of it. To want it. But she did. She wanted it all.

The question was, did he? She wasn't sure. Should she even dare to dream about a future with Ryker? She thought she was going to have that with Chad. Forever. But forever was a long time and their love, if it had been real, couldn't stand the pressure it had been under.

She wanted to have a big family to do things with. Bree thought she would have her parents around to be wonderful grandparents, and nieces and nephews to dote on from her sister, and Chad's family. Boisterous, loud, and loving. She had pictured that perfectly too, and now look what she had to show for it. Nothing. No one. Everyone she loved was gone.

She had kept her heart tucked in closely this last year, not letting anyone in. Not even Chad. Just when she thought it was safe, she opened her heart to Zylah, and look at what had happened to her. The thought made her sick. She had almost lost her too. The precious little life. She couldn't wait to have her back.

No, she wouldn't dare to dream anymore. She would just be content with Zylah and the house. She couldn't bear to lose anyone else close to her, especially someone like Ryker and what he represented.

If she let him in completely, she would fall hard. She couldn't let that happen. She wouldn't take the chance. She couldn't. She had to protect herself and the ones she cared for from this psycho.

She glanced at her calendar. Four days until the black moon. Would he really come for her? Bree had a thought, *what if she just offered up the money?* She didn't want it. He could have it if that's all it took to make him go away. She'd contact the lawyer and make sure the money went to Garth Jr. She would call as soon as she went through these photos.

Bree scrolled through the photos she had downloaded earlier and prepared to select a couple to use for her website. She started at the oldest and scrolled up. She had a few more from Assateague that she loved and couldn't wait to play with. She also wanted to get the ones she had taken today of Ryker and Sam and drop them into the folder she had created for Bolts & Beams.

She was scrolling to the end when a couple of Zylah caught her eye. She scrolled up. There were three. She selected the first tiny icon. Zylah was in her crate with her tiny paws perched up on the metal in anticipation. Tongue flopping out, looking happy. *She was so sweet*, Bree thought, *I don't remember taking it*. She'd taken some of her the day Ryker had brought her over. But this one? She looked at the date stamp. This one was taken . . . yesterday?

Surprised, Bree clicked to the next one, and her heart dropped. The cage door was open and Zylah was eating a raw beef patty off the tip of someone's fingers. Sickened, Bree advanced to the last one. Zylah lay flopped on her side, tongue hanging out, and eyes rolled up into her head. Her breath hitched. This was last night. That was the hand of the person that had poisoned Zylah. A new wave of sickening fear washed over her.

She picked up the phone and dialed Savard's number.

"Savard here."

"Detective, it's Bree Thompson."

"Yes, Bree. I was going to call and check on you and Zylah. How is she?" His voice was full of concern.

"She's doing better, but they are still keeping her for another day just to make sure."

"Glad to hear she's going to be all right. Now, what can I do for you?"

Bree cleared her throat. "I downloaded my photos off my camera today, and there are pictures of Zylah."

"What kind of pictures?"

"I left my camera here last night while I was out. Whoever poisoned her took pictures of her while doing it, with my camera," Bree finished, her voice a little shaky as she looked at the computer screen. Zylah's tiny face peered out at her.

"How many?"

"Three. Before, during, and after."

"Can you send them to me?"

"Yes."

He rattled off his email address, and Bree jotted it down. Then clicked on the three photos and attached them to his email, and clicked one more time sending them. "They're sent."

"Good. And the camera? Did you touch it?"

"I did."

Savard cursed under his breath.

"I'm sorry."

"No, it's not your fault. You had no way of knowing. Just don't touch it anymore. Chances are he had gloves on, or the prints have been wiped away, like everything else. But you never know. I'm going to send Kilpatrick over to dust it."

She heard him cover the mouthpiece and yell. "He's on his way."

Bree nodded even though Savard couldn't see her. "I'll be here. I'm upstairs in the studio."

She heard his email chime through the phone.

"Here it is."

There was silence as she heard him click.

"His hand is in this one. I wonder if the lab can close in on a print since it's partially visible," Savard said.

She heard him adjust the phone.

"Is there anything else?"

Bree shifted in her chair. "I'm going to call the lawyer, Heffner, and refuse the money. Let Snader have it. If he gets what he wants, surely he will stop."

"If you're sure you don't want the money, it may help. Or it may not. But if he thinks you're willing to give it up, who knows. He has to know we will still go after him."

"If he takes the money and leaves me alone, I won't press charges. I'll make sure the lawyer knows that."

"Bree, we can't just let him off. He's been stalking you for weeks; set fire to your property, vandalized your home, and almost killed your puppy. Not to mention he's threatened your life. We can't just let him go."

"We can, and we will if he promises to stop."

Savard cleared his throat. "We don't know what this guy is completely capable of, Bree. I found a couple of drunk and disorderly on his record and an arrest for a bar fight. I'm going back through his previous jobs and collecting all the info I can on him so we know exactly who we're dealing with."

"And who are we dealing with?"

"Someone who is a bit odd, stays to himself, is obsessed with the Black Shadow . . . and you."

• • • •

RYKER DROPPED HIS PAINTBRUSH in the empty can and raised his arms over his head and stretched out his back. "I'm out," he said to Sam. "How 'bout you?"

"Yep, just finished the last of it."

Both men stood back and surveyed the room. Bree had selected a warm stone gray that would set off the white painted cabinets with the dark brown rub through. The room glowed enchantingly with the inviting earth tone.

"Looks like we're ready for the flooring tomorrow."

Sam's phone chimed. He looked down and examined it. "Guess the appliances are arriving a little ahead of schedule."

Ryker lifted a dark eyebrow and reached for his water. "Oh?"

"Yeah, they were supposed to arrive tomorrow, but they had room on today's truck. They are out for delivery now. The problem is the truck won't get here until late, and I can't wait. I've got a family engagement."

"That's right, it's Mama Harris's birthday. No worries. I got you covered."

"You sure?" Sam asked Ryker, gathering the empty paint cans.

Ryker scooped up the drop cloth and wadded it into a ball. "Not a problem. Anything for Mama Harris."

Sam headed out to the truck, followed closely by Ryker. Both men had their hands full of equipment.

"More likely it's just because you want an excuse to stay here with Bree." He hefted the empty cans into the bed, leaned on the truck, and really looked at Ryker. "When are you going to admit you like her?"

"Who? Mama Harris? I love her," Ryker said unloading his armful.

"No, not my mother, jackass. Bree. I've never seen you like this with anyone."

"What the hell is that supposed to mean?"

"You can't seem to stay away from her. Every time I turn around, you're here with her."

"It's my job to be here, working on the house. Yours too."

"That's not what I meant and you know it. You've spent the night a couple of times."

"In the damn guest room. It's not like I'm sleeping with her."

"That's exactly what I mean. You can't keep your eyes off of her, yet you haven't made any move except for that slobbery kiss I walked in on earlier today."

"Fuck you. I'm an excellent kisser. Slobbery, kiss my ass." Ryker snagged a roll of paper towels out of the bed and chucked them at Sam's head.

Sam ducked. "If I didn't know any better, I'd think you were scared."

"Scared? Scared of what?"

"Of Bree. Of getting hurt. You're usually the one breaking hearts. Leaving a trail of crying women in your wake. She's different from any of the women you've ever dated. I think you're terrified of getting too close because you might actually have real feelings for her."

"Who the hell are you? And what have you done with that ass-hole Sam Harris I used to call my friend?" Ryker questioned with disdain.

Both men turned as they heard a car approach, and recognized Officer Kilpatrick. "Wonder what he wants?" Ryker said.

"I don't know. I'd like to find out, but I really got to go."

"Take off. Tell your mom Happy Birthday for me."

"I will. And think about what I said." Sam went around to the driver's side of the truck and climbed in. He stuck his head back out the window. "By the way, I invited Bree to the Shark Shack Friday night, just in case you didn't. I decided if you don't make a move on her soon, I will."

"She'd never go for your sorry ass," Ryker called after him.

Sam pulled away as Kilpatrick walked up.

"You guys finished for the day?"

"Yep, just cleaning up. Are you here to see Bree?"

Kilpatrick nodded.

"She's in the studio."

"Thanks." Kilpatrick strode off across the yard towards the carriage house.

Ryker went back into the house and cleaned his paintbrush out in the sink. He gathered a few tools, and stacked them in the corner, stalling. He wanted to go up and see if there was something new in the case, but Sam's words kept playing through his mind. He'd be damned if he would admit to Sam, or anyone else for that matter, that somehow Bree had gotten under his skin, and into his heart.

Instead of going to the studio, he walked around the house, assessing the work that they had done and had still yet to do. Spotting a couple of things to touch up, he went to the truck and grabbed a clipboard to take some notes. He was headed back in when the officer emerged from the garage.

"Still here?" Kilpatrick asked, walking towards his cruiser.

"Yeah, have a late delivery of appliances coming. Everything okay?" he inquired, tucking the clipboard under his arm.

"Had a couple of questions and an item to dust for prints. Nothing to worry about."

"Did you lift one?"

"A couple of good ones, but not sure if they're Bree's or the perps. Find out soon enough. Got to get back with this. Have a good night." Kilpatrick climbed into the car and drove away.

Ryker glanced at the carriage house and was about to walk over and find out what was going on when the delivery truck came up the driveway. "Guess it'll have to wait."

A half-hour later, with the truck unloaded, Ryker checked off the items on the invoice as they temporarily stored the appliances in the family room. He thanked the driver and went back into the house. Nothing left to do; he went in search of Bree.

He found her easily, outside sitting in her spot under the weeping cherry, gazing out at the rippling blue water. He eased down next to her in the other Adirondack chair.

"Beautiful day, turning into a spectacular evening."

She turned her head slightly, and a whisper of a smile played across her face. "Yes, it is."

"The appliances were delivered."

"I thought I heard a truck. How do they look?"

"They're nice. They'll be perfect with the cabinets and countertops. We're putting in the flooring tomorrow. Cabinets should arrive on schedule Thursday."

"It's really all coming together. You guys have done a great job so far. I couldn't be more pleased, Ryker, really."

"Glad you're happy. Just wait until the kitchen is complete. You'll want to thank me in more ways than one."

"Oh, really?"

He grinned wickedly at her.

"In your dreams, Mr. James."

Since she seemed upbeat, Ryker decided not to broach the subject of Kilpatrick and what he'd been doing here. Instead, he decided to focus on the evening ahead. "Do you have plans for dinner?"

"I was thinking cereal and milk since I don't have a working stove."

Ryker wrinkled his nose. "Cereal is for little kids."

"It is not," Bree retorted. "I eat cereal all the time."

"Let me rephrase that." He thought for a moment. "Cereal is for little boys and girls." He stood up and reached for her hand, pulling her out of the chair. "And you little girl, need more than cereal for dinner."

"You're calling me a little girl?" Bree asked in disbelief. "I saw you down a Yoohoo the other day."

"Chocolate milk is good for muscles." Ryker flexed his arms.

Bree reached up and poked at his firm bicep. "Hmmm, now I see why you drink it. Maybe if you drank one every day your muscles would get bigger, little boy."

Damn if she wasn't cute. It was all he could do not to reach out and pull her into him. He wanted to feel those lips on his and run his hands over her slender body.

"Do you know what my favorite game on the playground was?" He took a step toward her.

Bree asked coyly, "No, what game?"

"Boys chase girls. And do you know what we did if we caught them?"

"I'm afraid to ask."

He sent her a look that had her blushing.

"We tackled them to the ground and kissed them breathless. In our version of the game, it will be kisses and dinner. Wanna play?"

"Hold up. There's another angle to that game. We sometimes played girls chase boys."

"I like that version too."

"You didn't ask what we did when *we* caught the boys."

"Tell me," he said, taking a step towards her.

Bree stared him down, hands on her hips. "We punched them."

He laughed. "Figures. Only you, Champ. Well, since you've already punched me once and hit me with a door another time, I think we should play my version."

Almost daring her, he took another step as she stepped back.

"And being that I'm a fair man and *not* a little boy, I'll even give you a head start. How 'bout I count to three? Once I reach three though, all bets are off. One. . ."

"I'm not a little girl, Ryker."

"I'm well aware of that, Bree."

"You can't bully me into playing your silly, little game."

He cocked an eyebrow and smiled wickedly, dimples etched deeply into his face. "Watch me. Two."

She could see he was serious and weighed her options.

"You'd better run Bree, you're going to lose your head start. Unless you want me to catch you? Two and a half."

Bree ran.

He shouted, "Three! Ready or not!" Ryker couldn't help but grin as he watched her bolt towards the house. "Shit!" he cursed, realizing she was fast. Faster than he thought she would be. He took off sprinting after her. He should have known better. With a body like that, of course she could run.

He gained on her but not quite enough, she was going to reach the house before he got her. She made a mistake and looked behind her. It slowed her down just a little. He reached for her just as she pulled the slider open. He missed and she slipped in, yanking the door shut.

She shrieked in delight when she realized she had escaped by mere inches, and flipped the lock. "In your face! Ryker James! Cereal it is! Now . . ." she hissed. "You stop this, this instant!" she yelled at him breathlessly through the glass door.

"Never!" he said defiantly. He smiled wickedly drawing in a deep, badly needed, gulp of air. Who knew she was this much of a tease?

"Well, the game is over. I won. You lost."

"It's not over yet, Bree. There are other ways into your house."

She narrowed her eyes at him. "You're kidding, right? You're seriously going to make me run around and lock you out of this entire house?"

"You bet your pretty little ass I am. It's not over." Ryker grinned and took off.

Bree shrieked and darted through the kitchen towards the front door, jumping over tools.

Ryker only went as far as he needed to, to be out of sight, then doubled back and pulled his keys out of his front pocket. He slinked back to the slider and used a thin edge of his key to twist the latch, slid it open, and walked into the kitchen.

He saw her standing at the front door peering out. He laughed. "Guess I win."

She jumped and spun. With a smirk, she said, "It's not over until it's over, Ryker." She flipped the lock, flung the door open, and bolted.

This time he was closer and he knew what he was dealing with. He wasn't about to let her get away. A smile spread across his face as he ran. He was gaining. He reached out and grabbed her arm. He wasn't prepared for her sudden stop and they both hit the ground. Limbs tangled and breathless, he pinned her down in the long grass. Her chest heaved and he could feel her heart hammer against his.

She peered up at him under dark lashes, her cheeks flushed, and her breath ragged but still she smiled at him and literally took his breath away.

"You lose," he said, dragging in a ragged breath of his own. "Now for my prize."

He skimmed his lips over hers and nipped at her bottom lip, having the satisfaction of a little sigh escaping her. He dove in and took her mouth hostage. He went down fast. Tasting, teasing, tempting. She matched him kiss for kiss until they were both begging for air. He didn't want to stop but he had to. To save his own life and his heart. He had to pull back just so they simply wouldn't suffocate one another.

Ryker rolled off her, delirious from lack of oxygen and the pure intoxication she emitted. Flopping back on the grass, he stared up into the blue sky as the air slowly returned to him. Watching a big, fat cloud drift slowly across the sky, he regained his breath.

He leaned up on an elbow and looked down at her pretty face. "Looks like I definitely won that round. Wanna play again?"

She smiled a heart-stopping smile. "I let you win. I really didn't want to eat cereal."

He ran his thumb over her warm, soft lips, and leaned down, skimming them with his.

She put her hand on his chest and gently pushed him back. "You need to stop. I can't think straight when you kiss me."

"Really?" he asked intrigued. "Is it just when I kiss your lips? Or does it happen when I kiss other places too?" He bent down and kissed her forehead and cocked an eyebrow at her. "How was that?"

She shrugged a shoulder, apparently unfazed.

"I can do better. How about here?" He ran a trail of kisses down her cheek and nuzzled into her neck, his hands skimming over her bare flesh.

"Ryker, you need to stop. I can't think."

"Do you need to?"

"With you? Yes."

"Why? Why think? Just enjoy the moment. Be in this moment, Bree. Be with me."

He kissed her again. First, her lips, the small of her neck, and then the hollow of her collar bone.

She gently pushed him back. "I can't. I won't. Stop Ryker, please." She shifted. Tried to free herself but couldn't. "Let me up, please."

He looked wounded. "Why? Did I do something wrong?"

"No. Yes. I don't know. Just let me up, please?" she begged.

He let her go. Confused, he stood, extended his hand. "Give me your hand. I'll help you up."

She hesitated, then place her hand in his and he pull her up. As soon as she was on her feet, he let go and headed for the house.

Bree raced to catch up. "Ryker, wait." She pulled on his arm. "I'm sorry. You didn't do anything wrong. It's me, not you."

He turned to her, gone was the hurt, it was replaced by anger. It rolled below the surface of him like an undercurrent, unseen, but needing to be feared. "I would hope you would know by now I'd never do anything to hurt you. But by the look on your face a moment ago, I guess you don't." He shook her off, slipping from her grasp, and went straight to the truck. He climbed in and drove off without looking back, leaving her alone.

Chapter 34

He slunk through the dark. It was almost pitch black as the moon was barely more than a sliver. He crept along the edge of the reeds, keeping low and next to the brush that swayed in the bay breeze.

He tentatively slithered out into the open grass, staying low and moving slowly. He dug deep and willed his inner warrior to take control of his body so he could move stealthily and advance on the house.

He *was* Prince Kage Xyon. He moved like him. He thought like him. He advanced in the darkness towards what he thought of as the enemy. Bree Thompson.

He was a warrior. He thought back over the three teachings of a true warrior and tried to cling to them now.

The first was courage. Courage - to have the will to make it happen.

He had the will and the way. He was going to make Bree Thompson pay for what she had done. And what she had done was turn his own father against him.

His father. He thought of him with disgust. If his father had just remembered number two - loyalty. He spat on the ground. What had his father known of loyalty? He had let a sad, pretty girl turn his head and make him give away everything. If his father had remained loyal to him, to his own blood, he wouldn't have had to resort to this to get what was rightfully his. But no matter, he was a true warrior at heart and they did what was necessary.

He inched along the edge of the house and tried to embrace number three - fearlessness. Fearlessness meant having no limits on oneself. That's what he needed now. He felt the power within him shift as he came around the corner.

He knew the cop was driving by in the cruiser. They had been for some time now. All it would take was for one motion sensor to trigger and the whole yard would be flooded with light and the cop would probably come running with a gun in his hand. He almost wanted it to happen. He felt so alive, that surely, he could take one measly cop. But as quickly as he had the urge, he squelched it. He had a job to do. A mission. He needed to stick to the plan. And the plan was to terrify Bree Thompson, teach her a lesson, and ultimately get back what was rightfully his.

He reached the garage and felt around for the fake stone that held the hidden key that he knew was there. His gloved hand closed around it and slipped the key out.

Inserting the key, he turned the lock. The door whispered open. He moved through the darkened garage like the true warrior he was and crossed the glass breezeway without a sound, making his way down the foyer and to the stairs. Before ascending, he glanced out the window and watched the cruiser drive away. The cop had no clue that he was here, and now he was gone. Bree was utterly alone in the big empty house. He could do whatever he wanted, for as long as he wanted.

Now for the stairs and Bree.

The stairs would be tricky. He knew they creaked. He'd have to be nimble and light on his feet. Nothing Kage couldn't handle. He crept up on his tiptoes fast and quick. Reaching the top, a wide smile slithered into place. Her door stood wide open. Even from this distance, he could make out her sleeping form, and the soft rise and fall of her chest.

His heart was pounding at the thrill of being in her home. In her space. Adrenaline coursed through him like nicotine from a heavy drag on a cigarette. The excitement bubbled inside him and made him bold. He stood straight up and walked directly toward her room, not even trying to hide anymore.

Emboldened, he walked to her bed and stood over her, hovering, staring down at her sleeping form. She was pretty even though he despised her. Hated her. He could kill her now with his bare hands, he felt the power coursing through him. She wouldn't even know what hit her. In mere seconds she could slip from this world and everything would be restored. His power. His money. And his life. No more slinking from one job to the next. No more groveling or kissing ass. He would be free to do whatever he wanted, whenever he wanted. He would hold his world in his own hands. He smirked, as he held hers.

But if he killed her now then his whole plan would be for naught and a quick death was too good for her. No, he'd wait a few more days. He had plotted for weeks. He hated to give in to the temptation now and cheat himself out of his full glory. He had to be patient, diligent just a little longer.

He would stalk her these last few days and terrify the living shit out of her. And then he would take her, torture her, and kill her. In the end, she'd be begging for him to end it for her. And he would . . . in the shadow of the black moon just like he had planned.

He watched her sleep and wondered if her dreams were peaceful? He hoped not. He wanted her to suffer like his father had those last few months after the accident, losing himself to despair and depression.

He knelt down and made himself eye level with her, then slipped the item from his pocket and placed it precisely in the middle of the nightstand facing her. That's when he saw it. The scissors glinted in the frail light. He narrowed his eyes. If he was leaving something, why shouldn't he take something from her?

His hands were sweaty inside the gloves and shook slightly. Regardless, he picked up the scissors. Without hesitation, he reached across her pillow and snagged the end of her ponytail. He held the scissors just below the band as she stirred in her sleep. Adrenaline pumped through him as he hacked off a chunk. He felt giddy as he looked down at the soft golden-brown hair in his hand.

Running it between his fingers, he smiled deviously. He brought it to his nose and pulled in the sweet scent of her. The sight of her and the smell stirred something deliciously evil in him. He pictured crawling into her bed and having his way with her. It was tempting, very tempting.

It took all his will to stand. He watched her for a moment longer, anticipating her reaction in the morning. The shock that would be on her pretty face when she realized he had taken her hair.

That thought alone satisfied him. It would have to . . . for now. With one last longing look at her, he slipped out of the room, descending the stairs boldly, whistling as he clutched her hair in his hand.

• • • •

THE SUN WAS SINKING, and the ribbon of highway rolled on forever as Bree strolled down the middle. She watched a flock of birds shift and swoop over the wheat fields that lined the road. Bree could hear a semi approaching and glanced over her shoulder. She started to jog, to get out of the way.

Her heart started beating fast, she started to run as the tractor-trailer bore down on her.

Suddenly in front of her, she saw a minivan parked on the side of the road. Her sister stuck her head out the window and waved, calling to her, "Come on Bree! We've been waiting for you."

Frantic, she shouted, "Get out of the van!"

"What? I can't hear you. What did you say?"

"Get out of the van!" She ran as fast as her legs would carry her but the minivan didn't get any closer. Unlike the tractor-trailer, which grew closer and louder. It loomed large and daunting.

The driver laid on the horn. Over and over. The wail of the horn was relentless. She reached the side of the road just as the semi roared by. She could feel the heat of the engine, smell the diesel fumes, and hear the squeal of the tires as the driver locked the breaks.

All Bree could do was stand and watch as the semi fishtailed and skidded. She screamed when it exploded and fell back. Backward down a long dark tunnel. Falling head over heels into the abyss. Faces flashed by her in the darkness. Her mom. Her dad. Her sister. She reached out to them but they tumbled past. She cried out, struggling. Reaching.

Somewhere in the recesses of her mind, she heard whistling.

She woke with a start, her heart racing, and the Black Shadow theme song ringing in her ears. She groped for the lamp and switched on the light. She rubbed her eyes, trying to adjust to the light. She turned, then blinked and shrank back as she saw a torn photo taped together of her face.

She gasped and clutched at her covers. How in the world? How did that get there? She struggled to make sense of it. She recognized pieces. The corners she'd been finding . . . in the bathroom drawer, the kitchen drawer, and the one Sam had found in the basement. She could see it now. He'd been leaving them on purpose for her to find. But it hadn't been there when she went to bed.

He was in the house.

She reached out, careful not to touch the photo, and turned the light back off. She grabbed her cell phone and bolted to the bathroom. Flinging herself against the door, she locked it, then turned on the lights and dialed 9-1-1. She stared at her reflection in the mirror as the phone connected.

"9-1-1 what's the emergency?"

"This is Bree Thompson. I live at 10 Cypress Lane. Someone's broken into my house. I need the police. I need Detective Savard."

"I'm dispatching them now. Are you hurt?"

Bree started to shake her head no but then she shrieked when she saw it, "He cut off my hair!"

Chapter 35

Linda parked her car and got out. She stood looking up at the pristine white house with its gray clapboard siding and stone foundation while a couple of men from Bolts & Beams unloaded cabinets off of a truck.

Ryker came out of the house and crossed over to her. "What do ya think?" he inquired, standing beside her and looking up at the house.

"It's exquisite, Ryker. You've outdone yourself once again. It looks brand new but still possesses all its original character. I've always loved this house. Its peaks and angles, the unique charm with the widow's walk, the huge porch, and pillars. Not to mention the view."

She looked at the man beside her; saw his strong profile, his ruggedly handsome looks. Beneath that occasional rough demeanor, he had a heart of gold. "I'm sorry you didn't get the house. I truly am."

He shrugged, stuck his hands in his pockets. "I might not own it, but I got to help restore it. You made sure of that, and that's somethin'. For that, I'm forever grateful. I'll always be able to look at it from here or across the water and know that I had a hand in that." He turned and smiled at her. "It's a source of pride. That's enough for me."

She patted him on the arm. "I'm glad."

"What brings you out here this early?"

"Bree's taking our photograph. I want a team picture and individuals for the office and our website. It's been a while since we've updated. I thought I'd come a little early and get mine taken before everyone got here."

"I'd better let you get to it then."

"Is Bree in the studio?" She saw him stiffen.

"I don't know. Haven't seen her, but that'd be my guess."

"You're not still mad at her for buying this house, are you? If anything, you should be mad at me."

He half laughed. "No, I've forgiven her for that. As much as I hate to admit it, this house suits her. To top it off, she's made good choices, great selections in the materials and finishes. If she'd chosen poorly, I'd have been all over it, and it would have given me great satisfaction to argue with her about it. But I can't."

"Then what is it?"

A frown creased his forehead between his eyebrows and drew the dimples out in his cheeks slightly. "I can't forgive her for taking my heart and literally stomping on it." He sighed. "You best go in. I'm sure she's waiting. Check the studio."

Before she could say anything, he walked away. She watched him go. She'd

never seen him like that before. Ryker wasn't someone to give his heart easily. He was a love 'em and leave 'em kind of guy. Apparently, for the first time, the tables were turned.

Linda knocked on the carriage house door, then opened it slightly. "Hello? Bree? It's Linda. Can I come in?"

Bree stuck her head out the door from the top floor. "Linda, come up, please. You're early."

"I know. I'm sorry, but I wanted to get here before everyone else and get my picture taken first. Hope that's all right?" Linda said, climbing the stairs.

"Of course. I was just setting up before everyone got here. Please, come in."

"Why, my dear, it looks like you're ready. The place looks wonderful and I smell coffee. Can I have a cup?"

"Of course. Do you take it black? Or with cream and sugar?"

Linda set her purse down on the long wooden table. "Black is fine. I like a good strong cup. I do love this space, Bree," she said, taking a long slow turn in the middle of the studio.

"Thank you." Bree brought over the steaming mug as Linda turned to look at her.

Her hair was pulled back in a small bun, and her face was void of any makeup. There were dark circles under her eyes, and it looked like she might have been crying.

"Oh dear, are you not well? You look tired."

Bree half-smiled. "I'm fine, just exhausted. I had a rough night."

Linda took the mug and noticed Bree's hand tremble slightly. "Sit down a minute and tell me about it." She led her over to the reception area, and they sat.

"I couldn't. You came for a picture, not an ear full."

"Nonsense, I have all the time in the world. That's at least one of the perks of being your own boss. Now tell me."

"I don't know where to start."

"Does this have anything to do with a certain handsome man outside?"

Bree laughed. "I wish that's all this was, but it's not. It's way more. You don't want or need to hear all this."

"Please, hon," Linda said, gently patting Bree on the hand. "I want to help."

Before Bree knew it, she started to tell Linda. She gave her the whole story, from the moment she'd moved in until last night.

She gave Linda a weak smile. "I guess you weren't expecting all that, were you?"

"I most certainly wasn't. My dear, you've been through quite an ordeal. I can't believe you're still in this house. I would be terrified to stay here at night alone. I think I would be looking for somewhere else to stay until the police figure this whole thing out."

"But that's the thing. I love this house, this place. I want to stay. I have to see it through."

"You're quite right. This is yours. You can't let some maniac chase you off. But you have to be careful. You're risking your life staying here. Bree, I beg you to go to a hotel for a few days until Detective Savard can solve this."

"Hello?" a voice drifted up the stairs.

"That will be the others. I guess we didn't get your picture taken first after all." Bree stood. "We're up here. Come on up," she called. Bree turned back to the older woman. "Please don't say anything. Not a lot of people know. I'd like to keep it that way."

"Of course, hon." Linda turned her attention to the door as her employees walked in.

Chapter 36

Colette looked over at Bree as she drove. They bumped along down the lane.

"I think that style suits you. It's very professional-looking."

"You think so?" Bree asked, pulling down the visor, again checking her new haircut in the mirror. The stylist had evened out the jagged ends of her hair, cutting off at least another inch, so now her hair didn't even brush her shoulders. Her hair was the shortest it had been since her freshman year in high school.

She had pulled it into a tight bun this morning for the photoshoot, barely able to sweep it up. Examining herself again she decided it looked nice. "It'll take some getting used to."

Colette reached over and patted her arm. "It looks fabulous. And in a couple of weeks, it will really start to grow back, but in the meantime, enjoy the new look."

Tears shimmered at the edges of her vision. "I guess I was due for a new style. I just wished I hadn't been forced to get it this way."

"The main thing is that you're all right. It makes my skin crawl to think he was that close to you, hovering over you while you slept." Colette shivered. "It gives me the creeps. He could have done a lot worse, Bree. You're fortunate nothing else happened."

"I know. I can't imagine how he's been slipping by. The only thing I can think of is he's coming up from the water. It's the only way. And I had a hide-a-key out. He had to have found it. There was no trace of forced entry."

"I think you should spend the night at my house tonight. You shouldn't be here alone."

"Thank you, but I don't want to leave the house empty, and I'm afraid if I don't stay, I might make myself scared enough that I won't be able to stay here by myself ever again," Bree said as Colette pulled up in front of the house and shut the car off.

"Then I'll stay here with you."

"Would you?" She leaned over and hugged her. "I would be grateful."

"We can have a good old-fashioned slumber party! It'll be fun."

"I have to warn you. I don't have a couch or anything. And the only TV I have right now is in my bedroom."

"So? It's gorgeous out. We will have a fire on your patio and sit and talk until we're ready for bed." Colette glanced over Bree's shoulder at the two men by the truck. "And maybe if we're lucky, we can have company."

Before Bree could say anything, Colette jumped out of the car, waving. "Hey, Sam!" she called. "Hi, Ryker. How's it going?" She crossed over to them.

"Hey, Colette," Sam said, turning in her direction.

Bree let out a sigh as she grabbed her purse and got out of the car. She didn't want to see Ryker. Let alone talk to him, especially when she wasn't feeling her best. She was still shaky from the shock of last night and was still getting used to her haircut.

"What are you ladies up to?" Sam asked.

Colette batted her lashes at him. "Oh, you know. Just had a late lunch, did a little shopping. The usual."

Keeping her head down, Bree tried to buzz past. "Is six good, Colette?" she asked, trying not to stop.

"You bet. I'll be here. We're going to sit out back, light a fire. Are you guys busy? Maybe you want to join us?"

Bree was almost past them when Ryker stepped into her path. "What's with the hair, Champ? Get it cut?"

"Yes."

"Looks good. It's classy, sophisticated."

"Glad it meets your approval. Now if you'll excuse me."

"Are you inviting us over tonight or is Colette?"

She looked at him, met those deep pools of blue. "We both are, I guess. If you have nothing better to do, come. I can order some takeout or grill burgers on the new grill my aunt sent with my other things. It's going to be a nice evening." She shrugged. "Up to you."

"I think we can manage it." He reached out and delicately touched the tips of her hair, running his fingers through it.

She sidestepped him. "I have some things to get done. See everyone in a little bit. Thanks again, Colette." With that, she disappeared inside.

Colette slugged Ryker in the arm.

"Ow! What was that for?"

"Because you're a jackass, that's what. You just had to mention her hair, didn't you?"

"Why? I thought women liked that. It's always worked for me before. What's the big deal? It's new, and I noticed. I should get points for that, not punched."

"Seriously, Colette, he didn't say anything wrong," Sam chimed in.

"I guess you guys don't know." She glanced from one to the other.

"Know what?" Ryker asked, moving closer, obviously concerned.

"That guy, Kage, that's been stalking Bree. He broke in again last night."

"We heard, Linda told us," Sam said. "She's pretty shaken up, huh?"

Colette shook her head. "She's handling it pretty well, considering."

"Considering what? Damn it, Colette. Spill it," Ryker demanded.

"Considering he cut off half her hair."

"What the fuck? You're kidding, aren't you?" Ryker asked in disbelief, his blood ran cold.

"I wish I were."

"Linda didn't tell us that."

"Honestly, she probably didn't know, unless Bree flat out told her." Colette looked at Ryker. "Anyway, she called me and asked me to recommend a stylist. I picked her up and took her to mine. You should have seen it when she took it out of the little bun she had it in." Colette tsked. "It was all hacked off and uneven. Gloria had to take another inch to even it up. Bree was practically in tears. Gives me the creeps to think of him standing over her holding scissors." Colette shivered despite the warm sun.

Every inch of Ryker's being vibrated with disgust and terror. He wanted to punch something. The bastard was literally terrifying Bree.

Bree. He wanted to run in the house and grab her and hold on tight, and never ever let her go. He could kick himself for leaving her last night, especially in the way he had. If anything had happened to her, he'd have never forgiven himself.

Colette reached out to Ryker. "Are you okay?"

"Yes. No. Hell if I know."

"Wow. He's got it bad, hasn't he?" she asked, looking at Sam.

Sam grinned and nodded, "Yep. But he won't admit it."

"What the hell are you two talking about?"

Colette smiled at that. "Hey guys, I got to run. I'm going home to fetch some clothes. I'll be right back. You guys are staying right?" she asked, walking backward to her car.

"We'll be here," Sam indicated for both of them.

They both watched Colette disappear down the drive.

"Why don't you go in and talk to her?"

"I'm not sure she wants me to."

"When has what a woman wanted ever stopped you before?"

"You make me sound like a jerk. Is that what you think?"

"No. Most of the time you have your agenda, and it doesn't usually coincide with the other person's. This time though, you seem to actually be considering what Bree wants or needs." He shrugged. "I think that's a big step for you."

"Now I sound like I have the emotional capacity of a rock."

"Just go. See how she is."

"Yeah, I guess." With that, he stuffed his hands in his pockets and walked towards the house.

He found her with her head buried in the refrigerator.

She jumped when she heard him come in. She couldn't help it. Her nerves were shot.

"I decided on hamburgers. Hope that's okay?"

When he didn't answer, she straightened and proceeded to pull out everything she would need. Ketchup, mustard, lettuce, tomato, mayo, and pickles, she ticked off things on her mental list. Then put it in the basket. "Cheese, beef patties, and buns," she said out loud.

"Do you need help?" he inquired, coming up behind her.

She tried to keep her voice from quivering. "Sure. Can you take the basket? I need to grab the rolls and potato chips." She shut the fridge and turned to hand it to him.

He took it from her. His deep blue eyes met hers and locked. She backed up, away from him.

"I can tell by the way you're looking at me, Colette told you. I don't need your pity."

"I'm not giving you pity, I'm concerned. There's a difference." He put the basket on the ground and walked towards her. "You look like you could use a friend, and a hug."

She held his gaze but put her hand up to stop his advance. "Ryker, please don't."

"Why not?"

"Because . . ." she hesitated. "I'm afraid if you touch me, I'm going to . . ."

"To what?" he asked patiently. "Rip my clothes off and take me right here in the garage?"

That got half of a smile out of her. She couldn't help it.

His face creased heavily into a broad grin revealing his deep-set dimples. "I can see you're considering it." He glanced around. "That table could work."

She laughed. "Whatever. That's not what I had in mind and you know it."

"A guy can dream, can't he?" he didn't wait for an answer. "Then what? If I touch you what? What are you going to do?"

"Shatter into a million pieces. I'm barely holding it together. I can't handle your pity or your concern." She blinked back tears. "Or your touch."

"Then I guess we're going to need a broom because I can't be this close to you and keep my hands off you when you're hurting." Without warning, he stepped in and encircled her in his arms. She melted into him and shook. They stood in the middle of the garage clinging to each other while she trembled.

"I'm so sorry this is happening to you." He stroked her back. "If I could change it, I would." He kissed her forehead gently.

"I know."

He made the following comment so matter-of-factly she almost didn't realize what he said. "I'll kill the bastard if he touches you again."

She leaned back. "Ryker, no. It's not going to come to that."

"You're damn right. I'm not letting you out of my sight until Savard has him behind bars."

"What are you, my knight in shining armor?" she tried to keep it light. She could see anger festering beneath his calm exterior.

"Something like that." He leaned down and kissed her. When she didn't stop him, he did it again, running his hands through her hair and caressing her face. He smiled. "How about that table?"

She swatted him playfully. "Guess you'll never know if I would have." She tipped her head towards the window. "Looks like Colette's back," she said, indicating the car. She batted her lashes. "Grab the basket, my white knight. We have burgers to cook."

He groaned loudly and grabbed the basket.

Chapter 37

It was late, and all Linda wanted to do was go home and crawl into bed, but she couldn't. Not until she swung by the office and picked up the file for tomorrow. Her first appointment was at eight and an hour away.

She pulled into the lot and parked her car in front of the office. Everything was dark, except a couple of streetlights that hummed and cast small pools of yellow light over the large parking lot. The night air blew steadily across the open space giving her a sudden chill. Trash skidded across the blacktop, tumbling, seemingly tugged along by an invisible string. Linda slipped her key into the lock and went in, quickly going to the alarm system to disarm it. She was surprised to find it already off.

"I guess whoever was last to leave forgot to set it," she mumbled to herself, but returned to the front door and turned the lock.

She flipped on the light above the reception desk. Nervously she glanced around. Something didn't feel quite right. She tried to tell herself it was simply because she was overly tired and her mind kept replaying her conversation with Bree. The whole idea that someone was out there stalking Bree gave her the willies.

Nothing seemed out of place, but her heart quickened anyway. Looking over her shoulder she proceeded down the dimly lit hall to her office, the only sound was her heels clicking on the tile floor, echoing in the silent space.

She flipped the switch inside her office and circled around to sit at her desk. Getting to work, she sorted through the files looking for the one she'd needed. Linda stopped shuffling when she sensed movement in the hall. "Who's there?" she called.

There was no answer.

"Of course, there's no answer, you idiot. You're alone." Disgusted with herself, she went back to the task at hand. She found the folder and stood up, prepared to leave when she heard it again.

Her heart hammered in her chest as she clutched the folder to her. "Just get to the car," she told herself. "It's only your imagination."

She walked down the hall quickly, the click of her heels grating her nerves. She went out the front door, locked it, and got into her car. Linda sat in the still car waiting for her heart to slow down as relief washed over her. Thank goodness no one was around to witness how foolish she was acting.

"Oh damn," she said out loud. "I forgot to set the alarm and I need a sign for the yard. Guess I'll be going back in."

With a deep sigh, she got out, leaving her purse on the front seat, only taking her keys. Linda unlocked the door scolding herself for being so childish. She hadn't even turned the light off over the front desk or in the hall. She strode down the hall, heels clicking, and stopped at Greg's office. She knew he had the extra signs, reaching for the knob she found it locked.

She fished through her keys and found the master, unlocked his door, and flipped on the light. Piled in the corner, beside the bookcase were the signs. Still uneasy, she grabbed the top one and spun. In her haste, she knocked a box off the bookshelf. It hit the ground and split open, spilling papers everywhere.

"For goodness' sake!" Exasperated, she scooped up the papers which contained some photographs. "Can this night get any worse?" She flipped them over and tried to stack them neatly.

A photograph caught her eye. She gasped when she realized what she was looking at. She scrambled through the papers, digging out the other photos. One after the other, all of them, capturing the same person, unaware.

Linda's heart dropped. Her hands started to shake as she realized what she was looking at.

She had to get out of here. She shoved everything back into the box, placing it on the shelf just so. She grabbed the sign and bolted for her car. She didn't even bother to lock the front door. Her mind scrambling with what to do.

Running around the back of her car she popped the trunk, hefted the sign in, and was about to close it when she felt hands on her.

She shrieked and was rewarded with a fist to her back. She dropped her keys and gasped for air. Something was shoved into her mouth. Gagging she reached for it. Rough hands were in her hair. Gripping, yanking. Her head slammed into the trunk of the car. Her world spun. Her knees went slack. She bent forward and felt her arms being yanked behind her and roughly tied, cutting into her flesh. She was shoved forward and fell into the trunk face first, cutting her cheek on the metal sign. Hands grabbed her legs and flung them into the trunk. The lid was slammed shut, pitching her into complete darkness.

Chapter 38

Ryker stifled a yawn as he placed the cabinet in its spot. He hadn't gotten much sleep last night, lying in the guest room, listening to Bree and Colette whisper in the darkness. It had been all he could do not to go down the hall and scoop up Bree and deposit her in his bed.

He stood back and examined the cabinets that were installed so far. The white paint with a dark brown rub through looked elegant against the warm stone gray of the walls and the earth tones of the tile floor.

Ryker could hear Sam on the phone with a client and decided to take a break. The sunshine might wake him up and lift his grouchy mood. *Better yet, Bree would,* he thought, as he spotted her through the window. His mood already brightened just by seeing her. He went out to see if he could talk her into going out to dinner tonight.

"Hey, beautiful," he called coming up behind her.

She turned and smiled at him, his heart melted, and his mood instantly brightened.

"Look who I have," Bree stood and put the puppy down. Zylah bounded happily through the grass towards Ryker. Her little legs carried her as fast as they could.

He laughed at the sight of her. "Well, hello Zylah," he said, squatting down and petting her head. She dropped and rolled, wanting him to scratch her belly. He obliged, and her tongue lavished his hand with wet puppy kisses. Ryker grinned, creasing his whole face into it. "When did you get her? I didn't see you leave."

"About an hour ago. She was ready to escape when we got home, so I thought I'd come out here and work while she ran around."

Ryker glanced at the abandoned laptop. "And how's that going? Getting much done?"

"Not a thing," Bree laughed. "But I really don't care. I can't believe how much I've missed her." Bree tilted her head towards the house. "How's the kitchen coming along? I'm dying to see it, but want to stay out of the way."

"Good, the cabinets are gorgeous," Ryker said, flopping down on the grass. He reached for Bree's hand and tugged her down beside him. "You should know by now you're never in the way."

"Where's Sam? What's he doing?"

"He's on the phone talking to a client. Why don't you ask about me?"

"And what are you doing?" she batted her lashes at him dramatically. "Tell me please," she teased.

"I needed a little pick-me-up, some fresh air, a little sunshine, and a whole lotta Bree." He draped his arm around her waist and slid her closer. He stopped a whisper away from her. "Are you going to kiss me willingly or do I have to beg?"

He felt her lips curve into a smile and saw it reach her eyes. There was a sparkle in her summer-blue eyes that set his body humming.

"I would actually like to see you, Ryker James, beg. I bet you've never had to in your entire life."

"That's not at all true." He leaned in closer to kiss her. His lips brushing hers.

She put her hand on his chest, holding him at bay. "Give me an example."

"You're killing me here. You know that don't you?"

She smiled coyly but didn't move her hand.

"All right, fine."

He pulled her down into the grass. Her head lay on his arm and those blue eyes bore into his. Zylah crawled up in between, snuggling close, not wanting to be left out. Bree nestled her in.

"One summer night, when Sam and I were fifteen, we wanted to take the boat by ourselves. We knew some of our friends were going to be out moonlight boating down by Assateague Island and we wanted to go in the worst way. It was already dark and my mom said no. I begged and pleaded with her but she wouldn't give in. I'll never forget it. She just stood there on the front porch with her arms crossed and asked 'Did you sweep out the garage?' I shook my head no, and I promised I'd do it tomorrow. Then she asked about the grass she'd asked me to cut earlier. I hung my head in shame, and she said, 'If you'd done your chores, maybe I would have considered it. I guess we will never know now, will we?' I got down on my knees, pleading. It didn't matter, the answer was still no. She sent Sam home and went into the house. There was no further discussion."

"So? That's it? You didn't get to go?"

He shook his head. "Not that night. But the next weekend I cleaned out the garage. Took the garbage out, and mowed the grass without being asked."

"Did you get to go then?"

"Damn right I did." He laughed, "Guess I learned a lesson that week that my mom had been trying to teach me for years."

"And what was that?"

"Take out the obstacles in your way in advance. Then you're a lot harder to refuse."

"Hmmm . . . your mother sounds like a wise woman."

"She is. She also taught me that if I want something bad enough don't be afraid to take it." He reached in then and captured her mouth.

"Holy Hell! I go outside for a ten-minute phone call, and I come back in to see my help has disappeared. And low and behold! Where do I find him? Making out in the grass with a beautiful girl." Sam stood over them and smirked. "Next time you make the call, and I'll go find the girl."

At his voice, Zylah scampered over them and jumped at Sam, wanting attention. "Hey little lady," he said, bending down to pet her. Sam addressed Ryker, "Are you about done?"

"I hadn't even really gotten started. Go away, won't you?"

Bree blushed and sat up, then stood, brushing herself off. "Sam, your timing couldn't have been better. Ryker's distracting me from my work. I can't think straight."

"Oh?"

"Yeah, he thinks I have all day to lie around."

"Let's go, lover boy. You heard the lady. Break's over." Sam started back to the house.

"What the hell?" Ryker got to his feet. He had almost forgotten. "Have dinner with me tonight?"

Bree smiled. "If you insist."

"I do. Won't take no for an answer."

"There's one catch though."

"Anything. Name it."

"It has to be something that Zylah can come along to. I'm not about to leave her home alone. Not after what happened last time."

"Deal." He gave her a sly smile. "You know you just missed a chance to ask for just about anything, and I would have caved."

"I don't want much."

"But I do." He shot her a heart-stopping grin and started to walk away.

"Go. I need to concentrate on work."

That did it. He turned around and reached for Bree, snagging her around the waist, and pulled her in tight, and kissing her long and hard. They came up for air and he let her go.

"Now let's see if you can concentrate after that." He flashed another smile at her and jogged to catch up with Sam.

Chapter 39

Sheri shuffled papers as she checked her emails one last time. She was starting to get worried. She'd called Linda at least three times today only to get her voicemail. It wasn't like Linda not to answer. *She must be pretty ill,* she thought, as she cleaned up her desk for the day.

She clicked off the computer, stood, and stretched. Noticing the plants needed watering she went in search of the watering can Linda kept in the utility closet. Having located it, Sheri slipped into the kitchenette and filled it. She was watering the plants in the reception area when Tina came back.

"Hey, hon!" Tina called as she came through the door and flopped down on the sofa. "I am exhausted."

"How was your day?"

"It was good. I took my clients around to twelve different houses. I bet they spent at least a half-hour in almost all of them."

Sheri watered a fern in the corner. "Did you find a winner?"

"Yep. You'll never guess which one."

"The very last one?"

"Nope," Tina said, slipping off her heels. One by one they fell on the floor. "The very first house I showed them today. I honestly couldn't believe it when they told me." She rubbed at her sore feet.

Sheri looked at Tina. "Really?"

"Yep, said they needed to be absolutely sure. And now they are. Thank God! That was round two for them. I don't think I could have handled a round three."

Sheri smiled. "I'm glad you got the sale. When are they putting in an offer?"

"As soon as I can get my tired butt off this couch. They want to put it in tonight. I think it's a good solid offer too. Shouldn't be too much negotiating."

"That makes for a day well spent. Changing the subject," Sheri said putting the watering can back in the closet. "Have you heard from Linda?"

Tina got to her feet and hobbled to the reception desk. "Can't say as I have, hon. But I told you, I've been with clients all day. Why?"

Sheri shrugged, "It's probably nothin' but she hasn't texted or called all day. It was just that one text early this morning saying she was sick and to cancel her appointments. It's not like her to not check-in."

Tina frowned, a solid line creased between her eyebrows. "You're right. It's not like her at all. She must be pretty sick. I bet she's been sleeping all day. What did you do with her appointments?"

"Greg was able to take one. The others I had to cancel."

Tina turned as she heard a car door slam outside. "Speak of the devil," she mumbled under her breath as they saw Greg emerge from his car.

Sheri stifled a giggle as he entered.

He came in whistling. "Ladies, finished for the day?"

"Yes, we're just wrapping things up. How was your day?"

"Brutal. But I don't have to tell either of you that running around with clients is exhausting. I just need to grab a file for tomorrow and then I'm going home, put my feet up, and drink a beer," he said as he walked down the hall.

Tina rolled her eyes at Sheri. They could hear him whistling as he unlocked his office door and disappeared inside.

"I don't know about you but his whistling gives me the creeps," Sheri whispered.

Tina nodded. "Back to Linda. If it makes you feel better, I'll stop by her place on my way home. I'm a little concerned about her too. She usually doesn't get sick like this. Maybe I'll stop at her favorite place and get her some chicken noodle soup. My hubby is out of town tonight on business, I could use the company myself."

"That would be nice, I'm sure Linda will appreciate that."

"Appreciate what?" Greg asked heading out with a file tucked under his arm.

"Tina's going to stop by and take Linda some soup, make sure she's all right. Isn't that nice?"

Greg scowled. "Aren't you afraid you'll catch whatever she has?"

"Pish posh. I don't get sick. Except for when my gallbladder bursts," Tina laughed. "But I guess that can't happen twice since the little bugger's been taken out."

Sheri saw Greg cringe and turn to go.

"Do whatever you want," he called as he opened the door. "But if you get sick, don't say I didn't warn you."

"Duly noted, Greg. Duly noted," Tina said to his retreating back.

• • • •

BREE CLIMBED INTO RYKER'S boat and waited for him to hand Zylah over. She squirmed in his hands and desperately tried to lick every inch of him.

Laughing, Bree said, "Looks like she's excited to see you."

"I'm excited too, but I would prefer my kisses from you." He grinned, handing her the wiggling pup. He stepped in and unwrapped the lines.

Bree sat and let Zylah explore while Ryker started the engine. The minute the boat began to glide across the water, she came scampering back. Bree picked her up and held her tight. The little puppy placed her paws on the edge of the boat and let her tongue flop in the wind, clearly enjoying the scents that whisked by.

The water was as smooth as glass as they slipped across it and out of the little inlet into the open bay.

For a change, Ryker didn't open the throttle; he seemed content leisurely cruising along. Bree relaxed back into her seat and enjoyed the ride. The wind whipped her hair as the late afternoon sun streaked across the glistening water caressing her skin.

Ryker maneuvered gracefully between other boats, jet skis, and a few pontoons until he came around a spit of land. He aimed for a small swipe of beach and pointed the bow towards it. The boat came aground and lodged into the wet sand. Ryker cut the engine, grabbed the anchor, and threw it on the sand, securing them.

He turned to Bree. "Your very own beach, my lady."

"It's perfect."

"I'll get out and you can hand me Zylah. Better put her on her leash though, we don't want her running off. Who knows what she could get into."

Bree clipped the leash on her collar and handed her to Ryker. He held out the other hand and helped her out.

"Wanna walk a little before we eat?"

"Definitely."

Ryker set Zylah down and gave Bree the leash as they started down the little beach. They walked in silence for a little way, content to watch Zylah explore as far as her leash would let her. When he reached for her hand, she let him take it and relished the feel of her hand in his.

He nudged her with his shoulder playfully. "So . . . are we gonna do this thing or not?"

She glanced at him. "What do you mean? Do what thing?"

He stopped in his tracks and turned towards her. "This thing." He took his free hand and waved it between them. "Us. Are you and I going to be an us?"

He saw a smile play at the corner of her mouth and then noticed it turn down instead of up.

"What's the matter? You don't want it to be us?"

She didn't say anything, just looked at him with those summer-blue eyes.

"Talk to me, Champ."

She rolled her eyes at him. "You're never going to let that go, are you?"

"Nope." He linked his other hand through hers. "I'm serious. Talk to me."

She sighed.

"You have to know I'm crazy about you, don't you?"

Her eyes filled with tears.

"What is it, Bree?"

"It's just . . ." she shrugged and looked away. "Ryker, I can't."

"You can't do what?"

"I can't handle a relationship right now. It's too much."

"Why? What's too much?"

"This." She let go of his hand and waved it between the two of them as he had done. "Us. With all that's going on, I just can't."

"All that's going on?" he questioned. "You mean this stalker? Or is there something else?"

She acknowledged him with a glance. "Yes, that. And it's too soon."

"Too soon for a relationship?"

"Yes, I haven't been out of one for very long. And after my family . . ." she hesitated. Zylah tugged at the leash, pulling her. "My heart hasn't healed. I don't know if it ever will and I can't risk it." She let the puppy pull her away from him and started walking down the beach back toward the boat.

He stood there a split second and watched her go. He jogged to catch up, took her arm in his hand, and turned her around towards him. "Not this time, Bree. You are not getting out of this that easy. I care about you. Hell, I'm falling for you. Literally, head over heels. I'm not letting you walk away because you won't risk your heart."

"Let me go, Ryker. You don't understand."

"Then make me."

Their eyes locked. "I'm terrified and I won't risk you." There she said it. She hadn't meant to but she had anyway.

"That doesn't even make sense. What are you afraid of? And what do you mean you won't risk me? I don't understand."

"I told you, you wouldn't."

"Then help me understand it."

"I won't risk your life. I won't risk losing you. I couldn't bear it, not again."

"You won't lose me. I'm here to stay." He pulled her in close and wrapped his arms around her waist. "Trust me, please?"

"What if something happens? What if this Kage or Garth whatever you want to call him comes after you? He almost killed Zylah. What's to stop him from hurting you? If he knows you're important to me, he may go after you next. I could never live with myself if that happened. I'm bad. I'm a jinx. Everyone I've ever loved is either dead or gone. I can't lose you too. I just can't! It's too much and I'm scared."

She leaned her head onto his shoulder and wept. He held on to her and let her cry, stroking her back while Zylah jumped and whined at their feet.

After a while, her tears subsided and she pulled back, glancing up at him. "I'm sorry. It's just been too much."

"That's understandable. You have every reason to be scared, anyone would be. Hell, I'm terrified for you. When I think of him standing over you with a pair of scissors, what could have happened . . ." He shook himself. "I can't even think about it." He ran a hand gently over her cheek, caressing it. "But you need to think

MELISSA ROOS

with your head and not your heart. It's not you." He hesitated. "Your family . . . that was an accident, pure and simple. That wasn't even the truck driver's fault, he was sick." He swallowed hard and pressed on. "His suicide isn't on your shoulders either. That was all him. His guilt at taking three lives and the sickness in his body was too much for him. Your ex-boyfriend? Now that's on him too. He couldn't handle the pressure and took the easy road out. He didn't deserve you. And Zylah? She survived. You got her to the vet in time." He looked down at her. "Did I leave anyone out?"

She shook her head not surprised at the edge of irritation that was in Ryker's voice. Unable to look directly at him, she gazed out at the bay and watched the steady lap of the waves, avoiding.

"I'll take your silence as an acknowledgment that I'm right." He lifted her chin and locked eyes with her. A smile spread across his face. So deep and wide his entire face creased and his dimples winked out. "So now that we've established that I'm the wise one, I want to back up a moment."

She rolled her eyes at him again. "Back up to what?"

"Are you saying you love me?" He ran a thumb across her damp cheek, wiping away a lone tear.

She wiped at the other side with the back of her hand. "I didn't say that."

"Oh," his grin widened further if that was possible. "But I think you did." He looked down at the antsy puppy. "Don't you think that's what she said?"

Zylah gave a short bark and jumped around, wrapping the leash around their legs.

"See? Even Zylah agrees. You said you love me."

She denied it. "She's not agreeing, she wants to be let loose."

"Oh, she's agreeing and you can't deny it. You're in love with me. Just admit it, Bree." He tugged her in tighter, her hips pressed against his. "You want so badly to deny it but you can't."

She'd be damned if he would trick her into saying it. She hadn't, had she? No, she hadn't. She knew better. When and if she said it, he'd know it. That didn't mean she didn't feel it. She was definitely on her way if not already headed in the direction of deep, everlasting love. Love as she'd never experienced before. And that terrified her just as much as losing him did. Damn him for twisting her words and making her have to try to deny it. Because she couldn't.

"Cat got your tongue?"

"You're just trying to fluster me, aren't you?"

"Don't change the subject."

The puppy barked and pulled on her leash. "We should eat. Zylah's hungry."

He examined her face. "No more tears?"

"No," Bree said haughtily. She looked at his face, saw the concern there, and couldn't help herself. She knew she was in deep despite the fact that he infuriated her. It was all she could do to keep from reaching up and pressing her lips to his but she didn't, knowing that would only add fuel to the fire, proving his point.

"Good. We can eat but we are going to come back to this conversation. It's far from over." He tugged her forward towards the boat. "Have I ever mentioned how cute you are when you're mad?"

"Has anyone ever told you how infuriating you are?" she retorted.

"Let's just say you're not the first one."

"That I believe."

Ryker laughed all the way to the boat.

Chapter 40

Tina strolled up the curving walk to the front door and knocked. She waited, when there was no answer, she pushed the doorbell. Still nothing. "That's odd," Tina said, shifting the hot soup to the other hand. She rang the doorbell again, then dug through her purse for a key. She unlocked the door and nudged it open, calling out. "Linda? It's me, Tina. I'm letting myself in, hope you don't mind." She didn't hear a response so she opened the door wider and went in. "Linda?" she called. "I brought soup. Your favorite."

She eased the door shut, flipped on a light, and glanced into the living room. The couch was empty. "Are you in the bathroom?" Tina asked, talking loudly. "I'm just going to take the soup to the kitchen. Come out when you're done."

With the ease of an old friendship, Tina turned the light on, comfortable in her friend's spacious kitchen. Setting the soup on the counter, she shrugged out of her jacket and laid her keys on the table. Tina looked around. Something didn't feel quite right. The place was spotless. Not that Linda didn't keep the house clean regularly, but when she was sick? That didn't make sense. There should be an empty mug, a dirty plate, or even a wadded-up tissue somewhere. But there wasn't, not even a crumb.

The place felt empty, she'd swear no one was home.

Then a thought occurred to her. What if Linda had passed out or fallen in the shower hitting her head and she was laying there unconscious. That had her moving.

She walked down the hall calling her name. "Linda? If you can hear me, say something. Or knock on something so I know where you're at."

Tina went into the bedroom and found it empty. The bed was made and everything was in its place. The bathroom door stood wide and the room dark.

She checked the other bedrooms and found nothing. Going back into the living room, she stood still and listened. The house held an eerie silence. A chill ran up her spine.

Where could she be? Maybe she ran to the store or the doctor. She tiptoed through the quiet house towards the garage and then scolded herself for being so silly.

She opened the door and stood mystified as even in the darkness it was obvious the car was there. It loomed large in the small space. She stood at the top of the stairs and peered into the darkness.

"Linda?" Her voice quivered, echoing in the room and bouncing off the hollow walls. She could almost swear she heard Linda answer. She called again. "Linda? It's me, Tina. Are you here?" The stillness of the space and the looming darkness made her uneasy, but then she heard it. A muffled cry for help.

Tina reached for the light switch. "Linda?" she questioned louder. Before she could locate the light, she was hit from behind. A quick shove had her toppling forward. She missed the riser and tumbled down the steps. Tina landed in a heap at the bottom of the stairs, clutching her ankle as pain shot up her leg. She looked up and saw a dark form moving fast towards her a split second before her head split and light burst in her right eye. The roar in her inner ear was unbearable and she shrieked in agony. The room tilted. She heard her name called from somewhere far away, and slipped into the darkness, trying to escape the pure unbridled pain.

• • • •

SAVARD STARED INTO the darkness while his wife breathed deeply beside him. He wanted to sleep, needed to, but for some reason, the peaceful rest that he craved wouldn't come. Instead, he lay still, trying hard not to disturb his very pregnant wife. He knew that lately, sleep had not come easily for her either.

A million things ran through his mind. Everything from mowing the grass, to calling his mother, and a hundred other tiny nuisances kept pecking away at his brain. But he knew the real reason he couldn't sleep. Kage.

He knew it as sure as he knew the rhythm of his wife's breathing. He was close to solving this case but an obvious clue eluded him.

Savard kept running through the list of names Bree had given him in his mind but no one stood out to him.

Maybe if I count sheep, he thought. More often than not, his mind had a way of working through his problems, his subconscious sifting through facts, sorting it all out for him. He decided to give it a try. He'd try anything at this point. *One sheep. Two sheep. That's just dumb,* he thought. Better to just count backward from a hundred.

Frustrated after only a few numbers in, he abandoned the idea altogether. He thought back to the conversation he had with Bree about the list she'd given him. Other than the obvious names, Bree had mentioned in passing that someone else on the list had once had family in Kansas too. But for the life of him, he couldn't remember who.

He rolled to his side and stared at the clock. The red numbers bore into his corneas until he closed his eyes and could still see the numbers on the back of his eyelids.

Maybe he should drink some warm milk or better yet a shot of bourbon. He flipped the covers back and slipped out of bed, careful not to disturb his wife, he tiptoed out of the room.

In the kitchen, he went to the liquor cabinet, grabbed the bottle, and filled a shot glass to the top. He downed it in one swallow, savoring the liquid gold burn as it slid down his throat and felt it hit his gut. He knew it would be a few minutes until the bourbon worked its magic, so he decided to fire up his computer and work.

He went into the office and closed his door. He turned on his computer, typed in his password, and waited for it to connect to the Wi-Fi.

He yawned, leaned back in his chair, and clicked on Google. He glanced through his notes and the list Bree had given him. Greg Carpenters' name caught his eye. Savard decided to see if he could do a little research on him, maybe get lucky with a photo to put a face to the name. He typed in Gregory A. Carpenter and real estate, and waited. He got two hits. An older gentleman and a younger man in his early thirties from Coastal Realty here in town. He clicked on the older man first.

Savard enlarged the photo. The older Gregory was late fifties, with silver-streaked hair and deeply etched lines around his mouth and eyes. Sharpe Realty was listed as his place of employment. The name clicked in Savard's brain. *Wasn't that one of the places Snader Jr. had worked?*

He opened another tab and pulled up the file on Snader's past employment. Sure enough, Sharpe Realty was on the list. Savard refreshed his page and went back and clicked on the younger man. They had the exact name, and there was a familiar look to him but he didn't resemble the older man at all.

Savard enlarged the photo of Greg Carpenter at Coastal Realty. *Hmmm . . . what were the chances?* He tapped into a secure website and dug a little further but he came up empty-handed. Prior to Coastal Realty, there was nothing on Carpenter, it was almost as if he hadn't existed before. He went back to the little blurb that accompanied the headshot. He skimmed it . . . *new associate, welcome to the firm . . .*

On a hunch, Savard pulled up the headshot of Snader and placed it side by side with Carpenter's. He leaned forward and compared faces.

Chapter 41

Pissed, he drove exactly the speed limit. He couldn't risk getting pulled over in Tina's car. He could have beaten that dumb woman bloody, but he had settled for a quick kick in the ass, the stairs had done the rest. Now that was two frickin' bodies he had to worry about. It was only supposed to be the one. Bree. But damn if it hadn't given him great satisfaction to see Tina lying there helpless in a heap at the bottom of the steps. She had let out one hell of an ear-splitting scream when he had nailed her in the head with the hammer. It hadn't lasted long. She lost consciousness almost immediately.

He hadn't bothered to tie her up, he had heard her ankle snap as she tumbled down the stairs. He knew it was shattered as he saw the grotesque way it lay, barely attached to her leg. There was no way she was putting any weight on it even if she ever did wake up again.

He had smirked at the sound of Linda's muffled screams. He toyed with the idea of putting her out of her misery but didn't. He liked knowing she lay there in the dark, alone, injured, and frightened.

She deserved it and so had Tina. For all the times they had bossed him around, for making him do the grunt work, and for rolling their eyes at him when they thought he wasn't looking. He hoped they both died in pain and agony.

He pulled over into the parking lot of a strip mall to ditch the car. There were a few others in the lot and he assumed they were late-night workers so the car wouldn't stand out. At least not right away. For good measure, he switched out the license plate with a car in the row over.

Feeling better he started down the street towards the bus stop, whistling to himself.

Now for Bree.

• • • •

THE SCREAM RIPPED THROUGH him like a knife being plunged into his heart. He bolted from bed and raced down the hall to her room. He grabbed her up off the bed as she flailed about.

"Bree!" he yelled, running his hands over her, frantically looking for injuries. Finding none he let out a breath. Relieved he said, "You were having a nightmare."

Bree choked back a sob and clung to him.

He held her close, feeling her heart pound against his chest as she shivered in the cool evening air that blew in through the open windows. A sheen of perspiration gleamed against her damp skin.

"It was just a nightmare," he repeated. "You're safe here with me." He rubbed her back as the bad dream dissipated and their hearts slowly returned to normal.

Hearing the commotion, Zylah raised her head out of her basket. She padded over and put her tiny paws up on the edge of the mattress. She couldn't make the jump by herself so Ryker let go of Bree with one arm and scooped the puppy up, snuggling Zylah in next to her.

"There. Now you have your tiny bodyguard." Ryker tried to put a little distance between them. Despite her terror, now that he knew she was all right, he could only think about how beautiful she looked. A lesser man would take advantage. It was all he could do to squash the urge to do just that.

Bree sat in the middle of that big four-poster bed surrounded by pillows white as snow and her skin glistened gold against them. Her thin blue cotton camisole might as well have been sexy lingerie as far as he was concerned because he couldn't imagine anything or anyone being sexier.

He had to remind himself that she was vulnerable right now, and he didn't want to take advantage. But he sure as hell knew it was going to be difficult going back down the hall and leaving her here looking like that.

"Are you all right now?"

"I'm fine," she said, shaking off the last of the nightmare. She petted Zylah lovingly.

He cleared his throat and reached for the pup too. "Wanna talk about it?"

She shook her head no. "I don't want to relive it. It's already starting to fade."

"Okay," he hesitated, not wanting to leave but afraid to stay. "Can I get you anything? A glass of water maybe?"

She placed her hand on his arm. "I'm fine, Ryker. Really." She smiled at him in the darkness. "You don't need to worry."

He nodded. Stood and turned to go.

"But I'd feel better if you stayed."

"Really?" he asked unsure. "You want me to stay here?" he pointed at the bed. "With you?"

She nodded. "Only if you promise to keep your hands to yourself. Can you do that?" She patted the bed beside her and pulled back the covers.

He crawled in beside her and lay down, not quite sure if this was a trick or not. "I can control myself if you can. I'm a man of steel when it comes to self-control."

She slid Zylah, who was already asleep to the bottom of the bed, then scooted closer to Ryker. He lifted his arm and she snuggled in, draping an arm over his stomach. "I'm going to hold you to that." Bree laid her head on his bare chest and closed her eyes.

"You're killing me here. You know that don't you?"

She smiled into the darkness. "I certainly do. You'll just have to deal with it."

He wrapped both arms around her tightly, then kissed her head. "Just you wait; I'll return the favor somehow."

She laughed. "I expected no different. Good night, Ryker."

"Good night, Bree." He held her close as he stared off into the darkness savoring the feel of her warm slender body next to his, pulling in the soft sweet scent of her, content to have her safely tucked in his arms. He may have to control himself but this sure beat the hell out of the guest room. Now that he was in her bed, he had no intentions of ever leaving it. That's something she'd have to deal with.

Chapter 42

It was still dark as she eased out of bed, careful not to disturb him. Safely out, she bent over and pulled up the covers. He looked so handsome and peaceful lying in her bed. She felt a pang deep in her heart, unlike anything she'd ever felt before. Was he really hers? If so, was it too good to be true? Did her heart dare to dream?

Sighing, unable to resist him, she leaned in and kissed him softly on the mouth. Without warning his eyes snapped open and he snagged her around the waist. In one swift move, he had her back on the bed and tucked neatly under him.

He grinned wickedly at her. "I made it all night keeping my hands to myself and being good. Now I want my reward." And he took it.

His mouth took hers in sweet seduction. Tasting, tempting, toying, and imploring her to take what he gave. When he moved from her lips to her neck she sucked in a haggard breath. "Ryker, please," she hissed. "You need to stop. We need to stop." It came out of her mouth but she really didn't want him to. There was no force behind the words and she knew he knew it.

"Why?" he teased, going back to her lips.

"Because."

"I'm going to need a lot better reason than that," he said, placing kiss after kiss down her neck and across the hollow of her collar bone. He flicked down the strap of her camisole.

"Because," she had to think fast while she still could because her body was turning to putty in his hands and her mind was going blank. All she could think of were his lips on her skin. The feel of his strong hands. The weight of his body on top of hers. "Because I want . . ."

"Tell me what you want, Bree," he whispered.

329

She gulped, trying to concentrate. "I want to . . . to show you something." There, she got it out. Just barely.

"Show me what?" he asked.

"We have to hurry or we'll miss it." She tried to wiggle out from under him.

"I was planning on taking it nice and slow. But if you want it quick, we can always do it again." He flashed a grin.

She socked him in the arm playfully. "Very funny. Now let me up. We have to hurry."

He rocked back in disbelief. "Seriously? I thought you were kidding."

"Well, I'm not." She slid out of bed, suddenly cold after being completely engulfed by his heat. She grabbed a sweater and tugged it on. "Be quiet so we don't wake Zylah. She is still so weak." Grabbing an Afghan from a pile of blankets near her door, Bree waited for him.

"Where are we going?" he asked gruffly, clearly put out.

"To the roof. Come on." She tiptoed down the hall and stopped by the attic stairs, shivering in the cool air. She motioned for him to follow, so he did. They ascended the flight of stairs barefoot. Then crossed the attic to the spiral staircase that led to the widow's walk.

She paused at the door, unlocking the latch. He waited behind her, impatient.

"Let's go back to bed where it's warm. I'm begging you. Please? I'll make it worth your while." He wiggled his eyebrows at her.

"I promise it will be worth it."

"It better be," he said grumpily.

She patted him on the cheek and planted a firm kiss on his lips. Before he could react, she turned and raced up the stairs. They went up into the pitch black and the frigid air. They emerged into the small glass and clapboard room. The world around them lay still and dark.

"Here," she indicated the small bench. "Sit. The show's about to begin." He did and she draped the Afghan around him. He scooched back and she sat between his legs. He wrapped his arms and the blanket around her, snuggling her in close.

The quiet surrounded them, and the stillness was like a tranquil blanket itself. They felt like the only two people on earth. Slowly, at the vast edge of the horizon, it became a spongy darkness and the stars started to wink out.

Birds started to chirp below in a chorus of chatter. The sun crept over the horizon. Just a mere shimmer at first but then quickly growing. Ebony turned to a deep navy, then violet. Purple seeped into scarlet and a big orange ball of fire emerged from behind the black wall of water that shimmered and swayed.

All around them the world brightened. The darkness that had stretched long and wide began to retreat. Curling back and shrinking from the light until it was nothing. Moments later, the night was only a memory.

They both stayed completely still watching as the earth awoke from its slumber, a spectacular sight. Ribbons of violet, scarlet, and coral bled into tangerine, saffron, and amber. A ball of fiery canary yellow took its place in the east as magnificent as a gold medal around a victor's neck. The night, at last, relinquishing its hold on the horizon.

"Wasn't that beautiful?" she whispered looking out at the bay, Ocean City, and the vast ocean beyond.

"Yes, but nothing compared to you." He kissed her neck.

"I could stay here forever. Just like this. With you."

"We can. It can be you and me. Forever."

She didn't want to believe him, because if she did, and he was taken from her, she wouldn't be able to handle it. She said nothing, just relished the thought in her heart, tucked away safely.

"Do you come up here often?" he asked.

"Yes and no. I try to get up here at least once a week. Sometimes I bring my camera. Other times I just sit and watch. It's breathtaking and I never get tired of it. And somehow . . . somehow if I've had a particularly rough night . . . it just soothes my soul. Makes me feel whole again." She laughed softly. "I guess that sounds crazy, huh?"

"Not at all. Everybody needs something or someplace to go when they need to rejuvenate. I go out on my boat. But this . . ." he looked around in awe. "This is damn good. I would take this view and you, any day." He hugged her a little tighter.

She didn't know how long they sat there as the sky continued to brighten and the details on the buildings in Ocean City became clear. Bree enjoyed the simple warmth of his arms and the blissful contentment of being with him until she became aware of a faraway bark.

"That must be Zylah. She's going to need to go out."

They descended the stairs quickly, hand in hand, and found Zylah in the hallway outside the door. She greeted them happily.

Bree bent down and petted her. "Need to go out?"

Zylah barked once.

"Come on then," Bree said, walking towards the stairs.

Down in the kitchen, Ryker went for Zylah's leash. "I'll take her out if you make coffee."

"Deal."

• • • •

HE WOKE TO THE MUFFLED sound of his name.

"Joey? Where are you?"

He stirred but couldn't quite wake up.

"Joey? Joseph Savard! I need you!"

He lifted his head off his desk and sat up stiff and sore, with a paper literally stuck to his cheek. Savard rolled his shoulders and stretched his arms and neck trying to work out the kinks, then slowly peeled off the paper. He must have fallen asleep working, he mused. The light filtering through the blinds was spongy at best. His computer was still but hummed in sleep mode.

"What time is it?" he wondered. "What was I doing when I fell asleep?" He thought he had heard his wife call but couldn't be sure. He moved the mouse and his computer sprang to life. Snader's face popped up on the screen and instantly his research came back to him.

"Joey?" she called. "Where in heaven's name are you?"

"I'm in the office, babe!" he called back loudly since the door was closed. "So much for sneaking into the bedroom and going back to sleep," he murmured. "I'll be out in a minute and put on coffee."

She came bursting through the office door. "Forget coffee. We have to go." Her hair was mussed and her pajamas were rumpled. "It's time."

"Time for what?" he questioned, still blurry-eyed.

"The baby. We need to go."

"What?" he asked in disbelief. "It can't be. We have at least three more weeks until you're due."

"I don't care how many more weeks we have," she hissed between clenched teeth. "I'm telling you it's time."

"How do you know?" he stood now, completely alert.

"I started having contractions and was hoping they were just those Braxton Hicks contractions or false ones . . ." she hesitated, sucking in a haggard breath, clutching the doorframe as one racked her body. "But now it doesn't matter. My water broke. We need to go."

He crossed to her in full emergency mood. "Okay. I have to change. And get the bags. Do you want to change?" he asked, taking her arm.

She nodded. "My pajamas are soaked. I want a shower but I don't know if I have time."

"Let's get you out of those clothes. We'll call the doctor and ask." He punched in the number and put it on the dresser, pushing the speaker button so they could hear it ring. He helped her out of the oversized shirt, pants, and underwear. Snatched clean, comfortable clothes as the doctor answered. "You talk while I get the bags."

He heard bits and pieces as he pulled on jeans and a T-shirt, then brushed his teeth and splashed water on his face. He had to get in contact with Kilpatrick and let him know what he'd found out last night. But surely it could wait a few hours. Just until after the baby came or didn't. Maybe this was a false alarm, and then he could handle it himself.

She clicked off the phone and looked at her husband as he came out of the bathroom. "He wants us to come right over."

Savard nodded and went to his wife. "Let's get you dressed first. You can take five minutes for yourself." He helped her into her clean clothes and handed her a hairbrush.

"Brush your hair, and pull it back out of your face. You'll thank me later; otherwise, you'll be cursing yourself for your hair getting in the way."

She calmly did as she was told.

"Now, look around. I have your bag and mine, is there anything else you want?"

"No, I don't think so."

He smiled at his pretty wife. He didn't think he could ever love her more than he did at this very moment. He held out his hand to her and smiled broadly.

"Let's go have us a baby."

• • • •

"SON OF A BITCH!" HE swore out loud, watching him through the telescopic lens. "Does that fucking guy live at her house? What the hell was he doing out walking the damn dog this early in the morning?"

He bent over and picked up a shoe and flung it across the room. "How in the hell am I ever going to get her alone when fucking Ryker James is her damn bodyguard 24/7?"

Pissed, he paced back and forth across his tiny one-bedroom rental. He was tired of this fucking crackerjack box he called home. He needed things. Thing's money could buy. Money that was rightfully his by birth.

He could feel the power starting to build inside him. The black moon was coming. He had to take her tonight. But first to deal with Ryker James.

He could kill him.

He wanted to with all of his being. He despised him for all he was. His good looks, his charm, and his ability to get women. He wanted to watch Ryker writhe and squirm as he drained the life out of him, then took his woman while his body lay dying. But wait . . . maybe death was too good for Mr. James. Maybe he needed to stay alive so he would be aware that Bree was taken from him.

He smiled to himself.

If he could just sidetrack him. Keep him busy and out of the way until he had Bree. Then let him live with the pain of knowing she was gone.

One of the phones on his table vibrated. He walked over and checked it. That's when the idea came to him. He knew exactly how he would deal with Ryker James.

Chapter 43

The day passed quickly despite the early start. The cabinets were in, the hardware was on, and the appliances were installed. There was a small crew measuring for countertops now that the cabinets were set, and Sam and Ryker did some touch-up work on the trim, the toe-kick, and the moldings.

They knocked off late for lunch and Ryker went in search of Bree. He found her in the studio hard at work, Zylah asleep at her feet.

"Hey, beautiful," he said, rapping on the frame of the door that stood wide open. She was dressed simply in a faded navy T-shirt and a pair of worn jeans. Her short hair hung loose, falling around her face, framing it. Her feet were bare and one foot bounced slightly in time to the beat of the country song playing in the background.

She looked up at him and blinked, then smiled. "Hey, yourself."

He shook a brown bag at her. "Wanna share my lunch?"

She eyed him suspiciously. "Okay. What's up?"

"Why does something have to be up?" he came closer and perched on the edge of her desk. "Can't I just come up here and check in on you?"

"You can but . . ."

"But what?"

"But you didn't call me Champ. Or even Bree for that matter. You called me beautiful."

"Because you are." He leaned in and brushed her lips with his teasing, tempting. He eased back and gave her a sly smile. "There's more where that came from. Wanna take a break and sneak off somewhere?"

"I'm working and I thought you were too."

"Work, work, work. You sound like Sam. I wanna play."

His hands traced down her arms, resting on her hands. He took them and pulled her up and into him. He locked her in between his legs and laced his fingers at the small of her back. "You take my breath away every time I look at you," he said casually and had the instant satisfaction of seeing her blush.

"Now you're really overdoing it."

His hand slipped up her arm and caressed the side of her face. She pressed her face into the warmth of his palm.

"I'm not doing nearly enough where you're concerned." He looked deep into her blue eyes that shimmered like pools and almost drowned with longing. "You're coming to the Shark Shack tonight, aren't you? Sam said he mentioned it to you."

"He did. I thought I would but I don't want to leave Zylah home by herself. Not after what happened last time." She looked down at the sleeping pup who had worn herself out on their long walk. She had splashed in the water, raced after a ball, and chased seagulls until she was too tired to walk back up the yard to the house.

The vet said she was fine, but Zylah was tiny to start with, and the poison clearly had taken its toll on her small frame. She looked too thin and sometimes her legs trembled, and she tired so easily.

Ryker didn't give her a chance to back out. "We can go together. I'll pick you up at seven."

He didn't want Bree alone. Cops driving by and a small helpless puppy were not enough protection. Too many things had already happened, he wasn't taking any chances.

"Didn't you hear me? I'm not leaving Zylah."

"I heard you. Trust me, I have that covered. One thing at a time here. You haven't heard from Kage again, have you?" he asked, concerned.

"No, I haven't. Maybe he's given up. I told you I called the attorney, right? And I refused the money."

Ryker nodded.

"So, chances are we're worried about nothing."

"Have you signed the papers yet giving up your right to the money?"

"Well, no, but . . . "

"But nothing. As far as I'm concerned, he is still out there. And still after you. Money or not, he's fixated on you, and won't slink off into the shadows of the black moon quietly. He's gone too far. Invested too much time and energy into harassing you."

Bree tried to ignore the little tickle of fear that started to build in the pit of her stomach. "You're wrong. He only wants the money. Once he has that, he'll leave me alone. You'll see."

"I hope you're right." He had his doubts and could see she did too. There was fear in her eyes. She masked it well, but he could still see it, feel it, shimmering just below the surface. He let it go for a moment, reaching for his sandwich. "Since you seem like you don't wanna play, we might as well eat. Come on, before Sam texts me that I'm taking too long."

He unfolded the bag and pulled out a sub, a bag of chips, and an orange. Ryker handed her the orange. "Can you do the honors?"

"Sure." Bree peeled the orange while Ryker split the turkey sub.

"I think we will be finished here around five. Thought I would go home, shower, and then come back for you."

Bree handed him a slice of orange. "I'm not leaving Zylah," she said, popping one in her own mouth.

The puppy raised her sleepy head, hearing her name. Deciding it wasn't worth it, she lay back down.

Ryker acted like he hadn't heard her. "Pack a bag because tonight you're staying at my place."

She bristled. "Yeah, I don't think so. I'm perfectly fine here. I won't be told what to do like I'm a child."

Ryker knew she would resist, he was prepared for it. "You don't have a choice. I already put Zylah's bed in my truck along with the crate, her food, and some of her toys. From now on you will be with me twenty-four-seven until Kage is caught."

"Do you think you can just decide? Just like that?" she asked in disbelief. "Don't think I don't know what angle you're playing here. You're trying to scare me into your bed." She stood so she could distance herself from him. "It won't work. I'm not going to sleep with you."

He chewed thoughtfully. "You will." Ryker looked her square in the eye. "Maybe not tonight but somewhere down the road. I won't force you if that's what you're thinking. I don't play that way. I care about you and I'm going to protect you until this thing is over. Like it or not." He stood now too. "And I know you don't. You're afraid, and you have every right to be, but I'm telling you I'm in this for the long haul."

He put the wrappings of the sub in the paper bag and snagged another slice of orange. "I'm not going anywhere, Bree." His phone chimed. He glanced down at it. Frowning. "Damn it. Except maybe to another jobsite. Looks like Sheri needs me to check something out for Linda. She says it's urgent." His phone chimed again. "Here's a text from Linda too, it must be important."

He dug his keys out of the worn front pocket of his jeans, selected a key, and worked it off. Ryker reached for Bree's hand, and before she could protest, placed it in her palm. "Just in case I don't get back in time to meet you."

He went over to the little pup that had woken up, bent down, and petted her. Her jaws stretched wide in a yawn. She nuzzled Ryker's hand, loving the attention.

"And as some added insurance to make sure you'll come, I'm taking Zylah with me. I'll drop her at my house where she will be safe. You can enjoy the evening and the music without worrying about her."

Bree eyed the key in her hand. "And what am I supposed to do with this?" She held it up between two fingers like it was poisonous.

He flashed a grin that creased his entire face. "Disappointed I am that you know not what you hold. You use it to unlock a door. Not just any door mind you. *My* door. I'll have you know, that has been a highly sought-after item over the years. And you, my dear Bree, are the first to ever acquire it. Use it wisely."

His humor was lost on her. "By wisely, you mean to let myself in and make myself comfortable, correct?"

"Something like that." He almost added that it was also the key to his heart but couldn't quite make himself go that far. Some things needed to be said in the soft romantic moments, to be truly appreciated. And this wasn't one of those moments.

Linda texted again. URGENT in all caps.

"Look, I gotta go. If I'm not here at seven, go to the Shack without me. I don't want you here alone."

"I'll be fine."

He snagged her and pulled her in close. "You're more than fine. But I want you safe." He kissed her again, long and hard.

Ryker pulled back, looked down into her pretty face, and couldn't remember what it had been like before she came into his life. He asked as nicely as he possibly could, "Promise me? That's all I ask. Please?"

She relented, nodding.

With one last kiss, he released her and walked back over to the dog. "Okay, then I will meet you there if I'm not here by seven." He scooped up the little cocker spaniel. "Zylah will be safe at my house and you have a key if you feel the need to check on her ahead of time."

Before she could protest, he turned and disappeared down the stairs, her puppy tucked safely in his arms.

• • • •

SHERI STOOD OUTSIDE the rental house and waited for Ryker. The wind had shifted slightly in the last hour and the air was chilly. A shower had passed leaving everything wet. She hugged herself inside her sweater and hoped Ryker hurried. She should have opted to wait for him in the car.

"If he's not here in the next minute or two, I'll go back to the car," she told herself. But to her relief, he pulled up.

"Hey, Sheri," Ryker called, getting out of the truck.

"Hey, yourself."

"What seems to be the problem?"

She shrugged. "I'm not sure. Linda just texted and said we needed to get over here asap."

"I'll just grab my toolbox out of the back."

Sheri unlocked the front door. Water gushed out as the door swung outward. The living room was flooded.

"Oh my!" Sheri exclaimed, doing a little dance, trying to keep her shoes from getting wet. "What in the world happened?"

"Pipe might have burst somewhere up above," Ryker said, looking up as water rained down. "Stay back or you're going to get soaked."

"You don't have to tell me twice! These are brand new boots!" Sheri exclaimed.

Ryker chuckled and scooped her up out of harm's way. "Can't have a shoe emergency." He carried her down the stairs and to her car. "Go back to the office. I got this."

"Are you sure?" She leaned over and examined her new suede boots. Tsking a little as she noticed a few drops of water. "I paid full price for these too," she pouted.

"No sense ruining perfectly good boots."

Sheri beamed. "Ryker, you're my hero." She reached up on tiptoes and placed a kiss on his cheek. She batted her lashes at him. "I'll see you later at the Shack?"

"You bet. Be there as soon as I get this cleaned up."

"Maybe you'll take me home after?" She let the invitation linger in the air between them.

He waited a heartbeat and contemplated the offer. A few months ago, he would have been tempted, and probably wouldn't have even hesitated. But now? Things were different. Bree had changed that. Now all he wanted was Bree.

"Sheri, I'm sorry but I can't."

A flicker of disappointment raced across her face. "Can you at least tell me why? I thought maybe . . . maybe we had a little thing? But I might have misinterpreted."

"There's someone else."

"Would that be Bree?"

"Yeah, how did you know?"

"I've seen how you look at her, how you act around her."

"Look, I'm sorry if I led you on."

"No worries, Ryker. To say I'm not disappointed would be a lie but I'm a big girl with new boots. I'll be fine."

He laughed. "They're fine boots. I am sorry. Still friends?"

"Always."

He leaned in and hugged her.

She was the first to break the connection as tears filled her eyes and threatened to fall. She climbed into the car without looking back at him and drove away.

Ryker went back into the house shaking his head, feeling like a cad. Sorry he had hurt her.

Slogging through the house towards the kitchen, he stopped in disbelief as water poured over the edge of the kitchen sink and sprayed in the air from the faucet. Water dripped from the ceiling and the walls. Within seconds Ryker was soaked as he turned off the water. He looked around, *what a mess.*

He texted Sam and asked him to have one of the guys bring over the wet-dry vacs and their industrial-sized fans. Having sent the text, he set to work.

• • • •

SAVARD SAT DOWN, EXHAUSTED. He smiled at the sight of his beautiful wife asleep in the bed, his newborn son snuggled in next to her. It had been a long slow process for her, and the labor intense. So intense he didn't feel like childbirth classes had prepared him. He'd felt stupid with the whole breathing thing, the *he he he's* had made him lightheaded. The sight of all the fluids and the head crowning made him more than a little nauseous. But somehow, he had managed to stay on his feet and watch his child come into the world. Whole and perfect. Ten fingers. Ten toes. A nose as cute as a button, jet black hair, and a dimple in his chin. He was small and perfect. Savard couldn't have been prouder. He leaned back now in the recliner and closed his eyes. Content and happy.

He briefly succumbed to a light slumber when he felt his phone vibrate in his back pocket. He was tempted to let it go but suddenly realized he hadn't thought about work all day except for the brief text he had dashed off to Kilpatrick in the wee hours of the morning.

Easing out of the chair he tiptoed across the room. In the hallway, he answered. "Savard."

"Tell me you've had that baby by now?"

He smiled at the sound of Kilpatrick's voice. "Yep. He's here. All five pounds and four ounces of him. Head full of hair and a healthy appetite. Little Joey."

Kilpatrick laughed in his ear. "Lord help your wife if he's anything like you. Question though, is he the mailman's baby? We know he didn't get any hair from you."

Savard ran a hand over his shiny bald head as he walked and grinned in spite of himself. "Funny guy. What's up? I know you didn't just call to ask about the baby."

"Yeah, sorry to bother on such a special day and all but we have a situation. I'm not sure if or how it would connect but I wanted you to know right away. Tina Vincent from Coastal Realty is missing. Her husband Chuck reported her missing a few hours ago."

Savard ducked into an empty waiting room and closed the door. "What makes him suspect that she's missing?"

"He hasn't talked to her since last night. She was working late, which is normal if he is out of town. Tina told her husband she was going to stop and get some soup for a sick friend, drop it off, and check on her."

"Who was the friend?"

"Linda Lauer, owner of Coastal."

"Friend and coworker home sick. That doesn't sound unusual or of great concern."

"No, but the fact that he didn't hear from her later is. They always call each other and say goodnight no matter how late."

"So . . . Tina stopped by, maybe fell asleep on the couch taking care of her sick friend. It happens."

"Not to them. The husband's beating himself up because he didn't press the matter last night or have someone go over and check on her. It seems she never made it home. When he got home this afternoon the house was exactly the way he left it. He was the last one to leave yesterday. He found the house empty, his newspaper and his coffee cup still on the table where he left it. Apparently, Tina is a clean freak. She would have never left those things out. He called into work, and they said she hadn't been in all day, and they hadn't heard from her either, except for one short text in the morning saying she was ill."

"Work didn't question it?"

"No, they knew she was stopping by Linda's. They just assumed she got whatever Linda had. Funny thing is, Chuck, the husband, drove past Linda's. The house is quiet, shades are drawn, doors locked. He swore no one was home. Which had him puzzled because Sheri, the receptionist, said Linda had texted her late this afternoon, still ill."

"Why would Sheri lie?"

"Maybe she's not. Maybe Linda is really texting her."

"Or maybe someone has her phone and is using it to make it look like it's Linda."

"Maybe."

"Find out what kind of car Tina drives and put out a missing report on her." Savard rubbed his head and thought about what he had found out last night. Garth Snader's face floated through his thoughts. "Where are you?" he asked Kilpatrick.

"I'm at the station. Why?"

"Get me Linda Lauer's home address and meet me there in thirty. Something about this isn't right."

Chapter 44

B ree got the text a little after six, Ryker wasn't going to make it by seven. Sam was gone, and so was the rest of the crew. The house was quiet, and she longed to hear Zylah's little feet pad across the floor.

She debated what to do. Should she pack a bag and stay at Ryker's? Or should she skip going to the Shack and just go get Zylah and snuggle down with her in front of the TV for the evening? Bree replayed the conversation with Ryker in her mind and cringed realizing she had promised.

Pulling a bag down from the shelf of her closet, she carried it to the bed and stared at it. What was she doing? Was she crazy?

She wasn't crazy, she was in love. She paused. *Could she really be? In love? With Ryker James?* Her heart lurched at the revelation. That scared her just about as much as Kage.

Bree circled around the bag like it was a snake, coiled up and hissing, ready to strike. *Should she? Or shouldn't she?*

She paced. And bit her thumbnail. *If she went willingly what did that say? Did it say she was needy? Desperate? Did it say she was scared to be alone? Or did it simply say she was being smart and protecting herself?* She told herself it was the latter. Wanted to believe it. Had to.

Begrudgingly, she started to pack. "Nothing sexy," she told herself. "Basic comfort clothing. Basic hygiene needs. Make a list. . . a list."

She smiled to herself. It had actually been a few days, maybe even a whole week since she had felt the need to make a list. "Toothbrush, toothpaste, deodorant." She stopped. "I should take a shower. Shave my legs. . . In case. . . in case what? In case I end up in bed with him. Damn it."

She cursed herself and Ryker. What was he doing to her? She was a strong independent woman. Well, she had been, before. Before the accident. Before the loss of her family. She was becoming one again. How dare he interfere with that unknowingly.

Bree went into the bathroom and turned on the shower. She stripped, leaving her clothes in a pile, and then adjusted the tap. She scrubbed her head and washed her body. Then stared at the damn razor. Hating herself, she reached for it and shaved her legs.

Finished, she toweled off. Suddenly it hit her. Maybe she *should* take all the sexy stuff. Torture the man, while she did everything in her power to keep him at bay. That would serve him right.

Happier, she started to pack her bag. Then stopped. She owned absolutely nothing sexy. She stood mortified. She couldn't be sexy to torture him even if she wanted to.

In the end, she reached for clean and comfortable anyway, leaning towards cute. She sighed heavily as she zipped the bag shut.

Who was she kidding? Ryker didn't think of her that way. He looked at her as just another notch on his bedpost. "Which is fine," she told herself. "I can't love anyone anyway. That's how I lose them, by loving too much. I won't have anything happen to him. Whether he loves me or not, I simply couldn't bear it."

She'd go to the Shack, have something to eat. Mingle a little, because she promised she would. She'd even go to Ryker's, sleep on the couch a couple of days, just until the black moon was over. Then she would take Zylah and go home.

She only had to get through the weekend. Tuesday she would sign the papers releasing the money and this whole scary mess would be over.

• • • •

PICTURING LINDA TIED and bound in the trunk of her own car, he wondered if she was still alive. Did she lie there in the unforgiving dark and weep softly to herself? Or did she fight against her bonds, rip the flesh from her skin and scream with all her might? Oddly, both gave him comfort.

Did she know it was him who had done this to her? Did she live each hour, each minute in fear, wondering if he would return? What frightened her more? The thought that he would come back or that no one would? Ever.

Then he pictured Tina literally feet from her friend. Still and lifeless, lying crumpled at the bottom of the stairs on the cold hard cement. Blood pooled around her head from where he struck it. Her leg twisted at an odd, unforgiving angle.

It was a shame she never knew what hit her. That *he* hit her, and he took great pleasure in it. She would never roll her eyes at him again. She would never talk down to him. It was he who had overpowered her.

It made him smile to think of them. To think of both, lying there suffering, half-dead, in pain, in and out of consciousness, sick with fear.

He had an urge to do one more. To do it again. He craved one more victim before he dealt with Bree Thompson, his ultimate prize. One more target. He had already set the wheels in motion.

She had no idea she was being stalked. No idea she was about to suffer and that she was the last link in his chain. His chain to capture Bree.

He stood now in her house, tucked back in the corner of the dark cramped pantry. The door cracked just enough so he could see out. Watching. Waiting for her to come home.

Adrenaline coursed through him and he willed himself to be patient as the key turned in the lock.

She entered the house and dropped her purse on the table. Her back was to him and he slithered out of his hiding place. She sensed him and spun. It was only a split second but he saw the flicker of panic before the first blow connected with her face. Her strawberry blonde hair whipped as her head snapped. She staggered back and hit hard against the cabinets, a knob digging into her back. Sheri shrieked as he came towards her.

"Please don't!" she cried. Her knees gave out and she slipped to the floor, dizzy and in pain. "There's money in my purse. Take it! Just don't hurt me."

"I don't want your money."

She looked up at the sound of his voice. "You?"

His glasses were gone and his eyes were an eerie blue. "Greg? Aren't your eyes brown? What are you doing here?" she questioned.

The back of his hand connected with her face. Her lip split and her eyes welled with tears of pain as she shrieked.

"I ask the questions."

He was dressed all in black, from head to toe, a tattoo of a black moon on his bicep just below the hem of his short-sleeved T-shirt winked out as he moved.

She gasped, "It's you. You're Kage." She looked into his crazed eyes and fought panic. "All this time? It's been you harassing Bree? But why?"

"She stole what was mine. Took everything from me. My father. His life. He ended it because of her. And my rightful inheritance. My birthright. And tonight, I get it back."

"I don't understand?"

"I don't expect you to. It's way above your pretty head."

"But why are you here? What do I have to do with what's happened between you and Bree?"

"You're going to help me."

"I won't help you hurt her." Sheri tried to stand.

"It's safer on the floor. I suggest you stay there." He pulled a chair out and sat, watching her. "She took something from you too."

Sheri shifted on the floor and inched back further against the cabinet. "She hasn't taken anything from me."

"Really?" he questioned. "I beg to differ." She flinched as he pulled something out of his back pocket. "Look at this."

He held up his phone. On the screen, there was a picture of Ryker carrying her down the stairs at the rental only an hour ago. He swiped and she was kissing Ryker, swiped again and there was another photo of him hugging her.

"How did you . . ." she couldn't complete the thought. "You followed me?" she asked in disbelief. "You flooded the house."

He grinned slyly. "Very good. For a blonde, you're not as dense as I thought you'd be. Now let's get what we both want, shall we?" Coming forward off the chair, he crouched down in front of her.

"I won't help you. I don't care how much you think I want Ryker, I won't do anything to help you get back at Bree. She doesn't deserve it no matter what you say she's done."

"Fine," he sneered. "If you're not with me, you're against me." His fingers grabbed hold of her hair and slammed her head into the cabinet behind her. Her world spun. He yanked her up and twisted her around, pinning her to the ground. He put his knee in her back and wrestled her arms into position while she squirmed and screamed. He wrapped a zip tie around them and yanked it tight. She bucked and twisted while he struggled to do the same with her legs. Once immobilized, he got off of her.

Tears streamed down her face. "Please don't do this," she sobbed. "What are you going to do? People will come looking for me. I was supposed to go with the group to the Shack tonight. They'll know something's wrong when I don't show up."

He dumped the contents of her purse onto the table and snagged her phone. "Don't worry. I've got that covered. But I can't have you screaming and getting someone's attention." He pulled out a pocket knife and held it to her cheek, then ran it down her neck.

She whimpered.

"I think I'll leave you alive for a while. I may find another use for you yet." He grabbed a roll of duct tape and sliced off a piece with the knife, placing it over her mouth. He left her on the kitchen floor, bound and gagged. But still alive.

Chapter 45

Voices. *Were those voices?* Her mind was fuzzy, her throat scratchy and raw, and her eyes burned from staring into the pitch black. She heard it again. The sound was muffled but it was definitely a man's voice. Was it him? She shrunk back in fear. *Dear God, please don't let it be him.*

If he opened the trunk there was nothing she could do. There was no way to fight, her arms and legs had long since gone numb.

Wait. She heard more voices. Yes, she was sure of it. She tried to scream but all that came out was a tiny squeak almost inaudible to her own ears. She tried again, but her throat was so sore she couldn't get it out. There were too many, they would never hear her. She had to move. She had to make some noise. Tears welled in her eyes and her body shook as she willed her body to move but nothing happened. She began to panic. *Would they leave without looking in the trunk?*

She couldn't let them. Linda knew if she was in here much longer, she would die. She almost wished she would. The waiting was torturous, endless, mind-numbing.

If I can just move my legs and kick the side, she thought.

Linda concentrated on just her feet and willed them to move. All her energy poured down into her feet. They were so numb they burned like they were on fire. She imagined herself kicking the side of the trunk. Over and over again. She couldn't be sure but she thought her legs moved a little. Then a little more. They inched further across the black abyss until she swore, she felt the tips of her toes touch the interior of the car. She jerked to a stop as a racket came over her head.

Suddenly, she realized it was the garage door opening. She waited until it stopped and she was plunged back into the quiet. Were they gone? Her heart wrenched. *Please God let them still be here!* She heard them go by her head, the shuffling of feet, standing, and talking. She swore someone even leaned on the car. That's when she let loose. With all her might she screamed and kicked out.

"Did you hear that?"

"What?"

"Listen."

There was only silence except for a little street noise.

"I swear I heard something."

"I can't hear anything."

"Did anyone check the trunk of this car?"

"I don't think so."

"Hear that? It's coming from inside."

"Pop the trunk."

Savard was hit first with the smell but as the lid swung up, he saw a woman bound and bloody, pupils widely dilated, staring back at him.

"Linda?"

She let out a croak barely above a whisper that sounded like yes behind the thick material stuffed in her mouth.

"You're safe now. I'm Detective Savard." He reached in and touched her gently on her face. "I'm going to take the cloth out of your mouth." He slowly worked it out. "We're going to get you out of here. Paramedics! I need them now! And something to cut these zip ties off with. Hurry!"

Linda closed her eyes as relief washed over her.

• • • •

THE NIGHT WAS UNSEASONABLY cool, and getting colder. Bree parked at the Shark Shack and got out when Colette walked up.

"Hey, girl!" Colette gave her a hug.

"Hey, yourself. Are you taking your purse?" Bree asked, glancing at Colette's shoulder.

"Nope, left mine in my car."

"I don't want to keep track of mine either. But what about your keys and your phone? I don't have any pockets."

"I put my keys on a lanyard and hang them around my neck. I have an extra one in the car if you want it?"

"That would be great."

"Hang on I'll grab it."

Bree waited while Colette retrieved it, tucking a credit card and a twenty inside her phone case. She clipped her keys to the lanyard, then hung them from her neck and slipped them under her little white tank top. Her cotton blue and white checked button-down was tied in a knot at her waist and covered the bulge of the keys. "That's great. Now if I only had a place for my phone."

"Do what I do. Stick it in your bra."

Bree laughed. "You're joking, right?"

"Nope, I put it on vibrate and tuck it in. Try it. It beats the heck out of carrying a purse. See."

Bree watched her tuck it in and was surprised it wasn't even noticeable.

"Now you."

"Well, I have a little less material to work with than you do, but I'll give it a try." She did as she was told and was surprised how well it fit.

"See? What did I tell you? And with that extra shirt on you'll never see it. Let's go. I'm starving."

Colette linked her arm through Bree's and started towards the Shack. "I thought maybe you would come with a hot date on your arm. Heard through the grapevine Ryker's been spending a lot of extra time at your house. What's up between you two? Anything serious?"

Bree shrugged. "I'm not sure."

"When I spent the night the other night, I sure got the impression he was."

"Was what?"

"Serious." Colette looked at her friend's blank face and laughed. "You really have no clue, do you?" When Bree remained quiet, Colette continued. "Serious about you, silly. Apparently, everyone but you knows it."

That comment had her insides warming. Maybe he really was into her, more than she thought. More than she dared to hope. Maybe she wasn't just another conquest to him. Her heart did a little happy flip.

They could hear the music pumping out of the building even before they got close to the back door.

"This is going to be fun." Colette glanced at Bree and placed a hand on her arm. "Before we go in, tell me. How's everything, really? Have they had any leads in your case?"

Bree sighed. "Thank you for asking, but I really don't want to talk about it tonight. I just want to have some fun."

"Then that's what we will do. Have nothing but fun. We need to look for Sam. He said he would save a table." Colette opened the back door of the Shark Shack and music poured out.

The parking lot had been full but the party room was overflowing. Hard country twang filled the air with a bass beat that shook the ground. The tables that were scattered around the edge of the great expanse of the room were filled. Bree and Colette looked around for Sam in the throng. He waved from across the crowded room and they threaded their way to him.

The air was warm in the room so jackets and sweaters were off and draped over chairs, voices were raised to be heard over the music, and drinks flowed. There was a mixture of people already on the dance floor.

The twang of a guitar echoed as the music died just as they reached the table. Sam stood and kissed them both on the cheek. "Glad you guys are finally here. I was starting to get dirty looks for holding this table by myself."

Colette laughed looking him up and down. "I'm sure it was more likely women were wanting to join you." She glanced around. "But seriously, where is everybody?"

"Ryker is still at the rental house cleaning. Apparently, the place is a disaster. I don't know about Sheri. She should have been here by now."

"Looks like we should have gotten in line for drinks, the line is a little long but seems to be moving."

"I'm glad you didn't, gives me an excuse to get up and go get them. What would you like?"

"I'll have whatever's on tap," Colette answered.

"Same."

"Be right back."

Colette glanced over her shoulder and watched Sam disappear into the crowd. She grabbed Bree's arm and leaned in close. Her eyes gleamed with mischief. "I think I already know the answer, but I want to make sure. Are you into Sam at all? Or are you definitely into Ryker?"

Bree smiled. "I'm definitely just into Ryker. Why?"

"I kind of have a thing for Sam."

"No? Really?" Bree questioned trying to feign surprise.

"Ha, ha, very funny. So, I'm not subtle."

"Line must not have been as long as we thought. Here he comes."

"Looks like he found a friend." Colette nodded in their direction.

"Hey, Greg," Bree said, accepting the beer from Sam. "I didn't know you were coming."

He took the seat next to her. "Sheri mentioned it this after-noon. Pretty good crowd here already. The dance floor is crowded."

"Where is Sheri?" Colette asked as she took the drink from Sam and made room at the table.

"She had to help Ryker at the rental house. Something about a pipe bursting, I think. I would guess she'd be here soon. Can't imagine they wouldn't have it under control by now. Unless . . ." Greg raised his eyebrows behind his glasses.

"Unless what?" Sam asked leaning in closer, unable to keep a slight tone out of his voice. "What are you implying?" he asked again.

Greg glanced from Sam to Bree, then shook his head. "Nothin'. I didn't mean anything. You know, she probably just went home to get changed and maybe relax a little. We've been swamped at work with both Linda and Tina out sick."

"I'll give her another half hour and if she's not here I'll text her."

The band rolled on into another song, setting the fast-paced mood. Lights flashed, bouncing off every surface, and bodies packed onto the dance floor.

"Oh! I love this song!" Colette exclaimed as the crowd shifted and started to form lines. "Let's dance."

She grabbed Bree's hand and tugged her out of her chair to-wards the dance floor. They fell into line with the others and began to clap and move in rhythm to the song. It took a couple of tries but soon both women were in sync stomping, turning, and gliding with the rest. One song ended and without hesitation, the band flowed into another suitable for line dancing and the crowd carried on. By the end of the second, Bree and Colette were laughing so hard, they were exhausted. When the band announced they were going to slow things down they gladly headed back to the table.

Colette sat down next to Sam, wiggling in closer, while Bree took the chair beside Greg. The minute Bree was situated; Greg draped an arm behind her chair. She instinctively sat a little straighter, not sure what to think of the gesture.

"I can't believe Sheri is missing this! She loves to dance."

"Ryker too. That job must have been more of a mess than he let on. It's not like either one of them to miss this sort of thing."

Bree felt a little twinge of jealousy course through her. *What if they were together?* "You should text Sheri, make sure everything's okay," Bree said, trying not to overthink it.

"I will."

"I'm going up for another round. Does anyone want anything?" Greg asked. He leaned over close to Bree, his warm breath tickling her neck. "Can I bring you back another?"

She shifted slightly away from him in her seat and smiled kindly. "I think I'm good for now but thanks for asking."

He ran a hand down her arm and gave her hand a squeeze. "I'll be back soon."

Sam watched the exchange while Colette texted Sheri. "I think someone has a crush on you."

Bree looked at him and shrugged. "It's harmless, and I'm not interested."

Sam gave her a cheesy grin. "Because you're interested in Ryker instead?"

"I never said that."

"You didn't have to. I just hope Ryker gets here before Greg asks you to dance."

"He won't. It's not like that."

Sam held her gaze. "I'm telling you it is for him. He's gearing up for it. He needed one more drink for a boost of confidence. But after he's finished, I'm telling you he's going to ask. The signs are all there."

Colette glanced from Sam to Bree. "He's right you know? I've noticed before how he watches you. How he talks to you."

"He talks to you and Sheri, too."

"Yeah, but not the same way he does you. He's flirting with you, with us it's just necessary conversation."

"You both are exaggerating."

Colette straightened. "Here he comes."

Greg placed his half-empty beer on the table, stood next to Bree, and held out his hand. "Wanna dance?"

Bree looked up into his brown maple syrup eyes and hesitated. Were they right?

"She would love to but she can't," Sam spoke up.

"And why not?" Greg asked, not taking his eyes off of Bree.

"Because she's dancing with me." Sam stood and pulled out Bree's chair. "Come on."

Bree practically sprang to her feet and let Sam lead her out onto the dance floor. Safely in his arms, Bree relaxed. "Thank you. I owe you one."

Sam gave her a spin, out and in. He laughed. "You totally do. No worries. You'd do the same for me, I'm sure."

"I totally would," she agreed. "If Greg asks you to dance, I'll sweep you away."

Sam laughed and spun her again.

"You really should be dancing with Colette."

"I know. Believe me, I plan to as soon as Ryker gets here and can keep you safe."

"Ryker doesn't need to protect me from Greg."

"Maybe not, but he told me not to let you out of my sight for long tonight. He's worried about you, Bree. We all are. He thinks that this whole Kage thing is about to go down."

Bree shrugged, unsure. "Maybe. But if Ryker is really worried, why isn't he here?"

"I'm sure he's still at the jobsite, or maybe needed to go home and clean up. He'll be here soon."

Bree looked at the other couples that slowly circled the floor, swaying to the music, and decided to ask. "You don't think Ryker and Sheri might . . ."

Sam cut her off before she could finish. "I don't. He cares about you."

At that moment Bree felt her phone vibrate next to her chest.

"Hang on," Sam said, letting go of one of her hands. "This is probably him." Sam dug his cell phone out of his back pocket. "It's a group text from Sheri." They stood in the middle of the dance floor, heads together, while he pressed on the text message. A picture came up of Ryker carrying Sheri in his arms, her head thrown back in laughter.

Bree snagged the phone from Sam and scrolled down to the next picture. It was Sheri kissing Ryker.

There was a pit forming in her stomach. She couldn't believe her eyes. Her hand shook slightly as she scrolled again to the next one. Ryker holding Sheri. The words underneath said it all.

Not sure if we're going to make it tonight.

"There has to be some explanation, Bree."

"Yes, I saw it. They're not coming." She shoved the phone back at him. "Excuse me."

Before Sam could say anything, she darted through the couples on the dance floor and disappeared into the crowd.

How could she be so stupid? She believed him. Trusted him. She had even packed a bag to stay the night . . . and he had her puppy.

How dare he think he could stand her up and still get her into his bed later? Tears blurred her vision. *Stupid. Stupid.* She was so stupid.

Bree pushed out the back door and into the dark cold night. The door slammed closed behind her and cut off the roar of the band. She tried to think. *Where had she parked?*

She walked fast down the rows of cars, thinking. She'd go directly to his house. It wouldn't matter if they were there. She'd go in and get Zylah, and walk out. Simple. He couldn't stop her. She corrected herself, *he wouldn't stop her.*

She unlocked the door of her SUV and climbed in. She lay her head on the steering wheel and let out a sob. *How could she have been so stupid?*

She jumped as someone rapped on her window.

"Sorry, Bree," Greg said sympathetically, giving her a reserved smile from behind the glass. "Didn't mean to scare you. I hope you don't mind but I saw you run out. I called out but I guess you didn't hear me."

She quickly wiped her eyes. "I'm fine. I'm just tired and want to go home."

"Okay, if you're sure?"

Bree nodded. "Thank you, Greg."

"I'll talk to you tomorrow?"

"You bet."

He backed up and she stuck her key in the ignition, and turned it but nothing happened. "What?" She tried again. Nothing. And again. Still nothing. "Aaaaaa!" she cried. "Just my luck!"

"Everything okay?"

"No. My car won't start."

"Do you want me to call a tow truck?"

She got out of the car and slammed the door. "I guess, but with the way my night's going I'll probably be sitting here for an hour." She choked back a sob. "I just want to go home."

He reached out and touched her lightly on the shoulder. "I can take you home. We can come back tomorrow in the light and deal with your car. How does that sound?"

"Are you sure? I don't want to take you away from the Shack and the band. They were pretty good."

"I'm sure."

Bree hesitated, feeling bad about accepting, "If you're sure?"

"I am. My car's over here." Greg took her arm, guiding her in the direction of his vehicle.

• • • •

RYKER SLOGGED ACROSS the flooded basement in water up to his knees, cursing to himself. How in the hell had this happened? They had finished this project less than a week ago. All that time, money, and material ruined, wasted.

Linda would have a fit when she found out. He wouldn't blame her. She probably wouldn't believe it either, not until she saw it for herself. Hell, he couldn't believe it and he was standing in the middle of it. There was no rhyme or reason to it. Someone deliberately went through the house and turned on every faucet, plugged every drain, and overflowed every toilet. But why?

That was the million-dollar question. What was there to gain from flooding an empty rental house? Insurance money? That made no sense. Linda was the owner. She paid the insurance, she had nothing to gain by wrecking it. In fact, she had a ton to lose. The revenue from leasing out the house, money for repairs, materials, and not to mention that her insurance bill was going to go sky high after this.

The water had been turned off hours ago but that hadn't stopped the water from running down the walls and seeping into the basement. He stood in the center of the room and looked around, disgusted and disheartened at what he saw. His phone vibrated on his hip. He answered on the second ring.

"Hello?"

"What the hell, Ryker?"

"Glad to hear your voice too, Sam," he said sarcastically. He could hear the music blaring in the background. "What's with the attitude? You're at the Shack having fun while I'm here slaving away."

"Is that what you're doing? You sure as hell could have fooled me."

"What's that supposed to mean? I'm literally standing in water up to my knees and you want to chastise me for having more fun than you?"

There was silence on the other end. If it hadn't been for the steady wail of a guitar Ryker would have thought Sam had hung up.

"So, you're not with Sheri?"

"What? Hell no. She left hours ago."

"But she sent us pictures of the two of you. Kissing. Hugging. You carried her across the yard. Looks like fun to me."

"What? I didn't . . ." He started to deny it but then remembered. "Oh fuck."

"Are you telling me that didn't happen?"

Ryker scrubbed at his face, suddenly very tired. "It did. Why would she do that? And who did she send them to?"

"Me, Colette . . . and Bree."

"Son of a bitch. Bree saw them?"

"Yes. What were you thinking?"

"It was harmless, I swear. Sheri was here and she had on new boots. She didn't want them ruined so I carried her out so they didn't get wet, that's all. And she kissed me. I didn't kiss her back. This doesn't make sense though. It was just the two of us and she didn't take any pictures."

The thought crept into his mind. Had she set him up? Had someone been watching them in hopes to get them on camera so his relationship would be ruined with Bree? Would Sheri do that?

He was pissed. "Let me talk to Sheri."

"She's not here. We thought she was with you."

"Well, she's not. Like I told you, she left a couple of hours ago. Put Bree on."

"Can't do that man. She took one look at those photos and stormed out of here."

"Son of a bitch!" Ryker slammed his fist into the wall. Then started to pace back and forth like a caged animal. He could hear the men working above. Hear the suction of the machines as the water was pulled into the tubes, guzzling, draining, drawing water from the floors.

He turned and was about to go up the stairs when something caught his eye in the corner of the room, floating in the water.

"Ryker?" Sam questioned in his ear. "What's happening over there?"

"Hold on a minute." He slogged through the water and came upon the item bobbing in the water. He reached down and grabbed the figurine, unable to comprehend what it was. Fear snaked through him unlike any he had ever felt before. "Where in the hell is Bree?"

"I told you she ran out."

Ryker held up the item to the light. It was an action figure. Not just any action figure either. It was Kage Xyon.

In an eerily calm voice he said, "If he doesn't have her, he will soon. This was a setup. Kage is behind this whole thing. It was a way to get us apart tonight . . . And it worked."

Chapter 46

"You know he's really not worth it."

"Who?"

"Ryker."

"How do you know I'm upset about Ryker?" Bree asked Greg.

"I was sitting at the table when Colette checked her text messages. I saw the photos. The ones of Ryker and Sheri."

"Oh, I didn't know you knew. You must think I'm stupid." Bree tried to make light of it, tried to laugh it off, but couldn't manage it.

"I don't think you're stupid," he paused, "Just gullible."

The word stung, so Bree didn't answer, she just stared out the window and watched the buildings go by. They crossed over the bridge, leaving Ocean City behind.

Since she didn't say anything, he went on. "A guy like that, a girl like you. It would never work. You need someone that would appreciate you. Someone who would watch you." He reached over and put his hand on her knee. "Someone like me."

That got her attention. She turned and looked at him, then down at his hand resting on her knee. She tried to shift in the seat. "Greg?"

"You and me. I think we would make a good couple. Don't you?" His hand rubbed her thigh.

Uh-oh. She tensed. A tiny prickle of fear lodged in the pit of her stomach. She shouldn't have gotten in the car with him. Sam had tried to warn her but she really hadn't taken it seriously. *Just be straightforward with him,* she told herself. *He'll appreciate honesty.*

"I like you, Greg." She reached down and lifted his hand off her leg. "As a friend. But that's all. Just a friend. I hope you understand."

"I understand."

He was quiet while he drove. So quiet, for so long as the minutes ticked by, Bree thought that was the end of it.

"You think you're too good for me. Is that it?"

"What? No, of course not."

His fist struck her face and ricocheted off her cheekbone. She cried out, seeing stars.

"Don't lie to me. I can tell by the tone in your voice you're patronizing me. You think I'm an idiot. Well, I fooled you, didn't I? Who's the idiot now?"

She gasped in shock and held her throbbing face in her hand. "Greg, I'm sorry. I'm not patronizing you. I don't know what you mean?" She gulped, biting back pain. "How did you fool me?"

He laughed a deep dark laugh, took off his glasses, and threw them on the dashboard. "All this time and you still don't know?" He looked at her in disbelief. "I took you for a lot smarter than that, Bree. Look outside at the moon. Tell me what you see."

She glanced outside through watery eyes and saw nothing but stars, then realized he'd turned away from the direction of her house. He was headed somewhere else.

"What do you see, Bree?"

"Nothing but stars and a few dark clouds. There's no moon tonight. It's just before the . . ." her voice trailed off.

"Before what?"

There was just something in the way he asked the question that had her shrinking back in her seat.

"A new moon? Is that what you were going to say? That would make it the second new moon in a month. And what's that called? Do you know? Huh, Bree? Do you know?"

"A black moon," she answered softly.

"Very good, Bree."

"But the new moon is tomorrow."

"Yes. Tonight, it's in shadow."

"You're Kage?" she asked in disbelief, then really looked at him without the glasses. It took her a moment. Her mind flashed back to the picture Savard had shown her. In the picture his face had been quite a bit fuller, the hair lighter and longer, and the eyes blue but still, if she really looked, she could see the resemblance easily. She cursed herself inwardly for not seeing it sooner. "Why?"

"I think you know why. You have something of mine. Something that's rightfully mine. You stole it from me and now I'm going to take it back."

"Is all this about the money?" she asked in disbelief. "Didn't you get my messages? I left messages with your lawyer. I don't want the money. I have papers coming . . . tomorrow," she lied. "I'm signing the money over to you. You can have it. I don't want it."

"Don't lie to me. You want the money. Everybody wants money. Even you. How else are you going to pay to keep that pretty house of yours? Not with your pathetic little photography business. Certainly not. You need *my* money. You want *my* money. That's why you tricked my father into giving it all to you."

"I never did such a thing."

His fist connected with her jaw a second time and her head struck the side window.

"Quiet! You did. You bat your pretty little eyes at him, made him feel sorry for you, and he gave you *everything*. Left you everything in his will that was rightfully mine. It was MINE!" he shouted. "He cut me right out without even a second thought, and gave it all to you." He grabbed the front of her shirt and shook her fiercely. He let go when he had to take a sharp curve, grabbing at the wheel.

Her vision blurred and her head pounded but she could still make out the road. She saw another curve coming up and noticed he started to decelerate to take it. Slowly, she reached for the door handle. Bree groped in the darkness trying desperately to find it. But it was gone.

He laughed when he realized what she was doing. "Give me a little more credit than that. I'm always one step ahead of you. I've thought of everything."

Her heart was beating so fast she could barely breathe and her head was pounding. It felt like he'd hit her with a two-by-four instead of his fist. She could feel her lip starting to swell and just below her eye was puffy. She was afraid if he hit her again, she would lose consciousness. It was so hard to think.

She took her time trying to form the right words, to say the right thing. "What are you going to do with me?"

He reached over and she flinched but instead of hitting her, he caressed her face, running his thumb down the side of her neck. She cringed and her stomach did a flip, the slow possessive caress was worse than being punched.

"I'm going to kill you, in the shadow of the black moon just like I planned."

A wave of panic surged through her.

He must have felt her tense because he smiled. "But I'll keep you alive," he paused, "For now. At least until the papers come through. If there really are papers. Are there, Bree? You didn't just make that up did you, to save your ass?"

"No, I didn't," she said truthfully.

"Good. Not only does your life depend on it but so do three other women's."

"What other women?"

He smiled wickedly as he navigated the backroads. All signs of urban life had long since disappeared. The road narrowed and the trees thickened.

"What if I told you, I have Linda," he paused for effect, "Tina, and Sheri . . . bound and gagged in an undisclosed location?"

"You're bluffing. Prove it."

He laughed coldly. "I don't have to prove it. It's my word against your conscience. It's you that puts them in jeopardy if I get caught. I'll never reveal their location. After I'm safely away and I have my money, I'll send an anonymous text to the police."

"I don't believe you have any of them. Especially Sheri. She's with Ryker."

"Like I said, gullible. Did you actually look at those photos?" He didn't wait for her to respond. "Sheri didn't take those photos, I did." He let that sink in for a few minutes. When she didn't say anything, he continued. "She left shortly after that little romantic encounter with Ryker. I followed her. Let's just say she didn't get far," he laughed at that. "I'm the one who sent those photos . . . from her phone."

He pulled a phone out of the front of his shirt pocket and waved it. "This is Sheri's." Then dropped it back in. "Linda and Tina's are in the glovebox. You can look if you don't believe me."

She tentatively reached forward, afraid he might hit her, but when he didn't, she opened it. There in the little compartment were two cell phones just like he said. She pulled one out and turned it over in her hand, pressed the button, and waited.

He laughed again. "Did you actually think I would tell you where there was a phone if it worked? Both phones are dead."

He turned off the paved road onto a dirt path that was tucked back in and meandered further into the trees. With no moon, it was pitch black. All light had been snuffed out and the trees crowded in. There were branches reaching out, scratching and clawing at the car like the boney fingers of the dead. They bumped along slowly. As he rolled down his window, she could hear the roar of the ocean off in the distance.

"Where are we going?" Bree demanded.

"You'll see." He leaned down and pulled a pistol out from underneath the seat. "This is what the old man left me." He held the gun up for her to see. "You got a million dollars and I got a gun." He laughed and shook his head. "The irony of it is I'm going to use this gun to get back my million dollars."

He made a sharp turn around an outcropping of trees, the car lights slicing across the foliage. Suddenly, a crude hut came into view. It was nestled into a hill and overgrown by climbing vines and scrub brush. It gave Bree chills just to look at it.

"How did you find this place?"

He half laughed. "Linda. She had the property listed and then the client changed his mind. I had to drive all the fucking way out here to pull the sign. Working at Coastal Realty paid off in more ways than one. It gave me this little gem," he pointed at the shack. "And it gave me complete access to you. What were the odds that I would get you as an actual client?"

He shut off the car and got out and walked around the car. He grabbed the handle and yanked the door open. "Get out."

Bree didn't move. "I'm not going in there."

"The hell you're not." He yanked her up and out by her arm, tossing her forward.

She stumbled and hit the wet ground. She felt movement inside her shirt as her cell phone slipped out of her bra and slid down her side. Her tank top was tucked into her jeans keeping it from falling out. Bree scrambled to her feet, wrapping her button-down shirt tightly around her, and looked up into the barrel of a gun.

"Don't even think about running."

He shoved her forward and into the hut. The place reeked of dampness and decay. Bree had to cover her nose to keep from sneezing.

Inside, he struck a match and lit a kerosene lantern. As the light filled the small hovel, Bree gasped at what she saw.

Photos. She inched closer, hundreds of photos . . . of her.

There were some with her and Ryker or maybe Sam. In all cases, the men had been all but scratched out. There were some of her sitting by the water, or walking Zylah. And then there were the ones of her inside, taken through the window. Her skin crawled with the sickness she saw around her. Her hand went to her mouth, holding back a sob, as she saw the ones of her naked. They were enlarged and grainy, but clear enough to see everything.

Fear lodged in the pit of her stomach and started to grow. It grew so fast that a wave of nausea overtook her.

He came up behind her and ran his hands through her short hair. "Looks like we have a lot more in common than you thought, huh Bree? Do you like my display? I'm a damn good photographer, aren't I?" He glanced at the photos. "Even better than you."

He edged closer and sniffed her hair, which sent a chill racing down her spine. He stroked her face and ran a thumb over her swollen lip. She cringed.

"I'm not sorry I hit you. You deserved it. But I am sorry your pretty face is marked up." He leaned in close and whispered in her ear. "How does it feel to know that I've seen you naked? To know that when you thought you were alone, I was watching?"

She didn't hesitate, she jabbed an elbow into his chest and stomped on his foot. He shouted and cursed, grabbing her. She punched him in the throat while he clawed at her. She slipped free and ran for the door. But that was as far as she got.

Chapter 47

Ryker punched numbers into his cell phone and desperately waited for it to be answered.

"Detective Savard."

"Savard, this is Ryker James."

"Ryker. What's wrong?"

Ryker could barely contain himself. He ran out of the house and jumped in his truck, soaking wet. "He's got Bree."

"Wait. Who?"

"Kage!" Ryker threw the action figure onto the dashboard. Jamming the keys into the ignition, he punched the gas pedal down hard and tore off down the road.

"Where are you?"

"I'm in my truck headed to the Shark Shack."

"Why?"

"That's where Bree is or was . . ." his voice trailed off.

"I'll meet you there. But slow down so you can get there in one piece, and tell me what happened . . . from the beginning."

Ryker mentally tried to turn down his temper, but when he did the fear rushed in, like a tidal wave crashing the shore. It rushed in, then pulled back, leaving the beach swept smooth and raw. That was him if the anger was gone; he was left with nothing but pure raw fear. He clung to the anger like he would a lifeline.

Ryker tried to piece the day together and where he had gone wrong. *Why had he left Bree alone? What the hell had he been thinking?* Then it hit him. Linda.

The text from Linda had sent him to the flooded house. Was she Kage? That didn't make sense. He spared a glance at the figure wedged into the front of his dashboard. But how else could this be explained? Linda would have had access to the house and ultimately to Bree. But why?

373

"Ryker?" Savard questioned. "What's happening? Why did you stop talking?"

Ryker physically shook himself and jerked the wheel to stay in his lane. "I was thinking. . . I'm having trouble concentrating but I think . . . I can't believe I'm even going to say this out loud . . . but I can't think of another explanation."

"Just say it," Savard said calmly.

Ryker grunted, feeling despicable for even thinking it. "I think . . . Linda Lauer from Coastal Realty is involved somehow. She texted me this afternoon and sent me over to the rental house. If it hadn't been her, I wouldn't have gone." The reality of that hit him hard. "I wouldn't have left Bree for anyone else. I didn't think I would be gone very long and Bree was with Sam. So . . ."

Savard was silent for a moment. "More than likely, it was someone who knew that was the case. They knew you would go because Linda asked you to. They knew exactly what button to push and what you were walking into. Not an easy or quick job."

Disgusted, Ryker made the turn. He ran the next light, not buying it. "It came from Linda's phone. And from Sheri. How do you explain that, if it wasn't her?"

"This may come as a shock to you, but I know for a fact it wasn't Linda. She's in the hospital. I just left her only a few minutes ago. I promise you it wasn't her." He paused, "Linda has been locked in the trunk of her car for the past two days. I was there when she was found."

That hit Ryker hard. "What? Are you kidding me right now?"

"No. I wouldn't joke about something this serious. She was bound and gagged and thrown into her own trunk."

Another wave of fear washed over him. Linda was like a mother to him. "Is she okay?"

"She's dehydrated and banged up pretty good, but everything should heal. How far are you from the Shack?"

"I'm pulling into the lot now."

"Me, too."

"There's Sam in the far back corner."

"I see him."

Both men pulled in from opposite directions, parked, and jumped out of their vehicles. They crossed to Sam and Colette.

"Hey, man. Her car is here but we haven't been able to find her," Sam said, looking from one man to the other.

"She's not answering her cell either," Colette added.

Savard immediately took charge. "Tell me exactly what happened."

They ran through it quickly for him.

Without hesitating, Savard quickly called for backup. Then he asked, "Was anyone else with you guys tonight?"

"Sheri was supposed to meet us but she never showed. We assumed she was with Ryker."

"I told you that was hours ago." Ryker ran his hands through his dark hair exasperated. "Let me see the text that you guys got."

Ryker hastily grabbed Colette's phone and swiped through the pictures. "Son of a . . ." There was Sheri with her arms wrapped around him as he carried her out of the house. His heart dropped when he slid to the next one with her kissing him. He had to admit it looked bad. It looked like they were involved. He thrust the phone back towards Colette. "Why would Sheri do this?" He could only imagine how Bree had taken it. She had suspected that they had a thing all along, despite the fact that he had denied it. This would only confirm her fears.

Before Colette could reply, Savard took the phone from Ryker and scrolled through the photos. "Well, it's obvious Sheri didn't take them. The question is who did?" Savard looked from one to the other. "Have any of you seen Greg Carpenter?"

"He was here a little while ago. Might still be inside." Sam indicated the Shack with a jerk of his thumb.

"I don't think so," Colette added. "I saw him hurry after Bree."

"Yeah, he was hitting on her earlier so that wouldn't surprise me."

That got Ryker's attention. "What do you mean he was hitting on her?"

Sam shrugged. "He was moving in at the table and then he asked her to dance."

"And did she?"

"No, I saved her."

Ryker swore. "Really? Then where the hell is she?"

"I don't know, man. I told you she ran out."

Ryker grabbed the front of Sam's shirt. "I gave you one job to do." They stood toe to toe as Ryker clutched his shirt, seeing red.

Savard stepped in, literally got between the two men. "This will get you nowhere, Ryker. LET HIM GO! This isn't Sam's fault or yours."

Disgusted with himself, Ryker released Sam and took a step back. "I'm sorry. It's just . . . if anything happens to her . . ."

Sam shook his head in understanding.

Savard turned as a couple of squad cars pulled in. "I'll be right back. Nobody leaves."

Ryker perched himself on the hood of a car completely distraught. His jeans were wet, his body ached, and his mind was jumping from one thing to the other. He thought of Linda in the hospital and imagined her tied up and in the trunk of a car for two days. Is that where Bree was right now, held hostage somewhere, beaten and bloody? He tried not to think about it because when he did it literally made him sick to his stomach.

Colette came over and put her hand on his arm. "Are you okay?"

He shook his head no.

"Ryker, please don't be mad at Sam. She left so abruptly neither of us had time to react."

"I'm not mad at Sam. I'm furious with myself. I knew the new moon was getting close and I still chose to leave her. I didn't think I would be gone long. And it was for Linda." Ryker looked up at Sam for understanding. "It wasn't Linda at all."

"It wasn't?" Sam questioned, clearly surprised, "Then who?"

Ryker shrugged his shoulders. A lump lodged in his throat. "I thought Linda was home sick but instead . . ." he didn't know if he could actually say it out loud. He swallowed the lump. "She wasn't sick. She was bound and gagged in the trunk of her car for the past two days. Savard was there when they found her a few hours ago."

Shocked, Sam asked, "But what about all the texts?"

"Whoever did it, has or had her phone. I still don't understand all of this."

"Then what about Tina?" Sam questioned. "She went over to check on Linda and came down with the same thing."

Ryker straightened. "Who told you that?"

"Sheri."

Savard returned with a couple of police officers. "They're going to go in and search the place for Bree and Greg Carpenter."

"Why Greg?" Colette asked.

Savard signaled to the men and they headed for the building. "We have every reason to believe Greg Carpenter has been posing as Kage, the person that's been stalking Bree all this time."

• • • •

BREE SCREAMED AS HE tackled her from behind. His knee ground into the small of her back and she felt something crack.

"Hold still you bitch!" he screamed.

She bucked and thrashed around on the dirt floor, trying to get out from under him. He slammed her head into the hard-packed floor, causing her eyes to tear and her head to swim. It dazed her enough for her to go lax just long enough for him to get her wrists together. He leaned to the left side, reaching for something. She wrenched her right arm out and clawed at the ground.

He flipped her over and she flung dirt in his face. He struggled to hold her in place looking crazed, shrieking, and pawing at his eyes.

Shoving him off, she scrambled for the door. Reaching for the handle, she heard a click.

"I wouldn't open that door if I were you."

"Are you going to shoot me in the back?" she asked, her hand hovering above the crude latch. "Is that how Kage Xyon would kill his enemy?"

He laughed cruelly. "Part of me likes that you're a formidable opponent. The others were easy targets. You're strong, cunning, and manipulative. Your good, but I'm better." He paused. "We don't have to be enemies. We could be lovers instead."

A shiver ran up her spine. She turned slightly so she could see him. He stood feet apart, arms raised, and the gun pointed directly at her, dirt coating his face.

"Really? You want to be my lover?" she asked in disbelief. She outwardly shivered, repulsed by the idea.

"I've always been torn between wanting to kill you and being attracted to you. I have been since the first time I saw you."

Maybe if she could just keep him talking, buy a little time, she might be able to figure a way out of this. She forced herself to ask, trying to keep the edge of fear out of her voice, "Which was where?"

"At the funeral." He saw a flicker of doubt run across her face and he smiled. "Yes, I was there. I sat six rows directly behind you.

You were a vision in black. Those blue eyes of yours shimmered like sapphires as those crocodile tears fell."

He'd been around even then? "Why were you there?"

"To see exactly what my father had done, and to whom. I kept track of you ever since then. And it's a good thing I did too. When I learned about the will, I followed you across the country." He ran a hand over his face. "I got a job with Coastal Realty when I came to town. They were the biggest and the best around, they were hiring, and I needed information. Information on you I couldn't find without being connected. I needed to use their system to keep an eye on you. I wanted to know if and when you bought something with my money. I wasn't sure how it was all going to work out. If you were going to buy or rent, or just stay for a few weeks. I'd been keeping track of you through your stupid website; but once here, I was struggling to keep tabs on you. It was all new territory for me."

A sneer spread across his face. "I thought I'd lost you for a while. But imagine my surprise when Sheri all but handed you over to me on a silver platter. Some would say it was sheer dumb luck. But me? I say it's a power. A strong dark power that's in me."

All this time he'd been there, somewhere in the shadows. Lurking, waiting. A wave of desperation swamped Bree. She swallowed hard trying to keep calm and keep him talking.

"Your father was a good man. It was an accident. I didn't even blame him."

"Maybe you didn't . . . but I did." He shifted. "We have the same name. Did you know that?"

Bree shook her head.

"My name is Garth Snader Jr." He took a step towards her. "When it first came out in the news, about the accident, people thought it was me. The damn journalists didn't put in the senior. I got dirty looks and phone calls; reporters knocked on my door. People were talking about me behind my back at work, whispering, gossiping. They didn't care about the facts or who had actually done it. Do you have any idea how that might feel?" He didn't wait for her to respond. "Even after I set the record straight, they still stared and whispered."

"I'm sorry, I never realized."

"Of course, you didn't. You were in your own little world, wallowing in your own pathetic grief . . . People were always whispering. They think I didn't know."

"I know how that feels. People talked about me behind my back too."

"Yes, but they pitied you. Me? They thought I was a killer. Even though it wasn't me, and I had never ever driven a semi in my entire life. They said things like; he had to be drunk, or maybe he was on drugs, that's why he couldn't keep control of his vehicle. Even after I thought I set them straight, that it was my father and not me. That he had a seizure, he was sick, not drunk, people still wouldn't let it go."

"I'm sorry you had to go through that."

"Then you . . . you wouldn't take help from my father." The gun had slowly started to lower as he was talking. As if realizing it, he brought it up level with her chest. "You killed him. Did you know that?"

"No, I didn't. He had a brain tumor. He was dying."

"You're right, he was, but because of you he took his life sooner and left you everything."

"I didn't ask him to. I told you before, I don't want his money."

"My money you mean," he corrected. "*My* money."

"Yes, your money." She hoped she didn't sound patronizing or desperate. "If you let me, I would like to make it right. I was trying to do that. I tried to tell you before that I have the papers coming by courier tomorrow. All I have to do is sign them and the money is yours."

"What time?"

"What?"

He stepped closer. "What time is the courier coming?"

"Oh? Umm ..."

"You're not lying to me, are you, Bree?"

"No, I'm not," she said, sounding more confident than she felt. "Sometime in the morning."

"They're coming in the morning? On a Saturday?" he questioned, clearly not believing her. "Why would they come on a Saturday, Bree?"

"Because I asked them too. I wanted to get this done as soon as possible. I told you the money doesn't matter to me."

He waved the gun at her. "Move away from the door."

"Can't we just go back to my house and wait for the courier?"

"The answer is no. Do you think I'm stupid? I don't trust you. I'll go back and wait, you'll stay here. That way if you lied to me, I'll know exactly where to find you."

"I didn't lie."

"Then it shouldn't be a problem. Now move. Get over here and sit in this chair."

She stood still and tried to focus on everything around her. Her ears trained on the silence, she heard the steady pitter-patter of rain start through the thin walls, and defiantly said, "No."

"What did you say to me?"

"I said no. I won't just sit in that chair so you can tie me up. I won't be bullied into being a hostage."

She could feel a rush of air as the bullet whisked past her head and ripped a hole the size of a fist in the rotten wood behind her.

"I'll kill you right here and now. Don't tempt me."

Her body shook with fear. But she didn't move.

"Do you want to meet your maker?"

He fired another shot on the other side. Despite herself, she shrieked.

"GET IN THE FUCKING CHAIR, BREE!"

She didn't move but stood there trembling.

"When I'm through with you, you're going to wish you had died in that van with your parents."

"Believe me, I already wish I had. That was the absolute darkest time in my life. Nothing that you do to me can be worse than losing my family."

"We'll see about that."

The shot ripped through her leg. Screaming, she crumpled to the ground. He stood over her with the gun pointed at her head, his hand shaking with pure fury.

"I could finish you right now," he said coldly.

She thought of her family and then of Ryker. The picture of him with Sheri in his arms was burned into her mind.

She whimpered, "Go ahead; I've got nothing to live for."

He kicked her in the leg where the blood seeped through her jeans, and then in the ribs. She screamed as the pain seared up her leg. His hand grasped her hair and yanked her head back.

"Dying is too good for you. You can lie there in the dirt, in the dark, and pray that you bleed to death before the flames burn you alive. You're going to go out the way your family did, in a ball of fire. I'm going to get those papers and if by chance you lied to me .. . so, help me, Bree. I will come back here and use your charred body for target practice."

He kicked her again just because he could; she lay still and lifeless. He took out a cell phone and sneered. "I'm going to send your prick of a boyfriend the last photo of you he will ever see. Smile for the camera, Bree." He snapped the photo, grabbed the kerosene lantern, and without looking back, he left, plunging her into darkness.

Chapter 48

They fanned out and covered the Shark Shack as quickly as possible looking for Bree and Greg Carpenter.

The crowd was thick, the music loud.

In his gut, he knew. "She's not here," Ryker stated, cornering Savard. "We're wasting time."

"We had to rule out the possibility," he shouted above the wail of a guitar. Savard led Ryker out the back door and into the parking lot. "But you're right. It looks like they're both gone."

Disgusted, Ryker paced back and forth. "What the hell are we going to do?"

"I have police officers at checkpoints leaving Ocean City. Other officers are patrolling, looking for Carpenter's car on side streets, and a unit is at his house if he tries to return."

"What if he already has her out of the area?"

Ryker picked up an empty can and flung it into the dumpster behind the building, frustrated. His phone chimed. He looked down and saw that Sheri sent him a message and two attachments. He groaned. "What the heck is she sending now?"

"Who is it?"

"It's Sheri. I can't deal with her right now."

Savard moved closer. "Open it."

Ryker looked at Savard and contemplated him for a moment. He pressed the message with his thumb. First came the words.

Which one will you choose?

The attachments downloaded. The first one was Sheri. It was a close-up of her face. Her eyes were wide with fear and there was duct tape across her mouth.

The anxiety that Ryker had been holding back by sheer willpower exploded as he scrolled to the next one.

Savard saw him turn white as the blood literally drained from his face. "What is it?" he demanded, reaching for the phone.

Ryker staggered back. "It's Sheri . . . and . . . Bree. He has them both."

The picture of Sheri was bad, but the one of Bree was horrific. She lay crumpled into a fetal position on dirt. Her eyes closed. Face bruised. And blood staining her jeans. Ryker's heart practically stopped at the sight of her.

Sam and Colette emerged from the building. "No sign of him," Sam started to say but stopped short after taking one look at Ryker. "What's happened?"

Savard spoke, "Carpenter has Sheri *and* Bree."

Colette gasped and turned into Sam. He gathered her in, trying to comfort her.

"What's it supposed to mean? Which one will you choose?" Sam asked over Colette's head.

"He wants you to think that you have to choose, that you can't save them both. Colette, do you know Sheri's address?"

She choked back a sob and told him the address.

Savard dialed and spoke quickly into his phone barking out orders. He hung up and looked at the threesome. "They're going to track the phones he's using, and they are headed to both Sheri and Bree's now." He directed his attention to Sam. "Take her home. Ryker will be in touch if we hear anything."

"Call me if you need me."

Ryker nodded and gave his best friend a weary smile. "I will." He watched them walk away then turned to Savard. "Where are you going?"

"I'm going to go over to Bree's. I have a hunch Carpenter will turn up there before too long."

"I'm coming."

"I assumed as much. Let's go."

They drove in silence while Ryker stared at Bree's photo. It tore at his heart to look at her. Delicate and beautiful even in this disheveled state. She was so strong-willed, independent, and now? She looked broken. What if she didn't make it? Would she die thinking that he didn't love her? All because some deranged man took a few photos of him with another woman. Something so innocent turned to use against him and break her heart. If anything happened to her, he would never forgive himself. Never.

They were crossing the bridge heading out of Ocean City when Savard's cell phone rang.

Savard punched a button. "Talk to me, Kilpatrick. What did you find at Carpenter's?"

Kilpatrick's voice came at them through the speakers. "It's him all right. He has the whole collection of Black Shadow action figures lined up on his window sill except for one, Kage Xyon."

"He left that for me to find in the flooded rental." Ryker spat. "That son of a bitch!"

"There's a box full of photos of Bree Thompson and a large camera set up on a tripod. It's pointed out the window directly at the back of the Thompson house."

"Are you sure?" Savard asked.

"Yes, I'm looking through it now."

"Do you see anything?"

"The house is dark, but it's definitely Thompson's house. Wait . . . There's someone moving inside."

Savard grabbed his radio, calling the squad car that was in route. "Suspect may be in the house. Meet me on the road. We will go in silent, no sirens, no lights." Savard turned his attention back to Kilpatrick. "Keep me posted, I want to know every damn move he makes."

• • • •

BREE LAY CRUMPLED IN a ball on the dirt floor. Her entire body pulsated with white, hot pain. Smelling smoke, she struggled to sit up. She shifted slightly and saw the first small tongues of flames curl under the side of the shack.

With great effort, Bree raised herself off the floor. Her head swam and bile rose in her throat from the wave of nausea that hit her as she moved. She didn't think she could stand, so she stayed on the floor and prayed it would pass.

She delicately reached down, touched her thigh, retracting her hand quickly when she felt the sticky, warm substance on her jeans. The denim was soaked through with blood and the metallic smell burned her senses.

She needed something to stop the bleeding. The only thing she had was the shirt on her own back. She struggled to get it off and shivered in her thin tank top. Bree jumped as something hit the floor directly behind her. She'd think about that in a second.

Diligently she wrapped the shirt around her thigh. Cinching the sleeves tightly, she bit her lip to keep from screaming as pain raced through her.

She clenched her teeth, sweat broke out across her forehead as she felt along the dirt floor, trying to find what dropped. Her hand closed around an object she knew well, she cried with relief.

Tears sprang to her eyes as she felt the crack down the center. The screen was shattered but stayed lit and came back every time she pushed the power button. She tucked it into her bra and started to crawl towards the door.

Bree inched along on her hands and knees, dragging her left leg. She was drenched in sweat when she finally reached the door.

Gripping the handle hard, she pulled herself up and prayed it wasn't locked. Leaning on the rickety wall, she was surprised when the door easily swung open. Almost giddy with relief, she stepped out into the cold night.

Bree shivered against the cool air as smoke curled out along the ground like fog as the damp wood continued to slowly spark and burn.

Stumbling forward, she tried to get her bearings. She was losing too much blood. Her strength was drained, her mind foggy. She had to think. If she was quiet and listened, maybe she would be able to hear a passing car.

As her ragged breathing slowed, the night sounds came rushing in all around her. She heard the sway of branches, the rustle of leaves, an owl hooted, and there was a crack of a twig as a creature roamed. Behind it all, at the very edge of the night, she heard the roar of the ocean.

"The ocean," Bree whispered. She felt it call to her, pulling her forward. She took her first step in the direction of the ocean. Her thigh was on fire and blood dripped down her leg, but she kept moving. Drawn by the sound, and the need to see it one last time.

Chapter 49

The call came in as Savard cut the engine and the lights, stopping at the edge of the road, signaling for the other patrol car to do the same.

"What's the update?"

Ryker could hear the voice on the other end but couldn't make out the words.

"I see."

"What's happened?" Ryker demanded. "I need to know! Is it Bree? Or Sheri? Linda? Tell me!"

"They found Sheri bound and gagged at her home. She's bruised and has a concussion, but otherwise fine. Linda is fine. I'm sorry, but Tina didn't make it."

Ryker sat still in stunned silence. His voice was low and hung on the edge of despair. "And Bree? What of Bree? Did they find her too?"

"No, not yet. We need to get Carpenter, he's the key to finding her."

Savard got out of the car without looking at Ryker. Addressing the two officers he said, "From now on all communications will be through headsets. Kilpatrick still has eyes on the suspect from across the bay. He's in the kitchen. Kilpatrick says he's alone. We don't know if he's armed. We'll go in from here on foot. Down the drive and then come at the house from different directions to make sure we keep him contained. We've lost one life; I don't plan on losing another. Am I clear?" The officers nodded.

"I need a headset," Ryker said.

Savard turned to him. "You'll need to stay here in the car and wait for us to secure the suspect."

"Like hell, I will. If you didn't want me here you should have left me at the Shack. I'm going into that house whether you like it or not." Ryker took a step towards the detective. "I have a huge stake in the outcome."

Savard hesitated. "I'll give you a headset on one condition."

"Name it."

Savard stepped up close and got right in Ryker's face. "You will do exactly as I say when I say. Don't think I won't hesitate to handcuff you and haul your ass back to the patrol car if you don't."

"You have my word."

Savard gave the nod and one of the police officers hooked Ryker up. "I won't give you a gun and I won't have you running off halfcocked. Bree's life depends on your cooperation." He gave the orders and said, "Move out."

They slunk off into the dark. Ryker went to his assigned area and squatted in the brush at the back of the house.

The voice in his ear came in low. "He's on the move inside the house."

"How long until you're in?"

"Seconds."

"Advancing on the front."

"No visual on the suspect."

"Suspect is moving towards the front of the house."

The voices were coming in fast. Ryker couldn't keep straight who was talking. There was a piercing smash of glass, both in his ear and in the distance. There was shouting. Two shots were fired.

"Suspect is armed."

Yelling. Cursing.

"He's on the move."

"I repeat, the suspect is armed."

Two more shots pierced the silent night.

"He's headed to the back of the house."

"We got a runner!"

Carpenter burst through the back door, running. With no hesitation, Ryker took off at full throttle sprinting across the yard. Carpenter never saw him coming. Ryker tackled Greg at full speed, knocking him off his feet. With the force they landed a full ten feet from where Ryker made contact.

Pinned to the ground Carpenter lost his grip on the gun. Ryker raised his fist, ready to pound the life out of him, but he was stopped with the arrival of the others and Savard's direct order.

"Ryker, don't! We have him surrounded. Let us take over."

Carpenter laughed wickedly. "Ah, too bad, James! You can't hit me, even though I know you want to."

"You're lucky they're here. Otherwise, you'd be dead by now." Ryker climbed off him and the two officers hauled Carpenter up.

Greg laughed hysterically. "You're all talk, Ryker! I don't think you have it in you."

"Read him his rights."

Ryker took a step back, trying hard to control his anger.

"You may have me, but you're too late for Bree. She died alone. Broken. Thinking you didn't love her."

Ryker swung. There was a bone-cracking sound as his fist connected with Carpenter's face. Greg's nose shattered in a burst of blood and cartilage.

Savard grabbed Ryker and pushed him back as Greg wailed in agony.

"Ryker, enough! We still need him alive if you want to find Bree."

Ryker staggered backward seeing red, as white-hot fury coursed through him. He couldn't think straight. His heart felt like it might break as he thought of Bree dying alone, thinking he didn't love her, all because of a damn message on her phone.

A little thought niggled at the back of his mind. What was he forgetting?

"Arrest him!" Greg wailed. "He assaulted me! He broke my nose!"

"You broke your nose when you fell face first."

Ryker suddenly remembered. "That's it!" he shouted. "Why didn't I think of it before?"

"What?" Savard demanded as Greg was cuffed.

"My phone," Ryker pulled it out. "I was trying to call her but instead I should have tried to track her."

"Track her? How? The department is searching for a signal but it may take some time."

"You'll never find her. And even if you do, it will be too late. She was practically dead when I left her," Carpenter sneered as they hauled him towards the cruiser, blood dripping down his front.

"Not if you have a specific app and share your location with each other." Ryker swiped through his apps. He explained, "I turned it on in our phones a few days ago but we haven't used it. I totally forgot about it." He touched the little green circle with the blue triangle app. Bree's avatar popped up. He touched her avatar and instantly the map shifted and zoomed in.

"There! There she is!"

"Let's go."

Ryker and Savard took off in a dead sprint.

"You're too late!" Carpenter screamed. "She's dead! Dead! Do you hear me? Dead!"

• • • •

HER SHOE WAS FULL OF blood. It slid, slipped, and sloshed as she stumbled across the uneven ground. She fell down and lay there dazed, unable to comprehend how she had gotten there. The light drizzle had stopped. Through the leaves of the trees, Bree could see the twinkling of stars and an impression of the moon. The shadow of the new moon. A black moon. She laughed deliriously at the irony of it. Greg had gotten his wish, she would die under it.

How beautiful that ghost of pale gray rock looked, the hint of it, just the slightest shade lighter than the velvet black night. She wrenched herself up on her elbows as pain ripped through her body, and knew she had to get out from under the trees. Bree had to make it to the beach, no matter what it cost her.

There was a crack of branches to her left and behind her. She wasn't alone. There was something in the dark. She knew something was there, but couldn't fathom what lurked in the shadows. If it was Greg, wouldn't he just come out after her? She glanced over her shoulder with great effort. Was it her imagination or were there big dark eyes staring at her? Watching. Waiting to see what she would do next.

Somehow, she managed to stagger to her feet and tried to put those eyes out of her crazed mind. She felt feverish and dizzy but the crash of the surf called to her, pulling her forward. Coaxing her on.

She smelled brine and salt before she could see it. The slow steady roll of the ocean waves foamed and gleamed in the dark night, sparkling as the sea tossed and turned. She shivered as she emerged from the tree line and the salt air kissed her feverish skin.

Bree fell at the edge, where the forest met the beach. Dirt mingled with sand. It was cold and coarse, a mix of stone, pine needles, and sand. She crawled on her hands and knees, dragging her leg, desperate to get to the water.

She collapsed face-first into the sand. With one last great effort, Bree groaned as she rolled onto her back and stared up into the immense heavens.

She thought of her parents and her sister. Had they suffered like this? Her heart hurt. Bree prayed it had been quick and painless for them. Tears seeped out of her eyes as she replayed the van leaving the road, saw it flip end over end, land, and burst into flames. She was too exhausted and overwhelmed with emotion to even try to wipe away the flood of tears.

She looked at the shadow of the moon, a mere suggestion of what was to come, and thought of Ryker. Was he looking up at it now too? Could he see it? Did he wonder where she was? Would he know that she had loved him? In such a short amount of time, just the span of a couple of months, she had grown to love him. With all of her heart.

Bree chastised herself. Why had she wasted so much time being scared and holding back? Would she ever get to tell him? Would she hear his voice again? Or feel his touch? The thought that she wouldn't, had her letting out a sob, wrenching her battered heart.

The cry drew attention. Over the crash of waves, Bree could hear soft footsteps on the sand. It was a soft steady cadence. The end must be near because she was hallucinating now. How could she not be? Enchanting ebony eyes as black as the night, and as big as saucers, peered down at her. Something warm and wet nudged her arm.

She closed her eyes as the fever rocked her body. It hurt too much to have them open. Or to think. At least she was on the shore, near the water, her one refuge these past months. She drifted off, racked with pain, to the lull of the ocean and the warmth of what felt like a silky blanket caressing her. Her last conscious thought was of Ryker and the first time she'd seen him... on the beach at sunrise.

• • • •

"SLOW DOWN. THERE HAS to be a road somewhere close," Ryker said, his voice full of terror.

Savard slowed the car and eased down the road, the headlights cutting through the dark night and the dense trees.

Ryker sat on the edge of his seat praying they would find her in time, all the while searching desperately for a break in the woods.

"There!" he shouted.

Savard slammed on the brakes.

"You passed it! Back up! I'm sure that was a road."

Savard put the car in reverse.

"There!"

He turned the car down the dirt road. Branches scraped the sides of the car. The road wandered through the trees for almost a half-mile. Savard made a sharp turn around an outcropping of trees. He slowed the car as the lights rested on a small crude shanty that burned.

Savard hadn't even put the vehicle in park when Ryker jumped out, running for the shack.

"Bree!" Ryker yelled as he yanked open the rotten door and smoke poured out.

"I need a flashlight," Ryker called. Savard was beside him, instantly shining the light.

"Bree?" Ryker coughed, choking on smoke. It was just one room. It had a dirt floor and everything was coated in a thin layer of mold and wetness. The place was empty except for a lone chair, tongues of flames licked the corner. There were no windows and the smell of decay and rot hung heavy in the air as the smoke swirled and lingered. But the walls . . . the walls caught his attention . . . they were lined with photo after photo of Bree. "Sick bastard."

"She's not here," Savard said, stating the obvious. He shone the light around the room and saw a pool of blood. "But she was," he held the light steady. Then moved it across the trail of blood to the door. "Looks like she walked out of here after he left."

"She must still have her phone on her, I don't see it," Ryker said, stifling a cough.

They came out of the shanty. "Hold up, we need a first aid kit and another flashlight."

He turned back and looked at the little shanty. "That bastard tried to burn her alive," Ryker stated, the realization finally hitting him. He was suddenly weak at the knees when he thought of how close he'd been to losing Bree in a fire. If it hadn't been for the pure raw dampness and passing showers the place would have probably been completely engulfed in flames by now.

Instead, she was somewhere else, lost in the woods, bleeding to death.

"Hurry, damn it!" Ryker shouted impatiently.

Turning their attention to the blood trail, the men followed it with the flashlights. Ryker called her name over and over again until he was hoarse as they followed the sporadic blood through the forest with the icon of Bree getting closer to his. They were almost on top of each other now.

"There," Savard pointed as the light glinted off something shiny. He reached down. "Her phone, she must have dropped it."

"But where the hell is she?" Ryker cursed. He glanced around seeing nothing but trees. "How far could she have possibly gotten losing this much blood?" He swept the immediate area with his flashlight, desperate. That's when he heard it. "Listen."

"What? I don't hear anything but the roar of the ocean."

"Exactly. If Bree heard it, she would head straight for it." Ryker knew it like he knew the color of her eyes. She was close, he could feel it.

Ryker took off sprinting through the brush calling her name, not even bothering with the blood trail anymore. He stopped short as he broke through the trees and came out onto the beach.

The horizon began to lighten. The pitch-black became a dark inky gray as pale light started to spill over the edge. Ryker scanned the empty beach in the spongy darkness when his eyes stopped on three lovely creatures. Ponies. There were two lying down on the beach while the other one stood guard.

Sensing him, the one standing turned and looked directly at Ryker. He whinnied and stomped his foot, pawing the wet sand. His breath coming out in hot puffs of misty air.

The others turned their heads, sensing him too. The larger one pawed the sand again and the others stood up. Ryker took a step towards them and they took off running in the opposite direction. It took a moment for Ryker to register that there was something on the beach. Seeing the still and lifeless form, his heart wrenched. He ran across the sand and dropped to his knees beside Bree as the water rushed in and rolled her gently.

She was wet, shivering, and bloody but she was alive. He stroked her battered face and whispered her name. "Bree?"

Her eyes fluttered.

"Savard!" he shouted. "She needs an ambulance!"

Savard came running shouting orders into his phone. "They're going to send a helicopter, it'll be faster. We'll never get an ambulance through those trees."

Bree opened her eyes for a brief moment and smiled a heart-wrenching smile at him.

"Ryker?"

"I'm here. It's me. You're safe." He cradled her in his arms while Savard wrapped her in a blanket.

"The sun's coming up," she whispered, her voice barely audible. "I knew you'd come." Her eyes fluttered closed and remained that way.

"Hang on, Bree. They're coming." He kissed her feverish forehead. "I've got you and I'm never letting you go. Hold on for me. I can't lose you. I *won't* lose you. Not now. Not ever."

Epilogue

The air was cool and crisp, a perfect autumn morning. The sky was dark. The hint of first light was a secret the horizon kept as they cruised along the water in the Shadow. It wouldn't be long until the world would brighten around them.

Ryker steered the boat towards the shore of Assateague Island. The beach was bare except for a few wild ponies that stood out near the edge of the water, waiting on the sun. Bree smiled when she saw them and thought of that night, months ago. Had it not been for a trio of horses that had ventured across to the mainland at low tide, and been caught there by the rising water, Bree wouldn't be here now.

She had loved to come and watch the ponies before, but now they meant so much more to her than anyone would ever know. Except for Ryker. They had literally saved her life.

That night, almost five months ago, had gotten unseasonably cold. She had been wet and feverish, and without their body heat, she wouldn't have survived and Ryker wouldn't have found her in time.

She tried not to think about that now as she watched Ryker maneuver the boat so it would run aground on the beach. She braced for the impact, then waited while he cut the motor and jumped off. She threw him the rope and he tugged it further onto the beach as the ponies raced off.

She discarded the blanket she was wrapped in.

"Hurry now. First light is in a few minutes."

Ryker grinned up at her with his dark hair rippled in the wind. No matter how many times she looked at him, her heart always did a little flip. He held out his arms and swung her down from the boat, placing her delicately on the sand.

She had her camera in her hand and quickly uncapped the lens, pointing it in the direction of the horses.

The sun broke at the edge of the world, stretching its rays over the deep dark waters. Bree captured it from the moment the first rays shattered the darkness. She angled her body so she could get the ponies in her lens. Widening it as they turned to look at her. They watched her, curious, as she photographed them.

Ryker stood by her side, silent. She was so beautiful, so graceful. Loose strands of her golden-brown hair whipped out around her as the wind toyed with them. He was content just to watch her work, and simply be in her presence. He let her work her magic with the camera as she moved away from him.

There wasn't a day that went by that he wasn't thankful he'd found her in time. He shuddered to think back and remember just how close he had been to losing her, watching her life slip away, right before his eyes. She'd lost so much blood, and her body was ravaged with fever. It still made his own blood boil to think that Carpenter had kicked her so hard he'd broken her ribs and given her a concussion, let alone shot her and left her to die. But she was strong and resilient. If you looked at her now you would never know she had been a breath away from dying in his arms.

He thought about the endless hours he had endured while he waited for them to remove the bullet in surgery, or the blood transfusions, waiting for the fever to break, and her bones to heal. He had stayed by her side and only left when forced to. And then he couldn't go home. He went to her house and replaced the windows that had been broken, walked, and held Zylah endlessly just to be near someone else that loved Bree too.

That made him think of Tina and the devastating loss her husband had endured. He couldn't even fathom how hard it was for Linda either, that while she was bound in the trunk of her car, her best friend lay only feet away dying or already dead.

He physically shook, scolding himself for letting that nightmare into this special moment. For now, he had the girl he loved right in front of him. And he intended to keep it that way.

The world around them was getting brighter by the minute. Colors changing, fading, shadows shifting. It reminded him of the first day he saw Bree, on the beach wearing his leather jacket, photographing the rising sun. She had stolen his breath away that day. And now she had taken his heart.

At that moment she turned to him. Blue eyes shining, cheeks pink from the cold. She shivered and ran towards him. "Wasn't it spectacular? The colors. The waves. The horizon." She didn't wait for him to answer. "And the ponies. It was as if they wanted me to take their picture. I would swear they almost posed." She laughed despite herself. She reached out to him, suddenly concerned. "Ryker, what's the matter?"

"Nothing. You must be freezing."

"I'm fine." Bree shivered uncontrollably.

He laughed. "Liar. Here, take my jacket." He shrugged out of it.

"Then how will you stay warm?"

He eyed her knowingly. "I'm sure I can think of a way. You can thank me later. Properly." He handed her the jacket with a devilish grin.

She ran her hands lovingly over it. "I do love leather. You're not afraid I'll steal it, are you?"

He smiled. "I know where you live if you do. Here let me." He helped her in. She was immediately engulfed in warmth, and the heat and scent of all that was Ryker James.

"There. Better?"

"Much."

He raised her hand to his lips, kissing her icy fingertips. "Your hands are frozen. There are gloves in the front pockets. Why don't you put them on?"

She reached in. "There aren't any gloves. There's only this." She pulled out a little black box. Turned it over in her hand and looked up at him.

He knelt right there on the sand. Delicately took the box from her hand and flipped it open. Bree gasped as a large diamond winked out at her.

"From the minute I laid eyes on you I knew you were something special. I couldn't stop thinking about you." He looked up into her blue eyes and saw tears shimmering at the edges. He cleared his throat, and wasn't sure if he could go on, he wasn't good at the sentimental stuff, so he abruptly changed tactics. "Your eyes pierced my soul, and your fist connected with my face."

"Ryker!" Bree giggled.

He grinned coyly at her, melting her heart even further.

"You might not have stolen my jacket but you certainly stole my heart. And I've been trying desperately to get it back ever since."

She pulled him up off his knee. "Do you want it back?"

"What?" he asked, confused.

"Your heart . . . Do you want it back?"

"No . . . I want yours."

"You already have it."

He took the ring out of the box and slipped it on her finger. "I love you, Bree."

"I love you too, Ryker James."

As they walked down the sand towards the rising sun, the water rushed in, then out again. That's where they stood. Hand in hand. Heads bent together. At the edge. At the brink of a new beginning.

Acknowledgments

I want to thank a few people for making this book possible.

To my very first readers: Ryan and Kristy. Without you willingly reading my stories in their roughest form I might not have the courage or strength to keep going. I sit on pins and needles nervously anticipating your first reactions.

To Rachael, who willingly devoted her free time to the first edits to make my story better, more cohesive, and the overall flow, from start to finish.

And to Delaney and Elliot for reading into the wee hours to find any additional plot holes or mistakes that may have been overlooked. Not to mention Jeanne for answering my endless question via email, text, or phone call.

I also wanted to thank my new ARC team Melissa, Melisa, and Pam. Thanks for noticing those last little details. The team may be small but you are mighty!

I couldn't have done it without any of you. You have my sincerest gratitude, respect, and love.

Last but certainly not least, as always to my family for patiently waiting while I type one more sentence and believing I can accomplish anything. You have all my love.

About the Author

Melissa Roos graduated from Iowa State University. She was born and raised in Iowa, has lived in Maryland, and now lives in Lancaster County, Pennsylvania with her family. Her first novel, You Can Hide, was published in 2020.

• • • •

THANK YOU FOR TAKING the time to read my book. I hope you enjoyed reading it as much as I did writing it. I would be thrilled if you connected with me on social media or by email.

To connect with me visit:

Facebook: Melissa Roos
Instagram: Melissaroosauthor
Website:http://www.melissaroosauthor.com
Email: authormelissaroos@gmail.com
Leave a review and sign up for my
email so you'll be the first to know what's happening.
Thank you
&
Happy reading!
Melissa

Don't miss out!

Visit the website below and you can sign up to receive emails whenever Melissa Roos publishes a new book. There's no charge and no obligation.

https://books2read.com/r/B-A-EHDP-YBPPB

BOOKS 2 READ

Connecting independent readers to independent writers.

67879821R00229